SING
EL

Adam Lively was born in Swansea in 1961 and studied history and philosophy in England and America. He has published three novels, *Blue Fruit* (1988), *The Burnt House* (1989) and *The Snail* (1991), and a pamphlet in the CounterBlast series, *Parliament: The Great British Democracy Swindle* (1990). He was selected as one of the Best of Young British Novelists 1993. He lives in London, with his wife Diana and their children Jacob and Anne.

BY ADAM LIVELY

Adam Lively

SING THE BODY ELECTRIC

A Novel In Five Movements

VINTAGE

Published by Vintage 1994

2 4 6 8 10 9 7 5 3 1

Copyright © 1993 Adam Lively

The right of Adam Lively to be identified as the author
of this work has been asserted by him in accordance with
the Copyright, Designs and Patents Act, 1988

First published in Great Britain by Chatto & Windus Ltd, 1993

Vintage
Random House, 20 Vauxhall Bridge Road, London SW1V 2SA

Random House Australia (Pty) Limited
20 Alfred Street, Milsons Point, Sydney
New South Wales 2061, Australia

Random House New Zealand Limited
18 Poland Road, Glenfield,
Auckland 10, New Zealand

Random House South Africa (Pty) Limited
PO Box 337, Bergvlei, South Africa

Random House UK Limited Reg. No. 954009

A CIP catalogue record for this book
is available from the British Library

ISBN 0 09 932281 1

Printed and bound in Great Britain by
Cox & Wyman, Reading, Berkshire

For Diana and Jacob

Be not afeard: the isle is full of noises,
Sounds and sweet airs, that give delight, and hurt not.
Sometimes a thousand twangling instruments
Will hum about mine ears; and sometime voices ...

William Shakespeare, *The Tempest*

All I know about music is that not many people ever
really hear it. And even then, on the rare occasions when
something opens within, and the music enters, what we
mainly hear, or hear corroborated, are personal, private,
vanishing evocations. But the man who creates the
music is hearing something else, is dealing with the roar
rising from the void...

James Baldwin, 'Sonny's Blues'

I

15 September 2064

Dear Sister,

Imagine our hero leaning out of a carriage window, hills rushing past his head. Suddenly he sees the sea, and all the emotion that has been bubbling about his chest during the long journey bursts forth in a single triumphant cry. Tears well in his eyes as he retracts his head and shouts the happy news to his startled travelling companions. He clasps the hand next to him, waking an old dowager who has dozed through the entire journey. He pokes his head out of the window again and cries to the driver, through the buffeting wind, 'Faster, man! Can't you see the sea?'

''Nother twenty miles 'fore you'll see the sea, sir,' says our lugubrious charioteer. 'That's just a pond.'

As the poet so bitterly wrote: 'Imagination withers into the truth.' Our hero strains his tear-filled eyes, and it does indeed transpire that those oceanic vistas were no more than the play of light on a roadside pond, a stagnant puddle where some damned stream has trickled its wretched last. Thus are our ships of fantasy wrecked upon the rocks of reality. Our hero slumps back into his seat, ignores the smirks of those ordinary souls around him, and gazes petulantly out at the passing scene.

Now it is almost dark. A chilly night lies ahead. Silver-white clouds billow past a full, gothic moon. The hooves of the horses clatter along the road. The wheels rumble, and our hero looks up at the branches of the roadside trees, tossed

3

hither and thither by the wind. He can hear them knocking, like dead men's bones. He imagines himself as Schubert's winter traveller, fleeing from lost love:

> Every stream will reach the sea,
> Every sorrow too its grave.

He dreams of frozen rivers, barking dogs, loving words carved on lime trees. He falls asleep.

Falls asleep! Two days' journey spent yearning, thirsting, aching for that first sight of the sea, and at the climactic moment he falls asleep! The body is a fickle vessel.

He is woken by the dowager, who is patting his hand and telling him kindly that they have arrived. The other passengers are already unloading their luggage. Our narcoleptic hero thanks the old lady, curses himself, and wipes the grains of sleep from his eyes. He is in the courtyard of an inn. The horses are being led away to stables, while the weary coachman leads himself to a mug of ale. Our hero stands beside the coach and breathes deeply. Yes. He can taste the sea!

I can taste it still. As I write, I pause to look out of the window, over the red tiles of the rooftops, to the limitless grey horizon beyond. My mind leaps out over the scudding waves, unfettered and faithless. I think of how that aesthetic adventurer Hector Berlioz felt when he was writing his *Roméo et Juliette*.

> Oh, the ardent existence I lived during that time: I struck out boldly across that great ocean of poetry, caressed by the wild, sweet breeze of fancy ... I felt within me the strength to reach the enchanted isle where the temple of pure art stands alone under a clear sky.

I, too, feel the strength now to make the journey. Perhaps, one day, Berlioz and I shall dance a tarantella together around the columns of that temple.

Enough of these fantasies. News is what you demanded of me, and news I shall give you. I have, as you may have gathered, arrived in Wellfleet and taken up lodgings in the household of a certain Mr and Mrs Grindley, in the Old Town. They have a son, a daughter and – most important of all – a working piano to which I am allowed access 'at all reasonable hours of day and night'. I have been here scarcely three days, but already Mr and Mrs Grindley seem to have cast me in the role of eligible bachelor. They are at pains to allow me access to their daughter Priscilla (at all reasonable hours of day and night, of course). Already I have been engaged to give the maiden piano lessons in lieu of a quarter of my rent. But have no fears: your brother will not be ensnared. Miss Grindley has forearms like haunches, and she laughs like a horse. I may be able to teach her to smash out octaves on the keyboard, but she will never teach me to be her husband.

The Grindley house is in one of the many terraces on the slopes of the two long hills that cradle the Old Town. My first morning, waking early, I tumbled out of bed, galloped down some steps, then along a rain-washed street – arms spinning joyfully like a windmill – and was at the seafront inside two minutes. Here there is the fishing beach – the soul, lungs, eyes and life blood of the Old Town, where the fleet of some forty vessels is hauled up safe from the water on the shingle. Spread out over an area of some four acres is a glorious confusion of nets, huts, boats, men stamping their boots, barking dogs, ropes and cables, floats, buoys and markers fashioned out of every conceivable object, cruel cages for catching crab and lobster, bottles, bits of old iron, a million seagulls, and all the detritus regurgitated by the swelling, ceaseless sea. This place is paradise. Here is life. When the cannon is fired that signals that the lifeboat is about to go out, the million seagulls rise with a million squawks and circle round and round. The first time I witnessed this phenomenon, I stopped dead still in the street – everyone around me was going on with their business – and burst into song. I couldn't help it. I don't even remember what I sang – it came to me there and then. I stared up at those swirling, soaring birds and was suddenly filled with – ah, but who can solve these mysteries? The birds, the wind, the noise around me gave me the song. Or perhaps song, wind, birds and noise, all erupting into that unrepeatable moment, had a single source. Who knows? Why need to know? Father would no doubt have a theory. If he had the chance, he would kill the whole universe by slow, rational explanation.

Beyond the West Hill is the New Town. According to Mr Grindley – who prides himself on knowledge of all kinds, local and universal – this area was once a marshy wilderness known as 'Little America'. It was drained and colonised, and now functions as a resort for the tourists who flock here each summer to take the sea air. I have ventured into the New Town only twice, but have already developed an antipathy to it. There is something demeaning about a place whose *raison d'être* is to provide visitors with aimless pleasure. It provides a distraction, a place built on the philosophy of the eternal present – as though the present moment were a rag which could wipe clean both past and future. Abhorrent idea! When I step into the New Town I feel my soul soiled by it, and when I return to the workaday wonders of the fishing beach I find I can breathe again more easily. Something over there suffocates me. The honest toil of the fishermen is a living reproach to its abysmal pleasures. I have seen tourists venture over the brow of West Hill to the Old Town, and imagined I could fathom in their eyes a kind of shame as they looked down on what life can and should be.

Enough. I'm sounding like a bishop. Next time I write, I shall give you some real, *musical* news.

Your loving brother,
Paul

6

Dear Sister,

In my last letter I promised you an account of the town's musical life. Well I have met the town's musical life – his name is Monsieur Grenier. Have you heard of Grenier? I suppose not. He had his flash of fame some twenty years ago, and then the flame went out. He has lived here ever since. His music is thoughtful, teasing, physical, but all in a very French kind of way. Scrape the surface and you'll hear Boulez, even Debussy. Like all those Frenchmen, he has munched on the Orient like an old cow. Wisps of raga and gamelan dangle from his sensual lips. Now he ruminates not in an attic – I was disappointed to discover – but in a spacious and dusty room in a house at the vent-end of the Old Town, a mile from the sea.

The house, which stands in a dignified position at the top of the East Hill, is owned by one Clifford Patrick, an hairy man whose brightest attribute is a beautiful young wife. The couple, who are going up in the world, moved into this villa a couple of years ago. And soon after they moved in, in a notable act of patronage, they gave over one of their best rooms, together with the sea view it affords, to this musical celebrity, rescuing him thereby from the dingy digs where he'd been rotting.

I went there a few days after my arrival, on a muggy afternoon, and was greeted at the door by Madeleine Patrick. She led me with due reverence up the stairs and into his august presence. Monsieur Grenier is enjoying his Indian summer. He met me in a batik shirt, undone to his cavernous navel, looking for all the world like a colonial Balzac. To my relief, he had not the least notion who I am, but ushered me in anyway and served me with some green tea while Mrs Patrick withdrew. The tea had leaves the size of postage stamps floating in it.

When I said that poor Grenier's flame had gone out, I was referring merely to the flame of fortune and fame, not the spark of creativity. Grenier still composes. A large table was littered with the evidence of numerous projects. He has recently completed a series of piano miniatures – 'Vapours', I think they were called – and he did me the honour of playing me one of them. Unfortunately, his instrument was so excruciatingly out of tune, and the piece itself so short – or 'evanescent', perhaps I should say – that it was difficult to form a judgement. Or perhaps Monsieur Grenier eschews the equal temperament and has his piano specially tuned to some obscure raga? Life is full of mysteries.

When he discovered that I too was a composer, Monsieur Grenier begged me to return the favour and play for him some of my own music. I replied that there was nothing I could play him, since I had never written anything for the piano alone. My music was all dramatic, and all written for large instrumental or vocal ensembles. And since it relied for its effect on shifting texture and coloration, nothing could be gathered by banging it out on a piano. Being a Frenchman – *timbre* is, after all, a French word – Monsieur Grenier was completely satisfied with my argument. From that moment, I think, he admitted me to his brotherhood.

It is, of course, an exaggeration to say that Monsieur Grenier alone constitutes the local musical life. Having tacitly admitted me to the brotherhood of composers, Monsieur Grenier complained to me at length – as composers will – about the musicians available to him. The town's Philharmonic Society, he announced, was a dinosaur, a lumbering, small-brained creature that would expire of its own inertia – and if that didn't happen, it should be swept out to sea by a deluge. (I suspect Monsieur Grenier had spent many happy hours elaborating this picturesque analogy for his own amusement.) As a – if not revered, then at least respected – *vieux de la vieille*, Monsieur Grenier had been commissioned on two occasions by the Society. On both of them, he told me, his delicate scores had (the dinosaur analogy marched on) 'been trampled by those idiotic musicians until there was nothing left of them but dust and fragments'. After the second occasion he had vowed never to have anything to do with the Philharmonic Society again.

But times were hard, royalties from his days of fame only trickled in – and after all, a man had to eat. (And Monsieur Grenier looked like one who had to more than most.) The 'vultures' of the Philharmonic Society had returned to him with a request for some dances and occasional pieces for their winter subscription series. What could he do but accept? Even now the vultures were circling around him, demanding the scores for rehearsal. It was insufferable. He hadn't spent his youth trekking through the jungles of Java, notebook in sweaty hand, to end up writing waltzes for Sunday afternoon tea dances! The task was so distasteful that he did anything to distract himself from it. Hence 'Vapours'.

Nothing in this tale of woe alarmed me, for I didn't come here in the hope of finding musical sophistication. Sophistication was what I was feeling when I left New Venice. Sophistication was what was spoiling me. My operas oozed sophistication, which is what bought them popularity with that fashionably philistine audience. I have fled to the sea to find myself and my Art. It is only in the midst of Nature that one can shed the shackles of sophistication and discover Nature and authenticity in oneself. If the local orchestra is made up of untutored musical peasants, then so much the better. I shall exalt them to stamp in rhythm. They want dances? Then dances it shall be. I'll make them dance till their tea tastes like gin.

But back to Monsieur Grenier, ruminating all the while on life's injustices. It was uncomfortably hot in his apartment, and the old man – to broach a delicate subject – was not without his own, all too physical, 'vapours'. Perhaps this was the result of a lifetime's indulgence in peculiar green tea. At any rate, I asked him, as tactfully as I could, whether it would

9

be possible to open one of the windows to let in some fresh air. His refusal was vehement. He never, he said, opened the windows. The noise from outside disturbed his concentration, and that would be quite insufferable. He had to have absolute silence, 'in order to hear the secret harmonies that lie hidden deep within my mind'. So the windows stayed shut. I smiled understandingly and sipped my hot green liquid, sweating in the fetid fug.

Enough of Monsieur Grenier. I will tell you of the other people I have met here. First my landlords, the Grindley family. The strapping daughter, Priscilla, I mentioned in my first letter. She has an air of unchannelled, crude energy. I look on her as one might a handsome horse – admiring its size and proportions, but not wanting to get too close for fear it might accidentally jump on one's toes. What she thinks of me, I have not the least notion. We have had one conversation. I think it was about seagulls.

It is a mystery from whom she has inherited her animality. About the father there is something of the philosopher, something weak and vascular. Tall and thin, he stands rather too close to you when he is conversing. On several occasions I have been forced up against walls to escape him. His teeth, yellowing and crooked, are barely covered by his lips, and his breath smells. He is a thoroughly well-meaning fellow, and his conversation is painstakingly informative. I fear he has seized on me as a source of intellectual stimulation. If I make this sound like a dubious privilege, it is because Mr Grindley's mind moves in rapid and mysterious ways. Let me give an example. The other morning, passing each other in the hallway, we had the following curious exchange. I give it in full, verbatim:

Myself (breezily): Good morning, Mr Grindley.
Grindley: I've been meaning to ask your opinion, Mr Clearwater. Do you think there are universal moral values?

10

Myself: Let me see . . . 'Universal' is not a word I'm fond of . . .

Grindley (coming closer): But we all eat, we all have basic needs. I was trying to argue this with my wife this morning, at breakfast.

Myself (backing towards the door, jocularly): Ah, imponderables for breakfast. Not a healthy diet, Mr Grindley.

Grindley (in pursuit): Cannibalism! That's the crux of the matter. How can universal moral values survive if people will eat each other?

Myself (flung over my shoulder in flight, attempting a light-hearted exit): Well, it's been good to discuss it with you – universally good, indeed. I hope you haven't been putting Mrs Grindley off her breakfast.

Mrs Grindley – now there is an imponderable. Nothing, I warrant, could put her off her breakfast. As spherical and sphinxine as her husband is tubular and tendentious, she sits Buddha-like in the kitchen and picks cake crumbs from the many folds of her floral dress. By a curious leap of thought, it struck me the other day that she would have made an admirable partner for Monsieur Grenier, had he stumbled across her sitting cross-legged like some totem in the jungles of Java. But that was not to be. Her destiny was to lie with Mr Grindley. And thus, no doubt, it will ever be. Her world is warm, certain and secure.

It is a mystery how this curious pair could have sired their children. Their son, Reuben, exudes healthy physicality to a greater degree even than his sister. And in contrast to his father, he has a tendency to back away from his interlocutor. I have approached him on a number of occasions because he works on the fishing beach and I am anxious to gain an entrée to that world. But each time he answers me curtly and retreats, eyeing me with a blend of suspicion and antagonism. This uncalled-for coyness has led to some ridiculous scenes, with myself chasing the lad around the room much as his father

11

chases me. It would be amusing to get the three of us together one day. We could trip a merry *pas-de-trois*. Perhaps Priscilla could play Monsieur Grenier's waltzes for us on the piano while Mrs Grindley takes green tea with the composer.

Since my meeting with Monsieur Grenier, the weather has turned fresh and windy again. Every day, at around noon, I go down to the beach and walk along the sea as far as the pier, opposite the New Town, then back again to the fishing beach. Everything here depends upon the rhythm of the tides; we could all happily throw our clocks into the sea. The boats can only be winched back on to the beach when the water is high, and it is at high tide, around the middle of each day, that they return from their fishing expeditions. For the smaller boats, these trips have begun before dawn. The larger ones set out at sunset and trawl through the night. On their return there is a sense of relief. Wives and children come down to the beach to greet them, bringing food and bottles of the local beer. The atmosphere is one of carnival. The men are tough, strong and weather-battered. They leap in and out of the boats in their heavy thigh-length boots. They throw boxes of gutted, twitching fish to each other. They run up the beach from the sea, stamping the shingle to secure the lines. They shout orders to each other, haul on ropes, toss a child on to their shoulders. Everywhere there is movement, yelling, laughter. I walk through it in a kind of daze, as happy a man as has ever lived.

With love,
Paul

5 October 2064

Dear Sister,

How are you all? Even as I sit here, looking out across the rooftops towards the sea, I can imagine what you are all doing. You, Jean, are roaming somewhere through the city, soaking up its neurotic atmospheres. Mother is at some snobby, geriatric gathering. And father is with Milstein, trying to work out how the whole thing went wrong. I'm afraid I don't envy your life in New Venice. I'm done with the fashionable vacuity of that place. Here I've found something real. When it became clear that the ever-retreating Reuben Grindley was not going to give me an introduction to the world of the fishermen, I resolved upon a direct approach. Knowing me so well, you will understand my nervousness. A morbid sensitivity can seize me which makes any rebuff – makes even the anticipation of a rebuff – an exquisite agony. But I had to go through with it. Already I was acutely aware of my singular position as an outsider in this communal, close-knit world. I hardly knew which was worse – to be ignored, or to be the object of curious, sidelong glances. Of course, I had seen Reuben Grindley a few times on the beach, but always at a distance, in a group. And he never made the least attempt to acknowledge me. So I began to look for some friendlier face to approach. On a couple of occasions I made tentative steps towards some man who was working quietly alone, mending nets or tending to some obscure object. But at the last moment my nerve would fail. The fellow would get up and walk away, or he would look up at me with an expression that I interpreted unkindly. And so I would lower my eyes and pass on.

This continued for several days. And then, one morning, I woke to find that my mood had changed utterly. (You well know how sudden my changes can be.) I found myself brimming with confidence, with warmth and fellow-feeling. I was able to laugh at my awkwardnesses. I tumbled out of bed and dashed down to the beach, much as I had done on that first morning. The boats were all out at sea, but there were still a few men on the beach. Each boat employs a 'shore boy' who stays behind to look after the winching gear and prepare everything for the vessel's return. 'Shore boy', incidentally, is

13

a delightful misnomer, since they are all middle-aged and elderly gentlemen. Putting to sea is so physically taxing that fishermen have usually retired by the age of forty, to be replaced by a son, nephew or younger brother. On retiring, some of these veterans become 'shore boys'. (What an encyclopedia I have become! You have the wise Mr Grindley to thank for all this information.) Anyway, some dozen of these 'shore boys' were scattered across the beach, buttoned up against the wind, like a flock of crows scavenging a rubbish tip. I marched straight up to the nearest one – a grizzly-looking customer who was sitting on a lobster pot doing nothing in particular – and engaged him in a breezy, hail-fellow-well-met kind of a conversation. I discussed the weather, the remarkable changes it had undergone, and its future prospects. I told him how much I liked the town, how beautiful the hills were, how eager I was to learn about the life of the place. I gave him news of my health, enquired about his, and rounded the whole thing off with a paean of praise to the local beer. Then I gave him my hand and told him my name.

'Oh, I knew that,' he replied laconically. 'You're the gentleman that's lodging with Reuben Grindley's family. You're down here every day, ain't you? I seen you.'

So there I was. Without doing anything beyond wander around, I had become a fixture in the local scene: the-gentleman-that's-lodging-with-Reuben-Grindley's-family-and-comes-down-here-every-day. If that was to be my role, I would play it with pride.

'And you're a composer, ain't you?' he added. 'Come down here to do your composin'?'

Somehow I preferred plain gentleman-that's-lodging-with-Reuben-Grindley's-family. But if I was to be the fishermen's composer too, then so be it. I would make them proud of me.

I asked him if he'd introduce me to some of his colleagues.

'No need for that,' he remarked matter-of-factly. 'They know who you are. Nothing happens here without everyone hearing about it.'

'I meant,' I persevered, 'that I'd like to talk with them.'

'Oh,' he said, looking at me dubiously, 'I see. Well, you can talk to them yourself, can't you? Don't need me to go 'troducing you. Like I said, they know who you are.'

'Of course,' replied I, brightly. 'How stupid of me.'

So when they returned, I fearlessly ''troduced' myself to the crew of my new friend's boat. And perfectly affable they were, too. Of course, they were rather too busy – what with hauling up the boat and unloading the catch – to contribute much to the conversation themselves. But I think I kept up my end of things, covering some of the same ground as I had gone over with the 'shore boy'. What fine men they are! Chatting with these rugged individuals on the windswept shingle, I felt a million miles from the hothouse of New Venice. How I pity you pallid, wilting orchids who live there, barely seeing the light of day and feeding only on your own perfervid imaginings. A man like Frank Cottimi would be blasted away by this wind, would be blinded by the bright, sea-splintered sunlight. In the middle of talking to these fine specimens, I stopped and found myself thinking of Cottimi's productions of 'nautical' operas – *Les Pêcheurs de Perles, Der Fliegende Holländer, Billy Budd, Peter Grimes, Moby Dick*, even (God forgive me!) my own *Crooked Timber of Humanity*. Cottimi is celebrated for his crowd scenes, but the thought of those dozy, nose-picking lumps of lard that one finds in the choruses of our theatres impersonating real seafaring men was too much. I burst out laughing. I explained to my new friends what it was I found so funny, and I think they found it amusing too.

By now I was feeling so far accepted by the fishermen that I ventured to ask whether I could go out with them one day.

'No chance of that,' said one of them. 'You can get a pleasure boat from the pier. We don't take passengers.'

'But you don't understand,' I persisted. 'It's not just that I

15

want to go out to sea. I want to do it in a *real* way. I could help you gut the fish.'

The man laughed. 'You ever gutted fish?'

'No, but I could practise it beforehand. I have nimble fingers, from playing the piano.'

The fellow laughed. 'You might end up with no fingers at all by the time you got back.'

I didn't press my case then, but I had far from given up hope. I am determined to strike out boldly across that great ocean. If ever I return to the city, I promise, it shall be as a salt-crusted, wind-wrinkled veteran of the waves.

Old habits die hard, or perhaps it was just the thought of those portly tenors in their spotted handkerchiefs. As I was walking back from the beach, looking up the hill at that villa where Monsieur Grenier ruminates so claustrophobically, an idea for an opera came to me. I'll tell you more when I've chewed the cud. (Evening: I give my first piano lesson to Priscilla Grindley. She rides the instrument like a horse, stamping the sustaining pedal as though to spur it on. She neighs bracingly at her own blunders.) But I haven't come here to write operas. *Pure* music, instrumental music, that's my goal now. Lately I have been thinking more and more about Berlioz, 'caressed by the wild, sweet breeze of fancy', sailing out over the horizon 'to reach the enchanted isle where the temple of pure art stands alone under a clear sky'. I join hands with him across the centuries and dance – but not to the music of time, for what do true artists do if they do not defy time, thumping their drums in mockery, drowning out the measured tread of the years? Already I have in mind a kind of *Sea Symphony*. No seagulls (muted trumpets, string glissandi, etc), but a unified, *spiritual* expression of the feelings aroused in me by this marvellous place. When I was in New Venice, turning out those operas, music was something ready-to-hand, close to me, to be *used*. Now it feels much further off – over the horizon, something to be *attained*. This symphony that I talk about – this summation of all that I feel about the pounding waves, the slippery shingle, the spray dazzling in the morning – I feel it to be something *beyond* me, in the sense of something transcendent. Perhaps, also, in the sense of something I will never be able to do.

Now to my main news. I have had my first encounter with the Philharmonic Society. It was not a happy meeting, and I fear our relationship is to be that of two mountain beasts hurling themselves headlong at each other. One of us must tumble into the abyss.

I had seen posters around town advertising 'A Rich Feast of Music. An Orchestral Extravaganza' in the Everyman Theatre, opposite the pier. I duly went to the box office and purchased a seat in the front row. I wanted to examine at close quarters these musicians with whom I would have to deal. The evening of the extravaganza arrived, and taking an early supper with the Grindleys, I left the house and made my way along the front towards the theatre. A gale was blowing. The flags and banners outside the smarter hotels on the front flapped and cracked. The moon lit the foaming white break-ers that pounded the shingle. Beyond the breakers – beyond the pier, which lifts its skirts above the waves on stilts – there was an inky-black immensity. I stopped and gazed out at it, pondering the immeasurable depths of the darkness, the inhuman distance travelled by those waves that expended themselves on the beach below me. Ah! I would happily have spent the rest of the night listening to that merry music of nature – the sudden, whirling *crescendo* as a fresh gust whip-ped in off the sea; the grinding *lento* of the waves. Indeed, it might have been better if I had stayed outside.

The Everyman Theatre is built to a curious design, being wide, flat and shallow to the stage rather than deep and tall. The whole place is heavily carpeted (in a virulent red), which makes the acoustics as rewarding as a cardboard box. A full house (the capacity is about five hundred) might have improved the sound, but in the event only about a quarter of the seats were occupied. The audience for this extravaganza was scattered across the hall in small groups, complaining loudly about the weather, sniffing ostentatiously, and taking off coats – then putting them on again, then taking them off and wrapping them around their shoulders, then arranging them over the empty seats in front. All wore expressions of frumpish dissatisfaction, as though fully prepared to find the forthcoming fare neither rich nor a feast.

The musicians of the orchestra began to take their places, wandering on in ones and twos. They looked, if anything, even more disconsolate than their prospective victims across the footlights. Frowning, they studied the meagre audience, then consoled each other with none too subtle head-shakings and eye-rollings. They then set to work rubbing their hands, to restore life to cold, corpse-like flesh. The oboist blew down his instrument, producing a sound like an asthmatic goose, examined his reed for a few moments, and shrugged his shoulders. I took my place in the front row, which was otherwise empty.

The posters around town had been singularly uninformative as to what delicacies would make up the forthcoming feast. A single sheet of paper handed to us at the door was more helpful, though not much. The most substantial item on the programme was the opening one – the Overture to Mozart's *Magic Flute*. Thereafter the programme degenerated rapidly, with Duncan Ritchie's Piano Concerto *From the Cairngorms* – the kind of Hibernian fog that was produced much earlier and more effectively by a German Jew (Felix Mendelssohn-Bartholdy). The second half was made up of a dismal collection of popular tunes and medleys, concluding with *Merrie Dances* by someone called Montgomery Hummingbird. It looked like being a long evening. In the event it was not.

The conductor, a severe and matter-of-fact-looking lady in her fifties, walked on to the platform and acknowledged the trickle of applause with a curt nod. I have always believed that, at least at the beginning of a concert, musicians should

18

be encouraged in their labours. So I clapped vigorously and turned around to encourage my fellow members of the audience. The conductor gave me a baleful glance and opened the score. (That should have forewarned me; what self-respecting conductor needs a score for a masterwork like *The Magic Flute*?) I leaned forward in my seat, my chin resting on my cupped hands, and awaited the unfolding of Mozart's sublime drama.

It did not so much unfold as fall apart. Those majestic opening chords, so redolent of esoteric ritual, require the utmost precision and unity to gain their full effect. The approach adopted by the Philharmonic Society was, shall we say, rather more relaxed. The conductor waved her baton loftily in the air, as though she were pointing out some interesting feature of the theatre's interior decoration. The orchestra, taken aback by this gesture, scrambled in an undignified manner to get aboard the first chord. First on deck was the second horn, little more than a schoolboy, who had been watching the conductor with a nervous, hawk-like eye from the moment she had walked on to the platform. As soon as her hand moved, he blew down his instrument with all his might, producing a loud approximation to an E flat. Violins, flutes, violas, clarinets, cellos and all the rest clattered aboard after him. The conductor evidently found this grotesque cacophony entirely satisfactory, for she repeated her vague wafting motion for the two pairs of mighty chords that follow. The results were broadly similar. This leaky tub was launched.

After the third pair of chords, as you may know, Mozart's music dissolves into sublime mystery. Beneath the stirrings of the violins, the cellos and basses heave gently, while the wind interject with blasts that echo the opening fanfare. Now the Philharmonic Society had a novel interpretation of this passage. They opted for syrupy muddle instead of sublime mystery. There was an old fellow in the second violins whose favourite key, I suspect, is G major. At any rate, he was clearly struggling with Mozart's unreasonable and perverse requirement that all the musicians play in three flats. In order, perhaps, to disguise his difficulties, he employed a lavish, wailing vibrato and such a generous use of audible slides between notes that it seemed as though he might be playing the entire part with a single, greased finger. None of this would have mattered too much if he had not also played extremely loudly. Fixing his part with a look of steely determination, he dug his bow deep into the strings, as though the music were some particularly obstinate mollusc that he was trying to prize from its shell.

Mozart's slow introduction ends, as you know, with the music sinking down and dying away, until the violins break out, *piano*, with the bustling main theme. On this occasion the introduction did not so much die away as peter out. The conductor, disdainfully dismissing the last chord, turned on the violins and began thrashing the air impatiently with her baton. The violins, surprised by this turn of events, responded by sticking their heads further into their parts and pushing their bows backwards and forwards in a vigorous, business-like manner. The aural effect was that of a bunch of alley cats scampering from some evil-minded pursuer. The conductor, clearly feeling that they were not scampering fast enough, glared at them and thrashed the air even more impatiently. The music gathered pace, like a boulder building momentum as it rolls downhill – except that a boulder would suggest something clear-edged and well-defined. This was more a ball of soft, ill-defined stuff – an enormous ball of fluff, perhaps, with bits hanging off and trailing behind. By the time of the bassoon's entry – that bold cantus firmus that upholds Mozart's edifice – the music was going at a headlong, reckless gallop. The poor bassoonist's eyes looked fit to pop out with exertion and alarm. By now, the whole orchestra was a seething mass of frantic, meaningless activity, like one of those ugly nests of insects you find when you lift a stone.

Now I can look back on all this with some wry detachment. But at the time I was myself a seething mass of pity and rage – pity for the memory of that great genius, and rage at the insult that was being inflicted on it. But there was worse to come. Technical incompetence and sloppy musicianship I can just about stomach, if at least an honest, though bungling, attempt is being made to stay faithful to the score. But what I have never, and will never, tolerate is the practice of 'improving' a score by cutting it or altering some aspect of its instrumentation. As though anybody could 'improve' upon what Mozart had written! The orchestra stumbled through the rest of the exposition, botched the Masonic wind chords that echo the opening, and then launched on the development. Here Mozart bends the fugal theme through a succession of rapid modulations, perhaps intending to suggest the symbolic journey of initiatory trials that Tamino and Pamina undergo in the opera proper. Here, also, the orchestra were at their execrable worst. If E flat major presented insurmountable obstacles for my old fellow in the violins, B flat minor was an impenetrable, esoteric mystery. He glared at the music ever harder, attacked his instrument ever more fiercely. But he might equally well have been trying to interpret a manuscript in Mandarin Chinese for all it meant to him.

All this, as I have said, I was prepared to forgive. But at the stretto – where the fugue is tightened, the home key reached and the triumphant re-exposition prepared for – an unforgivable crime was committed. With a flourish of her baton, the conductor introduced a gratuitous roll on the timpani. This grotesque addition was presumably intended to provide some dramatic 'colour'. As though Mozart needed lessons in drama or colour! This was too much. I had reached breaking point. As soon as I heard the offending noise, I got to my feet and – half-turning to the audience behind me, so that the whole theatre might hear me – I said in a loud voice, 'That drum roll is not in Mozart's score.' Then I sat down again.

As you can imagine, this intervention had a galvanising effect on the proceedings. All eyes were upon me. Muttered conversations erupted. The music chugged on in a distracted, mechanical kind of way, but every musician was looking down at me with various expressions of horror, annoyance and amusement. Of the conductor, since she had her back to me, all I could see was that her ears had turned a livid red colour – whether from anger or understandable shame, I could not tell. For myself, I was sitting quite impassively, content to have registered my protest and listening attentively now for any other artistic abominations. And what an abomination there was to come! Even now I can hardly believe it, can hardly credit even the most reckless of musical vandals with such a piece of aesthetic nihilism. *They had added cymbal clashes to the final chords.* Even as he did the disgusting deed, I glared at the miserable individual assigned this task of butchery, and thought I detected in the glance that he returned me a look of hangdog apology. When the last chord died away, a deathly hush fell on the theatre. The conductor remained facing the orchestra. It was almost as though they were expecting me to say something else. I was in no mood to disappoint them. I stood up and, addressing the conductor and orchestra, said in a loud voice, 'Those cymbal clashes are not in Mozart's score. You have insulted the memory of a great artist.' With that I turned on my heel and marched out of the theatre. Behind me I left only an awful silence.

My jangled nerves needed the soothing balm of nature. I walked by the sea. The wind beat ceaselessly against me. Here was real music, here was the pounding of the waves, the screaming of gulls in the darkness, the wind roaring through the empty streets. I took deep, gulping breaths of the salty air, to cleanse myself of the false artificiality of the theatre and of that 'Orchestral Extravaganza'.

News of the evening's events in the Everyman Theatre had

already reached the Grindleys when I returned. The family was excitedly awaiting my arrival.

'There's a young gentleman here to see you,' said Mr Grindley. 'He's in the front room.' Leaning even closer to me, until he was practically kissing my left cheek, he added, 'A gentleman of the press.'

I entered the Grindley's parlour, and a young man about eighteen years old leapt up from his seat to greet me.

'Mr Clearwater? Pleased to meet you. My name's Wilkins, Thomas Wilkins – ' he gulped, as though short of breath – 'of the *Wellfleet Observer*.'

As we shook hands – his was clammy, and took mine in a nervy, claw-like grip – I studied his face. It had something familiar about it – small brown darting eyes; a wide forehead, a rather over-sized nose; an unattractive, thin-lipped mouth slashed slightly off the horizontal across the lower portion of his face.

'You don't have a relative who plays second horn in the municipal orchestra, do you?'

The beady eyes lit up. 'That's my younger brother, Jim. That's why they give me the music notices. You see, normally I do the courts. I don't really know anything about music, to tell the truth. But they think because I've got a brother who plays in the orchestra, I must have some inside knowledge. To tell the truth, it's usually a bit of a bore doing the music notices, except when something like this happens.'

He was fond of that phrase, 'To tell the truth'. It punctuated everything he said.

'Like what?' I said.

'What you did this evening.'

'So you were at that apology for a concert?'

'To tell the truth, it ended after you left. Everybody was talking and arguing with each other. The orchestra couldn't carry on. It's the biggest thing to happen at a concert here for years.'

If I had known I was releasing such a bombshell, I might

23

have thought twice. Thomas Wilkins himself, I now saw, was fit to explode with suppressed excitement. He kept bobbing from one foot to another, while those alert, bead-like eyes watched my every movement with the same hawkish intensity as his younger brother had watched the conductor. I felt that I had only to make the smallest of unexpected gestures and Thomas Wilkins would emit some extraordinary noise, or fly out of the window like a coiled spring.

'So you think this would make an exciting story for the newspaper?'

He nodded vigorously. 'I could get it on the front page. It would be my first story on the front page. If I could just ask you a few questions . . .'

'Very well, then. Take a seat, Mr Wilkins.' I had taken a liking to this young man and his ambitions.

We sat down at the Grindleys' table, and I allowed Thomas Wilkins to interrogate me. I told him about my operas, about the motives that had provoked me to leave New Venice and come to Wellfleet, and I told him why I had made my protest at the concert. Wilkins, bent over a notebook, licking a stubby pencil from time to time, took all this down with furious rapidity. At the end of half an hour he snapped the notebook shut.

'Thank you, Mr Clearwater,' he said, getting up and making for the door. 'I've got to get back for the last edition.'

And our young scribe did indeed get his byline on the front page. The paper was handed to me with infinite solemnity by Mr Grindley at breakfast the following morning. Then he withdrew, to leave me to ponder the immensity of what I had done. 'CONCERT ENDS IN UPROAR' proclaimed the headline, across six columns. Beneath that, Wilkins had done his job well:

The Philharmonic Society concert in the Everyman Theatre last night ended in uproar when eminent composer Paul

Clearwater, 34, who was in the audience, stood up and denounced the orchestra's performance.

The musicians had just finished playing Mozart's well-known overture, *The Magic Flute*, when Mr Clearwater stood up and accused them of 'insulting the memory of a great artist'. Earlier in the performance he had made a similar intervention. After making his remarks, Mr Clearwater stormed out of the theatre. Mrs Cynthia Tuck, conducting the orchestra on this occasion, attempted to continue the programme, but the audience was in too agitated a state, and the concert had to be abandoned. She later described the incident as 'unprecedented' and 'disgraceful'.

Mr Clearwater, who is living in the Old Town, moved to the Coast from New Venice two weeks ago. He has gained a considerable reputation in the city as a composer of operas. Among his well-known works are *Ulysses* and *The Crooked Timber of Humanity*. In an exclusive interview with the *Wellfleet Observer*, he revealed that he had made his protest because of his anger at deliberate alterations that had been made to Mozart's score.

'Mozart's score is a sacred text,' he said. 'It is divinely inspired. To alter it by adding drum rolls and cymbal clashes is like retouching an Old Master by pouring a tin of paint over it. As a composer myself, I know the agonies that go into the process of creation. I felt it my duty to protect the great Mozart from this philistine onslaught.'

So, dear sister, do not imagine that life is dull for me here, or that your brother is living the life of a quiet hermit. For this was not the end of the story. No sooner had I finished reading Wilkins' handiwork, than Mr Grindley approached the breakfast table again, bearing a note which had just been delivered. It was from Mr Roland Hinchcliff, President of the Wellfleet Philharmonic Society, and it asked me to call on him at the earliest possible opportunity.

As you know, I have never been one to shirk a battle.

When Art must be defended against the forces of darkness, I will always enter the lists with a joyous heart. I prepared to seek out Mr Roland Hinchcliff immediately. But first, I thought, it would be as well to know my enemy. I sought out Grindley. He was in the kitchen, reading – no doubt for the tenth time – Thomas Wilkins' account of the previous evening's events. His wife sat in her usual chair by the stove, grazing on some buttered toast and seemingly oblivious to the momentous events unfolding around her. Priscilla Grindley, situated at the sink, stared at me with an awful, drooping jaw.

'Mr Grindley,' I said, 'what can you tell me about Mr Roland Hinchcliff? I've received an invitation from him.'

Mr Grindley pondered the question with the utmost gravity. 'Mr Hinchcliff is a *very* respected man in the town,' he said. 'He is a lawyer and a councillor.'

'And President of the Philharmonic Society,' I added.

'He is said to have a fine tenor voice.'

Now I knew my man. In the evolutionary ladder of musical life, tenors rank with the amoeba or primitive one-celled protozoan. Amateur tenors who are lawyers, small-town politicians and puff themselves up as patrons of the Arts are like amorphous blobs of protoplasm, barely qualifying as musical life at all. I had no fears of Mr Roland Hinchcliff.

His house was a large detached building in the New Town, some half a mile from the sea. I was led by a housekeeper into the ground-floor office, where Mr Roland Hinchcliff presided over a large desk, an expanse of green carpet and row upon row of identical leather-bound volumes. A fire crackled in the grate. He got up and placed his hand in mine.

Now I can tell a lot from a person's handshake. Roland Hinchcliff let his hand merely rest in mine, as though it were on loan. When I had released it, he took it back carefully, with interest. He is in his fifties, with strands of long, silver hair tucked neatly behind each ear. He wears thick pebble spectacles and has prominent lips which are pushed forward in a pout of creamy satisfaction, as though he were perpetually sucking on some delicious confection.

Tea was served. Mr Hinchcliff supped it noisily and held each mouthful, savouring it, before swallowing. Between these operations he made small talk. As you know, I have never been able to stomach idle chat – all that whittering on about the weather and one's health. I got straight down to the point.

'If,' I said, 'you have invited me here to demand an apology for my protest at last night's concert, you're wasting your time. I stand by every word I said. Indeed, there are a few more which I wish I'd added. The crime committed last night was unforgivable.'

'My dear fellow,' he interrupted, leaning across his desk and waving his hands about in a placatory manner. 'Apology? I wouldn't dream of such a thing. I'm sure you were quite justified in what you said. Quite justified. Unfortunately, I wasn't able to attend last night's concert myself – I had an important meeting – so I'm unable to judge for myself. But I'm sure you were quite justified.' He slurped some more tea. 'However, you may, on reflection, wish to make some allowances. We are a small town. To someone of your musical sophistication, we may appear a little – how shall we say? – *primitive*.' He gave me a conspiratorial smile. 'Please don't rush to judgement. The Philharmonic Society strives to do its best with the meagre resources available to it. That's why we send up a hallelujah when someone like yourself appears in our midst.' He leaned back in his seat and looked at me as though at some sublime natural phenomenon. 'Your reputation precedes you, Mr Clearwater. Composer of *Ulysses* and *The Crooked Timber of Humanity*, recipient of the Médaille d'Or of the New Venetian Academy of Arts.' He raised his eyebrows and opened his hands, as if to say, these things speak for themselves. 'Of course, some people in the town may be saying that you were intemperate last night, but those of us who presume to have some inkling, some distant sympathy for the artistic temperament, will be more understanding. The artistic temperament, I know, is an impulsive and intemperate thing. God forbid that it should be otherwise. We lesser, humdrum mortals respect and cherish that. So, let's have no more talk of apologies.'

Don't think that I was taken in by any of this. If hypocrisy is the compliment paid by vice to virtue, aestheticism is the insult paid by philistines to Art.

'If apologies are out of order,' I said, 'then presumably you summoned me here for some other purpose.'

'Simply to meet you. I'm *such* an admirer of your work. And talking of meetings, I would love to arrange for you to meet our other resident musical celebrity, Monsieur Louis Grenier.'

'Monsieur Grenier and I have already met,' I said.

'How charming. You must have had lots to talk about. Did he mention to you some music that he is writing for the Society?'

'For the winter subscription concerts. Yes.'

'And did he tell you how he was progressing with the music?'

'He said . . . But Monsieur Grenier can speak for himself. I'm sure you'll get your music.'

'Mr Clearwater, I wish I shared your optimism. Every time I visit Monsieur Grenier, he sits down at the piano and plays me some phrases and melodies that he says will form the basis of the music. Some of them are quite delightful, but it's no substitute for having the scores. We must begin rehearsing this music soon. The winter subscription concerts are a very important part of our calendar. They're immensely popular. Now I was wondering if you might be able to help us out of our little difficulty. The problem with Monsieur Grenier seems to be that although his head teems with ideas, he just can't get them down on paper. I was wondering – if you worked with Monsieur Grenier, you might be able to help him realise his ideas. Of course, we'd recompense you appropriately.'

I stood. 'Mr Hinchcliff,' I said, 'you seem to be labouring under a misapprehension. I am a composer, not a secretary. I do not take dictation.'

Hinchcliff stood too, and his hands went through their placatory motions again. 'Oh I know, and *what* a composer! Of course, we are most anxious to play your own compositions at the Philharmonic Society. In fact, I was envisaging your assisting Monsieur Grenier as a kind of preparation for that. If you were to help us – perhaps even conduct the performances – it would serve as a good introduction to the orchestra. Your first meeting with them didn't, perhaps, strike the right note.' He laughed.

I could see right through Mr Roland Hinchcliff and his blackmail. Yes, dear sister, that was what it was. Either I was to do Grenier's dirty work or I would be frozen out of the musical life of the town. Now, it has never been my desire to be frozen out of anything. I sat down again and asked Hinchcliff how much he would pay me. Perhaps you think I gave in too easily? But the idea of lending form and substance to Grenier's vapid melodies amused me. Besides, my royalties are dribbling away. It was necessary not to be ostracised. After a few minutes' discussion, we had reached an arrangement. Hinchcliff said he would draw up a contract, then presented me again with that precious hand of his. I shook it and left.

> Your affectionate brother,
> Paul

16 October 2064

Dear Sister,

My life here has settled into a pattern. In the mornings I work, at noon I go down to the fishing beach, and in the evenings I play the piano and sing to the Grindley family.

Occasionally, I visit one of the ale houses in the Old Town. A dull life? A humdrum life? Not at all. I shall tell you in due course of some remarkable stirrings.

But back to routine. The mornings are devoted to sketches for my forthcoming *Sea Symphony*. I am in that wondering, febrile first stage of planning, plotting and projecting, that time when everything can be included, when the whole world is simply there to be expressed.

'No sound is dissonant which tells of life.'

I feel like a vessel into which the world is being poured. When I go down to the sea every day, I am filled with the sunlight and wheeling gulls, and with the strange metallic sound of the tide tugging at the shingle. When it is stormy, I sometimes go up on the East Hill, from where you can see the whole of the Old Town, and beyond it the West Hill, and then the New Town, and the pier, and beyond that the Coast stretching away. The mountainous waves far below crash on to the beaches, the raking rain mingles with the spray. The whole town is engulfed in a great cloud of water, as though the sea were stretching out to claw it off the land and into Neptune's clammy bosom. Up on the hill, the wind buffets me, forcing me to hold my hat down firmly on my head. These storms occur once or twice a week, but exhaust themselves quickly. I dash back to my lodgings to write some music.

Perhaps you will be surprised that I should take my inspiration so directly from Nature, given all that I have said about coming here to write a purer, instrumental music. Perhaps I should go along with Stendhal: '*La musique, qui est le plus vague des beaux-arts, n'est point descriptive à elle seule.*' But Stendhal was a diplomat. He knew nothing about music. Only someone imprisoned by words could write that music is '*le plus vague*' of the arts. Myself, I like Mendelssohn when he remarks that 'What any music *I* like expresses for me is not *thoughts too indefinite* to clothe in words, but *too definite.*' And I would go further. (Don't I always go further?

Don't I always go too far?) Music expresses something too definite to be expressed even in Nature, something that has a clarity lost when that something merely exists, bloated, obscene in its materiality. Those waves crashing on to the beach, the spray, even the wind buffeting around me – through their *movement* those elements express something definite and transcendent, but only dimly, because they are cloaked in vague, material forms. This is what Arthur Schopenhauer is trying to get at – in his heavy-footed, German way – when he writes that 'music is distinguished from all the other arts by the fact that it is not a copy of the phenomenon . . . but is the direct copy of the will itself, and therefore exhibits itself as the metaphysical to everything physical in the world, and as the thing-in-itself to every phenomenon.' The world is embodied music. But again I would go further. What is this talk of 'copying', of 'exhibiting' and 'expressing'? Music does not merely 'copy' or 'express' that primordial movement whose dim shadows flicker around us. It *is* that movement. When I see a woman's hips swing to ease her passage through the crowd, when I hear the wind snapping the flags on the seafront, then I am experiencing the echoes of a piece of music. It is *that* piece of music that I wish to compose. Like Faust, I yearn to

> . . . learn what holds the world together
> There at its inmost core;
> See the seeds of things, and power.

As you see, I have been ruminating busily over these elevated questions, and munching daintily among the tough and bitter weeds that writers have managed to push up in these fields. Poor fare. Sometimes, I confess, it distracts me from the real work of composition. Sitting in my room, I can spend hours gazing out to sea – can even feel for a while that I have a conception of that Absolute that I seek – but find by the end

31

of the morning that I have written nothing. Sometimes I do feel it is beyond me.

But all this is too morose. I can and will write the damned symphony. Already the thing is taking shape in my mind. The first movement I see most clearly. An arrival, the 'thing-in-itself' (to borrow Herr Schopenhauer's coagulation) of which my own happy feelings on arrival at the coast were merely an expression or 'copy'. A definite movement – not without its hesitations and holdings-back, but swept on again by winds of change and exuberant hope. The second movement. That is dimmer as yet. But it is fast and dark, with a hard, jarring note, like the wet, heaving otherness of the ocean itself. Perhaps it will have about it something of the dark, satanic scherzos of symphonic tradition.

And so on. I won't elaborate further, for fear that you will think I have given up music altogether in favour of merely writing about it. Well, I *have* been doing music, and in a severely practical form. Back to routine. Every afternoon I wend my way to Monsieur Grenier's house to take dictation. I approached this chore at first with a heavy heart, leavened only by my affection for Grenier's eccentricities. But in the event it has proved a happy task, surprising in its challenges and the bizarre turns it takes. Monsieur Grenier was not at all offended by Hinchcliff's suggestions that I should assist him with getting his compositions down on paper. Indeed, he leads his life at such a level of atmospheric elevation that I think he barely noticed the change. He sits at the piano and ripples out a *sonorité*; from time to time a theme pokes its head out, only to withdraw again whence it came. Since the sustaining pedal on Monsieur Grenier's piano seems to be permanently screwed down, it becomes difficult to pick out individual notes. To clarify matters for me, Grenier embroiders his improvisations with bizarre verbal descriptions. '*Une vague de chaleur déferle sur les violons*,' he will cry rapturously as another pentatonic mush flutters down from the top of the keyboard. These verbal arabesques continue even when – which is often – he gets up from the piano to pour himself a fresh cup of green tea. My own grows cold beside me on the table. Before me is a stack of manuscript paper on which I am attempting to realise Grenier's dreams. Fortunately, the old fellow seems to allow me a considerable degree of creative latitude (latitude in exchange for lassitude, one might say). At the end of each afternoon I show him what I have done, but he gives it barely a glance. He merely congratulates me and presses on me another cup of green tea.

At present we are working on what is to be the centrepiece of Grenier's presentation to the Philharmonic Society, his *Waltz of the Clouds*. God knows what will happen when Grenier hears it in my version, played by the Philharmonic Society orchestra. Imagine Johann Strauss living to hear Schoenberg's version of the *Blue Danube* waltz. Except that this will sound like Erik Satie reorchestrated by Berlioz.

Monsieur Grenier sees clouds in a very different way from myself, perhaps because he only ever sees them through a pane of glass. His clouds are very tame, cotton-wool affairs. The sad fact is that he never sets foot outside his house. Several times I have encouraged him to accompany me down to the beach to meet the fishermen whom I have made my friends. Each time I suggest it, he is seized with horror and flaps me away with his large, flipper-like hands. 'What am I doing with people like that?' he remonstrates. 'I am an artist, a composer. What am I doing with people who are so . . . crude?' It takes Monsieur Grenier considerable effort to summon this last word from his limited English vocabulary, and when he has blurted it out he smiles broadly, pleased with himself at having found so much *le mot juste*. I smile back. It is impossible not to like the old fellow.

But back to the fishermen, and to the stirrings that I promised you at the beginning of this letter. These are exciting times in Wellfleet, and once again I find myself at the heart of things.

A few evenings back, I was invited to a soirée at Mr

Roland Hinchcliff's house. It was the kind of event that mother would have loved, a gathering of the highest of Wellfleet's *haut monde*. Red carpets, twinklings of polished silver and conversation as brittle as bone china. Miss Grindley had been pressed into service to sponge my most sober dress suit, and I arrived at Mr Hinchcliff's feeling as trussed up and apprehensive as a chicken at the door of the oven. I have never, as you know, enjoyed these social ordeals.

But with three brimming glasses of sherry swiftly downed, I began to unbend. I plunged into the maelstrom. There were some twenty-five people present, of whom the first I was introduced to was the wife of the mayor. This was a hearty, rather engaging lady (bosom like the continental shelf, mountainous hips, jowls drooping to form a quivering cleft) who was already familiar with me from having been present at the infamous concert in the Everyman Theatre. 'Didn't know what on earth you were talking about,' she drawled to me now, 'but it was a beastly cold evening and I was damned grateful to get home early. "Well done that man!" I thought to myself.' This was a disarmingly straightforward perspective on the evening's events. I liked her for it.

As Roland Hinchcliff steered me around the company, introducing me, I began to appreciate the frisson of notoriety that now surrounded me. For Mr Hinchcliff, I was now Exhibit A in his case for the sublime volatility of the artistic temperament. 'Mr Clearwater is the saviour of the Philharmonic Society,' he announced, paddling me on the back. And he followed up each introduction with the following, sotto voce: 'But mind what you say to Mr Clearwater, or he'll interrupt you, and then you'll be sorry.' Whereupon he would leave me, and I would face his guests with an embarrassed and apologetic grin. That grin never left my face.

Fortunately, we were soon summoned to supper. But before we settle down to eat, I give you the principal characters in the company:

Roland Hinchcliff: See above.

Mary Hinchcliff, his wife: A small woman, with small features and a disapproving glance. Cropped brown hair. A novelist might describe her as 'mousey'. She only spoke to me once – to ask if I had had enough sherry. She spent the rest of the evening arguing with the servants.

Freeman Du Cros, the mayor of Wellfleet: Possibly the saddest-looking man I have ever seen. He has large-lidded, watery green eyes and a long, lugubrious face. His mouth bears a slight but permanent twist of pained surprise. His long body is folded up in his seat in an attitude of languid repose that says, with a sigh: 'Everything is simply *too much*.' The only perky thing about him is his moustache, whose whiskers taper elegantly up either cheek. But they merely serve to show up the absurd mournfulness of their setting. Unfortunately, Mr Du Cros's character is not nearly as diverting as his appearance. Indeed, he would be very interesting if he only kept his mouth shut. As soon as he opens it, he reveals a mind of numbing dullness, a mausoleum for secondhand, rock-like certainties. These are delivered in a voice of gravelly, awful rectitude, and attended with reverence by everyone else. He is in his fifties, has made his money from property and the hotel trade, and is the most powerful man in Wellfleet.

Barbara Du Cros, his wife: See above. The engaging lady with the aversion to icy theatres. Some people pick the strangest partners.

Clifford Patrick: The hairy man of whom I have spoken. Like Du Cros, a hotelier, and a man who sees himself going up in the world. He is in his late thirties and heavily built. He has coarse features and prominent, bushy eyebrows. His hair is rough and curly, like a dish scourer.

Madeleine Patrick, his wife: It seems inappropriate to leave this lady to last, because one's attention is inevitably drawn to her before all others. She is young, attractive, intelligent and – I suspect – quite unscrupulous. Though still only in her middle twenties, she has an unnerving maturity about her.

Her facial features are full and sensual, and her long dark hair is pinned up with studied carelessness, so as to allow wisps of it to fall down her gracefully curving neck. There is something cruel about this over-ripened bud, something cruel in her laughter and the things she laughs at. I suspect she is bored with her husband, who is older than her, and that she treats him rather roughly – and that he rather enjoys this. At first I assumed that she had only married him for his money, but then, watching them together, I detected a coarse, perhaps destructive bond between them. I imagine them enjoying a very active conjugal life, but without tenderness.

Picture this sextet of principals, then, occupying the head of the table and the centre of attention. Seated further down are the rest of the company, a nondescript bunch of hangers-on: the chorus. Between the two groups, occupying a kind of no-man's-land, is myself. As soon as we have sat down, the chorus sets up an ostinato of inconsequential chatter. The percussion department is busy as bottle greets glass and soup spoon makes the acquaintance of soup bowl. Meanwhile, the principals are still arranging their napkins on their lips and swapping pleasantries. They have more of everything, including time. Eventually they too turn their attention to the soup, and for a few moments a silence of engaged activity falls on the table. Then steps forward, figuratively, one of the chorus. In the programme he might be billed simply as 'Gentleman in yellow waistcoat'. A baritone. He is sitting closest to the principals, opposite me.

'I hear,' he says, directing his remark at Du Cros, but with an eye to the whole company, 'that *you know who* are having a "demonstration".' The word 'demonstration' is pronounced in an accent heavy with irony and mock presumption.

Freeman Du Cros merely nods, concentrating on the consumption of his soup. But the subject of yellow waistcoat's cryptic remark is of general knowledge and interest. Mrs Du Cros says, 'I have the greatest difficulty in understanding these people.' Everybody waits expectantly, but Mrs Du Cros has nothing more to say on the subject.

The baritone from the chorus, in an embellishment of his initial theme, attempts to entice the principals into song: 'I was wondering, Mayor, whether you would allow this "demonstration" to proceed?'

Du Cros grunts into his soup, then wipes his whiskers with his napkin and says, "Course they can demonstrate, if it makes them feel better. Get the thing off their chests. Won't do them any good in the long run. Corporation's made its decision.' He returns to his soup.

'I'm sure that we're *all* grateful that Mr Du Cros won't let himself be bullied,' says Mrs Hinchcliff, looking around the table darkly.

'Excuse me,' I said, 'but could someone tell me who "you know who" are?'

Madeleine Patrick laughed. 'What an innocent you are, Mr Clearwater,' she said.

'Not an innocent,' I replied levelly, 'just a newcomer.'

I hadn't intended this to be the least funny, but for the chorus it was clearly a devastating piece of repartee. They chuckled appreciatively as their soup bowls were removed and replaced with steaming plates of roast beef.

'Well, let me assist in the education of a newcomer,' said Mrs Patrick, leaning across the table towards me and lowering her eyes. ' "You know who" are the nasty fishermen who live down by the beach. These nasty fishermen mess up our nice clean town and make it smell of fish. They litter the place with their boats and nets and all their other nasty fishing stuff. And they have nasty accents. And if there weren't any nasty fishermen, then lots more people would come to stay in our nice clean town and spend their money. Your hotels would be full, wouldn't they, Freeman?'

Before Mr Du Cros had the opportunity of replying to this interesting suggestion, Clifford Patrick interrupted, 'My wife likes to turn things into a joke, Mr Clearwater, but actually it's a serious issue. The fishermen are getting hot under the collar because the Corporation is planning new sea defences. We've voted to extend the groyne between the pier and the fishing beach. This would build up the beach in front of the New Town, helping the development of the tourist trade. That's where the future of this town lies, not in fishing. The fishermen have just got to realise that.'

There were murmurs of approval all round the table for this. But not from me. I was having some difficulty following what this business was about – my glass had greeted the bottle so often as to become an old and dear friend – but what I did understand I didn't like. 'These fishermen of whom you talk,' I announced in a loud voice, 'are my dear friends.'

'Ah,' cried Roland Hinchcliff gleefully from the top of the table. 'The artistic temperament. Didn't I say?'

'And if my friends need help,' I continued, 'I shall give it to them.'

'Even if they don't want it?' asked Mrs Patrick.

'You'll find them a rough lot,' put in Mr Patrick.

'Perhaps we should move on to the dessert,' said Mrs Hinchcliff, grittily.

'A declaration of war!' exclaimed Mr Hinchcliff. 'How romantic.'

'I can never understand what this fellow is talking about,' drawled Mrs Du Cros.

'And anyway, the matter is closed,' droned Mr Du Cros.

This sextet succeeded in completely silencing me. What a vocal ensemble they made – from Madeleine Patrick's flighty coloratura down to Freeman Du Cros's basso profundo. I could not compete with them. So I sat back to enjoy Hinchcliff's fine white wine and strawberry mousse. But I had no intention of letting the matter of the fishermen and the sea defences rest. Next morning, I sought out Jacob Grindley to gain some enlightenment. He said that as it happened he had recently been applying considerable thought and attention to these groynes. It was a matter of considerable importance to the town, as was now being realised. Indeed it was Mr Grindley's opinion that the consequences would be even more far-reaching than the Corporation had hitherto admitted.

With the help of a plan of the seafront laid out on my desk, Mr Grindley proceeded to explain to me what was afoot. It was all rather technical, but I will try and give you an abstract of what I could understand. (If you remain mystified, perhaps father might be able to explain it. He must know about these things.) Anyway, the purpose of these groynes is to catch the shingle as it is pulled along the coast by the current, thus enabling a beach to accumulate. At present there are half-a-dozen of them along the seafront at Wellfleet, each consisting of a stone wall projecting approximately forty yards out from the promenade into the water. At low tide these groynes are fully exposed. Only one of them is at present more substantial than this, and that is the one at the very eastern edge of the town, at the end of the fishing beach furthest from the New Town. This one projects some sixty yards out to sea. Its importance – and that of the other groynes – is shown by the state of the coast immediately beyond it to the east. There, because the drifting shingle has all been trapped before the town, the cliffs are exposed and subject to considerable erosion. Fortunately, nobody lives there.

This is how things stand at present. The Corporation's plan, which was passed comfortably in a vote several weeks ago, is to strengthen and extend two of the groynes to a distance of one hundred yards. These groynes are the ones immediately to the west of the fishing beach and another further along towards the pier. This will have the effect of building up a greater area of beach in front of the New Town. The fishing beach will not have such increased protection, and thus will diminish in size by proportion. Indeed, according to Mr Grindley, the fishing beach will not only diminish in size proportionately, but also in actuality. Such is the increasing strength of the storms and currents along the coast during the autumn and winter months, that unless the existing groyne at the eastern end of the fishing beach is strengthened and enlarged as well, the beach will suffer significant depradations.

Following this masterly exposition of the physical facts of the matter – illustrated with much drawing of diagrams – Mr Grindley proceeded with a fascinating analysis of the political forces working to bring about this state of affairs. The Wellfleet Corporation, which exercises jurisdiction over Old and New Towns, is apparently dominated by a clique of men who thrive on the tourist trade – hoteliers, restaurateurs, impresarios of various sorts. The purveyors, in short, of all the false glitter that I loathed in the New Town. The head of this clique, of course, is Freeman Du Cros. By log-rolling and various other forms of manipulation, this group was able to secure large majorities for its proposals concerning the new sea defences. The handful of councillors who raised tentative objections on behalf of the fishing community were overwhelmed. It was Mr Grindley's judgement that the fishing interest lacked political sophistication. (That alone would no doubt damn them in father's eyes.) He explained how the fishing community had originally been attracted here, as to other places along the Coast, by Utopian ideals. They would live close to Nature. They would dispense with the machines, systems and organisations that had crimped and cramped the soul of modern man. Even now these ideals were kept alive by certain individuals. Grindley gave the example of his friend Matthew Rimmer, 'a philosopher of the school of William Morris'. Grindley himself was in sympathy with these ideals, but on the other hand (such is the balance of his mind, the judiciousness of his judgements) he could see how they had harmed the interests of the Old Town. They had blinded the fishing community to the importance of political organisation, which in turn meant that the fishermen had been backward in fighting for their rights within the existing political structures of the Coast. For years, he said, Wellfleet Corporation had been passing measures inimical to the interests of the fishermen – restricting their activities, forcing them off certain areas of the beach. For, from the Corporation's point of view, balanced against the consideration that the fishing beach had some value for its 'quaintness' were the weightier ones that visitors might be put off by its 'unsightliness' and the fact that it took up a significant section of the seafront that might otherwise be given over to mindless frippery. The ultimate aim of certain leading figures in the Corporation, Mr Grindley feared, was the complete eradication of the fishing community.

Grindley's analysis struck me like a thunderbolt. Here was a cause which no lover of liberty and humanity could ignore. Grindley had given me the eyes with which to see through the smooth phrases of Du Cros, Hinchcliff, Patrick and the others. Thinking back to the night before, I felt nauseous at having drunk their white wine and eaten their strawberry mousse. Now, thanks to Grindley, I knew on which side of the barricades I stood.

It is evening now and I write by a single guttering candle, exhausted from having composed all day. Grindley's revelation to me concerning the oppression of the fishermen put a kind of fire in my belly, and I have been able to compose more freely than for some time. Everything else has been forgotten. Monsieur Grenier has had to vaporise without me. But tomorrow I shall go down to the beach and talk to the fishermen. I shall offer them my solidarity, my fraternity, and whatever help is in my power. Why have my friends not mentioned this matter to me before now? They need my assistance. What is an artist if he cannot help those among whom he works?

> Yours in love and resolution,
> Paul

Dear Sister,

I still receive no reply to my letters. With mother and father, I could always predict what they were going to say – but you, Jean, I could always listen to. Please write. Is it that I am not forgiven for leaving New Venice so suddenly? The city had become for me something dark and hard, something that enclosed without giving comfort – something like a trap. In my claustrophobia, I began to long for open skies and horizons, for wind on my cheeks. I often used to walk to the very western edge of New Venice, to look out across the water at the mountains beyond. There at least I could escape the closed-in feeling of the city, those passages, canals, arcades and courtyards. There were no indoors and outdoors in New Venice, no feeling of freedom when you stepped out of the door. Even the air felt bricked in. That's why I used to walk out to the Fondamenta Nuove. Did you know that there are seagulls there, wheeling over the open water? I suppose they come over the mountains from the Coast.

The story of New Venice is almost the story of our family. I've known no other place. Strange, then, that when I looked out across the water I felt nostalgic for something. I can hear you laughing at that. Cottimi would laugh too.

Cast out the Gods who have usurped my power and return to my laws. Return to nature from which you have fled; she will console you and dispel all those fears which now oppress you. Submit to nature, to humanity, and to yourself again; and you will find flowers strewn all along the pathway of your life.

Well, I have followed Diderot's good advice. I have returned.

I have submitted myself to the Coast. I want to believe in the Coast utterly, and have found encouragement in the fishermen and their daily struggle to catch a living from the sea. Their life is real, tangible and authentic. I feel my own life become more real by contact with them.

All of which is a preamble to saying that, true to the resolution of my last letter, I have offered them my solidarity and support. On the morning after I had written I went down to the beach, just when the boats were in, and presented myself to a group of them. I told them that I was making myself available. Every atom of my mind and body would be devoted to their cause. They told me about the march that was to take place the following week and suggested that I come along to that. Now that was all well and good, but I wanted to do more. It suddenly occurred to me that a protest march needs a protest song, an anthem to raise the spirits and rally the troops. I put this to them and, meeting no opposition, considered it approved. Fired with enthusiasm. I walked back to my lodgings and within the hour had come up with something suitably stirring:

> A fisherman, he can't be told
> 'Bout rain or fog or sleet or cold.

> Chorus: *O save our shingle, save our beach,*
> *Our need for groynes we've come to teach.*

> He sails at dawn, he sails at night,
> The snow and storm he has to fight.

> *O save our shingle etc.*

> He feeds the people of this coast
> With fish to boil or grill or roast.

O save our shingle etc.

His livelihood is just the boat
That keeps him and his crew afloat.

O save our shingle etc.

His boat he drags up on the beach
Safe from the sea's destructive reach.

O save our shingle etc.

Without the groynes the beach would go,
Be swept away like melted snow.

O save our shingle etc.

The council's plans mean certain doom,
For the fishermen there'd be no room.

O save our shingle etc.

For the fishermen no beach at all,
Just pubs and hotels wall to wall.

O save our shingle etc.

The starving child and weeping wife
Cringe beneath the burghers' knife.

O save our shingle etc.

So men and women stand together
For groynes for all to fight the weather!

O save our shingle etc.

To go with this Brechtian ditty, I composed the kind of jaunty march that Weill himself would have been proud of. I envisaged it as a call-and-response song – like a Negro spiritual – with a Mother Courage figure, standing in a cart, rousing the crowd of fishermen who march around her. The overall effect, in my mind at least, was quite striking.

In the event, unfortunately, I had to play Mother Courage myself. I had hired the church hall and advertised a rehearsal, so that people could learn the song before the big day, but only two old men turned up. One was tone deaf, the other stone deaf, and both, I suspected, had come in the hope that an open rehearsal might include free beer. But I was not disheartened. The tune was simple enough, and with a following breeze the crowd could pick it up on the day.

The big day arrived, and I arrived at the fishing beach with the cart and driver that I had hired for the occasion. A crowd of some five hundred people milled about, some of them carrying banners fashioned out of old sheets and fishing nets. No one seemed to be in charge, and a half-hour passed before, by an act of collective spontaneity, we started moving off along the front towards the New Town. I directed my driver to a place near the front of the march and, standing, tried to rouse the crowd to song. This, I may say, took a good deal of nerve – not least because, what with the cart constantly stopping and starting as the procession shuffled forward, it was exceedingly difficult to keep my balance. To begin with, the crowd was singularly unresponsive, even despite the hearty 'All together now!' with which I prefaced each chorus. I must have been through the damned song a good half-dozen times – by which time we were almost in the New Town – before I began to get some murmured response. In order to rouse them further and keep them all singing in time, I took my hand from the rail of the cart and began conducting them. Result: when the cart next stopped, I was thrown on to my backside. Much hilarity.

The demonstration proceeded into the main square of

the New Town. Gulls wheeled overhead and the smart villa gleamed whitely in the pallid sunlight, the railings in front of them grinning at us like malevolent black teeth. When everybody had filed into the square, there was something of a hiatus. Because I, in my cart, had been near the front, I now found myself at the top of the square, with the crowd facing me.

'What happens now?' I asked a man who was standing beside the cart.

'We all go home again.'

'Is that all? What about speeches?'

'We don't want speeches. That's undemocratic. Smacks of people thrusting themselves forward.'

I had been crouching to speak to this fellow. When I stood up again to stretch my legs, I felt the gaze of many eyes on me. Being higher than the rest, up on the cart, I formed a natural focus of attention. In that moment, something strange happened to me. I fear you will laugh at this, sister. In that moment, I felt a sense of . . . destiny. It was rather like the moment when you are standing before an orchestra, baton in hand, waiting to begin, and you feel the music come upon you as something inevitable, something irresistible. You raise your hand to get the orchestra's attention almost with resignation, almost wearily, as though carrying a burden. It is a gesture that is not so much demanding as demanded. But I can hear you laughing by now. If you were here to speak, you would tell me that this is just a fancy way of saying I felt a sense of power. Yes, I'll admit that power is involved. But it is not power as you are thinking of it or as the fishermen fear it, not the power simply of one person over another. It is the power of a climax to a great symphony, when all that has gone before, all those gradually gathering forces, demand *this* and no other. That is not power for the sake of it. The trumpeters forge their mighty sound not just to prove that they are strong fellows with healthy lungs that can blow long and hard. There is something beyond any of them at stake. Again I felt that sense of transcendent force

46

that I feel when the wind buffets me on East Hill. Or perhaps you still dream of a world without power. Without even *that* kind of power? What world would that be? A world without Art, without inspiration, without dreams? What *is* this world that you dream of, sister?

I have strayed a long way from the fishermen. Whatever it was that steeled me to it, I began to speak to the crowd. And miraculously, a hush fell on my audience almost as soon as I began to speak. I could hear my voice echo around the tall, white villas that enclose the square. Only the gulls vied with me, screeching as they glided backwards and forwards across the cold sky. My speaking was such a thing of the moment, so little anticipated, that it is only with great difficulty that I can recall it. But it went something like this: 'Friends, fishermen. I understand that nobody was going to speak today. But it seems right that somebody should say something. Words are needed to mark an occasion like this. Of course, I realise that I have no claim to be the one to say those words. I am a newcomer in your midst. Several weeks ago I came here from the city in search of a life that was true and honest, a life that could provide inspiration for my own work of composing music. I have found that life here on the coast, in the movements of the sea, in the wind and the rain – and in you, my friends. I sail out only across seas of my own imagining, but you sail on the real sea, the sea that rolls and tosses you and clogs your hair with salt. I celebrate you for that. Every day you put yourself in the hands of the sea. You submit yourselves to Nature. There is nothing nobler. Surely, friends, you will find flowers strewn all along the pathway of your life.'

At this point, I found myself quite overcome with emotion, and had to stop for a few moments to blow my nose, wipe my eyes, and generally recover myself.

'Friends,' I resumed, 'there will always be those who will look down on you and oppress you because you labour and have rough hands. I know. I too, in my different way, dirty

47

my hands with the stuff of life. But the people who despise us do nothing. They risk nothing. They gain nothing. They are scared of life, and we have nothing to fear from them. Remember, friends, that when Our Lord sent his only son into the world, it was among fishermen that he found his first disciples. If we stand as one before the Corporation, they will never be able to impose their will upon us. Friends, the future is yours!'

With all due modesty, I must say that this speech garnered considerable applause. I waved it away self-deprecatingly and raised a clenched fist. The crowd turned round and began to make its own way back along the front towards the Old Town. I tried to get some singing going again, but by this time it was beginning to rain.

Next day I went to the fishing beach and gained some impression of how my performance had been received. I think they have hopes of me. One or two of them commented that they were aware of my being acquainted with Du Cros and the other Wellfleet burghers. I think they are beginning to look on me as their representative in those salons of power.

These weighty matters have filled so much paper that I find I now have no time to tell you of Monsieur Grenier's vaporisations and other musical doings. They will have to wait for another occasion, for now I must run to catch the post.

With love,
Paul

9 November 2064

Dear Sister,

Forgive me for not writing sooner. Whirlwinds of activity surround me, stirrings as irresistible as the winds that whirl around our sea-perched town. I promised you news of my musical doings. My communal ruminations with Monsieur Grenier have been issuing in completed scores, which I have been delivering to my copyists as I complete them. For that task I have engaged two of the younger members of the orchestra: Jim Wilkins – who you will remember as the enthusiastic horn player and younger brother of the journalistic Thomas – and Janet Truss, a dumpy girl with dull eyes and cascades of beautiful red hair who sits in the violas. For the young people concerned this is a blissfully happy arrangement, since it is obvious that young Wilkins adores the ground upon which young Truss treads. Now they have a perfect excuse to remain closeted together in warm intimacy for days on end. The erotic charge in the air does, however, blunt the urgency of the copying. More than once I have burst in upon this love-nest to find young Wilkins' pen dangling limply from his fingers as he gazes, chin in hand, across the table at his Ideal. So deep are his sighs that if you put a horn to his mouth they would produce a round passionate note.

As fast as the vapours wafted from Grenier's brain and were fixed beneath my pen, I delivered them into the sweaty hands of the young lovers. And so I scurried back and forth between these two centres of languid inertia. The programme gradually began to take shape. The *Waltz of the Clouds* remained in a rather amorphous state, but enough of the other pieces were orchestrated and copied for a first rehearsal to be called. Now, the venue for the rehearsal was the old ballroom at the end of the pier, a place of beautiful, faded grandeur. I love the fantasies of plaster, the cornices like wedding cakes, and all of it finished with a romantically peeling lacquer of blue and pink paintwork. On the terrace outside fish gloomy anglers, who turn every now and then to peer in through the steamed-up windows at the assembling orchestra. Beneath the wooden floorboards you can hear, far below, the sea. A soft rain is falling. As the musicians dribble in and start arranging themselves, I sit at the back of the hall and listen. Outside the windows there are only the hunched figures of the anglers, and beyond them, in every direction, the heaving, white-flecked greenness of the sea. Every now and then the wind changes, a gust sweeps off the sea against the pier, and rain patters against the windows. Somewhere on the pier behind me a door bangs shut in the wind.

It was the closest I had come to being out at sea. The magic of the place flooded me. I felt myself shiver with every shift in the direction and strength of the wind, dissolve with every distant crash of a breaker. But gradually, more mundane sounds began to impinge on this aquatic reverie: the out-of-tune open strings of a violin being stroked; a cello plucked; a rippling scale on a clarinet; a trombone belching quietly in the background. With a sigh, I stood and approached the orchestra to begin the rehearsal.

But before we could begin there were some preliminaries. I introduced myself and went through the usual pleasantries about what an honour it was to be working with them, etc, etc. This was rather farcical, since they already knew perfectly well who I was. There was none of the hostility I had been fearing, but instead the odd look of interest and amusement. Most, though, seemed indifferent. Introductions over, I talked a bit about Monsieur Grenier's compositions, praising them lavishly and explaining the particular problems in interpreting 'these exquisite, gem-like scores'. All this was part of a Machiavellian plan I had concocted to prune some of the dead wood I had observed in the orchestra during that disastrous concert in the Everyman Theatre. I explained that the delicate, gossamer-like quality of Grenier's orchestration demanded a reduced string body. On the other hand (I didn't have the heart to sack anybody), the fecundity of his aural imagination, the dazzling variety of timbres he called upon, demanded an enhanced percussion section. These additions would provide the flecks of colour, as in a pointillist painting, that would bring the whole composition to life. (In fact, of course, I had written these percussion parts myself, and in such a way that they would be scarcely audible behind the rest of the orchestra.) The delicate and precise execution of these percussion parts, I added, required musicians with decades of orchestral experience.

In this way, with infinite cunning and diplomacy, I was able to winkle out a handful of the more decrepit and slap-dash string players – including the old Mozart-mauler in the second violins – and install them safely out of harm's way at the back of the orchestra and behind an array of triangles, wood blocks and miniature gongs. Everyone was satisfied. We were ready to begin.

With these changes, the Philharmonic Society orchestra became a much more competent band of musicians than had appeared that night in the Everyman Theatre. With a clear beat, most of the string players could keep time well, and there were one or two excellent soloists in the wind section. The first clarinet had a luscious tone, even if he did tend to linger on any scrap of melody and perform altogether too flamboyantly. But these were good faults, the kind that could be channelled to artistic purpose.

The first piece that we rehearsed was the 'Arrival and Sacred Dance of the Spirits of the Air', which Grenier intended as a kind of overture to the rest of the music. It is perhaps the closest that Louis Grenier's fluttering and mias-mic musical imagination could get to a fanfare. Imagine for yourself Handel's noble 'Arrival of the Queen of Sheba' shrouded in fog and you will have caught something of its spirit. The approaching spirits of the air are represented by pulsing chords in the wind section – somewhat reminiscent of the second movement of Beethoven's Eighth Symphony, only smoother and with richer harmonies. These begin *pianissimo* (difficult to do, but surprisingly well achieved by the Wellfleet musicians) and build to a solid *forte*. Meanwhile, the cellos have entered with long, single notes that disintegrate into the beginnings of a melody. The violas take over, then the violins. The first flute detaches itself from the body of the wind and performs a series of flutter-tongued arabesques. And so forth.

The musicians read all this with remarkable efficiency, and I was able to let them simply play through it, to get a feel for the notes. I must admit that my mind began to wander as I conducted. (I had grown over-familiar with the music from having worked on it so hard with Monsieur Grenier.) I couldn't help thinking of the real, natural sounds of the wind, and how I would have attempted a more subtle representation of them than Monsieur Grenier had achieved. To use the wind instruments *en bloc*, building from *pianissimo* to *forte*, struck me as – to use Grenier's own word – 'crude'. In the Violin Concerto by Edward Elgar there is an accompanied cadenza in which the orchestral string players are instructed to play *pizzicato tremolo*, strumming the strings of their instruments with the fleshy parts of their thumbs. The effect gives a magical depth to the sound. That is the effect I would use to represent the wind approaching over the water, with waves of *pizzicati tremoli* sweeping across the strings, dying away, then surging up again. The wind itself is invisible, which is why Grenier's portrayal is so crude, but one can represent the vibrations and tensions it creates. The eerie, thrumming strings could be the riggings of boats humming in the gathering wind. Then I thought of a whip-crack, to represent a flag or banner snapping in the wind. Grenier's picture was too soft, too lacking in 'harsh reality'.

These meditations, pursued while I dutifully beat time, began as idle, technical thoughts as to how I would have tackled the problem Grenier had set himself. But as I pursued them, I began to consider them more seriously, in relation to my own *Sea Symphony*. And all at once I saw the first movement of my symphony clearly, saw how the wind would dominate it, blow through it constantly, with gusts that would suddenly shake up the musical materials to create new and expected patterns. I had thought of it hitherto simply as a human arrival (*my* arrival) at the Coast. Now I saw that it was the arrival, too, of the wind, and with it of that transcendent force or inspiration that brings music into being. My symphony would be a hymn not just to the sea, but to music itself.

Meanwhile, throughout these fanciful thoughts, the orchestra was continuing to muster Grenier's Spirits of the Air, and was now encouraging them to dance. Grenier is capable of writing good, well-sprung dance music, but in this instance his idea of dancing – perhaps because unencumbered Spirits of the Air were involved – was to create as much frantic, directionless activity as possible, like someone running on the spot, or a doodle drawn by a neurotic. I think Grenier may have had something Mendelssohnian in mind, but the result was muddle. The first violins scampered up and down their fingerboards, then the second violins followed in canon; the clarinet warbled on high, the bassoon grumbled below. Grenier may have been trying to write a fugue, but it was evident that the passing years had taken their toll on his grasp of that demanding form. The only point of clarity in the music was a strutting, dotted figure that was passed from one instrument to another. As the orchestra got more and more lost in Grenier's sea of notes, the musicians latched on to this figure as a drowning man might snatch at a piece of passing driftwood. It came at me from all directions, in no way corresponding to what was in my score. The music fell apart, and the musicians, exhausted and bewildered, put down their instruments and laughed. From that moment, any vestige of frostiness that might have existed between the orchestra and myself was swept aside. We got on famously.

This happy occasion took place on the day before the fishermen's demonstration, the dramatic unfolding of which I recounted in my last letter. The rehearsals continued after the demonstration, of course, but I found myself preoccupied now by these public affairs. How can I convey to you, sister, the sense of weighty responsibility that was descending on my shoulders? This is something quite new for me. As you know, I never involved myself in politics or public affairs in New Venice. Frank Cottimi looked after that side of things, defending our productions against the philistines in the Municipal Department of Culture. I had work to do. And besides, I was always confused in New Venice. I could never discover the political battle-lines. Things slipped through your fingers as easily as the water through the canals. No, to fight a battle there have to be sides. It you tried to draw the political battle-lines in New Venice, you would end up with a scribble as convoluted as the canals and alleys that make up the physical structure of the place. Here things are much simpler. Everyone knows which side they are on, including myself. My sense of the rightness of the fishermen's cause sustains me. My only doubts have concerned my own ability to fulfil the role of leadership that has fallen into my hands. But never underestimate the invigorating effects of a sense of righteousness. It clears the head as powerfully as a blast of the fresh sea air.

I think of the wonderful phrase 'natural justice'. How true and just a phrase it is! There *is* something natural about justice. It is as pure, unadorned and bracing as a gull wheeling across a cold blue sky. It is as unarguable as that. I think of Handel's music – the way, when one listens to it, one feels opened to the acknowledgement that it could be no other way. It is inevitable, but not in the sense of trite or 'predictable'. When it moves towards a noble cadence, it is justice that is being fulfilled. To argue against it would be as futile as reasoning with a tree that it should stop growing.

So that when I approached the offices of Mayor Du Cros a few days after the demonstration, to argue the case for the fishermen, I felt very much as I had done that night when I walked away from the Everyman Theatre along the wind-swept seafront. Then, the falsity and artificiality of the concert was smashed in my mind by the natural music of the storm. Now, the selfish power of the Corporation would be smashed by the natural justice of the fishermen's cause.

But please don't think that I have been so naive as to suppose that a sense of righteousness would be enough. I have been putting together a case for the fishermen that would impress the most hard-nosed of lawyers. I say 'I', but most of the work on this aspect of the affair has been done by Jacob Grindley. I find myself rather ashamed now of the way I ridiculed this good man in one of my letters. He is in fact a genuine man of science, a gentleman of diligent learning and fathomless curiosity. If his conversation takes a surprising turn sometimes, those abrupt transitions are no more than traces left by the trajectory of his swift and lofty mind. Within this limited, small-town sphere, he is something of a Galileo.

Jacob Grindley has become my indefatigable and invaluable assistant. He has prepared for me a substantial dossier that puts forward the fishermen's case in unarguable terms. It includes numerous diagrams and calculations that show beyond doubt the catastrophic effect that the council's plans would have on the fishermen. Every week that passes strengthens our case, as gale after gale is swept along the coast. Without the protection of a more substantial groyne, the fishing beach would eventually be swept away by this onslaught.

Everything about Du Cros's office spoke of stuffy stiffness and falsity, from the stout, leather-clad volumes standing like pillars of rectitude on the bookshelves to the mayoral robes draped around a clothes horse by the door. On the walls hung badges and chains of office. Gulls soared and dived beyond the window, but they made no noise. It was as quiet as the grave in that mayoral office. Freeman Du Cros sat amidst his finery, bearing his usual expression of tender and regretful sadness. He opened his mouth and revealed his gravelly coldness.

'What do you want?' he growled, looking at me with his brimming eyes.

I sat down on the chair opposite him and placed Mr Grindley's bulging dossier on the desk between us.

'I've come to seek justice for the fishermen in the matter of the groynes,' I said.

'Won't do any good,' he snapped back. 'Corporation's already decided the thing. Still, if you want to get it off your chest . . .'

'If,' I began, 'the Corporation go ahead with their plan for a new groyne at the western end of the fishing beach, it will mean the destruction of the beach and disaster for the fishing community.'

'Poppycock. Won't make the least difference to them.'

'But I heard the way you were all talking that night at Mr Hinchcliff's. You *know* that it would be ruinous for the fishermen.'

'Balderdash. I never heard anyone say that. Who said that? Give me chapter and verse.'

'It was the mood of the whole conversation.'

'Mood? Moods won't stand up in a court of law.'

'I'm not talking about a court of law.'

'I'm glad to hear it, for your sake.'

'If you would only examine the evidence that I have compiled here, I am sure you will reach the same conclusion as I. I'm appealing to your sense of natural justice.'

In reply, Du Cros grunted and told me that if it made me feel better I could leave my evidence with him. I should come back at the same time tomorrow for an answer.

Well, I went back to Du Cros the next day and got my answer. He saw no reason for the matter to be referred back to the Corporation.

You can well imagine the state of despondency into which this harsh decision cast me. As is my wont, I sought solace in Nature. I walked down to the sea's edge, where all was calm and the waves lapped and teased at the shingle. The sea always seems to act as an echo for my own emotions. In turbulent moods it seems a great panorama of conflict and variety, with waves jostling and swathes of light and shade passing swiftly across the scene. But I looked out across the waves now and saw hopeless uniformity, a monotony of heaving water, a desert.

There's a place at the eastern end of the fishing beach called Rock-a-Nore. Its name captures something of its wild and romantic spirit. Beyond the last groyne, o'ershadowed by the cliffs of East Hill, are savage outcrops of rock, swirling pools and jagged headlands. Great boulders of the soft brown limestone lie where they have fallen from the eroded cliff. The place is a grim, sublime battlefield of the elements. This would be the fate of the Old Town were the fishing beach to go. I remained here for a long while, gazing at the rocks and at the mournful sea. It was almost dark when at last I turned my back on the heaving waves and headed for home.

> Calm and deep peace in this wide air,
> These leaves that redden to the fall;
> And in my heart, if calm at all,
> If any calm, a calm despair.

Back at my lodgings, I sat down with Jacob Grindley and told him the sad story of my rebuff.

'That is unfortunate,' was his mild reply.

'Unfortunate?' I cried. 'It is an insult to justice and humanity.'

'Perhaps,' said Mr Grindley, 'it would be as well to approach the matter in a different way.'

'What do you mean?'

'In a siege, if the fortress cannot be taken by frontal assault, one uses more indirect methods, one tunnels beneath the walls. With regard to Mayor Du Cros and the council, it might be as well to look for some point at which you might have some influence or leverage. Mr Hinchcliff, for example. You are having some dealings with him over the Philharmonic Society. And Mr Hinchcliff is not without influence upon Mayor Du Cros and the Corporation. Perhaps that would be a fruitful area of exploration.'

In a flash of light I saw where Grindley's thoughts were leading. I clasped his hand in mine and thanked him. He murmured modestly in reply and begged to be excused, for the hour was late. When he was gone, I took out a pen and paper and began this letter.

The world now lies deep in the bowels of night. My head is a ferment of sparks and movement, as new hopes and resolutions penetrate my consciousness like shafts of bright, revealed sunlight. I will present Hinchcliff with an ultimatum; either he bring about a change of heart by the Corporation, or I will withdraw my services as conductor of the Philharmonic Society orchestra and arranger of Monsieur Grenier's music. We are now in the final rehearsals for the winter subscription concerts, and were I to withdraw it would almost certainly mean their cancellation. The burghers of Wellfleet value their entertainments, and Mr Hinchcliff values his position as President of a smoothly running Philharmonic Society. This blackmail will present him with a hard choice. If he decides to let me go, at least I will have made my stand. I can do no other. But now I must sleep. Already I feel the bonds of wakefulness slacken. Beyond my window, the world is beginning to stir 'Under the opening eyelids of the morn'.

Your ever-loving brother,
Paul

Dear Sister,

Do you remember my writing, weeks ago now, that the thought of Monsieur Grenier ruminating in his room had given me the idea for an opera? That was the germ, and now I have caught the disease. My fever is high.

This sudden relapse into artistic fervour occurred about a week ago, when I went to visit the venerable composer. I had not seen Monsieur Grenier for a while. My transcriptions of his vapours had long been completed. Even the evanescent *Waltz of the Clouds* was now fixed in ink. There were a number of small points I was keen to consult him on, and I also wanted to press him one more time to attend at least the final rehearsals. Hitherto he had waved aside all my invitations to hear the orchestra play his music. I was rather proud of the results of my labours and, in my affection for Grenier, wanted him to have the satisfaction of hearing his imaginings realised. But my principal reason for wanting to see him was the ultimatum that I intended to present to Roland Hinchcliff. Since my actions might result in the cancellation of the subscription concerts, I felt myself honour bound to gain Grenier's agreement before proceeding.

I was greeted with the habitual bowl of green tea. Monsieur Grenier was in a state of lassitude, a victim of torpor. He collapsed on to his chaise longue, held out his hand to indicate that I too should sit, then closed his eyes and sighed.

'Increasingly,' he murmured, 'I find reality failing to live up to the demands of Art.'

Since this observation clearly lay at the end of a long and wearying round of thought, I forbore from pointing out that Art itself is composed of the stuff of reality. Take away that stuff, and you are left with the ghost of the memory of an abstraction. But the remark was so charmingly in character, so well within the ample Grenier mould, that I could not help but be delighted by it. Already the disease was taking hold. My temperature was up.

'There are a number of small points I wanted to check with you,' I said, consulting the folder of manuscript on my lap. 'matters of rhythm and tempo.'

'Please no,' he interrupted in a distressed tone. 'I leave all that in your capable arms. I am drained.' He took another gulp of tea. 'I cannot bear to go through it all again. My thoughts have flown the nest. Let them find perches where they will.'

He smiled with satisfaction, though this pleasantry sounded a little rehearsed to me. I closed the folder.

'All this tinkering and revision,' he continued. 'I have not the energy for it. During these days I am all the time creating, creating. Through my agony I bring these creations to birth. Am I expected also to nursemaid them?'

This was hardly a prospectus for responsible artistic parenthood. But before I could say anything in reply, Monsieur Grenier had heaved himself to his feet and was staggering across the room to his piano, the tails of his untucked batik shirt flapping behind him.

'All the time it is create, create, create,' he said, striking a large, glutinous chord. 'It pours from me. This piece I have called "Twelve Ways of Looking at a Vacuum".'

With a sigh of my own, I put the folder of music on the floor, my feet on the footstool, and let Grenier's music pour over me. What poured over me more than anything else was Louis Grenier's laboured breathing. His music contained enough silence to fill several vacuums of its own. And each one was a blessed relief, for his piano was excruciatingly out of tune.

'Your piano is rather out of tune,' I said, when one silence had lasted so long that it could only mean the performance was at an end.

Grenier, sweat dripping from all chins, shook his head weakly. 'It doesn't matter,' he said. 'The thought is there.'

'But I don't know how you can bear to hear your music like that. It sounds dreadful.'

Grenier looked at me as though waking from a dream. 'Sounds?' he murmured. 'Bear it?' He looked down at the piano, as though noticing it for the first time. 'I never play it these days, except when you come to visit. Look, it is so dusty.' He blew on the keyboard, and a large brown cloud billowed into the still air. 'Why should I need to play it? I have all the sounds in my head.'

'But you haven't even written them down.'

'They are written in my mind. I do not need the pen and paper.'

'But they can't possibly be music while they're stuck inside your head,' I said with some exasperation. 'Look, why don't you come along to one of the rehearsals and *hear* some of your music? You could hear it as others hear it.'

'I do not want to hear it as others hear it,' he said grumpily, returning to his chaise longue. 'I like only the way *I* hear it. If I keep the music locked inside my head, I have the perfect audience, *n'est-ce pas*? There is nobody coughing or cleaning his nose or thinking about his dinner. My music is heard as it should be heard.'

'But it isn't heard,' I protested. 'There's just silence.'

'Ah, but all music comes from silence, *n'est-ce pas*? What is music without silence?'

'But it can't be *just* silence.'

'*Just* silence? What is wrong with silence? There are many kinds of silence. One day I will compose a beautiful silence.'

I should add that all this was said without a trace of humour. Grenier was quite serious. For my part I found it quite surreal.

'But, Louis,' I said, 'music is sound. What else can it be?'

He looked at me scornfully. 'Music comes from silence, it returns to silence. Silence is the thing it points to, its purpose, just as the purpose of life is death. The most perfect piece of music would achieve that silence. It would escape the prison

61

of sound. It would rid itself of sensuousness and achieve silence. *N'est-ce pas?*'

Of course, I was familiar with all this as an idea. Bridget Lampion tried to express it in operatic form some years ago in her *En Attendant Godot*. But what alarmed me was that Grenier was treating it not merely as an idea but as a way of living.

'There was something else I wanted to ask you,' I said, to change the subject. 'I am considering a course of action that may lead to the cancellation of the subscription concerts.' I explained to him, as briefly as I could, the problem of the groynes and how I intended to fight the fishermen's cause. He regarded me with weary incomprehension.

'You must do as you wish,' he said when I had finished. 'I leave the matter entirely in your hands. It is of no consequence to me any more. When the music leaves my head, it ceases to be mine. It is of no consequence to me whether it is heard or not, provided I receive my money. As for your association with these crude fellows who fish in the sea, I do not understand it in an artist like yourself. And I do not share your enthusiasm for these sea walls. I do not like the idea of building walls to stop the sea. The sea is natural and free. May the sea run where the fancy takes it. But really it is of no consequence to me. We have talked of the matter enough. I am exhausted.' He took a deep, lingering gulp of tea.

I had mixed feelings on hearing this. I was happy, of course, that Monsieur Grenier had no objections to my going ahead with my plans. But there was something sad about Grenier that could not be ignored – sad, and at the same time sublimely ridiculous. Here, surely, was the theme for an opera. It had crossed my mind before how easy it would have been, should I have wished to do such a thing, to have passed off my transcriptions of Louis Grenier's musical meditations as my own compositions. Or, conversely, I could have written my own compositions and passed them off as his. And Grenier, I suspect, would not have cared one way or another.

And so the story came to me. An unworldly composer receives a commission from a rich patron. This elderly and distinguished composer has, like Grenier, taken to thinking that music exists in the head rather than as sounds in the air. Like Balzac's unfortunate Gambarra, *'il s'occupe nuit et jour à composer des opéras et des symphonies imaginaires, au lieu de chercher à gagner honnêtement sa vie.'* He finds himself struggling with the tedious reality of having to fulfil this mundane but important commission. In addition, his music is becoming increasingly strange and dissociated, moving on a trajectory of its own away from the conventions of his time and place. But he has an ambitious and unscrupulous servant who offers to work as his assistant on the commission. This assistant takes down the composer's original and moving themes, and harmonises and arranges them in a bland and conventional style. The rich patron, who had been alarmed at the increasing idiosyncrasy of the composer's music, is greatly relieved. He is delighted with the music that is being presented to him. The servant sees a way of fleecing his master. He tells the patron that the composer is lapsing into silence, and that it is in fact he who has been writing the music. The patron immediately transfers the commission from the composer to the servant, although they continue to use the composer's name publicly, because of the kudos attached to it. The servant conceals this fact from the composer and continues to use his themes (and be paid as his assistant). Then the servant discovers that he can just as well use his own bland themes. It makes no difference to the patron. So everybody is happy. The servant is rich, the patron has his unoriginal music. And the composer is no longer pestered by either of them. He can keep his music safely inside his head. Except that he is going mad and starving to death. That is how it ends. It will be called *The Commission*.

What do you think? The plot is convoluted and unlikely enough to be that of an opera. The whole thing will, of course, be thoroughly eighteenth century, with a plethora of wigs, purloined letters, overheard conversations and harpsichords. Perhaps one could have it that the commission itself is for an opera, thereby creating a delightful *mise en abîme*. The possibilities are endless. The setting is the composer's dusty and fetid garret. I would like a running gag involving the housemaid wanting to open the windows to freshen up the room. The composer can't stand the noise of the street outside, which breaks in upon the profound silence of his musical meditations. Flirtation is an essential ingredient of such an opera. I'm sure something could be arranged between the unscrupulous servant and the sun-loving chambermaid. The harpsichord, of course, is horribly out of tune. The composer's music, following its own weird trajectory, leaps forward through the centuries (witty references for the cognoscenti) while retaining an eighteenth-century flavour.

This parable of Art versus Commerce should appeal to the New Venetian public's peculiar blend of complacency and social guilt. I am sending you under a separate cover a rough draft I have done of the libretto. Show it to Cottimi. See what he thinks. If things get desperate I might even compose the damn thing. The thought of it interested me greatly for a few minutes as I walked back towards the seafront from Grenier's house. But as soon as I was back beside the crashing waves and the drag of the tide on the shingle, it seemed as empty and pointless as a crossword puzzle. I have my own commission to fulfil. It comes not from a rich and philistine patron, but from the sea, from the wind, from the sky and the waves. I have been commissioned by Nature, and she is a difficult and demanding patron. Her indifference is colder than that of any aristocrat. Yet she is insistent too, for every morning when I open my window she reminds me of the work I have not done.

But odd things inspire me. There was, for example, Louis Grenier's remark that the purpose of life is death, just as the purpose of music is silence. It has been a common enough idea, especially among those artists like Bridget Lampion who are also philosophers of exhaustion. But when Grenier said it, I felt the force of that idea in quite a new way. It is Time that brings death, just as it is Time that animates the wind, the waves and the growing trees. Time is the primordial movement whose dim shadows flicker around us. Time is the silence beyond Nature, the patron of us all. We scurry about to fulfil its commissions. But in truth nothing can placate it.

But I have a more immediate, practical commission from the fishermen, and now that I have secured Monsieur Grenier's acquiescence, I am better placed to carry it out. I decided that it would be amusing to ambush Roland Hinchcliff and present my ultimatum to him when he was least expecting it. I chose a day when, as Jacob Grindley assured me, the Wellfleet High Court was in session and Mr Hinchcliff was sure to be found there fulfilling his lawyerly functions. The rain was pouring on Wellfleet that day, running off the two big hills that dominate the town and down the cobbles and paving of the streets. The court is on the outskirts of the New Town, where the main road out of Wellfleet turns away from the sea and heads for the hills that separate the Coast from New Venice. It was some forty minutes' walk from the Old Town, over the West Hill then through the streets of suburban villas. But I minded neither rain nor walk, for my spirits were high with the open road.

The High Court was awfully imposing, standing with majestic serenity in its gardened grounds, dispensing justice across the cropped lawns and duck-laden ponds. And imposing too were the broad corridors and hallways within, containing knots of lawyers; flocks of craven petitioners; the accused – the sullen, the nervous and the amused; whispered last-minute instructions; the curious; shufflings of papers and breathless apologies; a shout of rebellious laughter; and a fat man in funny clothes who, standing at the top of the stairs, bangs his stick on the floor and calls out, 'Case of Beardsley now commencing in Court Number Two.' At which the whole human caboodle wheels around, seethes some more, and sheds a part of itself, which shuffles and pushes its way up the staircase towards the court.

If I were a novelist, I'd paint for you this dazzling scene of the whole panoply of the law, this microcosm in which 'life breathes, life suffers'. But I am no novelist, dear sister, so I will only tell you how I sought my own passage up the stairs – easing my way through that throng of hopes, fears, tears, recriminations and laughter – and inquired of the funnily clothed fat man where I might find Mr Roland Hinchcliff.

'Mr Roland Hinchcliff,' he announced, without taking a proprietary eye off the crowd that swelled about him, 'is in the tearoom.'

I struggled back down the stairs, against the tide, and then further down still, down into a conspiratorial underworld where policemen, lawyers, criminals, victims and all the other flotsam caught in the law's inexorable net sat hunched over mugs of tea and plates of sandwiches, where even the steam swirling from the urns spoke of labyrinthine complications and the tortured, tangled interconnectedness of human affairs.

Hinchcliff was deep in conversation with a man of ruffled, hirsute demeanour. It was clear that this was a meeting between lawyer and client. Respecting the confidentiality of such occasions, I was about to wait for Hinchcliff outside, when he saw me and beckoned me over.

'Mr Clearwater,' he purred. 'How wonderful to see you in this humdrum setting. Do join us. Mr Fergus and I were just discussing his case. Mr Fergus, may I introduce Mr Clearwater? You don't mind if he sits in on our discussion, do you? Mr Clearwater is an artist, so there are no dark corners of the human soul hidden from him. Is that not so, Mr Clearwater? Please, sit down. Mr Fergus and I have almost finished.'

He swilled some tea around his mouth, popped in a sandwich, and looked first at me and then at Mr Fergus. The latter – who, with hair sticking up at all angles and tie askew, had the appearance of having been dragged forcibly from bed that morning – looked at me with deep resentment, as though to say, 'I don't want you peering into the dark corners of *my* soul.'

'Mr Fergus,' continued Hinchcliff, 'is accused of embezzlement. The case has some interesting features. We were just discussing the vexed question of whether Mr Fergus should plead guilty or not guilty.'

'But I didn't do it,' Fergus croaked. 'It's that bloody accountant covering up for his mistakes.'

'Of course you didn't *do* it,' replied Hinchcliff, allowing a note of irritation to sour his creamy tones. 'The question is how you should plead. Quite a different issue. If you plead not guilty and the jury find you guilty, which is not impossible given the evidence against you, then the judge will take an extremely dim view. Extremely dim. Whereas,' he continued in brighter tones, 'were you to bite the bitter pill and swallow your pride, the judge I'm sure will send you home with merely a rap on the knuckles and a light fine. Is that not a more enticing prospect?'

Fergus had a perplexed frown on his face.

'I knew you'd see reason,' said Hinchcliff. 'Of course I can only take my instructions from you, but I'm sure that in this case you've made the right decision. Why don't you spruce yourself up a bit before we go up? Always helps to make a good impression. Run along now.'

Fergus got meekly to his feet and wandered towards the door.

'Of course I can only take my instructions from you, Mr Fergus,' Hinchcliff repeated over his shoulder. Then he turned to me and said, amiably, 'If you don't give these people a nudge in the right direction, they might never make up their minds.'

'You are no doubt aware,' I began, 'of the approach I made to Mayor Du Cros on behalf of the fishermen?'

'A very noble gesture, I thought.'

'Well it has gone beyond noble gestures now. Now is the time for action. And I require your assistance.'

Hinchcliff smiled incredulously.

'I want you to exercise your influence,' I continued, 'to get the Corporation to reconsider their decision.'

'Why on earth should I do such a thing?'

'Because if you do not, I shall refuse to conduct the winter subscription concerts. I shall also forbid my arrangements of Louis Grenier's music to be used.'

'Mr Clearwater, I am horrified. I am aghast. I had taken you for an artist. How can an artist abandon his work like that? Where is your sense of vocation? Where is your higher calling?'

'I will not be lectured about Art by you, sir,' said I, rising from my seat in a fury. 'An artist serves truth and justice.'

'For God's sake sit down,' said Hinchcliff, alarmed at the way I was attracting attention. 'Very well, I'll see what I can do.'

'I demand a written assurance from the mayor that the matter is being referred back to the Corporation. If I don't get that, the concerts will not go ahead.'

Hinchcliff thought for a moment. 'I'm really not sure I can do that. But I'll try. I'm seeing Freeman this evening. Meet me here at four o'clock tomorrow and we'll discuss it again. Now I must get into court.'

We parted, and I walked home again through the rain. It felt good to be back again amongst my friends, the elements.

I returned to the High Court the next day, full of trepidation, to discover that Hinchcliff had bowed to my demand. He came bearing a letter from Du Cros stating formally that the plans for the new sea defences would be referred back to the Corporation for reconsideration. I, for my part, agreed that the winter subscription concerts would go ahead as planned. Before leaving, I inquired what had happened to Mr Fergus.

'Four months in jail,' said Hinchcliff nonchalantly. 'Who'd have guessed?'

Poor Fergus. Perhaps now, Jean, you can see the kind of men with whom I do battle.

O happy day! Life, the world, the future – all stand before me, a piece of music crying out to be performed. I flick my baton and the winds whirl about me, blowing out the old and in the new. Rejoice with me,

> Your loving brother,
> Paul

24 November 2064

Dear Sister,

It is difficult, looking out at another storm sweeping in off the sea, to imagine what this place might be like in the heat of the summer. And I am thinking not just of its natural aspect, but also of its social fabric. Mr Grindley informs me that the character of the town changes utterly during the summer season. Wellfleet is anyway, by the standards of the Coast, a remarkably heterogeneous place, divided as it is between the fishing community and the burghers who receive the town's visitors. During the winter months these visitors are primarily the refined wealthy, who for long weeks come to sip from the subtle cup of out-of-season seaside pleasures. Long, melancholy walks in the rain along the front; readings of sentimental poetry in the dark and lofty function rooms of the Palace Hotel; tea dances on Sunday afternoons. Everything is expensive and consolatory. Mother would love it. The subscription concerts in the Everyman Theatre are an essential part of this fashionable calendar – hence Mr Roland Hinchcliff's anxiety that nothing should interfere with their smooth functioning.

During the summer season, by contrast, the rigorous rules of entry for visitors to Wellfleet are relaxed. Mr Grindley – who, for all his radicalism in supporting the fishermen, is something of a snob – describes it as 'an influx of the average, the great mediocrity, the ordinary'. The natural character of the place, he assures me, is thereby placed under great strain. That may be, or it may not. I have not seen it for myself and I am not prepared to speculate, since I do not share Mr Grindley's tendency towards theory. All I can speak of is the winter, and while I have not fallen for the discreet charms of Wellfleet's *haut monde*, I can enjoy from a distance their *penchant* for the elegiac. Sometimes, when a mist rolls in from the sea, if I forget myself and half-close my eyes, I can almost see the town as they yearn to see it – as a place of faded grandeur and watery regret, the air thick with sighs, the very buildings breathing 'the consolation of lost illusions'. But I only have to rub my eyes, stamp my foot, and think again of my friends the fishermen, and all those illusions are gone. In fact, I think I might prefer the rougher reality of the summer season.

The opening concert of the subscription series fell upon a starlit, magical evening. I fumbled nervously with the buttons of my dress suit (pressed by Priscilla Grindley) and paced my room, slicing and jabbing the air like some demented duellist as I ran through the music in my head. Once I shouted out in triumph as, in my mind, the violins executed an arpeggio with just the *élan* that I had spent hours of rehearsal trying to extract from them. Priscilla put her head round the door to see if I was all right; she thought she might have left a pin in the trousers when she was adjusting them. How I love it, this delicious agony of waiting for a concert to begin. It is like knowing in advance that the pleasantly unexpected is going to happen. The sensibility is heightened; the mouth goes dry; you frown, then laugh suddenly, without reason; you blink in the shadows as though dazzled by sunlight. You are rolling sober, delirious with lucidity.

I clattered down the stairs, humming, and sought out the Grindley family in their parlour. I needed company. It was an hour yet until I could decently leave for the theatre, and I needed faces and laughter. I needed noise and the cut and thrust of repartee. I needed to wave my arms about, to drink, to state outrageous opinions loudly, to tease and be teased. But I also needed to be still, to think about nothing but the music I was about to direct. So I needed others to fulfil those extrovert functions, that I might share in them vicariously.

Thus I burst in upon the Grindleys, a fury of contesting needs. They were sitting around the hearth.

'Priscilla,' I exclaimed, saying the first thing that came into my head, 'would you be so kind as to play for me again that piece you have been learning. You know, the bird one.'

For her piano lessons, she had been learning a piece of sentimental salon flummery called 'A Nightingale Sings by Starlight'. I forget the composer.

Priscilla neighed a nervous laugh. 'But I can't play it proper,' she said.

'Proper*ly*,' interjected her father.

'No,' I said, with a gay laugh, even getting down on one jocular knee, 'I implore you to play it for me *proper*, Priscilla. There is something about it . . .' I laughed again, lost for words, waving my arms about. 'You don't mind, do you?' I asked, looking round at the others. They looked back at me as though I were quite mad. Which I was.

I took a seat next to Reuben, the strapping son, while Priscilla Grindley settled herself at the piano and began to apply herself to the complexities of that eternal nightingale. I closed my eyes and conducted it to myself while she played. I was entranced. (Such was my excited state that I think she could have hammered out 'Baa Baa, Black Sheep' and I would have heard something wonderful in it. Indeed, perhaps it was in just such a state, before a concert, that Dohnányi heard the nursery rhyme and conceived his delightful variations . . . You can see how my mind was running on.) I began to hear in 'A Nightingale Sings by Starlight' things that I had not listened for previously. It was so replete with the clichés of the salon – the expiring glissandi; the splashes of exotic 'colour'; the 'yearning' leaps and 'flights of fancy' – as to become almost a wistful pastiche, a sad and humorous commentary on the follies of the genre. Do you know the beautiful 'Romance' from Edward Elgar's Violin Sonata in E minor? I was put in mind of it, for there the ageing Elgar quotes just these clichés of the salon (but in compressed form, containing intensity), as though remembering through a veil the excesses of his youth. It is a wonderful movement.

What rubbish I am talking! My brain was drunk. No sooner had I thought these convoluted thoughts – waving my arms about to Priscilla Grindley's plonking rendition of 'A Nightingale Sings by Starlight' – than I had lost interest in them and immediately began thinking of something else.

I opened my eyes and turned to young Reuben Grindley, who was watching me with frank amazement. I was seized suddenly with a desire to know this young man better, to explore, as Hinchcliff would have it, the 'dark corners of his soul'. I began to talk to him of music, to share with him the thoughts I had been having of starlit nightingales, of Dohnányi and Elgar, and of expiring glissandi among potted plants and leather upholstery. I expanded on these themes – embellishing them; twisting them into strange inversions; reorchestrating them – but all the time I was observing closely Reuben Grindley's reactions. He didn't give much away. I have written to you before of his retiring nature, and of how when I was interested in him as a means of entrée to the world of the fishermen he would flee from me. Since those early days I had not paid him much attention. But now he appeared to me in his own right, a mysterious and unfathomable object, like something fallen from another world or dragged up from the deep. I thought I could detect a flicker of interest in my rambling musical discourse, and leapt on it. At the piano, Priscilla Grindley was concluding her rendition of 'A Nightingale Sings by Starlight'. But that no longer interested me.

'Why, Reuben,' I exclaimed, interrupting my own stream of words, 'it never occurred to me before. You're a music lover. How obtuse of me! How little we know each other! Yes, now I can see that you *are* a music lover. You must come to the concert tonight. No, I absolutely insist. You shall be my personal guest. You shall have the best seat in the house. No demurring, Reuben. Mr Grindley, instruct your son. Come, let us go!'

All this was spoken in a frenzy of enthusiasm, as I leapt from my seat and practically dragged my artistic victim from his. To the accompaniment of some hasty exchanges between Grindley junior and his parents, I collected my cape and cane, and inspected myself in the glass for the last time. I was wearing my favourite and most flamboyant dress suit – the green velvet one with purple brocade. My shirt was purple too, and generously ruffled. The *ensemble* was finished with a cravat of Indian silk patterned in cream and maroon. As I swung my cape over my shoulders and allowed Priscilla Grindley to fasten it around my neck at the front, I detected in her expression a certain sadness. I thought nothing of it at the time, but in retrospect I can see that she was disappointed not to have been invited to the concert herself. Am I so heartless, dear sister? I can only plead ignorance. My nervous exaltation had blinded me. I was moving down obsessive, blinkered paths.

Reuben Grindley still lingered in the centre of the room, close to the bosom of his family. I took his arm and all but catapulted him out of the house into the night.

In the darkness of the street, with the waves pulling at the beach in the distance, my mood changed rapidly. Gone was the extroversion, the urge to talk and be talked to. The heavy, rhythmic swish of the distant sea seemed to summon me back to the music, almost to admonish me for neglecting it. I examined the scores in my head, running through complex passages and rounding difficult corners. I found myself altering the pace of my step as the tempo of the music I was hearing changed. My feet dragged funereally, then sprang forward. It was still too early to be going to the theatre, for I didn't want to be kicking my heels there before the performance. I headed towards the beach.

For half an hour I paced the shingle – singing, cursing, hurling wild looks into the darkness. Then I turned my steps along the front towards the Everyman Theatre.

There were greetings at the stage door from Roland Hinchcliff and his wife Mary, who seemed to be acting as House Manager for the evening – or perhaps she simply liked ordering people about. I was in no mood for chitchat, and was about to brush past them when Mary Hinchcliff said, 'We did not know that you would be bringing a friend with you.' She allowed a pause of disapproval before the word 'friend'.

I looked round. I had entirely forgotten about Reuben Grindley, who had been trailing after me during my abstracted wanderings. 'Why this is my friend Reuben,' I said. 'Fisherman and music lover. I want him to have the best seat in the house.'

'That is impossible,' said Mary Hinchcliff. If granite could speak, then she is what it would sound like. 'Every seat in the house is sold.'

'Then he must sit in a box,' I said. 'He can go in with you.'

'Don't bother on my account, Mr Clearwater,' said Reuben. It was the first thing he had said to me all evening.

'No, Reuben,' said I. 'I insist. Don't let yourself be bullied.' Then, to the Hinchcliffs, 'I insist that Reuben be allowed to share your box.'

'That is quite impossible,' replied Mary Hinchcliff. 'We are sharing a box with Mayor Du Cros and his wife.'

'Then you must all muck in together. You'll make a cosy party.'

'Impossible,' repeated Mrs Hinchcliff, looking disdainfully

at Reuben Grindley's boat-like boots, his salt-caked trousers and fish-slimed smock.

'Very well then,' I said. 'Reuben and I shall depart, and I shall make music at home this evening. I hope you enjoy your concert.' I turned to leave.

'Mary,' said Roland Hinchcliff, 'I fear we must concede defeat.

> 'Every dog shall have his day
> And every artist have his way;
> You can't expect a Bohemian
> To behave like an old academian.

'I was something of a poet in my younger days, Mr Clearwater.'

'So I see,' said I. 'Very youthful. And now, if you'll excuse me, I must prepare myself for the performance. I trust you will look after Reuben. We shall meet again in the first interval.'

With that I swept on down the stairs to the Green Room. It was giving me great pleasure to think of Reuben Grindley, in his fisherman's smock and boots, being elevated to the mayor's box. The idea appealed to my democratic instincts.

I have never been one to write about performances. They belong to the moment. I will only say that the opening concert of the series was a great success. There was the odd slip, but that was no more than what was to be expected in a long evening's music-making. And those slips were more than outweighed by the disciplined spirit and passion with which the orchestra performed. The musicians came to the hall champing at the bit, fully sensitive to the importance of the occasion. It only required me to provide a steadying hand. Only once or twice were their nerves too much for them. At the climax of the 'Dance of the Spirits of the Air', for example, Louis Grenier had conceived a delicate shower of scales from top to bottom of the orchestra. What with the

75

edginess of the players, this came out sounding more like razor-blades than rain drops.

I opened the concert with Berlioz's *Le Corsair* Overture. They played it splendidly. The violins' flashing scales at the opening were like lightning. As you know, I never 'inspire' an orchestra during rehearsals. Rehearsals are for untangling technical problems. But performances are different, a place where all rules – so long as they are already mastered – can be broken and transcended. With every fibre of my being, as I walk on to the platform between the ranks of violinists, the applause thundering across the bare boards of the stage, I try to communicate this uniqueness of time and place to my fellow musicians. I look round at them, wait for the audience to settle, and they look at me as they have never seen me before, in my green velvet dress suit with purple brocade. I flick my baton for the first beat at a tempo that is fractionally faster than that which they are used to, and this added electricity galvanises them. I sense a wave of exhilaration pass through them. All my gestures are faster, wider, slower, more urgent and larger than they have been in the rehearsals. The musicians are shocked into a new kind of playing.

It was a long evening. I wanted this concert to be not just another event in the social calendar, but an event that for years to come would explode into a million dazzling fragments in the collective memory of the town. It was to be an edifice of musical art, an ocean of sound, a single transcendent gesture that would reach from the canyons to the stars, from the gutter to the galaxy, from the darkest corners of the human soul to the most exalted realms of supernatural fantasy.

And so, I think, it was. I give you the programme in full:

Hector Berlioz	Overture: *Le Corsair*
Louis Grenier	'Arrival and Sacred Dance of the Spirits of the Air'
Frederick Delius	'On Hearing the First Cuckoo in Spring'

	and 'A Summer Night on the River'
Felix Mendelssohn	Overture and Incidental Music to *A Midsummer Night's Dream*

INTERVAL

Louis Grenier	*The Waters of Remembrance*. A Concert Suite
Edward Elgar	*The Wand of Youth* Suite No. 2
Anton Bruckner	Symphony No. 4, *The Romantic*

INTERVAL

César Franck	Symphonic Variations for Pianoforte and Orchestra
Camille Saint-Saëns	*Le Rouet d'Omphale*
Louis Grenier	*The Triumph of Abdiel*. A Symphonic Poem

Now perhaps you will see why the orchestra required such an extensive period of rehearsal. In the event, I think, my transcendent gesture may have overreached itself. The proceedings began at half past seven and were not through till one o'clock the next morning! The orchestra displayed remarkable endurance and resilience – rather more than did the audience, who trooped away at the end looking more than a little shell-shocked.

During the first interval I went up to the mayor's box, only to meet Reuben Grindley coming out.

'Thank you for the concert, Mr Clearwater,' he said. 'I enjoyed it.'

'You did?' I replied. 'Well, in that case I have good news for you!'

I led him back into the box and gave the Du Cros and Hinchcliffs a ticking-off for not lending him their programme.

The orchestra I was proud of. They were now a disciplined and able bunch. Saint-Saëns's spinning wheel spun off exactly as it should do, into airy nothingness. When Abdiel smote

Ariel, Arioc and Ramiel, the brass marked the event with a blast that blew away any sleepy cobwebs that Saint-Saëns' dream might have left on the audience. And when Abdiel –

. . . faithful only hee; among innumerable false, unmov'd, Unshak'n, unseduc'd

– made Satan himself reel from his 'mighty sword stroke', the enlarged percussion section celebrated the fact with a clattering that shook the burghers to their bones.

And myself? I think I made the impression upon Wellfleet's musical life that I was seeking to make. The entire concert I conducted from memory, and I performed the solo part to the César Franck myself, the pianist I had originally hired to do the job turning out to be rather heavy-handed.

There was a party afterwards at the Patricks' villa on East Hill. A favoured few, including myself, were driven up in carriages. The remainder of Wellfleet's bourgeoisie had to tramp up on foot. That they would do this at all at half past one in the morning was testimony to the strength of social obligation. I had wanted to bring Reuben Grindley along to the party, but he had fled at the end of the concert.

Three households in Wellfleet – the Du Cros, the Hinch-cliffs and the Patricks – vie with each other in point of the sumptuousness of their entertaining. With their performance after the concert, the Patricks won a battle, even if the war was not over. It was a handsome spread. I turned my attention immediately to the champagne, securing myself a bottle for personal consumption. It went with me everywhere. Given everything that was laid on, it was a shame that the guests were such an exhausted and dull-headed lot. I was very keen that Louis Grenier should come down and share in the triumph that was rightly his, but Madeleine Patrick – who seems to act as his nursemaid and guardian – insisted that he would be asleep and would not want to be disturbed.

So to liven up this dismal scene, I sat down at the Patricks' piano and hammered out some waltzes.

> On with the dance! Let joy be unconfined;
> No sleep till morn, when Youth and Pleasure meet
> To chase the glowing Hours with flying feet.

But every time I looked up, the guests were gazing back at me with frumpish disdain, crumbs dangling from their slack lips. The only point of life was Madeleine Patrick, who came over and joined me at the piano. It is a mystery to me how such a coarse and hairy man as Clifford Patrick could have acquired a wife of such extravagant loveliness as that woman. I began playing 'A Nightingale Sings by Starlight', so far as I could remember it from Priscilla Grindley's rendition so many music-filled hours earlier. I should say that I was spectacularly drunk by now, and that in this exhausted, exhilarated state, the somewhat flimsy charms of the salon-bound nightingale became unwarrantedly exalted in my mind. Madeleine Patrick was leaning on the piano, laughing, addressing some remarks to me as I played, glancing over her shoulder at her husband, who was talking to the departing guests. Each time she leant towards me, I found myself breathing deeply of the intoxicating, perfumed air of her décolletage. This atmosphere of abandoned sensuality fuelled my musical fantasies of the nightingale even more than the champagne, so that my fingers began dabbling in the stickiest goo imaginable of erotic 'exoticism'. Shimmering chromatic scales fell from the body of the melody like veils floating softly to the floor; come-hither crescendi ended in exciting anticlimaxes; modulations wrapped themselves around each other like writhing limbs. I blush now to think what I may have played. But it was meat and drink to Madeleine Patrick, who leant ever closer to me, laughing ever more fully. Some of her soft black hair had come adrift from its mooring on the top of her head, and at one particularly orgiastic moment of the music, I found it tickling my nose. With a spluttering, grunting sneeze of exhausted drunkenness and pent-up emotion, I blew it from my face.

Soon after that, the nightingale – grown to the size of an albatross – was popped back on to its perch. With a luscious, expiring arpeggio, I crashed down to the tail-end of the key-board and concluded my recital. There was something in the atmosphere of the room that told me, even through my inebriation, that it might be best to depart. Madeleine Patrick's unbuttoned interest in my music-making was in no sense innocent. The guests had all gone. Even as she flirted with me, she was exchanging glances with her husband, who was watching us darkly. I had no desire to be an instrument in the intra-Patrick trials of sexual strength. I hurriedly made my apologies and left.

Dawn was breaking over the town. My green velvet dress suit was crumpled and stained with champagne. When I got down to the fishing beach, the last of the boats was setting out to sea. The men heaved with their backs to the boats, digging their heels into the shingle to get a purchase. Then they were launched. One of the last men to leap through the surf and be hauled aboard was Reuben Grindley. I clambered up to one of the groynes and waved them farewell as they struggled away from the shore, tossed up and down by the incoming waves. Then I went home to bed.

> With love,
> Paul

7 December 2064

Dear Sister,

The winter here continues mild and damp, with winds that rake the town and send spray from the scudding waves billowing over the front. I watch this from East Hill and compare it in my mind to the way that the storms and tempests of musical inspiration batter at my consciousness. The sea is so alien. Its otherness is so vast and *watery*. It is said that our own bodies are composed in large part of the stuff, but this has always felt to me like one of those scientists' myths. We are animals of the land. The sea is another world, and its creatures are strange and horrible to us.

Let me illustrate this with a modest story. Every day I go down to the fishing beach at noon to watch the fishermen bring in their catch. The decks of the boats are littered with dead and dying fish – plaice, sole, herring, the ugly, gape-mouthed cod, the big conger eel. Occasionally the valuable halibut is caught, as big and round as a coffee table, and left to bleed in a barrel of its own. All in all it is a scene of terrible destruction, with the fish gasping and flapping, slithering along the deck as they attempt to escape the inescapable. No matter how many times I see them, I never overcome my sense of their strangeness. At one moment it can seem as though the very devils of hell have been hauled up from their hiding places to face the light of day in all their naked, unblinking ugliness. And then in the next, as the sunlight catches the rainbow scales of the expiring cod, it can seem as though they are angels – with all *their* alien beauty – that have been dragged so cruelly to earth.

Anyway, one morning I was talking to some of my friends while they boxed the fish. They kindly offered me one to take home for my dinner, and gutted it for me. Even after this brutal act had been performed, mysterious and beautiful ripples disturbed the fins that ring its body. It was a particularly fine day, the previous night's storm having blown new air across the town, so I decided to take a walk along the beach before returning to my lodgings. I had walked a few hundred yards along the shingle, engrossed in a passage of my symphony, when I received the shock of my life. To begin with I felt a movement in the basket in which I was carrying the fish. I looked down and saw that the creature had suddenly arched its back, raising a part of itself from the bottom of the basket. Blood trickled from the gash down its side where its entire innards had been ripped out some half an hour earlier. Then, to my horror, the thing launched itself into a spasm of slapping and writhing. I was about to release the handle of the basket, when with a last effort the fish jumped clean out of it and landed twitching on the shingle. I felt quite nauseous. For a few minutes I sat on the shingle and stared at this ghastly phenomenon. The fish was still now. The leap from the basket seemed to have exhausted it. (As though anything could be more exhausting than having your innards ripped out!) I rather wanted to leave this grotesque object on the beach and forget about it, but that seemed wasteful and cowardly. So I picked it up, and as I did so it arched its back again. It was only through the greatest self-control that I held on to it and put it back in the basket. The experience left me with slime on my hands and a slimy feeling in my soul.

The thing was still twitching and flapping when I returned to my lodgings and delivered it, with thanks, into the large and capable hands of Priscilla Grindley. She was not at all perturbed.

'Soon fix that,' she announced cheerfully and, holding its body down with one hand, sawed its head off with the other. The fish was still rippling and twitching as the knife cut through its flesh. Only when the head was fully off was it without any sign of life.

The ever-knowledgeable Jacob Grindley was on hand with a scientific gloss on my unpleasant experience. Flatfish such as the plaice are tough and muscular, and it is the undulating, flapping motion of their unwieldy bodies that carries them along the sea bed. Even after death, with the removal of the vital organs, nerve impulses in the form of electrical charges will cause the contraction of the fish's powerful muscles.

'One time I put a sole in the ice box,' said Priscilla, 'all gutted and cleaned, and two days later I opened the box and it jumped clean out on to the floor.'

I listened with rapt interest while Mr Grindley discoursed at length on the electric vitality of fishes – on the living batteries of the electric eel, which can deliver a grievous shock to a man, and on the lazy torpedo-ray, which will stun a five-pound salmon and then eat it at its leisure. I thought again about the electrical spasms of that plaice whose skin, its last shred of dignity, was even now being stripped away by Priscilla Grindley's knife. There, in those primal twitchings, was Nature at its strangest and most unadorned.

The coast is the point of contact between the human world and that other world to which we have access only through rupture and dislocation, which we can reach only by dragging its denizens up into our world and thereby killing them. Nature is alien to us, and yet we ourselves are part of it. (Here, of course is the mystery of mysteries: 'Who then will not wonder at this chameleon of ours, or could wonder more greatly at anything else?') Scientists may reach down through the waters of our own being to catch the very stuff of Nature, yet by that same act of hauling it up with their nets and tackle of concepts, laws, language and mathematics, do they not thereby destroy its vital force? Does it not lie beached, gasping and dying, in the harsh light and open, empty air of consciousness and reason? The 'thing-in-itself' (as Herr Schopenhauer so crudely puts it), the thing to which the scientists have no access, is that fish moving mysteriously through the watery darkness of its own privacy.

It is that that music can become. My symphony is a natural force battering at the house of my humanity, just as the storm-driven sea claws at Wellfleet. When I arrived here, so many months ago, I thought of my work, like Berlioz, as a temple standing on an island far across the sea. The clouds of inspiration would blow me across that sea to reach it. All that seems untrue now. A temple is too fixed and unyielding a thing, and also smacks of the supernatural.

My symphony, if it is to become that which animates Nature, must itself move. I see it now in the sea itself, in that restless otherness that heaves and shatters itself against the groynes along the front. I let the sea come to me. I let the music come to me. I sit in my lodgings and watch the rain and sea-spray run down my window. I let the ocean of music trickle down through every cell of my being. I let it fill me. I let it trickle down until it has reached the tip of my pen, the ink in my pen, the ink on my manuscript paper. It isn't easy. It seems sometimes that there are windows in this house of humanity – this *prison* of humanity – that are closed and fixed upon keeping the music out. I work for many patient hours at removing brick by brick the walls that hold those windows. Then I lose my patience and shout threats and curses, hurl bricks at those windows of my mind in order to smash them and let the wild music of Nature sweep through those stuffy rooms.

But don't think, dear sister, that I am falling into the trap that Louis Grenier blundered into long ago of 'describing' or 'expressing' Nature in music. For me, the relationship between music and Nature is quite the other way around: it is Nature that expresses music. In that sense it is true that music is like a temple that lies *beyond* the sea – but it is a strange, fluid kind of temple, a temple whose substance is Time. Like Time, it is transcendent but not motionless.

How abstruse I have become! Let me describe the progress of my symphony in more down-to-earth terms. Do you remember the rehearsal that I took in the ballroom at the end of the pier, my first rehearsal with the Philharmonic Society? Do you remember how, inspired by Grenier's 'Arrival of the Spirits of the Air' and by the rain and sea washing the windows of the ballroom, I conceived of Elgarian shimmerings of plucked strings? These I have now realised and completed. This unearthly sound – fluid yet drawn from taut strings, in texture neither string nor wind nor percussion – is the beginning of my symphony and a leitmotif that recurs in the first movement. This is the wind that blows through the movement, that gusts to blow the music into new configurations. It is not merely an accompanying figure, as Elgar made it, but a natural force that drives the music on.

In the second of the subscription series I conducted Mendelssohn's atmospheric Overture, *Fingal's Cave*. I have been meditating at length upon the vividness of its opening. The brooding, rolling figure in the bassoon and lower strings is evocative, of course, of the rolling of the waves, yet its effect derives too from its breadth and heroism. Its arpeggiated form has something of a dark, descending fanfare about it. All fanfares partake of the heroic, and so does the sea. Like a hero, the sea is wild and untamed, transcending the self-imposed limitations and scruples of burghers and bourgeoisie. It shames them. Perhaps it will seem wilfully perverse to you that I should see in the sea an image of leadership? But should not leadership have about it something of the inspirational, something of the heroic? And what could be more heroic than the sea, in all its strange and cruel vastness?

This, then, was the mood at which I was aiming as the winds, represented by the humming *pizzicati*, approached across the waves. This was the event whose arrival was presaged by that strange introduction: an episode of striding, o'er-leaping heroism, a theme that held aloft the key of heroism, E flat, like a banner. This is the tone and mood of the first movement. Not that it is not without its hesitations. The wind theme of thrummed strings returns to haunt the flow of the music, and the air is filled with atmospherics. At present I am working on a passage whose starting point was the climax of Grenier's 'Dance of the Spirits of the Air' (the passage which sounded in the orchestra's rendition like razor-blades rather than rain drops). Flute, bassoon, piano and harp swoop down through the music like the gulls that ride the air currents in front of the East Hill cliffs. I have watched them. I have tried to write music whose material expression would be those gulls – gliding, sometimes tumbling, then swooping quickly up again on a rising flow of air. I have tried to embody the crystal-clear chaos of all those birds diving, gliding along the line of the cliffs, tumbling with folded wings. To construct such counterpoint requires hours of patient work.

The essence of musical composition lies in the ability to work back and forth in one's mind from the smallest detail to the overall form of the work. A momentary or barely audible gesture made by third clarinet or double bass must have its unique relation to the whole conception. It is by such a to-and-fro movement between detail and form – I use dichotomies, for the sake of argument, that have no place in the artist's mind – that the composition itself is woven. When one begins a work, this weaving gesture is a large and strenuous one. There is much empty and uncomposed space to traverse. (Mozart was able to realise his genius because for him that space was already filled with detail. He could hold whole compositions in his head with ease.) But as the composition proceeds, the relation of the part to the whole becomes clearer, and the distance that has to be traversed by the relating gesture gradually lessens. I am now at the stage in my *Sea Symphony* when the progress of the first movement is beginning to clarify the form of the whole. It is as though, working through the first movement, I am on the prow of a ship moving through waters that are veiled with mist. As I move forward, the mist begins to clear ahead and slowly I begin to see where I am going. I know now that the symphony is in five movements. For the second, one must imagine the figure on the prow turning and going back into the interior of the boat. It is enclosed on all sides by the movement of the sea – perhaps one can even feel the sea beneath it, moving it – but in itself it is merely a room, or a series of rooms. Where the first movement has a freshness, the feeling of the wind and the sea sweeping it clean every now and again, the second is claustrophobic and stuffy with

86

the heat of human cerebration and artifice. It has the claustrophobia of a ship at sea.

My problem with this, however, is that I have never *been* in a ship at sea. The vaporetti of New Venice hardly count. If I am to fathom the thing-in-itself of which a ship at sea is the material expression (the more I repeat this philosophical formula upon which I have hit, the more ridiculous it begins to sound), then I must put to sea, if only once. Ever since coming here I have been asking my friends the fishermen if I might go out with them one day, but they are most unhelpful. I can't help feeling it's ungrateful, considering all that I am doing for them. Whenever I put it to them, I get the same reply: 'We don't take passengers.'

But I have machinations of my own, schemes and plots that will take me out to sea by an altogether different route. Not very *far* out, it is true, but at least I will have been there. The day after the first of the subscription concerts – after I'd slept off the effects of all that champagne and exposure to Madeleine Patrick's décolletage – I discussed with Jacob Grindley our campaign to secure justice for the fishermen. I had been thinking that what we needed were more facts to support our case. Facts are like diamonds. They can cut through any amount of cant and prejudice. Fortunately, it transpired that Grindley had been thinking along similar lines.

'Lobster cages,' he said.

Again the Grindley mind was moving swiftly.

'I don't catch your drift,' I said.

'Exactly,' he said. 'Lobster cages should be strong enough to catch the drift. I've worked it all out.'

And from beneath a tottering pile of books he drew a wad of papers, on each of which there was an impressive array of sketches, notes and mathematical calculations. They were as indecipherable to me as Egyptian hieroglyphics. It seemed that while I had been pursuing the political struggle on behalf of the fishermen, there had been no neglect on Jacob Grindley's part of the scientific aspect of the matter.

Jacob Grindley's ingenious scheme – which could have sat proudly in the *Notebooks* of Leonardo or *Principia* of Newton – was to quantify the drift of shingle from west to east along the coast, and by quantifying its movement in different places to demonstrate the effects of the groynes upon that movement. The instrument of measurement was to be a cage, one side open to the current, anchored to the bottom, whose mesh would be fine enough to catch the shingle as the relentless and unforgiving forces of Nature dragged it across the scene. By calculations far too complicated to explain – they involved, among other things, relating the size of the cage to the area and angle of incline of the whole beach – Jacob Grindley would be able to arrive at a figure for the total volume of shingle shifted in a given period by the combined effects of wind, current and tide. He would thus be able to project the effects on that movement of various possible configurations of groyne.

This shingle-catching cage was to be constructed out of twenty individual lobster cages – unhinged, opened out and secured together with strong wire. As soon as I knew what was required, I left Jacob Grindley and ran down to the fishing beach. There were always dozens of unused lobster cages lying about there. Unfortunately, it seemed that these lobster cages were suddenly in demand. Wherever I went, I was told that they would soon be needed to construct the traditional fishermen's arches for the New Year's Day parade. Even when I explained the purpose that I intended for them, I got the same reply. Not for the first time, I was sensible of a certain ingratitude. In the end I was forced to pay a shore boy the extortionate price of thirty shillings for twenty rather decrepit specimens.

And on another matter the fishermen were again most unhelpful and blind to their own interests. We had counted on one of their boats to do the job of transporting the shingle cage. Grindley had worked out the exact locations along the shore where measurements should be taken. A boat would take the cage out and drop it overboard, with floats attached to it to mark its location. Three days later the cage would be collected, Grindley would do his calculations, and the cage would be taken out again to a new position – and so on until the researches were completed. Unfortunately, none of the fishermen were willing to let their boats be used for this vital task. Everywhere I went I met the familiar response that their boats were not to be used for pleasure cruising. They were deaf to my pleas.

Some people, it seems, must have their best interests forced upon them. I have hired a rowing boat, and Jacob Grindley has instructed his son Reuben to row me out to drop the shingle cage myself. I will write soon to let you know how our expedition fares. But now I must go downstairs to help Jacob Grindley assemble our ingenious contraption.

With love,
Paul

17 December 2064

Dear Sister,

In my last letter I told you how I longed to go to sea and become a salt-encrusted veteran of the waves. Well, now I've done it. I've faced the power of the sea and lived to tell the tale.

Under the precise and scientific direction of Jacob Grindley, the building of the shingle cage was done. The structure was some twelve feet long, three feet high, and the same in breadth. The lobster cages of which it was made up had been first dismembered and opened out, then bound together and rehinged with rope and wire. The mesh on the bottom and sides had been made finer with more wire, so that no shingle could escape. One whole side was left open to allow the free entrance of the current and its pebbly burden. Jacob Grindley examined every joint carefully, until he deemed it stout enough to face whatever the watery deeps might hurl at it. Reuben and I loaded it on to a cart and wheeled it down the steep streets of the Old Town to the beach.

It was mid-afternoon, and the fishing boats were all safely back, their catches at the market and their crew at home or in the pubs. Jacob Grindley accompanied us as far as the front, but not on to the beach – the shingle, he said, hurt his feet and made his old legs tired. So we went on alone, and Grindley senior was to see the maiden voyage of his invention – if see it he did, for his eyesight was poor – at a distance.

I was heartily thankful for the presence of Reuben Grindley, since he seemed to be a man who understood boats and water and the sometimes problematic relationship between the two. It sounds the easiest thing in the world to launch a rowing boat off a shingle beach, but the sea is no pond. Implacable and unwelcoming, it attempts to throw off intrusion. There was little wind that day, but no sooner would we get a portion of the boat into the water, than a wave, with surprising force, would lift it up and deposit it back on to the beach. This happened several times, with the added complication that the shingle cage, balanced precariously across the gunwales (what a seadog I have become, to use such terms so lightly!) had to be held fast by main force, and threatened to overbalance the entire caboodle.

But then, with a last shove, with a scrambling and a shoving and a heave on the oars from Reuben, we were free of the fetters of land. For Reuben it was, no doubt, a humdrum and quotidian experience, but for me that moment was one in which the bases of existence seemed transformed. To find beneath you no longer the solid, unmoving ground, but the living sea – yielding at one moment, tossing you up the next – is a sensation that cannot but make you meditate on the frailty and insignificance of this rag, this tissue, called man. In that moment, I came to appreciate more sympathetically than I had done hitherto the fatalism of the fishermen, their inability to defend their interests or take control of their own future. What nonsense to talk of 'interests' or 'future' when faced with the mighty power of the sea! The force of nature is soaked into the grain of their lives, just as the passage of the wind is etched into their faces. Compare their world with that of Roland Hinchcliff, who carefully directs his purposes through the accommodating, artificial milieu of the law. No wonder they find themselves at his mercy! I clasped the shingle cage with renewed passion.

Still the waves rolled in upon us, and Reuben Grindley had to dig his oars deep into the water, bending his back to surmount the foaming breakers. Then we were in calmer waters. Reuben laboured on, the oars clattering in the row-locks, and I strained to look round at the beach as it slipped gently away from us. How profound was my sense of moving upon a different medium! The land was now merely an adjunct to the sea. Where beneath me once there had been solid ground, now there was water, bobbing and running about us, slapping the hull of the boat at every turn with liquid reprimand.

In the hand that was not clasping our precious cargo I held Jacob Grindley's diagram that showed where the cage was to be positioned. Consulting it from moment to moment, I gave the straining Reuben directions and cautioned him when he seemed to be wandering off course. Our destination was a point some sixty yards out from the groyne at the western end of the fishing beach. This spot, you will remember, would form the terminal point of the groyne under the council's proposals. Having attained our objective, Reuben anchored the boat and we heaved the cage over the side. Weighed down on its bottom with iron bars and an old kettle of Mrs Grindley's, it fell quickly, disappearing into the cold, green gloom. The line played out, until all there was to mark its presence were the cork floats we would use to haul it up again upon our return.

That night I conducted the third of the subscription concerts, a challenging programme that included the Interludes from Benjamin Britten's *Peter Grimes* and Louis Grenier's Tone Poem for Celeste and String Orchestra, *Dimly Remembered Breezes* (the title loses something in translation). But I was unable to render unto the music my undivided concentration. As though itself dragged down by weights, my mind kept returning to the shingle cage. Would the contraption work? What mysterious forces, beyond the reach of man, were working on it, even at that moment, down in that nether world? These same questions hung palpably in the air of the Grindley household, where daily life was carried on only under a canopy of suspense and speculation. For long hours Jacob Grindley and I sat in vigil over his plans and calculations, debating to exhaustion the respective influences of tide, wave, current, and chance. The labours of Hercules are as nothing to the labours of science. But on the third day the agony was over, for on that day, when the tide was at the exact same point as when we had taken it out, Reuben Grindley and I put to sea again and rowed the short distance to collect the shingle-catching cage. The task of bringing in our stony catch was one of exceeding delicacy, for one false move would result in the cage's precious burden being tipped back on to the sea bed and the whole experiment being wrecked. The cork floats had been carefully marked to indicate which ones we should pull upon first in order to turn the cage on to its back. This achieved, it could be pulled up with the open side to the surface, and thus the shingle saved.

Heaving the cage up was a labour both scientific *and* Herculean, and made it exceedingly difficult to keep one's balance in the boat, to boot. The reason for this was apparent as soon as the thing was aboard: we had garnered a rich harvest. All this was quite exhausting, but I think the most painful part of the whole operation for young Reuben Grindley was the reception we got when we returned to the beach. Our labours had been attracting attention, and there was a small crowd waiting for us when we brought the shingle cage ashore. Mr Grindley's machine was, as you may imagine, the object of much philistine and caustic badinage. Poor Grindley junior, faced with this onslaught from colleagues and workmates, remained silent, blushing to the roots of his eyebrows.

His father was waiting eagerly for us when we had hauled the barrow back up the streets to the house. The light of scientific truth glinting in his eye, he pounced upon the stones as a starving man upon bread. I watched as he took each one out, weighed it, and wrote in his notebook. They were like diamonds to him. To me they were precious too, each one a fragment of the whole, a piece of crystallised truth with which to shatter the brittle and transparent lies of the Corporation. Slowly they accumulated in a pile beside the cage. At the end of two hours the cage was empty but for a few strands of seaweed. Jacob Grindley put on his glasses and went inside, notebook in hand, to begin his calculations.

There was no rest for Reuben or me, either, for we had to load the cage back on to the barrow and take it down to the beach again. This time the cage was to be anchored some fifty yards off the fishing beach itself, and two hundred yards to the east of the groyne at the western end of the beach. In this way, Jacob Grindley planned to assess the effect of that groyne on the movement from west to east of the shingle. On the third day, again, we collected the cage, and Jacob Grindley counted and weighed the stones. He retired indoors to feed this new information to his proliferating calculations, and we took the shingle cage out again, this time to set it down towards the eastern end of the fishing beach.

Our scientific operations were attracting a fair amount of attention by now, and when, on the third day, we arrived back on shore from collecting the cage for this third time, there was quite a crowd gathered on the beach to welcome us. There were the usual quips and sallies from this chorus, but their number had been augmented by a group headed by the beachmaster. Their mood was altogether more sombre.

'I have to inform you,' said the beachmaster, 'that you are breaking regulations concerning fishing in the shore area and fishing from an unlicensed boat.'

'But we're not fishing,' I riposted. Reuben remained silent. 'Everybody knows what we're doing. We're measuring the movement of shingle with our shingle cage.'

More guffawing from the crowd.

'I don't care what you're doing,' said the beachmaster implacably. 'The fact is you're fishing from an unlicensed boat. I've received a number of complaints about that thing.' He pointed to the shingle cage. 'There's a grave risk of a boat grounding or fouling its nets on that thing.'

I didn't care for the way he referred to our shingle-catching cage as 'that thing'. 'For God's sake, man,' I cried, 'this is all for the benefit of the fishing beach. We're building a case we can put to the Corporation.

'I don't care what you're doing,' said the beachmaster. 'The fact is you're fishing from an unlicensed boat. I've received a number of complaints – '

'Yes, damn you. I understood the first time. Come, Reuben.'

There seemed no choice but to submit. We loaded the cage, with its burden of shingle, on to the barrow and wheeled it home.

That night I sat with Jacob Grindley while he worked on his researches. Spread out before him on the table was a plan of the shore, on which from time to time he drew arrows and wrote in figures. Between times he returned to his notebook to make further calculations, or wearily massaged his forehead, as though trying to stimulate his brain to still greater efforts. He was fascinating to watch. It was as though that judicious mind of his held in balance the very forces of

Nature, ordering them about on his charts as a general might command his forces on the field of battle.

'Will you be able to complete your calculations with the information you have?' I asked. 'It seems that we will not be able to take the cage out again.'

The old man sighed. 'Unfortunately not,' he said. 'To complete my picture I need a measurement of the movement of shingle here.' He pointed on the map to a point some seventy yards out to sea beneath the East Hill cliffs, three hundred yards beyond the groyne at Rock-a-Nore. 'Without that information, all our work will have been for nothing.'

'Then we must do it,' said I firmly, 'whether the beach-master likes it or not. We will do it in secret, at night.'

In readiness for our nocturnal mission, I engaged the services of the young horn-playing Jim Wilkins. Wilkins was to be our lookout. I detailed him to keep guard upon the groyne at Rock-a-Nore – the last groyne before the wild and rugged shore beneath the East Hill cliffs – and to blow his horn if he saw anyone approaching along the beach. Siegfried's horn call from *The Ring* was to be our alarm signal, and upon hearing it we would extinguish our lamp and remain quiet and still until danger had passed.

The laying of the cage was achieved without alarm or incident. The night was calm, the moon clear and full. The gulls were roosting, and the only sounds were the splash of our oars in the inky water and the ceaseless, metallic rustling of the waves as they pulled at the shingle on the fishing beach. As we steered round the Rock-a-Nore groyne, the dark shape of the East Hill cliffs began to loom over us. The moonlight caught the polished brass of Jim Wilkins' French horn, and for a moment it flashed out in the darkness. We could hear the gurglings and rushings of the sea working its many passages among the jagged rocks at the foot of the cliffs. With little more than a watery plop, the shingle cage was dropped to its resting place on the sea's bed. The job was done. With relief we turned the boat around and headed back for the beach.

Three nights after that we had to go back for the cage again. It was also the night of the penultimate concert of the subscription series. With my mind fixed on the task ahead, I could scarcely concentrate as I steered the orchestra through the complications of Grenier's *A la recherche du ton perdu*, and found myself hurrying through the *Siegfried's Rhine Journey* that concluded the programme. Even as the applause was dying away inside the Everyman Theatre, I was dashing out of the stage door with Jim Wilkins. The weather had changed for the worse while we were within. Rain lashed the front, and the wind sent spray billowing across the black and glistening street. The lamp that I carried swung backwards and forwards as we ran, tossing an arc of light up and down the buildings. The air was thick with the sound of rushing, pounding water.

We met Reuben Grindley on the fishing beach.

'It's no good, Mr Clearwater,' he said. 'We can't go out in this.' He had almost to shout against the noise of the wind rushing around us.

'But we must,' I said. 'If we leave the cage out there any longer, it'll ruin your father's calculations. We must fetch it in tonight.'

'Damn his bloody calculations,' said Reuben. 'I'm not going out in this.'

'Then I'll go alone,' I said, and began pushing the boat out into the waves.

'You can't even row the bloody thing,' he protested. 'And you'll get soaked.'

It was true that I was wearing only the green velvet dress suit that I had been conducting in. But nothing mattered to me at that moment save our mission. Turning on Reuben Grindley, I yelled, 'Are you coming with me or not?'

He shouted something angrily at me in reply – I did not catch what it was against the roar of wind and wave – and joined me in pushing the boat out. We jumped in, and Jim Wilkins watched petrified from the beach as we breasted the first waves and headed out into the tempestuous darkness. Thick swathes of cloud slid swiftly across the night sky, whisked along by the wind, and as they passed from before the moon, a shimmer of dim white light would be thrown from time to time on to the scene below. In one such moment, looking back to the shore, I saw a caped figure, the figure of a woman with a hood raised over her head, walk past Jim Wilkins and out along the groyne. She stopped. She was looking out to sea, watching our progress. I saw Jim Wilkins raise his horn to his lips and play Siegfried's horn call in a fine, bell-like tone that was carried clear across the water before being whipped away by the wind and smashed against the East Hill cliffs. But it was too late now to worry about being discovered, for all our efforts were bent towards keeping control of the boat. We were tossed high in the air, then pulled down deep into a trough as another wave towered over us. Already I was soaked to the skin, my dress suit clinging unpleasantly to me as though itself desiring to drag me down through the waves to my death. Every moment was a superhuman effort. I took one of the oars from Reuben Grindley and together we began to row out beneath the cliffs to where our shingle cage lay.

Despite the discomfort and danger – *because* of it, perhaps – my soul was filled with such a sense of exhilaration as I can find expression for only in Art.

'Blow, winds,' I sang at the top of my voice, hurling my defiance at the cliffs, 'and crack your cheeks! rage! blow! You cataracts and hurricanoes, spout Till you have drench'd our steeples, drown'd – '

'Shut up!' shouted Reuben Grindley. 'We're there.'

I had never heard him so voluble.

Seizing the cork floats, which were dancing wildly on the seething surface, we began hauling the cage up from its watery grave. Waves buffeted the boat, practically hurling us over the side. When the cage was safely up, lying across the gunwales, Reuben pulled the anchor aboard and we began to head for home.

But the storm was building to a yet greater climax. It seemed as though the whole sky were being hurled from one dark horizon to the other. The rain raked us as though shot from a gun. The more we struggled with our oars, the less headway we seemed to make.

'It's no good,' shouted Reuben in despair. And with a sense of sinking doom I knew exactly what he was going to say next. 'We're heading for the rocks.'

It was true. Every stroke of the oars seemed to take us backwards toward the gaping, jagged maw of the cliffs.

But there was worse to come. A wave, driving across the boat, caused the cage to slide on the gunwales, unbalancing the boat and causing it in its turn to list in the heaving water until it had almost capsized.

'We'll have to lose the cage,' shouted Reuben. 'It's going to sink us.'

He took hold of the cage and was about to push it off into the water, when I held him back.

'No!' I shouted. 'Our cause is lost without it.'

'We're going to die,' he shouted back, 'you bloody lunatic.'

We managed to pull the cage back till it was evenly balanced again across the gunwales, but by thus abandoning our oars for a few seconds we had allowed the boat to be drawn ever closer to the rocks.

'We need help,' shouted Reuben.

I remembered Jim Wilkins, waiting for us back on the groyne, and with all my might I shouted in his direction, into the wind: 'Wilkins! We need some help!' I repeated this phrase again and again. Filled as I was with that strange exhilaration that I have already described, I found myself singing into the nocturnal storm the march-like dotted figure that is tossed from instrument to instrument in

Mendelssohn's *Fingal's Cave*. By a strange fluke of Nature, or of Art, it fitted my cry perfectly:

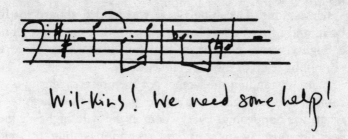

Lucky it is that I possess a lusty baritone. After a few repetitions, Siegfried's horn call came flying back across the water. Our plea had been heard. *Fingal's Cave* had saved the shingle cage!

We struggled with our oars against the current that was bending every effort to drive us on to the rocks. We were just beginning to think that my song had in fact gone unheard, when there was a mighty report, and all the sleeping gulls of Wellfleet, jerked rudely from their gullish slumbers, shot squawking and screeching into the air. We were saved! The cannon was fired! The lifeboat was launched!

And so were snatched from the jaws of destruction. The hull of the lifeboat loomed over us out of the heaving darkness. Men swung lanterns, shouted at each other, hauled on ropes. Reuben Grindley, half-dead from exhaustion, was pulled up into the arms of our rescuers. I was manoeuvring the shingle cage so that they could take that up as well, when one of the lifeboatmen shouted down at me, 'You can't bring that. Leave it and climb up.'

'Never!' I shouted, and gripped the cage ever tighter. 'If this shingle cage stays, then so do I. I will not be parted from it.'

'For God's sake,' came one voice from above.

'If you don't hurry up,' came another, 'we'll all be smashed on the rocks.'

'Let him bring the damn thing,' came a third. 'Then let's get out of here.'

It was done. The shingle cage was hauled aboard the lifeboat, and I followed it. Even as my feet left the rowing boat, a mighty wave swept it up and sent it crashing on to the crumbling teeth of the East Hill cliffs.

Notwithstanding the lateness of the hour, the firing of the cannon had brought a crowd down on to the beach to see what was happening. Everywhere in the wild night air there was nervous laughter, excited recountings, hugs of relief. Blankets were put around the sopping shoulders of Reuben and myself, and somebody produced mugs of steaming sweet tea. The identity of that caped and hooded figure was discovered – it was Madeleine Patrick. She came running up to me across the shingle, put her arms around my neck, and kissed me on the cheek. Then she was gone. I was in a state close to ecstasy, a kind of delirium – most of all because the shingle cage was safely ashore with not a pebble spilt.

I write this next day, after a sleep as long and deep as the sea itself. Downstairs, Jacob Grindley is counting the pebbles and making his final calculations. My memory of last night's events is as fresh on the sheet of my mind as the ink that even now dries on this page. Only one detail clouds and puzzles my exultation. It is a curious and delicate thing, and perhaps in my highly wrought state I merely imagined it. It concerns Madeleine Patrick. I could have sworn that – after she had kissed me on the cheek, and before she dashed away – she put her tongue into my ear and wiggled it about. Can this be?

> With love,
> Paul

Dear Sister,

Never before have I found a letter so difficult to write as this. Feelings of shame, unhappiness and foreboding overwhelm me. In my more rational moments I wonder why this should be so, for the events I shall describe – or rather *event*, for that in truth is what it boils down to – are not so very unusual or shocking. There is even a humour in the manner of their unfolding that I can smile at through my tears. And I'm afraid I feel too a sense of shocked excitement when I remember the matter. Do you remember that episode I told you of – the plaice that would not die, and how it left in my hand an unpleasant slime? Well, let that stand for my sensations at present. Something viscous and morally repugnant, a kind of moral slime, has been left on my hands.

It is particularly hard for me when I think of the pure and high ideals with which I arrived in Wellfleet. Are they now utterly corrupted and brought low? Can the ideal of Art survive a temporary victory of the baser instincts? Is it possible that music should remain confined by the Nature which it strives to transcend? These doubts swirl around my head in painful confusion. I feel myself posed before a great question, and I fear the answer.

Being quicker than me, you will probably by now have guessed the event to which I am pointing. But let me approach that cadence in my own time and in my own way. The note of high euphoria and exultation that accompanied the rescue by Reuben Grindley and me of the shingle cage, and our own subsequent rescue by the lifeboat, became a pedal point, a basso profundo, that rumbled through the following days. Of greatest importance was that Jacob Grindley was able to complete his scientific researches into the movement of the shingle, and hence muster a convincing case to show the detrimental effects on the fishing beach of the

Corporation's plans. For years Grindley had been measuring and monitoring the ever-increasing strength and frequency of the storms that ravage the coast here, and now he was able to put these observations to good use by showing how the rate of drift of shingle along the front would increase in the years to come.

Grindley's evidence, the distilled essence of his cogitations and our collective investigations, was collected together in one document which I presented to Mayor Du Cros in person four days after my adventure beneath the East Hill cliffs. It was accepted with good grace, and Du Cros assured me that the matter would be considered most carefully, and that a reply would be given soon after the New Year. It was too late, he said, for anything to be done about the matter before the Corporation suspended its activities for the Christmas festivities.

I was to catch sight of Freeman Du Cros on a number of occasions during that period, for the enhanced celebrity in the town given to me by the shingle-cage adventure – which was written up in exhaustive and lurid detail by Thomas Wilkins, complete with 'inside testimony' from his younger brother – made me the object of a large number of social invitations. I had made an exhibition of myself. It was during these seasonal junketings that the artificiality of life in Wellfleet began to irk me. What could express the elegiac, dying-fall bathos of the place better than these ceremonies carried on within the hollow casket of a dead religion? This antipathy of mine was all the stronger since I myself long ago discarded religion in favour of Art. Not that I conceive of anything of the sacral or sacramental about music, for that would be to imply something altogether too fixed. All Art is opposed to the doctrinal. No, music is transcendent, but not sacred. If that gives it an affinity to religion as traditionally imagined, then so be it. I am indifferent. And anyway, that is part of a larger argument between Art and sincere religion. The objection with regard to the Christmas celebrations at

Wellfleet concerns insincere religion – the clinging to outward forms and styles without penetrating their essence. Indeed, that could be said to be the pervading fault of the Coast.

But I welcomed any distraction from the painful suspense of waiting for the Corporation's decision. And so – despite their emptiness, and my own qualms about being served up like a delicacy to the burghers of Wellfleet – I accepted those invitations to their various seasonal celebrations.

And distracted I was. On several occasions I was persuaded to run my fingers over a keyboard. People were forever asking me to recount the story of how I was rescued from beneath the East Hill cliffs. And, everywhere I went, there was Madeleine Patrick. I was at a loss to know why she had taken such an interest in me. She is witty, vivacious and highly sociable, whereas I take a pride in these situations in being dour, peasant-like, slow and quite without the repartee that convention demands. Even so, she seemed to pursue me from one soirée to the next, drawing me aside and greeting my every monosyllabic response with gay laughter or nods of profound appreciation. I had imagined that her nocturnal visit to the Rock-a-Nore groyne might be an escapade she would want to keep quiet about. But not a bit of it; she talked of it volubly and in all kinds of company, including that of her husband. Clifford Patrick seemed quite unperturbed. She talked of how she had been keeping watch, having heard of our expeditions; of the wildness of the storm; of Reuben and me braving mountainous waves; of my singing and of the ringing tones of Jim Wilkins' French horn; and of my safe return 'like a real hero'.

'His hair was all curly from the salt,' she added on one occasion, and fondled my hair familiarly.

I was flattered by these attentions from an indubitably beautiful woman. And hence began my downfall. In mitigation I can plead only an excess of seasonal drink and my sense of exultation at completing the shingle researches.

These things weakened that austerity and asceticism that I maintain to be indispensable if one is to attain the most sublime and purest realms of artistic achievement. Fortunate it was in that regard that I had by now all but completed the first movement of the *Sea Symphony*. It lay upon my desk in a neat pile, and in blessed hours of quiet between junketings I leafed through it, playing the music in my head and making emendations here and there where what I saw did not correspond to what I heard. Only the end was not fully written, for I could not hear how to resolve the o'erleaping heroism, the gusts of thrumming wind, the oceanic downpourings, without falling upon bombast or striking a false note. It was clear to me only that such a movement could not conceivably end on a dying fall or 'feminine ending'.

The Grindley household was something of a haven at this time. They were having none of these Yuletide charades. Jacob Grindley is a scientist of the old school, an atheist and a man of the Enlightenment. For him, the phenomena of Nature obey their natural laws like well-behaved children. Everything in the universe operates by natural law, and the highest human calling is the scientific one of discovering its intricate patterns, of revealing the grid that locks the universe together in one harmonious whole. In the Arts, unfortunately, Mr Grindley takes no interest whatever, tending to regard me as a potentially promising pupil who has been seduced by frippery and degenerate pastimes. (He is, of course, far too courteous and deferential to air such thoughts openly.) But our minds meet on the broad and level ground of philosophy, and it is there that we have passed many a happy hour in jousting. By way of teasing him, I like to accuse him of being a secret Deist, of so elevating his natural laws upon the shoulders of 'objectivity' that they become, in effect, divinely granted. This never fails to raise from him a lather of anxious reassurance that this is 'not at all the case', and 'a quite unwarranted inference'. Nothing slips through his naturally legal net, he says, and there is an end of the matter. This seems to me to miss the point entirely, but when I argue this he tends to fall into a whereof-one-cannot-speak-thereon-one-must-remain-silent kind of a sulk. To mollify him a little, I tell him that what the two of us seek is not in actuality so very different, except that one of us seeks it through science, and the other through music. We both search in Nature itself for the Absolute, for that which animates mere sensuality, but whereas he finds that in law, fixity and regularity, I find it in movement, time and animation itself. If this does not entirely convince Jacob Grindley, it is usually enough to dissipate any ill-feeling caused by my jibes about Deism, and he will be happily off on some hobby-horse about the noumenal and the temporal, and my confusion of Kantian categories.

But it has not all been the heady matter of champagne and philosophy. On Boxing Day, in the afternoon, I had to conduct the traditional tea dance in the ballroom at the end of the pier. On this occasion Louis Grenier's *Waltz of the Clouds* received its premier, and I also included my 'Molly Bloom Dances', extracted from *Ulysses*, as well as the usual Strausses, Lehár and Tchaikovsky, etc. I have told you before how much I love the pier and the magnificent ballroom, which hangs like a belljar over the sea, a champagne bubble of music and celebration midst the wind and rain. The whole occasion was innocent and delightful, not least on my part for my meeting with Johnny Hunter, the manager of the pier, and his assistant Charlie Hawker. They have only recently arrived in Wellfleet to manage the affairs of the pier, but have already received a fair amount of attention – not all of it, on the part of the *haute bourgeoisie*, entirely favourable – as a couple of 'characters'. They work as a team, and are often to be seen hurrying along the front together to some meeting or business appointment. Much of the interest and amusement they arouse is occasioned by the very great difference in their physical and psychological types. For whereas Hunter is short, blunt, cocksure, and wears a straw boater, even in winter, Hawker is tall, elegant, courteous to the point of lugubriosity, and wears a top hat (even in summer, I have heard it said). I had some dealings with them over the arrangements for the tea dance, and found them to be a most amusing double-act. Hunter disparaged the event quite tactlessly and boasted about the more lucrative entertainments he could be putting on if it were not for the Corporation's backwardness, while his assistant openly reprimanded him for his vulgarity and humbled himself before me. The conversation left me baffled and amused, which was perhaps its intention. Clifford Patrick tells me that this is the manner in which they tend to carry on their business, and that they have a reputation in some circles for sharp practice. I have learnt to take nothing that any of these people say at face value, so have concluded that this antipathy of Patrick's to them is merely the general expression of some private interest. In my own dealings, I have found Hunter and Hawker quite amenable and open, and possessed of an efficiency that is unusual in this town. Everything was immaculately organised for the tea dance. The ballroom was made to look splendid, ample rehearsal time was allowed in the hall itself, and my musicians were provided with good facilities.

Indeed, the arrangements rather outshone those at the Everyman Theatre, where, on New Year's Eve, I presented the last of the subscription concerts. The programme included Sibelius' *Oceanides*, the orchestral suite taken from the opening scene of my *Ulysses*, Elgar's *Sea Pictures*, and a piece of juvenilia of Grenier's that I have unearthed, the jazz-influenced *Blowin' a Gust*. This last, I think, was a little daring for the Wellfleet audience. But at the New Year's Eve party held afterwards at the Patricks' house, I received many congratulations both for that evening's concert and also for the entire series. As a measure of appreciation, I was presented with a leather-bound copy of the concert programmes.

106

Again I asked Madeleine Patrick if Grenier might be invited down to share in the celebrations. I hadn't seen him for some time. She said that his health was poor, and that he detested crowds. But she did invite me back next day for a private audience with him.

So on New Year's Day, my head still cloudy with an excess of champagne the night before, I stumbled from the Grindleys' cottage up the hill to the Patricks' villa. Madeleine greeted me at the door in a voluminous dark blue dress. She always dresses in dark colours, to set off her luminous complexion.

She led me upstairs to Louis Grenier's room. I was shocked at how his appearance had deteriorated since I'd last seen him. His jowly face looked more sallow then ever, with a hint of grey about the eyes, and his walk had become a stiff, painful shuffle. He wore the same batik shirt as when I had first met him, heavily stained now with spilt tea, and his entire corpulent bulk was swathed in a grubby kimono. He all but devoured Madeleine Patrick when he greeted her, murmuring *'charmante, charmante'* over and over again like a mantra, kissing her hand, cradling it between his own pudgy flippers, patting it several times, then kissing it again for good measure. Green tea was served.

It was not hard to fathom the cause of his unhealthiness, for the air in his room was fetid and warm, despite the cold wind that blew outside. I knew from experience that it would be useless to ask him to open a window. Madeleine Patrick took a seat in one of his cavernous armchairs, and I slumped down on the couch. The combined effects of the warmth of the room, a lack of sleep, the excess of champagne and Grenier's green tea was making me feel more than a little strange. A kind of giddiness, mixed with a weakening of the joints and liquidation of the muscles, was beginning to overtake me.

Madeleine Patrick, meanwhile, was telling Grenier about my maritime exploits. Grenier listened to her narrative with a childlike wonder that was *charmant* itself. *'Quelle horreur!'*

and '*Mon dieu*,' he gasped at appropriate junctures. And then, when she had finished, he turned to me and said, with a sad shake of the head, '*Tu es trop farouche, mon vieux. Trop farouche.*'

It was, I think, the finest compliment that had ever been paid to me. Who could but be flattered to be named in alliance with such a word. My head tipped back on the couch, I found myself gazing at the ceiling and murmuring the word over and over to myself. *Farouche.*

'Only music can calm these tempests and excitements,' he continued. 'Come, I shall play for you.'

Leaning on Madeleine Patrick's arm, he shuffled over to the piano. Madeleine sat down next to me on the couch. I felt the springs sink and my own body be drawn by gravity close to hers.

Grenier began playing a barcarolle, the bass rolling along prettily below while the melody slid smoothly by on top. You will be able to gauge my weakened state, dear sister, by the fact that I allowed such a piece of music – the kind of saccharine noise that pollutes the canals of New Venice day and night – to move me. Granted the piano was still out of tune, but as I let my body relax and Grenier's barcarolle wash over me, it occurred to me that I had never given due credit to the sensual beauty of Grenier's music. His piano playing was teasing. It savoured the deliciousness of each phrase. I began to feel flushed and drowsy.

Madeleine Patrick also seemed affected by the music. She gave a deep sigh and tipped her head back, allowing the natural weight of her body to bring it closer to mine. Sitting together there on the couch, close to each other, it was indeed as though we were on a gondola being propelled slowly and lazily forwards by the motion of Louis Grenier's music.

Time passed. I could not say how much, nor when it was that I felt a softness upon my thigh. Madeleine Patrick's hand rested there, exerting a pressure greater than that merely of its natural weight. The barcarolle swelled romantically. I

turned my head heavily to look at her. She remained in the
same position – head tilted back and sideways towards my
shoulder; lips slightly apart, chest swelling as she breathed.
Her eyes were closed. Her cheeks were flushed, and beads of
sweat had appeared amid the down of her upper lip.

Grenier's barcarolle came to an end.

'I must lie down for some minutes,' he said in a soft, trem-
bling voice. 'You will forgive me.'

Madeleine Patrick hastily removed her hand, and we sat
up more properly on the couch. But we need not have bothered, for Grenier did not so much as glance at us. He moved
painfully away from the piano and deposited himself on a
chaise longue. Then he closed his eyes and fell into a deep
sleep.

For several minutes there was only the sound of Grenier's
snoring. Neither Madeleine Patrick nor I spoke, though a
kind of electricity was passing between us, a complex inter-
change of signal and response that seemed a language more
basic, stronger and vital than that which any tongue could
speak. At last the silence was broken.

'Play the piano,' she said in a broken, husky voice. 'I need
more music.'

We got up and went over to the piano. My legs felt heavy,
drugged, my mouth dry. She sat next to me at the piano,
touching me. I began to play, but my fingers felt like automata. My mind was a blank. Everything I did seemed to
come from blind, unreflecting instinct. I tried playing the
heroic theme from the first movement of my symphony, but
it came out sounding much slower than intended and *à la
Grenier* – swathed in voluptuous chords, engulfed in *une
vague de chaleur*. Madeleine Patrick's hand was on my thigh
again, moving. She began – I hardly know how to write
this with delicacy – to interfere with me. My symphony was
forgotten. My hands left the keyboard and fell on her. They
began playing a different tune. She undid herself, allowing
my fingers to play arpeggios on the ivory whiteness of her

breasts. She sank from the piano stool, lifting the voluminousness of her dress as she went.

And so Mrs Clifford Patrick and I did the carnal deed beneath Louis Grenier's grand piano, while the old composer himself snoozed in ignorance not ten yards away. I was much afraid at one point that I had woken him, for at a particularly passionate moment in the proceedings I hit my head on the underside of the instrument and set all the strings vibrating lusciously together. It sounded not unlike one of his compositions. But Grenier slept on. While I was deep within Mrs Patrick, Grenier was deep within oblivion.

If I can write about it with a smile now, it is only because laughter and tears are such close allies. And believe me, there have been tears over this matter. There are tears of shame even now, as I look back at the sentimental gloss that I find myself putting on such sordid transactions – all that tosh about gondolas and romantic swellings. There was nothing sublime or elevated in what occurred beneath that piano.

As I left the villa, I already felt the consciousness of what I had done weighing heavily on me. The cold, brisk wind seemed to slap my cheeks in reprimand, the gulls to shriek their derision at me. I wandered through the Old Town towards the sea, still caught in that distracted state in which I had left Monsieur Grenier's house. I had not eaten yet that morning. The only things to have passed my lips were Louis Grenier's tea and Madeleine Patrick's tongue. At one moment it all seemed like some dreadful dream from which I still might wake; the next it resolved itself into hard, irredeemable facts. I found myself standing before the clock tower in the High Street. I looked up at its face. It was noon. My heart was beating *prestissimo*. Everything about me unfolded slowly. Not far away, nearer the front, I heard the sound of many voices. I followed the sound, until there appeared before me a crowd. They were passing between the columns of great arches built of lobster cages, barrels, fishing nets, buoys, anchors, old ship's lanterns and a host of other

110

bric-a-brac of the sea. One of the arches bore a huge banner that proclaimed:

THE FLOWING TIDE IS *STILL* WITH US

I found something inexpressibly moving in this message of simple faith and hope, and tears welled in my bloodshot eyes as I watched the throng of fisherfolk – women in aprons, old men in their Sunday best, a child riding a donkey, fishermen in their smocks – pass beneath it. My tears were for myself as well, for I could not help but think that in some obscure way I had betrayed my fishermen friends. Wild and fearful thoughts invaded my mind: that I had been deliberately seduced in order to compromise the fishermen's cause; that Madeleine Patrick was in some sinister cabal with her husband, Du Cros and Hinchcliff; that even now they were huddled together, joined in cynical laughter at how high ideals could be brought low by base instinct. At any other time, in any other mood, I would have joined my friends and marched with them. But now I stayed aloof.

I watched until I could bear it no longer, then turned from that scene of happy, fraternal celebration, from the fresh and honest breeze off the sea that carried with it the damning, dancing laughter of children. I turned and fled for my lodgings, to bury myself in my work. But when I sat at my desk and leafed through the pages of my symphony's first movement, there were horrors anew. I remembered with nausea how I had played the theme from it so lushly for Madeleine Patrick, how I had *used* it (so I elaborated and plotted the incident in my mind) to seduce her, to draw her down beneath that piano. All the sublimity at which I had aimed crumbled to dust. I was desolate. I picked up the manuscript, was on the point of tearing it to shreds, then threw it aside and buried my head in my hands.

With love,
Paul

Dear Sister,

Over a month now since I wrote last, and for much of that time my spirits have been too low to contemplate putting pen to paper. But I am hopeful now that things are changing for the better, and am keeping myself more than occupied in putting an end to the first movement of the symphony. This task, which has been plaguing me without issue for some time is now forced to a resolution by the circumstances that I shall next narrate.

For a few days after the New Year I could hardly bear to face the world. Shame still hid me. I sat in my lodgings, before empty manuscript paper, and anxiously awaited the arrival of my daimon. That was the only company I desired. But the daimon never came, the manuscript paper remained empty, and in my idleness I found myself flicking back more and more through those pages that I had completed. I gazed on them with a dull and jaundiced eye, and it seemed to me that they were entirely lacking in beauty of sound. I could not imagine anyone taking pleasure in those pages. I compared them with Grenier's music, which for all its superficiality – as I had been given to think of it – did not *presume* upon the audience's attention. I had always thought that for all its surface glitter, Grenier's music lacked real, transcendent significance. But who was I now – I who had been so signally seduced by it – to deny the importance of material attractiveness? A fear grew in me that in trying to aim beyond the mere surface of things at the 'thing-in-itself', my music had fallen into abstraction. I wept as I riffled through the pages. I was surveying a wasteland.

But the outer world had its demands to make of me, and some ten days after the New Year I ventured out of my lodgings and bent my steps towards Mayor Du Cros's office.

The subject of this meeting was the Corporation's response to our submission respecting the groyne for the fishing beach. Already, as I walked through the familiar streets, I was feeling a sense of doom. The fate of the symphony and that of the fishermen's cause had become curiously enmeshed in my mind, and feeling so despondent about the one, I could not help but look gloomily upon the other.

This sense of foreboding was not alleviated by the sight of Freeman Du Cros's lugubrious face. He greeted me with the intention of a smile, but the execution of it was cloaked in pained, watery regret.

'May I congratulate you, Mr Clearwater,' he inquired, 'upon the success of the subscription concerts? You are an ornament to our town.'

'You may,' I replied.

'I'm sorry?'

'You may congratulate me upon the concerts,' I said with dignity. I was determined to put my best foot forward, and not to be intimidated by the majesty of Du Cros's office.

But Du Cros merely gazed at me with sad puzzlement, twiddling his whiskers. 'Let us get down to business,' he said.

'Has the Corporation examined Mr Grindley's researches?' I said.

'They are an exhibition of learning.'

'So you see the force of the fishermen's argument?'

'To an extent I do,' he said. 'We have decided to grant permission for the Rock-a-Nore groyne at the eastern end of the fishing beach to be strengthened and extended, to facilitate the build-up of shingle there.'

I leapt from my seat. 'But this is marvellous news,' I cried. I clasped Du Cros's languid hand and shook it vigorously. 'Thank you.'

'Of course,' he continued, 'there remains the matter of money.'

I sank back into my seat.

'Yes, Mr Clearwater,' he continued, 'I only said that in view of the evidence you have supplied, the Corporation has granted *permission* for an extra groyne to be built. The Corporation is not willing to incur the costs of such a project. The money for it will have to come from the fishermen themselves. It cannot possibly come from the public purse.'

'But the public purse is just as much theirs as yours,' I objected.

'The Corporation has made its decision.'

'And has the Corporation made an estimate of the amount it would cost the fishermen to build their groyne?'

He named a large figure, a figure so large that I knew immediately it would be far beyond the collective means of the fishing community.

'In effect,' I said bitterly, 'for all your talk of "permission", your reply is exactly the same as that which you gave me when I first approached you.'

'The Corporation has made its decision.'

'You've tricked me,' I said. 'You waited until the concerts were safely over, then merely repeated your previous decision. I don't believe that the Corporation has examined this fresh evidence at all.'

'What you believe is of little consequence,' he said. 'Our position is quite clear. Permission has been granted for the fishermen to extend their groyne, should they wish to.'

'You are an out-and-out rogue, sir,' I said, rising from my seat.

With a heavy heart I took this news back to Jacob Grindley. I bore my desolation back to my work and carried its heavy burden on my wanderings through the arid landscape of my symphony's first movement. Everything seemed quite without shape. I looked out from my window and saw wind and wave continue their relentless dance. They cared nothing about my symphony. The world would be the same without it.

There are moments in an artist's life when, pushed hard up against such a wall of hopelessness, a door suddenly swings open. Where before everything had been blank and formless, now there is an opening, a frame, a way through. Thus it was that I saw a way both to finish the movement and to help the fishermen. So intertwined had the two things become that it was a single door that was opened. I walked through.

I would organise my own series of subscription concerts to raise money for the fishermen's groyne. Art would serve justice. And the subscription series would open with a performance of the first movement of my symphony. As soon as the idea came to me, I was filled with such enthusiasm that immediately I knew how to finish the movement. I have mentioned before now the parallels between music and religion, but perhaps the greatest of these concerns faith. The most pious priest has nothing to teach me on the matter of faith. The priest believes in something because he thinks that it exists. But the composer has to believe in something while knowing that it does not exist, and that it can only be dragged into existence by the thin thread of faith that he has in it. Well, I had found my faith again.

The venue for these concerts would, of course, be the pier ballroom, that glass bubble of enchantment that hangs over the sea. What better place could be conceived for the coming to birth of my *Sea Symphony*? Without delay I arranged an appointment with Messrs Hunter and Hawker in their office on the pier. It was, in a way, a relief to be dealing with such unabashed men of commerce, rather than devious aesthetes (haters of Art) like Hinchcliff. The proposition that I put to them was that we should initially stage a single concert. At its conclusion, the audience, enticed by what they had heard, would be invited to subscribe to a further series of ten concerts. With the help of Jacob Grindley, I calculated prices such that, even taking into account the costs of hiring the hall and paying the musicians, there would still be a handsome profit left over for the fishermen.

Johnny Hunter, chomping upon his impresarial cigar, was at first adamantly opposed to the entire proposition. Fortunately, however, his assistant Charles Hawker was much more sympathetic, and indeed took my part against his master throughout the whole proceedings. With Clifford Patrick's dire warnings in mind as to the cutthroat ruthlessness of their business manners, I was pleasantly surprised at this.

Mr Hunter began by saying that the scheme was entirely out of the question, since they had their own plans for entertainments in the ballroom which could not possibly be disrupted. Charlie Hawker interrupted to say that none of these plans were finalised, and that they should give me a proper hearing as it sounded a promising scheme. I was a little surprised at this open disagreement, as it hardly seemed like the best policy, from their point of view, to present me with such a disunited front. I proceeded to lay out my plans in more detail, emphasising the recent success that I had had with the winter subscription series. When I reached the point of saying that I would book the hall initially for just one concert, in order to take subscriptions for the series proper, Johnny Hunter interrupted.

'Oh no, you don't,' he said. 'It's all or nothing. We can't just keep those dates free for you. Do you realise, we're taking bookings two years in advance? You'll have to come up with the money for all eleven concerts. We'll want that money up front before your musicians so much as step foot on this pier.'

'But Johnny,' said Hawker. 'How can you be so unreasonable? You can't expect Mr Clearwater to take that risk. How is he going to come up with that kind of money before he's even taken any subscriptions? And besides, even if he didn't take enough subscriptions, we'd still have time to take bookings for those evenings.'

He smiled at me in a friendly manner.

'Whose side are you on?' inquired Hunter, scowling.

'I just want Mr Clearwater to get a fair deal,' said Hawker. 'What if we asked Mr Clearwater to pay as a deposit a quarter of the overall cost of booking for the whole series. That would provide us with more than enough insurance.'

'No,' said Hunter, scowling through the window of the office at the waves. 'It's got to be the whole lot.'

Charlie Hawker looked at me with a frown of embarrassed irritation. 'I'm sorry about this,' he whispered. Then he said to Hunter, 'Well, a half then. That would be more than enough for us.'

Hunter was silent for a few moments, glaring at his assistant with ill-disguised hostility. Then he said, 'Very well, two-thirds of the total costs, in advance and in cash before the first rehearsal. And that is my last offer.'

'At least let him pay the money after he has taken the subscriptions,' said Hawker.

'All right, damn you,' said Hunter. 'Payment will be due a week after the opening concert.'

And so a contract was drawn up and signed. The sum of money to which it commits me is a large one, but the risk involved is small. It would be a sad comment upon my artistic faith in my first movement if I were not able to stake money on it. What is mere money to the breath and spirit of life that I have already squandered on it?

> With love,
> Paul

26 March 2065

Dear Sister,

My dear friend Louis Grenier has died. He passed away a few days ago in his sleep. Madeleine Patrick tells me that he suffered from a heart condition, and that he had known for some time that his end was approaching. It says much for Louis's stoical and elevated cast of mind that in all the many hours I spent with him, he let slip not a word of complaint or foreboding. He was a man for whom I had the greatest respect — as a spirit, a musician and an artist. I have shed many tears since I heard of his departure.

My distress is all the greater since, because I have been so busy preparing for my concerts, I have not had an opportunity to visit him since that dishonourable occasion when Madeleine Patrick and I misbehaved under his piano. It pains me that my last meeting with him should be connected with an event which I have tried to blot from my mind.

But for all that, the memory of this noble artist remains fresh and vivid. And his music, with its charm and its open, engaging appeal to the senses, will be hallowed wherever there are ears to hear and tongues to speak. My own music of late has not been uninfluenced by it in matters of texture and timbre. I have written to you previously of how his 'Dance of the Spirits of the Air' has found its echo in my evocation of the gulls wheeling and diving off the East Hill cliffs. More recently, while rehearsing my symphony's first movement for its première with the Wellfleet Philharmonic Society orchestra, I have noticed other parallels between the surface — the mere *sound* — of my own work and Grenier's music. We had another rehearsal yesterday, in the pier ballroom, and the similarities were made more uncanny by the knowledge of his recent death. It was as though his ghost were stalking the pages of my symphony. Of course, the experience of hearing one's own music played back to one is always uncanny. There are moments of quiet satisfaction, of confirmation, but what is more pervasive is a sense of unease. It is the uncanniness of *déjà vu*, of unnatural repetition, of the double. There were times, as I was conducting, when I wanted to stop the orchestra and say, 'That is all very well, it is even quite pleasant, but it is not what I *meant*.' But I am nothing if not a professional. I beat on.

I have decided that it would be a noble gesture to dedicate this concert to Louis Grenier's memory, and to include another performance of his youthful and energetic *Blowin' a Gust*. That is perhaps how he should be remembered. If towards the end of his life he played the role of aesthetic recluse, at least in death he shall come out and breathe freely again, reactivating that spirit that took him through the jungles of Java in pursuit of his daimon. That spirit is the same that places my Art at the service of the just and natural cause of the fishermen. It is fitting that they should be joined in counterpoint.

Frederick Delius was a great favourite of Grenier's. (For all that he chewed the cud of English pastoral, Delius was, after all, practically a Frenchman.) So I have decided also to include his *Sea Drift*, which should sound nicely on the pier. As for the rest of the programme, I have opted for Mozart, who always pulls the punters. His *Masonic Funeral Music* will open – though anything further from Grenier's tastes than that austere majesty would be hard to imagine – and the first half will end with the *Jupiter* symphony. My symphonic first movement will share the second half with Grenier's *Blowin' a Gust*. As a concert programme it is something of a potpourri, but at least it may stir the waters. I am, after all, angling for subscribers.

Not, I confess, that I am altogether at ease with my role of baton-twirling *rabouilleur*. That uncanniness of which I have spoken haunts me more than ever it has done before. I find myself envying Balzac's composer, Gambarra, who plays directly upon an instrument that can reproduce all the sounds of the orchestra. Not that the Wellfleet musicians are at fault, for they are faithful to the letter of what I have written. But can they be faithful to the spirit? No artist has lived who has not felt that cold, empty space that lies between conception and realisation. But for me, as I dutifully rehearsed the orchestra in my symphonic movement, there opened at times an awful, howling abyss. I shake my fists at the heavens and what do I get in reply? Mere sound.

You may wonder, dear sister, how I carry on in the face of such disappointment. The answer is that I keep my faith. A true believer does not lose his faith merely because he cannot share his good news with others. He retains his relationship with his God. And I retain my faith in my symphony. To blame it for my failure to communicate would be like a man of religion blaming God for his own misdemeanours. So my faith survives. It even grows.

And the contours grow clearer. The second movement, as I have written to you before, is moved by a sense of claustrophobia. I have in mind a piece of *Nachtmusik*. And the third movement, the slow movement? I hear it now as an elegy for Grenier – slow, swimming with sensuality, and not without its own feeling for the French.

The first movement? I realise now that I have not told you how the first movement *does* end. But let that wait. I am tired now, and haunted by strange repetitions.

With love,
Paul

15 May 2065

Dear Sister,

For the two months that have passed since last I wrote I have lived in a kind of limbo. All emotion, desire, energy, spirit has been frozen, and I have had to treat myself as an infinitely delicate thing, a thing for which a confrontation such as that with a blank sheet of paper would be too bruising to contemplate. I only force myself to write now because my situation is so desperate.

Do you remember that libretto I sent you, *The Commission*? Have you shown it to Cottimi? Does he think he can do anything with it? I find it demeaning to have to crawl to him in this way, but the truth is that I need the money desperately. Please ask him to do what he can to find a backer and to secure a *substantial cash advance*. I need the money immediately. I promise to come back to New Venice and write the score as soon as that is done.

You've probably guessed by now what lies behind all this. Yes, my attempt to act the impresario and put on a subscription series for the benefit of the fishermen has proved an unmitigated disaster. And because of that contract that I was insane enough to sign with Hunter and Hawker, I now find myself mired in debt.

When I wrote to you before the concert, I think I talked of that sense of disquiet, of the uncanny, that I felt on hearing my symphony's first movement being played. That feeling continued – got worse, indeed – as the big night approached. I found myself inflicting on the musicians a puritanical perfectionism that is foreign to my usual way of working. Hitherto it has been my practice never to berate or intimidate the musicians under my direction, but always to instil in them a sense of confidence in their own powers. For it is only with such confidence – and of course I mean *genuine* confidence, confidence built upon real ability – that a performance of merit can be attained. But as rehearsals for this concert went on, I found myself becoming more and more irritable, ill-at-ease and unreasonable with the orchestra. I made them play over and over again passages which they had already mastered, unable to express exactly what it was that I disliked about their rendition, but feeling only a vague, all-pervading aversion to it. This, as you can imagine, did not go down well. All this destructive fussiness, this sense of *wrongness* that haunted me, extended from my own music to the other pieces in the programme. Delius's *Sea Drift*, God knows, is a work with more than its share of potentially turgid moments.

121

But I made the poor Wellfleet musicians – and the chorus that had been assembled for the occasion – go through great swathes of it again and again, at achingly slow tempos, in order to check the tuning of each gelatinous chromatic chord. I think the poor baritone soloist almost burst a blood vessel. And in the case of the Mozart *Jupiter* symphony – where, it is true, insistence on precision is more of the essence – my dictatorial methods all but caused a mutiny. Do you remember the opening of the monumental last movement, when the four-note motif that is to become the object of every conceivable fugal manipulation is first introduced? The first violins introduce it *legato, piano*, while the seconds play a quickly rocking accompaniment. I must have made them play those bars thirty times. They could 'play the notes' from the very start, but with each repetition I heard something to dissatisfy me. The four notes were not wholly even and *legato*; they were too loud; there was too much vibrato; now it was not warm enough; now the balance with the accompaniment was all wrong. I began to get more irritated, hitting the lectern with my baton. (The kind of behaviour I would normally abhor. Violence of any sort is antithetical to Art.) The very sound of the violins – its physicality, its *presence* – was beginning to grate and set my teeth on edge. I rolled my eyes and made sarcastic remarks. To begin with the musicians took all this stoically, straining their concentration to meet my sometimes contradictory demands. But after twenty minutes of being berated, of playing the same phrase over and over again, there were audible grumbles. The wind and brass players began chatting to each other, ostentatiously yawning or reading their newspapers. After rehearsals, it was usually my practice to take tea with some of the players. But from then on I was shunned. A frostiness and mistrust had grown up between myself and my musicians.

I blame none of this on them. Had I been directing the very cream of the world's instrumentalists I would have felt the same, for what was disturbing me was the very physical *sound* of music. There seemed to me to be an excess, a superfluity, a sort of gross, crude *materiality* about it. Perhaps you will think it mad for a composer, of all people, to come to hate the sound of music. How could such a thing happen? But it is the lofty ambition of the composer to give expression to something beyond the materiality even of music itself. So music is doomed to fall short. There is a strand of austerity and asceticism in every true artist; and in music, by its nature, there is an element of excess, of crude, Dionysiac sensuality, that can never be purged. To want to purge it, as I did, is to yearn for silence.

These were the kind of thoughts that I entertained in order to rationalise and explain to myself the strange anxiety, the *nausée* that began to grip me during the rehearsals. I was, of course, a professional, and attempted to hide from the orchestra as best I could my sense of unease and panic. But orchestras are highly sensitive to the moods of their maestro. My unease quickly communicated itself, so that with each word I spoke, with every gesture of mine, I was undermining their confidence rather than building it up. And as a mechanism of psychological defence, they began to put a distance between themselves and me – treating my comments with scepticism, looking to each other for support, closing ranks, making jokes about me behind my back.

So, in short, as the big night approached, I was not the master of a happy ship. I knew all too well how much was riding on the success of the concert – and so did the musicians, for whom it meant a few weeks of gainful employment before the summer season – but my every last attempt to lighten the atmosphere fell flat. If I made a joke it came out as a dry cackle, and if I paid them a compliment it merely sounded condescending. With my theatrical background, however, I am a firm believer in the 'power of performance', the 'magic of the moment', etc. The fact that the concert was fully booked gave me heart. Before an expectant audience, the orchestra and I might yet put the past behind us.

The night of the concert saw another storm sweep across Wellfleet. It was indeed the kind of night when miracles might happen, when fresh winds could furnish fresh inspiration. '*Le vent se lève . . . il faut tenter de vivre!*' The pier hummed with burghers. They clutched hats and flapping coats, abuzz with the novelty of the occasion. I visited the musicians' green room and spoke a few words of encouragement, which were greeted with politeness. The orchestra shuffled on and, when they had tuned up, I followed.

It was about half-way through the opening item, the *Masonic Funeral Music* of Mozart, that the banging started. I had noticed just before I went on, stepping out on to the terrace to catch a last moment of natural inspiration before the performance, that the wind was strengthening. Huge black waves had rolled below me, between the pillars that hold up the pier. The skeins of foam on their heaving, distended surfaces were illumined by the gas lamps. Now Mozart's *Masonic Funeral Music* was interrupted by a low, metallic boom, not only heard but felt, vibrating through the body to the very teeth. It was an ugly sound, a very *physical* sound. The music continued, of course, but the Masonic magic was quite destroyed. I saw a few of the musicians exchange smiles of amusement. For a while there was nothing, and then another boom, like the first. I could sense a restiveness in the audience behind me.

It is almost impossible to re-establish the particular tension of a musical performance once it has been broken by some external distraction. In that sense, even if there had been nothing more, that first interruption would have ruined the concert. But the noise continued, becoming louder and more insistent if anything, and at unpredictable intervals. It revived all my feelings of disgust at the physicality, the *soundness*, of music itself. How pathetic that music, which should be the purest and most ideal of Art forms, is in actuality so fragile as to be shattered by so irrelevant a disturbance. Perhaps I should have halted the concert until the source of the noise had been sought out and eliminated. Yes, that might have been best. But I chose instead to grit my teeth and continue as though nothing were happening. And there is nothing so ridiculous, so pompous and artificial, as a concert where nobody is attending to the music. The whole thing becomes a charade. There are many quiet passages in Delius's *Sea Drift*, which was next on the programme, and when these formed merely a mushy backdrop to the distinct bangings from outside, there were guffaws of laughter from chorus, orchestra and audience alike. By the end of the Delius the entire event was becoming a joke. It seemed at moments as though I were the only one taking it seriously. At the end of the piece, which seemed as interminable as the ocean itself, there was a chorus of ironic cheers from the rowdier elements of the audience. There was little applause from the rest. Outside, that infernal noise boomed on.

As soon as the opening notes of the *Jupiter* symphony sounded, I realised what an appalling, cloth-eared piece of programming it had been. Who but a madman would pour the amorphous mass of *Sea Drift* into the space between two pieces of Mozart? What can I have been thinking of? It was at that point, I think, that I knew that the concert was doomed. I carried on waving my baton about in the approved manner, but my heart had gone out of it. And that resignation of mine communicated itself immediately to the musicians. They knew from then on that there was little point in even trying. The result was a shambles worse even than that rendition of *The Magic Flute* I had heard in the Everyman Theatre. How I wished, as we destroyed the *Jupiter*, that someone in the audience would have the courage to stand up and denounce the performance, as I had done that night! My arms went through the motions, like automata, but the rest of me felt only shame. The noise that the musicians made had little to do with music.

During the interval, I rushed out on to the terrace of the pier to see if I could discover the source of the noise that was ruining the concert. It was not hard to find. Leaning out over the railing, into the wind, I looked down and saw that a wooden platform, suspended by ropes from the girders of the pier, was swinging freely in the wind and crashing against one of the supporting pillars. This was the cause of that hollow, metallic boom.

I ran along the terrace to the pier office. Fortunately, Hunter and Hawker were both there. I explained to them the problem and demanded that they do something about it immediately, or the entire concert would be a disaster.

'That'll be those damned decorators,' said Hunter. 'They're giving the pier a new lick of paint. They promised to tie up their gear. I'll have words with them about this. Don't you worry, Mr Clearwater. You just get on with your music. We'll send someone along there right now to sort it out.'

Feeling much relieved by this, I returned to my dressing room and sat quietly till the end of the interval, attempting to restore my tattered nerves. Perhaps at least Grenier and I would redeem the evening.

Vain hopes! *Blowin' a Gust* came off well, for even if there had been noise from outside, it would have been drowned by Grenier's syncopated clatterings. But we were some five minutes into my symphony movement – the winds approaching across the sea, the strings thrumming in sympathy – when there was another loud metallic boom. This was followed by another, louder still. They were greeted with laughter by the audience. From that moment, my symphony was lost. How bitter an irony that the natural force of the wind, which had played so great a part in the movement's inspiration, should also have been its undoing! The bangings and boomings continued unabated. Clearly Hunter and Hawker had failed in their attempt to make fast the decorators' equipment. There was nothing for it but to complete the performance with as much dignity as could be mustered. There were points when, the audience having been placed in such high good humour by the evening's disasters, dignity was hard to come by. Towards the end of the movement there is a storm passage, when jagged argpeggios lash the orchestra like squalls of rain. At that moment, as a counterpoint to the booms and bangs below, a real squall swept the pier. The rattle of the rain against the windowpanes, and of the windows themselves in their frames, all but drowned out the squalls of Art, a juxtaposition that occasioned considerable merriment among the musicians. Again it seemed that I was the only one who was not laughing.

The applause at the end of the première of my symphony's first movement lasted ten seconds. I counted them. They barely gave me time to scamper off the platform. The audience – some still chuckling and joking with each other, others yawning – gathered their belongings and hurried out into the stormy night. The musicians departed too. On the lists deposited on the trestle tables in the foyer for people to sign up as subscribers, there were just seven names. Two of those were 'The Pope' and 'Wolfgang Mostfart'.

For me, this fiasco has meant financial disaster. I considered it my first obligation to pay off the musicians. What was left was not nearly enough to pay Hunter and Hawker what I owed them. Would that I had never signed that accursed contract! Already they are threatening to take legal action against me. ('We've got the best lawyer in town,' said Hunter smugly. 'Perhaps you've heard of Roland Hinchcliff?') The money I got for the winter subscription concerts, my savings that I brought from New Venice – all of it has gone, and still I owe Hunter and Hawker a huge amount. There is nobody here to whom I can turn. My life is in ruins. My friends on the fishing beach, for whom I was doing all this, shun me. Grenier is dead. I have not been able to pay my rent to the Grindleys for weeks. I can find no solace in my work, for I have not been able to think of a note of music since that disastrous night on the pier. My only hope of salvation lies with Cottimi. He must get a commission for the opera. Please do what you can. I place myself in your hands.

With love,
Paul

II

Paul, I suppose when I started getting your letters I assumed they'd dry up when you didn't get any reply. I should have known better. You're such an obsessive. I'm sorry, but I couldn't write back. Who *writes* any more? It's archaic. I might end up sounding like you do in your letters. So here I am. Of course, as soon as I mentioned the idea of recording a disk to send you, mother and father were on to me. They *had* to be included. You know how mother hates to be left out of anything. For her it would be like not getting an invitation to the ball. The pathetic thing is that, despite everything she's got, deep down she thinks of herself as a Cinderella. Self-pity's always been her strongest card. As for father, he wants to 'put you straight on certain matters'. So I think you'll know what to expect. Maybe we shouldn't be too hard on him. He's got a lot to be defensive about.

That's enough about our bloody family. There's something happening here, Paul. About a month ago, posters started appearing around the city. They're bright orange, and along the bottom, there are slogans in tiny letters. 'A Different Drum.' 'Music? No compromise.' 'Roots.' 'Straight from the source.' The slogans change all the time. No one knows what it's all about.

At first people didn't pay too much attention. They've seen too many tease campaigns. This was probably just someone trying to create a buzz for a new band. But there were so *many* of the damn things that you couldn't ignore them. And they kept appearing. Not just on the official hoardings, but plastered along the alleys and round the campos. Whoever was doing it was plugged into canal culture. And they've got money. A friend of mine moonlights fly-posting, and he says the people he works for get a thousand of these things a night. He reckons it's someone running for the Municipal who's out for the youth vote. Everyone's got a theory.

But then that's how a tease campaign works, isn't it? You get everybody talking about it, even if it's just to say they're sick of being mindfucked. I saw one of those posters today on the wall of the Santa Nicola de Tolentino. Above the slogan, someone had written 'The Palaces of Kings are Built upon the Ruins of the Bowers of Paradise.' The letters were done like flowers. I liked that.

People were expecting the pay-off after a couple of weeks, but it never came. The ads started flashing up on the telescreens in the clubs. 'I celebrate myself and sing myself.' 'I and this mystery here we stand.' 'An organ of your own.' 'Blow your own trumpet.' I was at an electric-flamenco night at the Palazzo Mocenigo and a fight started. Someone told me they were arguing about those posters. Like I say, everyone's got a theory. The neo-mafiosi are behind it. There's a new designer drug about to hit the market. It's the Municipal trying to mindfuck the whole city. That's what I love about this place. Something like this happens and it's like a shot of electricity through the whole system.

Everybody is talking about you. We had a small do in the hotel last week and I lost count of the number of times I was taken aside and interrogated. 'Where *is* your dear Paul?' 'Has he *really* gone to the Coast?' Darling, what could I *say*? You might at least have left me with an alibi. All I could do was put on my most demure smile and murmur to them that you had gone to the sea to find your inspiration among those darling fishermen. That *is* right, isn't it, darling? Jean gives me your letters to read. Sweet things. Madame Marie Donnelly — 'Queen of the Fenice Crush Bar' I call her, and your father can't stand the sight of her, poor woman — she came up to me and asked me *ever so* solicitously how I was coping with your absence, as though for all the world you'd been banished to the depths of . . . oh I don't know, think of some far-off place. You know I could never do geography. So: demure smile, inspiration from the fishermen. 'The theatre *will* miss him,' she says, with an I'm-so-glad-you're-putting-a-brave-face-on-it smile that quite turned my stomach. So, putting a brave face on it, I assured her that it was merely a case of *reculer pour mieux sauter*. Same smile from her. *Que dire*? Do tell me what I'm meant to *say* to these dreadful people, darling. It's so like you to run off without so much as a word.

How beautifully you describe your seaside hideaway! Those storms! You'll give us all nightmares. I go to unimaginable lengths to find out about this place of yours. Everywhere I go it's 'Wellfleet, Wellfleet'. People must think I'm quite mad. I was despairing of finding out *anything*, but then I met Peter Forrsteen, that quite *horribly* intelligent banker who your father knew in the old days. He told me that Louis Grenier is living there. Louis Grenier. Now there's a name from the past. There is a certain class of person, isn't there, who you just *assume* must be dead. But no, now that I think of him again I can remember him quite clearly. Of course, I was just a slip of a thing, so he wouldn't remember me, and I was quite in *awe* of him. It must have been in the Thirties. I have no head for dates. It was at the opening of the Teatro Moulin on the Zattere Al Ponte Lungo. I was wearing a peach dress with a daring plunge that Monsieur Grenier positively *feasted* upon. It was the time that I was deliriously pursuing your father. So *imagine* my joy when I read in one of your charming letters that you had become friends with dear Louis Grenier. He is quite enchanting, and I'm sure he writes perfectly beautiful music. You must tell him *all* about us. I know how you leave things out. All right! Your sister says my time is up. What a bully she is! Where can she get it from? No, don't answer that. But Paul, darling, I absolutely insist that you tell Louis Grenier all about us.

*

You would think, would you not, that your sister's education – not to say a modicum of common sense – might have made her realise the problems in sending a disk to the Coast. Even if it could be smuggled in, against all the Movement of Technology laws, how on earth would you be able to play it? And why is it always left to the man to point out the practical difficulties in these kinds of situations? So, Paul, don't think that your father shares your sister's naivety. I only agreed to speak on this disk because I've been thinking for a while anyway of airing my thoughts on certain matters. I have my own disk recorder running even as I speak. It has troubled me for some time that Milstein has never written his memoirs. I've often urged him to record his version of events for posterity, before it's too late, but he's always dismissed the idea as self-indulgent and individualistic. I don't agree. Milstein and I have suffered many smears and attacks, and we have a right to reply to them. But it seems that the task of doing so has devolved to me. When these thoughts of mine have been transcribed and published, they will form a final justification of the original ideals that inspired us to build New Venice. They will be a memorial of our times and a record of everything that has happened here to destroy our dreams.

As far as you are concerned, Paul, if this disk ever does reach you, there are a number of matters on which I would like to put you straight. Jean has shown me the two letters she's received from you, and I must say that I find your play-acting irksome. Since you seem to be living in a romantic, pseudo-nineteenth-century world of your own, perhaps we should start with some basics. The Coast, of which Wellfleet is a part, is an entirely artificial creation, a hermetically sealed region deliberately plunged back into a pre-twentieth-century idyll. It had its origins some fifty years ago, when communes started appearing there of people who claimed to have turned their backs on the modern world. The movement grew, and was taken up by the Parti Turquoise, those opportunistic advocates of Green Conservatism. In 2023 the Coast was officially established as the first Preserved Region – a living, breathing theme park where fantasists could act out their wish that the modern world did not exist. Many deluded people were attracted there. I suppose it appealed to that pathetic romantic historicism that was reaching its peak at that time, that odious and sentimental obsession with 'heritage' that was sweeping Europe. Behind it, of course, lay a reactionary, self-deluding deification of 'nature' and 'authenticity'. Marie Antoinette playing at peasants in the gardens of Versailles. I shouldn't have to give you these history lessons, Paul, but you seem to have fallen for that lie completely.

The Parti Turquoise attempted to hijack the plans for New Venice. In fact they plotted at one stage to make New Venice itself a kind of Preserved Region. Many of the people who flocked to New Venice in the Thirties, with their elitist and backward-looking ideological baggage, represented the worst kind of Parti Turquoise supporter. Most of them were friends of your mother. Of course, Milstein and I, in the course of long and complex political manoeuvres, had at certain times to make tactical alliances with some elements in the Parti Turquoise. Architecture on this scale is the art of the possible, of compromise – and none the worse for that, contrary to what you may think. Because at certain times, and for limited objectives, we made these political alliances, you will see it claimed in some quarters that the philosophy and aims of the construction of New Venice were the same as those for the establishment of the Preserved Regions. Nothing could be further from the truth. As evidence, let me read you a passage from Milstein's *Re-Renaissance*, which was published in 2032 at the height of these controversies, and when our plans were at last being realised. This is what Milstein wrote:

The concept of New Venice, and the way in which it pays homage in the most direct way possible to one of the van-

135

ished glories of European civilisation, is far from being an instance of reactionary, nostalgic *turquoiserie*. New Venice is much more than merely a copy of the old. It takes its basic shape, its overall design, its theme and atmosphere and inspiration from '*La Serenissima*'; but it will be above all a development of that theme, an enlargement and elaboration. There is nothing reactionary or merely 'backward-looking' in that. Indeed, every great advance in European civilisation has involved just such a reworking and transformation of intellectual and cultural materials from the past. The very word 'revolution' encompasses this sense of something that had disappeared into the darkness of the past being turned over, like soil, and brought back into the light of the present. The Renaissance – that upheaval of the human mind that launched our modern world on its giddying, unpredictable trajectory – had at its heart the bringing to light again of the achievements of the classical world, the blossoming of seeds that had been sown many hundreds of years before.

New Venice, in its construction and dynamic development, will be a celebration of that principle of human progress. It builds on the example of Venice – that Renaissance city; that city of Carpaccio, the Bellinis, of Titian, Tintoretto, Serlio and Sansovino – just as the Renaissance built on the example of the classical world. If the human animal can be said to have an 'essence' or 'nature' (but is it not the human paradox to be that animal whose nature is to have no nature, whose essence is to have no essence?), then it must lie in the exercise of this reflective, dialectical, transformative faculty. New Venice will embody that faculty in living stone, water and brick. It will stand as homage to the past and new life to the future. It will be a laboratory of culture, a seed-bed for the growth of some future Renaissance of which at present we can but dream.

I kept that book of Milstein's beside my bed for many

years. It sustained me through the long, day-in, day-out struggles that went into the physical construction of the city. It captures the heady idealism of that time.

I'm more bitter now. I can hardly bear to go out into the city these days, even though I've devoted my whole working life to it. I know what I'll find out there: loutishness, philistinism, fashion and hedonism. Milstein made the humorous remark the other day that in one respect perhaps we had been *too* successful in recreating the old Venice, that we had come too close to the original. After its high Renaissance, the old Venice entered a long period of decadence and decline. New Venice was simply mirroring that process in a compressed timescale; whereas the old had taken a couple of centuries to plumb the depths, the new was achieving the same in just a couple of decades. Nothing, he said, better illustrated the acceleration of history. Milstein elaborated on this amusing conceit by expressing a regret that we hadn't built New Venice on foundations as unstable as those of the old. Then at least it might be allowed, like its predecessor, to slip gracefully into oblivion. Unfortunately, we had done our work too well. New Venice was as solid as a rock, condemned to stand witness to its own humiliation.

Do you know what I hate most about this place, Paul? It's the infernal noise. Even up here at the top of the hotel, Milstein and I have to keep the windows shut or we can't hear ourselves think. It's not the motor boats in the canal that bother me. I don't mind the noise of machines. It's the blasted music. There's no escape from it. Everywhere you go you're assaulted by the noise of music. It drives me to distraction. When Milstein and I conceived the city, we thought it would be a city above all of the visual arts. We envisaged the look of the place being constantly transformed, in an organic process, by the development of the arts. The buildings themselves were just a beginning. They'd be changed by new frescos, new decoration, new sculpture. New buildings would go up. Instead, you look around you

137

now and all you see is decline and neglect. The visual arts are derided. It's as though people in this city had given up caring about their physical environment. Instead there's this obsession with music, this constant thumping and wailing, this 'universal language' that everybody chatters about. People prance about on the gondolas like monkeys, like half-crazed savages. When I think of all the work and idealism that went into building this place, and it's come to this. To hell with it all. That's what I feel like saying. To hell with it all.

That buzz is still here. I can feel it in the city. I felt it the other night when I went to a Fela Lahbib gig. He's the new African singer that everyone's talking about, when they aren't talking about those ads. His songs stick in the mind. He's become a kind of Messiah for a lot of people, especially the non-Europeans. Before he was discovered, he was selling trinkets in San Marco along with the other Africans. He's been there. His songs are about exile, homesickness, love. They're very personal, with a lot of beautiful, surreal imagery. He's become a kind of political icon. No doubt the commercial world'll latch on to him, but it hasn't happened yet. He's still a cult figure. He still belongs to canal culture. A Fela Lahbib concert is still an event with its own atmosphere and electricity.

It's atmospheres and electricity that fascinate me when I go to a concert, not the music itself. Take that Lahbib gig. There was a seriousness in the air that I hadn't come across before. His songs invite people to look around them and think. By the end the mood was almost downbeat. The more I think about that, the more I think it was something he deliberately engineered. Because you see the first set was different. He came on with a big, driving band behind him – rhythm section, horns, singers. Lahbib was dancing. The audience were dancing. There was a sense of release.

I should explain that there's been a strange tension building up on the campos over the past couple of weeks. If this thing is a tease campaign, it's certainly working. It's getting under people's skin. The graffiti scrawled on the posters gets more obscene every day, and the toasters are using the slogans to whip up the audiences in the clubs. The slogans change all the time, but there's one that keeps coming back. 'Sing the Body Electric.' This phrase was getting so familiar that it started being replaced with just the initials 'STBE' in tiny letters at the bottom of the posters and telescreens. Then sometimes these four letters would be scattered randomly across the poster, or there'd be stupid games played with them, things like: 'BETS: STBE = BEST'. People are getting annoyed. You hear them say that whoever's running this tease campaign's blown it because it's gone on too long. But the point is, they're talking about it more than ever. The campaign's feeding off the negative feelings that it's created.

While Lahbib's band was playing the first set, I had the feeling that all this tension was reaching a point of release. But it didn't happen. The band went off and he played the rest of the gig alone, sitting and accompanying himself on the kora. He still had the audience's attention, but there was a definite sense of anticlimax, as though he'd deliberately put a dampener on things. There was a strange mood when people drifted out of the club at the end – not like the exhausted, exhilarated buzz you usually get at the end of a gig. People were quiet.

I love crowds. They're a kind of music to me. That's why I love this city. Like you say, Paul, it's claustrophobic. Father hates crowds too. They're too noisy, too much of a muddle. He likes things cut and dried, black and white. Think of how he used the word 'European' just now when he was talking to you. We know what that means. The Parti Turquoise was always the party of 'preserving' Europe, of 'Europe for the Europeans'. They latched on to New Venice as a reaffirmation of 'European civilisation'. That old whitewash. And Milstein and father went along with that. To give them their due, they also argued that New Venice should be more open than the other European cities – a conduit for different cultures, a chink in 'Fortress Europe'. Father liked the idea of that because it was 'progressive'. But he can't deal with the reality. Chinese chanteuses? Somalian performance artists? Mongolian throat-singers? Cuban rappers? A Tower of Babel. A frightening cacophony. That's father's reaction. But to me it's beautiful, a beautiful, human music with its own harmonies. What could be frightening about that?

Sometimes I think I'm the only democrat in this family. I'm amazed by your letters. You couldn't give a fuck for those fishermen. They're no more real for you than a chorus in one of your operas. Father was right about Marie Antoinette. You won't find nature out there on the Coast. It's right here. I'm touched that you write me these long letters, but they confuse me. Why do you go in for all that self-dramatisation? Do you need to appear strange to people? You say you want to get back to something real and honest, but then you dress that up in costume. When you ran away from here to the Coast, you weren't escaping to something more authentic. The world you were going to was more artificial than the one you'd left behind. I understand you wanting to escape, because I've felt the same way myself. But you seem to think that there's *one thing* that when you touch it you'll know is real and without bullshit. Whereas I know that it's many things, in the interactions of many things. I've glimpsed them right here in the crowds of New Venice. Your trouble was that you spent too much time in the theatres with Frank Cottimi. It may have given mother something to boast about, but it stopped you seeing what's really happening. God knows, you didn't have to go to the Coast to find life.

So what's the other news? Father escapes by spending his whole time up in Milstein's penthouse, surrounded by the original blueprints of the city. God knows what they do all the time. Relive the old days, I suppose, and moan about how everything's gone wrong. I don't think Milstein's spoken to anyone but father for months. He loathes mother. She managed to drag them both down last week for some grotesque gathering in the ballroom. When they'd served their purpose, mother let them scuttle upstairs again. Otherwise people tend to forget that they're still alive.

Of course, they're all dead in a way. This hotel's like a mausoleum. But quite interesting, too, when the ghouls come out to rattle their bones. Mother still drifts around in her floaty dresses, going to parties, bitching about people. Only the parties are smaller now, and there are fewer of her set to bitch about. Most of them have died. Those that are left feel under siege. They hate what's happened to this city. But mother puts on a brave show, acting like it's still the Forties, when father was the toast of the town and New Venice was the preserve of what she calls the *crème de la crème*. The reason she's so manic is to convince herself that she's really still alive. That's why she'll sneak back in here to listen to what everyone's been saying about her. Well, she's welcome. She knows I never lock my door. It makes her very unhappy when she thinks she's not in control. That's why she really is finding it difficult to deal with your having gone. She doesn't know what to say to people.

Not that I feel sorry for her. It's too easy to feel sorry for mother. When I say she's unhappy, I mean she's acting in a certain way, to provoke a certain response. Sometimes I don't believe mother has an inner life at all. Her moods are patterns of behaviour dictated by external stimuli. She adapts to her environment. She's like a primitive life form, an amoeba or something. Quite sensitive in a way. And utterly selfish.

Paul, I simply *had* to have another word with you. Jean has doubtless been saying the most atrocious things about me. Please, don't believe any of it. I worry about Jean. It must be hard for a younger sibling, especially when her brother has been such a dazzling success. I've never felt that Jean has

141

found her *niche* in life. Perhaps it's not too late, if she can avoid becoming too bitter about things.

But then perhaps she's inherited that bitterness from her father. He's no doubt been on to you, complaining that New Venice is not what it was and that it's failed to live up to his expectations. Of course I agree with him in many ways, but there's no point in becoming bitter and twisted about these things. It is quite beyond me why he feels the need to do down his achievements. There is *nothing* so irksome as false modesty. Not a day passes here when I am not proud to have been associated, in my own humble way, with the building of this city. Yes, dear, I am proud to be your father's wife. It would be a sorry state of affairs if I were not. I have devoted my life to your father, and through him to New Venice. *Je ne regrette rien.* Only last night I was saying the same at dinner to some friends at the Palazzo Dandolo. We were eating out on the terrazzo – probably for the last time before the winter. Looking down the Grand Canal towards the Rialto, it looked perfectly lovely. I could not *imagine* anything more perfect. All the lights of the palazzi were reflected in the water. The boats were chugging along. There was music everywhere, and laughter and conversation. The chink of wine glasses. I can't think what your father finds to complain about. He's become such a curmudgeon in his old age. Sometimes I think he's lost all the poetry of his youth. But then perhaps he's just bequeathed it to you, my dear. There is such poetry in your letters! They never *fail* to delight me. I'm perfectly miserable while I wait for the next.

It's happened. The most wonderful thing has happened. Do you remember, a few years ago, a gimmick called the 'neuro-phone' came on the market? Perhaps you missed it. You miss a lot. There was a TV ad with a toddler hooked up to one of these things, and some classical music coming out of the speakers. The voice-over was something like 'Now he can make music with the big guys!' The idea of it was that you could just think of some music, imagine a tune or something, and the machine would pick up on your brain signals, reproduce them, and synthesise the sound. Hey presto. You could make your own music without having learnt a note of any instrument. It seemed like a neat idea, a great short cut. I remember they installed these big neurophone things in all the palazzo arcades. For a while there was a craze on them. Kids would hook themselves up and try to freak each other out with their private psychedelia. They'd try it on different drugs. I remember thinking at the time that it was a great concept, but every time you heard one of those neurophones it sounded dreadful, like someone unmusical splashing about on a synthesiser keyboard. Even when you got someone who was musically trained plugged into it, the results weren't as good as you'd get if you sat them down in front of a synthesiser. The craze lasted about a year, then people lost interest. Sometimes you still see them in arcades, but nobody takes them seriously any more.

Apparently the Synergise Corporation, who'd come up with the neurophone, lost a lot of money on it. In fact they'd put so much capital into the project that they couldn't just cut their losses and drop it. Their survival was at stake. They had to carry on and try to improve the thing. So that's what they've been doing on the quiet for the past ten years. Billions of ecus have been poured in, hundreds of research workers, and the result is this new thing that's suddenly appeared, the neurorch. *That* was what those ads were about.

Part of the problem with the neurophone, apparently, was that existing synthesiser technology was too crude to cope with the complex signals being fed into it. You had synthesisers that could represent pretty realistically the sound of a saxophone, or African drums, or a sitar. But you could tell that it was *representing* those sounds, it wasn't actually them. For one thing, it couldn't get all the noise that's part of the real instrument's sound – the noise of the breath going into the instrument, or the keys rattling. Or with the violin, say, there's that gritty sound of the bow biting into the strings, or the little imperfections in individual notes that make the sound human. The synthesised sound was too pure, too crude. So the quality of the synthesiser had to be a thousand times more refined, so that it could pick up all those little things like a catch in the voice, a change in the vibrato or the slightest suggestion of a bend in the note. It had to be able to do that at great speed, and not just with any existing type of instrument or voice, but with any sound that could be imagined.

They also had to refine the electrodes so that they really could pick up and locate every single brain signal, the firing of every individual neurone. A micro-computer was developed that would generate models of the brain states as they flashed by, and the synthesiser would read them and convert them into sound. Then the whole thing had to be reduced in size to make it easily portable.

All this means that, unlike the neurophone, the neurorch gives you access to your unconscious. With the neurophone, you had to consciously think of a tune and the neurophone would play it, the same way you'd play on a synthesiser. But there's music going on in our brains the whole time and we're hardly aware of it. It's a natural brain music, and the neurorch allows you to express it.

So anyway, all those theories about the ads were wrong. The pay-off came last night. All day yesterday the media was saturated with those slogans about 'Sing the Body Electric'. In the evening I was at the techno-tango night at the Club Camerlenghi, near the Rialto. It's a big place, with massive telescreens at each end of the main hall and banks of speakers on each side. On top of the speakers are video cameras turned on the crowd for watch-u-dance spots. All evening there'd been 'Sing the Body Electric' slogans flashing up on the telescreens. The crowd was singing them. Then at midnight the music stopped and the screens went blank. I thought it was a power failure. You could hear hundreds of feet shuffling in the dark. After a few seconds there was an explosion of light and sound. Friends told me it was the same everywhere – in the clubs, on the TV. There were psychedelic graphics on the screens, music blasting out of every speaker, and a voice-over intoning over and over again: 'Be natural. Be neurorch. Sing the body electric is here. Be natural. Be neurorch. Sing the body electric is here.' A heavy back beat started up, and on top of it there was gamelan, hi-life, zithers, gypsy violin, temple gongs, Beethoven, panpipes, punk, bagpipes, blues, whales singing, Appalachian fiddle, sitar, kids singing, nightingales, dolphins clicking, Charlie Parker. It was the most incredible piece of music I'd ever heard. It was world music gone mad. These different styles followed each other in waves, breaking over each other, mixing together. And all the time the voice-over kept saying, 'Be natural. Be neurorch. Sing the body electric is here.' Only sometimes it varied. 'Be roots. Be you,' the voice-over said. 'Sing the body electric is here.' It was done in a rhythm, like a mantra.

Then there were the visuals. On the screens there was a woman sitting crosslegged up a tree in a rainforest. The only thing she was wearing was her neurorch. It looked like a Walkman. There was a small box strapped to her waist carrying the computer hardware, speakers and batteries. She was wearing headphones, only these were electrodes and they were on her temples rather than over the ears. The camera did a close-up of her as she threw her head back and looked up at the sunlight filtering down through the forest canopy. She had a smile on her face and a dreamy look in her eyes. She was getting into her own groove. The camera moved closer and closer into her swimming-pool eyes and then suddenly you were moving through her brain. The editing was done cleverly, with shots cutting back to the forest. The tendrils of her brain cells were like the branches and creepers of the forest. There were flashes of light, the electrical impulses passing between the cells, that were like the flashes of sunlight filtering through the canopy of leaves. As the camera hurtled on through the brain, the film cut backwards and forwards between the brain and the forest, in time to the heavy back beat of the music. Then the camera burst out of the brain graphics into the electrode and the wire leading to the box at the woman's waist. The editing showed this by intercutting to the outside of the electrode, then the wire – travelling down it, down the woman's side. The camera appeared to shoot down the inside of the wire. Then the camera was inside the brain again, only this time it was the computer model of her brain, in the box at her waist. The camera moved through this quickly, then burst out through the speakers and you were back in the forest again and the sunlight flashing and glittering through the green leaves. Then cut to the woman's eyes, her face thrown back, staring up at the canopy, then the camera moved in again on her clear blue eyes. And you were inside her brain again, and the whole thing was going round again. It kept going round in that loop – the forest, the woman's eyes, her brain, the wires, the forest – while the Japanese flutes and balalaikas and electric guitars swirled around and the man's voice intoned over and over again, 'Be natural. Be neurorch. Sing the body electric is here. Be natural. Be neurorch. Sing the body electric is here.'

I left the club. The streets were alive. On the canals there were vaporetti decorated in the Synergise logo. They were selling the neurorchs. People were coming off wearing them, fiddling with the controls to turn up the volume. The air was already full of strange vibrations. It was like the whole city was humming, pulsing to a strange beat. I wanted to buy a neurorch myself, but I didn't have enough money. They're expensive. I thought of going back to the hotel, but I didn't want to miss anything. In a way I was happy to be on the outside of this, listening to what was happening. There'd be plenty of time to try it for myself. I spent the rest of the night walking around the city, calling on friends who'd already bought the neurorchs, listening to the crowds that were milling about the campos. The gondolas were busy all night, taking people up and down the Grand Canal. Groups of them floated by, everyone with neurorchs on their heads. Over the water came an extraordinary mixture of sounds – hummings, whistles, clicks, screeches, snatches of melody. It was the most amazing night of my life. Until you've heard it, you've no idea what it's like to listen to the sound of thousands of brains, thousands of individual brain-sounds being poured together. You have to come back to experience it.

The first time I saw the site of what was to be New Venice was in the spring of 2019. I was just a student then, and Milstein was the youngest ever professor to be appointed at the university. He was already a practising architect with a worldwide reputation. During the vacations he would invite some of his students to go on walking holidays with him. Of course, he had no wife or family, no ties except those to his work. The conversation on these walking tours covered many areas, from the arts to economics and science. But everything came back to architecture. Milstein was a man obsessed with the importance of the built environment. Nothing about the human animal could be improved, he believed, until that was got right. He still believes that. And so do I.

To be invited on one of Milstein's walking tours was considered a great honour, so you can imagine my feelings when I was asked in only my second year at the university. I think Milstein had been impressed by some drawings of mine he had seen at a departmental exhibition. He always attached the greatest importance to draughtsmanship. That spring that I was first asked, Milstein was going walking in the hills between here and the Coast. That was in the days before the Coast was dedeveloped, so those hills were the only part of the region where you could get away from the traffic and noise of modern life for a while. We returned to the same place later that year, in the summer, and for each of the subsequent few years. By which time, of course, the plans for New Venice were beginning to take shape.

I look back on those days with unalloyed nostalgia. The atmosphere in the group of students that Milstein gathered around him was frank and open in a way that I had never experienced before, nor have since. Looking back on that time, I find myself thinking of relationships I formed then that seemed as close to the ideal as such things can be. I often reflect on what a shame and waste it was that our group had to split up. There were relationships formed there that could have lasted for life. But we were young, we were on the threshold of brilliant careers. If I told you some of the names of members of our group, you would recognise – if you knew anything about architecture – some of the most important and revered names of the past half century. One by one they had their quarrels with Milstein and went their separate ways. Usually they said that he was too autocratic and fixed in his ideas. In the end, I was the only one left who kept the faith. I make no apologies for that.

May the first, 2019, was the day that I first set eyes on what was to be New Venice. May Day was important to Milstein. He had both a feeling for tradition and a firm belief in the socialist ideal. Only a year before, he had published a major theoretical work, *Building the Society of the Future*. He always marked May Day in some way, and that year we celebrated it by rising at dawn and undertaking a twenty-mile hike across the tops of the hills. It was a beautiful path, with views towards the Coast and, in the other direction, across the terrace of valleys that stretch inland. We set out at dawn, singing the Internationale. There were about a dozen of us. Milstein had been talking to us the previous night about the ideas that were to culminate in *Re-Renaissance* and the other theoretical works associated with the construction of New Venice. These ideas, and the vivid energy with which

Milstein had presented them, had kept me awake half the night. I'm sure the same was true of most of the rest of our party. As we walked, the debate was joined again as to the possibility and problems of regenerating man's social and spiritual life through the built environment. I found myself walking at the back of the column with Milstein, who was characteristically forgoing further debate on these heady generalities. Instead he was questioning me on a somewhat technical paper I had recently completed on the use of new materials in the manufacture of brick. I say characteristically, because one of Milstein's great strengths as an architect has always been his ability to switch rapidly from the social, artistic and philosophical context of his work to the most minute technical detail. He has never been one to forget that buildings are ultimately made up of individual pieces of brick, stone, glass, metal and plastic.

So while my fellow students strode on, spinning castles in the air, Milstein and I dawdled at the back and discussed the chemical composition of bricks. From time to time, Milstein stopped and pulled out his pocket book to make a note. We fell further behind. I know it's sentimental to attach undue significance to particular moments and to ignore the slower, deeper forces at work in any situation, but I can't help feeling that those few hours forged something between us that was to last a lifetime.

Up on the ridge there was a fresh breeze. About noon, when we were above a wide valley, Milstein suggested that we rest for a few minutes. The others were already a few hundred yards ahead of us by now. I must admit that I was quite flattered to be given such individual attention. We sat on the springy heather and stretched our legs, looking out across the valley.

'Tell me,' said Milstein, 'what do you see?'

I didn't at first take the question very seriously. I just murmured some banality about it being 'a lovely view' or something of that sort.

'No,' said Milstein. 'Look carefully. Tell me what you *see* down there.'

I can laugh now, looking back on it, but at the time I was very worried that this was some kind of test. I was very young and unsure of myself. I respected Milstein immensely. We all did. I scoured the valley below, trying to see what it was he was referring to. But as valleys go it seemed ordinary to me, though quite attractive. There were no buildings of particular interest. The most obvious man-made feature was a railway line that entered the valley from the hills to our right, crossed it, and disappeared again through a tunnel into the next valley. Much of the valley floor was covered with conifer plantations. They were crisscrossed with loggers' tracks. The slopes of the hills that surrounded the valley were studded with shrub-like trees and boulders. The valley itself was oval in shape and formed a kind of natural amphi-theatre. It was hard to judge the distances, but I guessed that it was about seven or eight miles at its widest and perhaps ten miles at its longest.

But I was quite at a loss what it was I was meant to be commenting on. Then Milstein saved me from further discomfort by saying, 'I see a city down there.'

I was initially rather dismayed at this. It smacked ever so slightly of megalomania – a charge to which Milstein was often subject, both then and subsequently. I had heard how the students at the university talked about him. The way he was now looking at a beautiful, peaceful valley and dreaming of building a city on it reminded me of their malicious par-odies. But I was misjudging him. When he used the word 'city', I automatically thought of a megalopolis, an ugly sprawl of roads and traffic spreading across the floor of the valley and clawing up the surrounding hills. Milstein, of course, had something very different in mind.

Paul, I absolutely forbid you to return to New Venice. This place has gone quite mad. It would only upset your musical sensibilities. You must remain on the Coast and compose your wonderful symphony. For a moment I can close my eyes and imagine it. It sounds like softly breaking waves. But then the noise from outside starts up again. You can't hear yourself think. You can't carry on a conversation. I'm quite certain that within twenty-four hours we shall all have been driven utterly insane.

I'm sorry, Paul. You must think your mother's gone mad already. This dreadful gadget has sent the city into a frenzy. It's awful. This *thing* that they wear over their heads makes loud, objectionable noises. They say it allows people to make music without any effort or application. They just think about it and it happens. What an absurd notion! As though anybody, just *anybody* could make music. As though music could come from anything but genius and artistic struggle. Oh Paul, it makes me weep when I think of you struggling in lonely isolation to produce your symphony, while here in New Venice every lout and hooligan on the streets is strutting around pouring forth aural pollution and thinking he can become a second Mozart, a second Paul Clearwater, just by flicking a switch! Call me a snob, I don't care. The whole idea is evil and barbaric. It's a kind of vandalism. I've always thought that there's something irredeemably vulgar about technology.

And of course the hilarious thing is that it doesn't work. All they can produce is meaningless noise and scrambled snatches of popular melody. But the point is that they *think* that they're now great artists, and so they drag everything down to their own impoverished level. People can't be bothered to *work* at anything. Above all, their small minds can't encompass the fact that beauty is transcendent. I know that you and I feel the same way about this, Paul. How beautiful is that temple you write about, Paul, far away across its sea of poetry! Myself, I sometimes think that the beautiful will always be beyond our grasp. Hence the sadness of life.

But there's no peace here for such sublime thoughts. Ever

since it was announced that this thing was on sale, the city has been a cesspit of noise. Your sister, of course, has been bursting with enthusiasm for it. I've hardly seen her since it appeared. So I took the opportunity to come in here and tell you the truth about it. Jean will no doubt sing the praises of this dreadful contraption. Don't listen to her. You must stay on the Coast until the enthusiasm for this *thing* has died down, as I have no doubt it will. Your own divine music must not be drowned out by the mooings of the common herd. (Yes, yes, I know. Call your mother a silly snob.) Please, stay on the Coast and complete your wonderful symphony. In the evening, when I've closed my eyes and listened to the departing tide lapping at the bank of the canals, I've almost imagined that I could hear it. So sad. So soft and wistful. So – but how can one describe these things in words?

I got the libretto about your friend Grenier. Cottimi, as usual, has been so busy that he can barely squeeze in anybody. In the end we fixed up for me to visit him at his new apartment off the Piazzale Roma, near one of the big car parks. 'This is where I feel at home,' he said, 'on the margins. I need to hear the sound of grinding gears.' The guy is such a pretentious dickhead. I suppose I could have posted your libretto, but I was interested to meet him on his own. Whenever I've met him in the past he's been with you. You two were such a double-act. Did you know people used to call you 'the duet'? I remember that routine you used to do together at parties, improvising arias and trading couplets like a couple of eighteenth-century rappers. But if I were you I'd be careful of Cottimi. Think of father and Milstein. Father hates Milstein. He always has. And he hates himself for having become the great man's sidekick. Johnson had his Boswell, Marx had his Engels, and Miles Milstein had our father. It would be a tragedy if it wasn't so pathetic. Milstein's always been a millstone round father's neck. So watch out, brother.

152

Anyway, I did what you asked and handed the libretto over. Actually I didn't have a bad evening. It wasn't even spoilt by him thinking I was making a pass at him. That was just one of those little misunderstandings. In fact, sex was the last thing on my mind, and all through supper I'd been waiting patiently for him to stop telling me about his theatrical triumphs so that I could get down to what I really wanted to talk about – the neurorch. There are ads for the neurorch everywhere. There's one they have on the TV that I like. There's a couple walking along a palm-fringed beach. The wind's in their hair and they've got their neurorchs on. The camera cuts from one to the other as they swap soulful sax licks. There's a bossa nova beat in the background. They lie down on the sand and start necking. As the surf sucks at them their musical grooves come together in a mellow big band riff. What gets to you is that the water doesn't fuck up their electrics.

And it's all over the news. There was footage in the bulletins yesterday of the South African President posing in traditional Zulu dress, in front of some drummers. He was doing a shimmy for the press and switching on his neurorch. There were shots of people queuing outside the stores in New York, and the President fooling around in the Rose Garden with his neurorch on. His dog had one on too. NVTV had a special feature on how 'with the launch of the neurorch, the eyes of America are on New Venice'. There was a shot of a guy sitting in his apartment watching film of a club scene in New Venice, with all the freaks dancing in front of that video of the woman up the tree in the rainforest. The camera panned around and caught Joe-six-pack's what-the-fuck expression. So the neurorch's really putting New Venice on the map.

I was tipsy by the end of supper. We were sitting side by side on a black sofa the size of a small car. Cottimi goes in for the kind of furniture that's either very large or very small. We were sipping tumblers of ice-cold gin. The sofa tipped us back, so that we must have looked like a couple of jet pilots going into a steep climb. At last I'd managed to get the conversation away from Cottimi's achievements and on to the neurorch. I was pleasantly surprised by the interest he was taking.

'So how does it actually work?' Cottimi said.

'It's like this,' I said. 'Your brain's made up of about ten billion cells called neurones. The membrane of the neurone is highly excitable. It transmits and receives messages in the form of impulses – electrical impulses.'

'I get it,' he said. He was leaning closer towards me. 'Excitable, huh?'

'Each neurone,' I continued, 'has a number of fibres reaching out from the main body of the cell. There are two kinds, dendrites and axons. The dendrites receive the impulses and conduct them back to the cell body, where they're added together. The axons transmit the response to the signal away from the cell body again. The axons can reach out over great distances, making lots of connections with the dendrites of other cells, creating pathways for impulses. Give me your hand.'

I took his hand and locked our fingers together. His were a bit clammy. With his other hand he took a gulp of gin.

'The brain is an interlocking network of these fibres, all carrying signals to each other.' I squeezed his fingers between mine, then half-released them again. I was beginning to realise by now what was going on in his head. 'The junction between the axons and dendrites,' I continued, 'are called synapses. At these junctions, there are tiny bubbles on the body of the axon, called synaptic vessels. These are filled with the transmitter substance, and release molecules of it into the synaptic gap, the gap between the axon and the dendrite. Are you with me?'

Cottimi nodded and sipped his gin, trying to look cool. But his eyes were waiting pathetically for my next move.

'The molecules cross the gap and attach themselves to the

membrane of the dendrite. Like this.' I put down my gin and let my fingers flutter across to land on his thigh. I was trying not to laugh now. 'This can cause the electrical potential between the inside of the dendrite and the synaptic fluid between the cells to change. If the potential reaches a certain threshold, the neurone that the dendrite belongs to is fired, and the electrical signal is passed. It's an all-or-nothing response. Understand?'

He nodded vigorously. 'It's turned on, you mean?'

'Yeah. The electrical charge builds up to a critical point, and if it reaches that point then the neurone's fired. It's a binary system.' I eyed him. 'Either it's turned on or it's not.'

I paused. I thought he was going to make a dive for me then. But no, he was waiting for me to make the move. That's Cottimi for you. He gets other people to do things for him. I suppose it's his instinct as a director. And usually he's pretty good at it, but not with me. I was getting bored. I heaved myself out of the sofa and went over to the picture window. There were no hard feelings. Cottimi's the kind of man who takes his chances when they come up.

I was standing at the window looking down at the lights of the city. The room was dark. Some New Wave Chinese Opera was playing softly on the sound system. Beyond the sofa, hovering over the polished floorboards, was a tastefully erotic hologram.

'This view makes me think of the neurorch,' I said. 'The city's like a brain. Imagine each of those lights are neurones. Each of the campos are like the cells, and the alleys and streets are like the fibres that connect them. The bridges over the canals are like the synapses, the connections. And the canals themselves are the blood and fluid that flows through the brain all the time, just like the tides wash through New Venice. Hundreds of years ago, scientists thought that it was the blood that carried the mind. But in fact the blood's only like a fuel. Whenever a connection is made, and a neurone fires, there's a rush of blood to that spot, to provide energy for it. Scientists in the last century tried using that to map brain activity. They introduced radioactive tracers into the blood to monitor its flow within the brain. But that technology was impractical for the neurorch. Electrodes are better. Back in the 1920s, Hans Berger put electrodes on the outside of the skull and found he could monitor gross changes in brain activity. Sleep and activity, that kind of thing. It was like a geologist with a seismograph. They've modified the sensitivity of electrodes so much since then that now every impulse can be individually monitored to build up computer models of the brain states.'

I could have gone on. Nothing bores me about the neurorch. But I could tell that Cottimi had had enough. The truth is that he's not really interested in anything outside the theatre. For him, the moment had passed. But not for me. I was standing at that window, looking down at the lights of the city, imagining each of them as a single brain cell firing on and off. I could imagine the whole city as a single organ of expression.

Life is on the whole a process of gradual accommodation, so that it becomes quite impossible to say when a particular change of situation or outlook began to take place. But just occasionally there come moments of which you can safely say, 'There did my life undergo a remarkable change.' Such a moment came for me when Milstein explained to me his idea of New Venice. The scales fell from my eyes and I can say in all modesty that I saw the valley exactly as he saw it. What he proposed was that it should be flooded to form a large shallow lake, and at the centre of the lake, attached to the 'mainland' by an umbilical cord of road and rail, would be a city built entirely on water. This city, set in the middle of the lake like a jewel, would itself be a curious oval shape, with a broad canal looping through it and dividing it into two halves. The two halves would fit together – as Milstein fancifully expressed it – like the yin and the yang, or like two animals curled up together. This was New Venice.

Milstein described it so vividly that I swear that on that warm May afternoon all those years ago I could actually see the buildings reflected in the choppy waves of the lake, the boats chugging out to the city's port. It was around that time that UNESCO had finally given up hope for Venice, so it was much under discussion, particularly among architecture students. Milstein liked using it in his lectures as an instance of 'urban engineering', and as an example of the cellular, organic growth and structure of the medieval city, a rebuke to Le Corbusier's prejudice that 'the curve is ruinous, difficult and dangerous; a paralysing thing'. I had noticed, also, that on our walking holiday he was carrying a copy of Ruskin in his knapsack which he would take out from time to time to read. But nothing had prepared me for that first revelation.

For a while, then, as he talked, I was blinded by the sheer audacity, the visionary nature, of what he was proposing. But it has always been my habit of mind – and its strength, I think – to move swiftly to an exploration of practicalities. I think that is why Milstein has always valued my assistance and guidance, and why, indeed, he singled me out in the first place as the sounding-board for his plans. Not that Milstein had not begun to explore these practicalities himself. He has never been one for mere pipe dreams. It transpired that he had been visiting this valley in secret for some months, and had obtained detailed maps and geological surveys of the area. There was a river, hidden from our view in the hills, that could be damned to form the lake. A canal could be cut through the lower hills on the far side of the valley to take overflow water away to the next valley. There was even a rising area of ground in the middle of the valley that Milstein had identified as a possible basis for the artificial island of New Venice itself. The geology of the valley as a whole was stable enough to support a limited number of smaller 'sub-urban' islands, should it be decided that these were desirable.

Indeed, the beauty of Milstein's plan was its *flexibility*. He had no wish to produce a blueprint for a city, to fix it in advance for eternity. Indeed, that would have been quite contrary to the principle of organic, cellular growth that he so admired about the old Venice. What Milstein wished to construct above all was a *culture* that would itself foster future development and change. There was a dynamic element to all his plans.

One drawback of the old Venice, considered purely as an 'urban machine', was its geographical position in a marine lagoon. During the early centuries of its existence it was plagued by disease, and up until the end – as my own father once told me of his visit to the place, before it was closed to the outside world – the canals could be overpoweringly smelly in high summer. This new Venice, by contrast, would lie in a lake of clear, fresh water, a lake considerably above sea level and swept regularly by breezes. It was while Milstein was talking about the lake that my mind began turning on practicalities. Tentatively – for at that time, as I say, I was much in awe of Milstein – I made a suggestion that was to take on an important role in the conception of New Venice. I pointed out that one of the *advantages* of the old Venice's position was that the twice-daily tides operated as a natural waste-disposal system, flushing out the canals and preventing the water from becoming stagnant. During the course of the city's development, sea gates had been built which accelerated the flow of the tide and thus accentuated this natural asset. I suggested to Milstein that it would not be impossible to produce a man-made version of this tidal flow for New Venice. Giant sluice gates could be built into the feeder river and outlet canals, and by opening and closing these at intervals, 'tides' could be created, providing a regular flow of water through the city. I had a minor interest of my own in such marine engineering. I was familiar with the operation of the Panama Canal, with the use of giant caissons, and with the Pirelli system of inflatable tubes that in the twentieth century had been proposed to protect Venice. Already I could see a number of ways in which the artificial tides of New Venice could be made perfectly feasible. I outlined these to Milstein. He was delighted with the proposal, cursing himself for not having thought of it before. Thus was born, on that glorious May Day, perhaps my single greatest contribution to the construction of this city. In some of the many books that have been written on the building of New Venice, you will find it stated that the system of artificial tides was an integral part of Milstein's original conception. This was not at all the case, and I sometimes feel that Milstein has not done all he might have to correct the misapprehension. It gives me some satisfaction to set the record straight now.

I got an invitation from Cottimi to the cast party for his revival of *New Year*. I suppose that means he's forgiven me for not seducing him. Either that or he was giving me a second bite at the apple. The party was being held on stage at the Miracoli, surrounded by canvas tenement blocks. It was the same set he used a couple of years back for *West Side Story*. Most of the cast were dressed in some costume designer's idea of urban hip – all black lycra, bandannas and leather thongs. They stood around in this stuff nibbling canapés and quaffing champagne. Cottimi was holding forth to his actors about the neurorch. He was telling them how it was bringing people out on to the streets. It was a catalyst. 'I see a seminal *moment* approaching,' he said. There were going to be riots. There was going to be trouble. He wanted to bring trouble into the theatre. He wanted to bring the neurorch into the theatre. He wanted his actors to go out on to the streets and experience riot, because riot was the ultimate street theatre, the ultimate political carnival. It was surreal to watch Cottimi spouting this rubbish to a bunch of actors done up as street dudes, while a guy in a white tuxedo glided around filling our glasses. But I suppose that's the theatre for you.

When Cottimi finished his lecture on the aesthetics of

159

street violence, a woman said, 'But isn't it better that people should live in harmony with each other? Shouldn't we look for the positive elements in things?' Her voice was slurred and had an American accent. There was an embarrassed pause after she'd spoken. A couple of the actors smirked, and the group that had formed to listen to Cottimi began to break up.

I'd been watching this woman from the moment I arrived at the party. You couldn't help noticing her, because she didn't fit in with Cottimi's radical chic crowd. For a start she had a suntan, which isn't exactly *de rigueur* in New Venetian fashionable circles. She'd been standing apart from the other guests, scoffing canapés and drinking heavily. When she'd said her bit and the people had started drifting away, she looked glum again and dropped her face into her wine glass. I felt sorry for her. I went over to her and said, 'I shouldn't worry. Some people prefer things to be apocalyptic. That way there can't be any doubts about them.'

'You mean they like the idea of violence?' she said.

'Of course they do,' I said. 'Things aren't real for them unless they end in blood.'

'I think the only things that are real are peace and understanding.' She said this quickly, and threaded her hair back behind her ear in a nervous, defensive gesture.

It occurred to me for a moment that she wasn't just drunk, but stupid too. But then I always find stupid people more interesting than intelligent ones. I started talking to her, and what with my questions and the champagne, she was soon in full flow. She explained how there was an order and harmony to the universe that was working itself out through everything that happened. Even awful things contained some seed or hint pointing to that future when the hidden order latent in everything would come to the surface. Like everyone else with a goofy theory, her main evidence for it was her own life. She came from a broken home, she'd had broken, failed relationships around the world (Cottimi was one of

160

these. That was why she was at the party.) and she drank too much. But through everything, she felt that her life was being drawn on to that sense of balance, harmony and peace that she listened for in everything around her.

It took her about an hour to tell me this, by which time Cottimi and his crowd had left. We were asked to leave too, because they were locking the theatre up for the night. We staggered out the stage door and started walking up the Calle Lunga. She was in a bad way from the drink. She was wearing a thin summer dress and she kept shivering in the cold. I asked her where she lived and she said on a yacht. By now I'd resigned myself to taking her back to the hotel and putting her up on a couch. But she kept walking, and kept talking about how she was only staying in New Venice for a couple of weeks and then she was going to sail away on her yacht again.

I felt sorry for her. When we came out on the Fondamenta Nuove she was walking quicker, still talking about that yacht of hers. I was trying to figure out how to get her home. The lights of the city were behind us, and you could hear the water of the open lake slapping the quayside. It sounds different from the water in the canals. We'd been walking along the quay for about ten minutes when she stopped. Sure enough, right where she'd said it would be, there was a yacht moored to one of the jetties.

She turned round and looked at me, very serious and sober all of a sudden. She said, 'I'm not always like this. I'm like a different person when I'm on my yacht.'

I went aboard with her and she went into the cabin to get some drinks. I sat on the deck with her. She was calmer. She *was* like a different person. I told her how you'd said in your letters that you used to come down to the Fondamenta Nuove to escape from the claustrophobia of New Venice. Then I told her about your little dramas in Wellfleet with the fishermen and the orchestra. I even got a laugh or two from her, though she laughed awkwardly, like it wasn't something she was used to doing.

Anyway the upshot of all this is that she's going to take this disk down to you when she leaves. She's got a disk player in the cabin, so you'll be able to listen to it there. I suppose if you're listening to this you'll be sitting in that cabin right now. I wonder what you're making of our courier. Her name, as you'll know by now, is Luisa Delaware. I think she's a bit of an airhead. She's spent too much time on her own, lying in the sun and gazing at the sky. It's got into her brain.

When I mentioned the problem of the disk, she said that she knew Wellfleet and she'd been thinking of going down to the Coast when she left New Venice. Did you know you can get down there through the canals? It's a roundabout route, but she's not in any hurry. 'A journey takes as long as it takes,' she says. That's the kind of stupid thing she does say.

As far as I can make out, she lives on the yacht the whole time, drifting from one place to another. She says she only visits New Venice every couple of years, because it's a hassle getting up through the canals. Most of the time she's at sea or in different ports where she knows people she can visit. She doesn't plan too far ahead. She told me she takes her cues from the stars. She talked about how that peace and order she was moving towards was mirrored in the stars, and how she'd reach it by following them. The weird thing is that I like her. She's a breath of fresh air after people like Cottimi.

Your father may have abdicated his civic responsibilities, but I am not without influence here. Jean may mock, but I still have my connections. And I'm not afraid to use them. I shall not rest until I've got those infernal neurorchs banned from public places. I've started a petition, and already I've gathered a number of *important* names. I have friends on the Municipal who'll listen to me. Clearwater is still a name that people respect in this city.

It occurred to me the other day as I was walking down the Riva Schiavoni, assaulted on all sides by the noise of those machines, that civilisation is built on a respect for the separation of public and private spheres. Your father would no doubt dismiss this as a commonplace thought, and be able to cite a hundred and one people who'd thought it before me. But it's true, isn't it, Paul? I know you'll understand. If people want to use this thing in the privacy of their own homes, then that's their business. One can only pity them. But they have no right to inflict on others the garbage that's swilling about in their heads. It's as though we allowed everybody to tip their household rubbish into the canals. Where would we be then?

My blood boils with righteous indignation. I don't underestimate the forces ranged against me, but I gain constant encouragement from your letters and the noble campaign you are fighting for the fishermen against those philistine burghers in Wellfleet. Like mother like son, Paul. We're two of a kind.

Do you remember our family trips up into the hills? That was back in the Thirties and Forties, when New Venice was being constructed. Milstein and I were devoting ourselves to it day and night. Occasionally, these days, I allow myself a moment of guilt that I did not spare more time for my family. Once a year, in the summer, we took a short holiday in those same hills that Milstein and I walked across back in 2019. Even then I couldn't really escape the city that we were creating. Every year I would return to that spot where Milstein had shown me his original conception for New Venice. From there I would look down at the progress of the city – the lorries inching across the floor of the valley, the tiny cranes swinging stiffly like matchsticks in the distance. And I was proud, too, to be able to share all this with my family, to be able to sit with my children on that hill and trace with them the outlines of their future.

Milstein never accompanied us when we went up to the hills. I think families made him uncomfortable. Most people made him uncomfortable, apart from professional associates like myself. Of course it's a familiar charge against socialists that they chase the dream of universal brotherhood at the expense of their own relationships. Rubbish. Many people fail in their relationships. And besides, Milstein could hardly be said to have had relationships at all, failed or otherwise. I did sometimes think that he had abstracted himself so much and projected himself so much into the future that he had lost touch with the people around him.

Of course, Milstein was very conscious in his writing of the dangers of abstraction. It forms a major theme of *Building the Society of the Future*. That is why the grounding of theory in history plays such an important part in the book. And anyway, Milstein was more than just a writer, a builder of intellectual castles in the air. Indeed, he always regarded his writings as merely a means to an end. They were never intended as monuments. Milstein was an architect, a builder of buildings, not merely of books and ideas. The only way to build the society of the future was brick by brick, by transforming the material environment in which people lived.

Thinking of idealism reminds me that in your letters you quote with enthusiasm that old German idealist Arthur Schopenhauer. No doubt you approve of his absurd ranking of the arts, placing architecture at the bottom and music at the top. Architecture he looked down on because it was too bound up with material reality. Music he looked up to because it had freed itself of the bonds of materiality. Or as Walter Pater wrote in his book on the Renaissance, a book that Milstein loathed: 'All art constantly aspires to the condition of music.' Rubbish. The true antithesis is not between the material and the spiritual, but between the social and the individual. There is nothing 'spiritual', nothing 'transcendent', about music. This new machine, this 'neurorch', demonstrates that beyond peradventure. It all comes down to the brain. That much is obvious. What interests me about the neurorch is why, historically, it should have been invented when it has. Inventions such as this don't appear from nowhere, from individual genius. They are made to fulfil particular social functions. The neurorch is merely another manifestation of the retreat into the individual that liberal so-called democracy has encouraged. Art, according to the liberals, is something to be *expressed*, just as one's body expresses bodily fluids. That is what this cult of self-expression makes me think of – viscous, slimy bodily fluids, like the puddle of saliva that sits permanently in one's mouth.

It's occurred to me that I haven't told you what it's actually like to wear the neurorch. I wasn't prepared for how *weird* it is. You know that moment of strangeness when you hear your own voice on tape, or you get a glimpse of yourself in a mirror when you're not expecting it? Well, imagine that moment prolonged. Or imagine having someone else say what you were going to say fractionally before you say it. The voice sounds like yours, and it says what you intended to say, but at the same time it *isn't* your voice, and you can't help feeling that that isn't what you intended to say. But this isn't just a voice, and there are no words. It's pure sound. You recognise it immediately as *your* sound, the sound of *your* mind.

Everything happens so quickly. You have to imagine that the uncanniness I'm talking about is being expressed at the moment you're experiencing it. It doubles itself. It's the speed of it that's so strange and so modern. When I switch my neurorch on, there's a part of me that's still trying to stay upright, like someone on a running machine that's going faster and faster. But my consciousness feels like it's skimming from underneath me.

People have said to me that it's like when you're high on drugs and your mind's running away with you. I suppose in a superficial way it is like that, but it makes me angry when I see how the neurorch's being marketed. It's *not* just a gimmick. When the tease campaign was going on, people thought it was building up to the launch of some new designer drug. That's how it's still being pushed. There's *more* to it than that. If people could only learn how to use it and how to *listen* to each other, it would be revolutionary. People spend so much time hiding behind words. Take the way father talks, with all his references and paradoxes and quotations from Milstein. It's all a way of hiding his real feelings – his hurt and anger. Every word builds a wall between himself and the real world. If he'd only try the neurorch, he could smash that wall down. He'd be a happier man. It's the same with you and your letters, the way you dress yourself up in flowery prose and snippets of poetry. Why do you want to hide yourself like that? The neurorch gives people a way of bypassing the old languages, with their hierarchies and deceits. If people would only learn to listen and understand, they'd be able to express themselves completely. And that would be a whole new beginning. A new life. A new equality.

I can only think about this clearly when I'm on Luisa Delaware's yacht by the Fondamenta Nuova. I've been going there a lot. There's peace and space there. Luisa's got her own ideas about the neurorch, of course – about how we'll all be able to tune into the same cosmic vibrations, and how the music of the spheres is buzzing about in our brains as well as out there in space. All that seems too abstract and religious to me. The neurorch's just a way people can express themselves, a better way than there's ever been before. You should try it. You go on about your 'struggle' to compose this symphony of yours, about how it's 'beyond you' and it 'transcends' your efforts. Well, come back and use the neurorch. If there's something inside you that you want to express, you'll find a way with the neurorch. Father only dislikes the idea of self-expression because at heart he's an authoritarian.

Just occasionally something happens that makes me think the neurorch's being taken seriously. Only of course it all gets channelled into New Venice's usual weird symbolic politics. Cottimi's been on at me to go out with him. He still wants to get me into the sack. Anyway, last night I took him to a Fela Lahbib concert. Cottimi had never even heard of him, though he pretended he had.

The atmosphere at the Lahbib gig was electric. Lahbib's followers have been trying to get him to put down his kora and use the neurorch on stage, but for some reason he's refused. And now the whole thing's getting a political edge. There's a minority of Lahbib's African support who are black fascists, and it's this group that's been leading the calls to get him to wear the neurorch. They say that if he'd use the neurorch on stage it would show his solidarity with them, his *blackness*, and that because he refuses he's selling out and setting himself above his audience. They've been handing out leaflets in the clubs and picketing his gigs. Last night things came to a head.

There were people handing out leaflets when Cottimi and I arrived at the Club San Moise. Inside we could see a few banners draped from the galleries. But Lahbib and his band came on and everything started normally. It was only in the middle of the second number that I became aware of something strange. At first I thought it was a syncopation that the band itself was putting into the music. Then I realised that there was a rhythmic chant coming from all round the hall. 'SING the body eLECTric. SING the body eLECTric.' When the band finished the number, the chanting carried on. They started the next song, but the chanting was getting louder all the time. Some rowdier groups in the galleries started up: BRING ON THE NEURORCH, BRING ON THE NEU-RORCH.' After a couple more numbers there was a hiatus. The music was being overwhelmed by the chanting that was coming from all round the club. The band stopped playing and I could see Lahbib talking to them. To mixed boos and cheers they all went off. At that point I thought there might be trouble. I could see two or three men at the front of the crowd trying to climb on to the stage, and being pushed back by security guards. But then Lahbib came back, carrying his kora. The crowd jeered. He sat on a stool and began playing his solo songs. The chanting had petered out when the band went off, and for a couple of minutes when Lahbib started playing there was a surprised silence. He was singing in a completely relaxed way, as though this were just any gig. The chanting started up again, quieter this time, but by now something else was happening in the crowd. I could see people rummaging in their clothing. Neurorchs started appearing. A lot of the clubs in the city have sacked their DJs and given themselves over entirely to the neurorch, but a few have stopped people bringing their machines in. The Club San Moise's one of these, but last night it seemed like most of the audience had managed to smuggle them through the security checks. Someone told me that the guards had been bribed. I can believe it. The whole thing seemed well-organised. People were pulling their neurorchs out from under their clothes and putting them over their heads. Already the air was full of those familiar, strange vibrations. I was watching the stage to see what Fela Lahbib's reaction would be. He was impassive. He just kept on with his set as though nothing was happening. About three-quarters of the audience had their neurorchs on by now, and it was almost impossible to hear him. I expected him to leave the stage at any moment, but instead he reached under his stool and pulled out a pair of headphones. This seemed organised too, as though he'd been expecting everything that had happened. He plugged the headphones into the sound system, then carried on playing. Now the audience couldn't hear him at all. He was playing for himself.

So that was the situation. Most of the audience were wearing neurorchs, and their brain-sounds were deafening in the confined space. Up on stage, Fela Lahbib sat under the spotlight, headphones over his ears, continuing to weave his intricate musical webs for himself. He looked a very lonely figure. There was no danger of violence now, but the situation did feel like a kind of stand-off, an irresistible force meeting an immovable object. Lahbib had cut himself off from his fans. He'd retreated into his craft.

He was still sitting up there on the stage, defiantly playing his kora to himself, when the audience got bored and started drifting out of the club. The evening had ended in anticlimax. But Cottimi was excited afterwards. He kept asking me about Lahbib, then switching back and talking about that libretto you'd sent him. I thought he'd forgotten about it, but now he was saying he thought he could see a way of doing it, though it would need some changes. He asked if I'd heard from you recently. Yesterday morning I'd got the letter from you telling me about how your concert had been a disaster and you owed all that money. I took him back to the hotel and showed him that letter, and all the others you've written me. I hope you don't mind. You know I don't believe in keeping things secret. I'm afraid he didn't take your problems very seriously. In fact he laughed. He kept telling me how you hadn't changed a bit, and how he'd like to put your adventures on the stage. He has a point. There's something performed about the way you write those letters. But at the same time I think you really mean them. I don't know whether to be pleased or scared by that.

Of course all art is a social construct. How could it be otherwise? Even this cult of individuality, this mania for self-expression that has attached itself to music, is a collective phenomenon. Either art recognises its own social nature, and hence realises its social potential and responsibility, or it retreats into obscurantism and quasi-religious intimations of transcendence and 'absolute beauty'. The latter, of course, is the path that you have chosen to follow. Your mother, in her silly way, encourages you in it. The other path is the path of architecture, which if one *were* so foolish as to rank the arts would come before music precisely because it integrates the aesthetic and social vision. Indeed, it demonstrates that the imagination and the social and political conscience are one. There is no division. Put like that, in mere words – which themselves contain elements of abstraction and hence 'aspire to the condition of music' – it could be one of the evasive, soothing formulations of the so-called socialist intellectuals. But the architect demonstrates the truth of it, the truth that lies beneath the words, in stone and brick, glass and metal – and, through them, in the lives of the people that inhabit them. That was the idea of New Venice, to *build* the society of the future.

Milstein's imagination was such that he could *see* the completed New Venice, as though from above, even while he was engaged in the minutiae of directing its construction. He didn't *need* to come on our annual trips up into the hills. I'm afraid I lacked that vision. I needed the reassurance of looking down on it and seeing it take shape. Perhaps in a way I didn't believe in it as much as him. I know he disapproved of my trips, though he was always too correct to say anything. He regarded it as a kind of weakness in me. And perhaps it was. I had a feeling of nostalgia for that place where he had taken me into his confidence and where the idea of New Venice had been born. Milstein never showed any desire to go back there. He is a severely rational man. He always looks ahead. As far as his personal existence goes, he has never shown any desire to go back. Ever, anywhere.

If that May Day when Milstein told me about New Venice was the greatest day of my life, the second greatest came on our final family trip up into the hills. New Venice was complete. The sluice gates had been opened, the valley was flooded. Twenty years of struggle had come to fruition. That summer was the last that the city was empty except for the workers and their families. Twenty years is a long time, but I can honestly say that looking down on it from that same hill, it looked exactly as I had imagined that first time: a large, beautiful dwelling, set like a jewel on the ruffled waves of an inland sea. Utopia visible. I can't believe Milstein wouldn't have been gratified to have seen it like that, the confirmation of all our hopes and battles. New Venice was at its best then, when it was a matter of hopes unbetrayed.

My pride, looking down at the city from the hills, was in part a purely technical one. But I also shared Milstein's social vision. Here at last was the city of the new Renaissance. Here was a city in which the citizens would live in cooperation both with one another and with their built, social environment. Of course, that view belonged to the time before the people moved into the city. New Venice was at its best when it was empty. It was the people who betrayed it.

Perhaps that sounds like the authentic voice of the socialist authoritarian. Didn't Brecht once sardonically remark that the communist East German government should dissolve the people and elect a new one? But I'm only speaking the truth. The people of New Venice failed to engage with their environment, with their city. They failed to care for it. Ideological greenery, that opium of the modern age, produced merely a mystification and idealisation of 'nature'. It obscured the importance of the built, social environment. The failure of New Venice showed that.

Because don't forget that the building of New Venice was not some alien blueprint imposed from above. It was a human project. Milstein and I were 'the people' just as much as those who moved in and tore apart our hopes for the city. The failure of New Venice was merely a temporary, tactical victory of the forces of regressive individualism over those of social progress. But the age-old struggle between the two cultures goes on. At the end of the twentieth century, that impossibly dark century, someone wrote, 'The old age is dead, the new is yet to be born.' Nearly a hundred years later, that's still the case. We're still in limbo, still searching. That age that had begun with the Renaissance, continued with the

Enlightenment and industrial revolutions, was over, buried in the rubble of the twentieth century. But the new age is yet to be born. We're still living off scraps of the old. But the change will come. The tide will turn. And New Venice, this dwelling of stone and water, will be there to receive it.

I remember those family trips into the hills. When I was a kid, I liked little things. I liked intricate, enclosed things, things you could imagine crawling into. That's what New Venice looked like from up on that hill – a nest that a small animal could curl up in. You were different. You were excited by the open space and the sky. We didn't get much of that in New Venice. I remember you running around, shouting, singing. Like me, you were in your own little world, but yours had been inflated by the sun and the breeze. You spread your arms as though you had the whole globe in your hands. My world was small and enclosed. I lay on my stomach, and with one eye I tried to follow individual yellowing stalks of grass into the labyrinth of blades and stems and roots. That was another nest. I could have spent hours exploring that tiny space, finding more and more hiding places in it.

Father made a big effort on those trips to fulfil his family responsibilities. It didn't come naturally to him. I remember him sitting beside me on that hill. 'Look at the pretty city,' he'd say. 'That's home down there.' Those words made a big impression on me. I remember following the direction of his finger down to that far-off stone and glass nest in the middle of the lake. There was my future, my life. My father was beside me, and down there, laid out like a children's game, was my life – something I could crawl into, something to make myself at home in. I look back at that kid on the hill, looking down at this city, her home, and it's like looking down at claustrophobia. That's what I aspired to – claustrophobia. When I was a bit older, I loved getting lost in the city. It seemed like down every alley there might be a place I'd

172

never been. And that place I hadn't been would lead to another. Doors opened and closed. There were canals and bridges, tiny squares and arcades and alleys that were like tunnels through the houses. There were courtyards, stairways, balconies, dead-ends, quays, sudden slices of water between the buildings. That was what we grew up in. It was a toy town that our father had built specially for us, a doll's house that I could crawl further and further into.

But recently I've realised that there aren't any places left in this city that I haven't been. The stupid thing is that I feel betrayed, as though a piece of magic I'd believed in had turned out to be a cheap trick. I know now that every time I open a door in this city there'll be another waiting on the other side.

Victory at last! You would not *believe* the amount of effort I've put into my little crusade. I'm quite exhausted. For three weeks I have done little but cajole and persuade, argue and plead. Of course, one would rather live a life of contemplation – how I envy your peaceful existence on the Coast! – but sometimes it is necessary to plunge into the noise and heat of battle in order to preserve peace. I feel I've struck a blow for civilisation. It has truly been on a scale with your own noble campaign on behalf of the Wellfleet fishermen. How sad I was to read of your setbacks! You must seek consolation where you can, and soothe yourself with the balm of music.

My own victory has not been total, though I have secured more than I dared hope for. It was gratifying to be reminded how much weight the Clearwater name still carries among New Venice's upper echelons. I was helped by a petition of over two thousand names which I had gathered among our more eminent citizens. Your father and Milstein refused to sign. They're being perfectly bloody these days. But even without them, we have persuaded the Municipal to pass a law which says that in public places these neurorch things must be fitted with earphones. I'd wanted to get them banned completely, but this is almost as good. The carabinieri have been admirably diligent in enforcing the new law. We now have the delightfully absurd spectacle of crowds of people wandering around not only with electrodes over their heads, but earphones as well. How *can* people be so foolish? It makes one wonder why they don't have done with it and put a bag over their heads. They're half-dead to the world already.

Jean, of course, is absolutely furious. She has become quite besotted with this machine. I'm afraid it may have something to do with jealousy at your artistic success. She honestly believes that everybody can be brought down to the same level at the flick of a switch. One can't help but feel pity for her. Please, don't tell her I said all this. It's just that I worry about her so much. It's so sad to see a young woman with no direction in her life, with neither career nor family. One can't help feeling that she's reaching for solace. But then, aren't we all?

Frank Cottimi here. Jean said it would be okay if I broke into this family gathering to send a quick message. The message is that your troubles are over. I'm getting things moving on *The Commission*. I had my doubts about your libretto to begin with, but now I can see a way of doing it. We'll use the neurorch on stage. The music will come straight from the actors themselves, straight from the situation, from the moment. Music is about the moment, and the moment is the only thing that counts in the theatre. All the rest is bullshit. Just think of the demands the neurorch'll make on the actors, the kind of discipline it'll require. They'll have to *be* the characters and *live* the situation. Totally. We're talking about the ultimate theatre. The focus will be totally on the theatrical moment. At one stroke we'll do away with the old hierarchy of composer and performer. It's *that* radical.

What we're really talking about here, Paul, is the final

democratisation of music. Opera was always potentially a radical art form, because it's based on the idea that music is for individual expression, it's not just a part of religious ritual or something abstract and beautiful. Anybody, from a Spanish barber to a Harlem hoodlum, can open their mouths and express themselves in music. It comes from them naturally. That was why Nietzsche was so suspicious of opera, because it was so democratic. He was right.

And now we've got the neurorch, and that democratic dream of music has come true. You wouldn't believe the energy we have here, Paul. This is a city that rocks with music, hums with music. If we in the theatre can't tap into that energy, then we're not doing our job. Take the old composer who wants to keep the window of his attic closed. I see him as a metaphor for the way high culture tries to shut out what's happening on the street. In the opera, the old composer lapses into silence and sterility. His servant uses the neurorch and gets the commission. I've been in touch with Synergise and I'm lunching one of their executives tomorrow. I'm hoping we'll get sponsorship from them. I was getting good feedback, and people have told me they want to sharpen the neurorch's profile a bit, to show that it's not just a gimmick that'll be forgotten in six months' time. We could get serious money behind this project, Paul. It raises the tie-in to the level of an art form.

There's another reason why I'm fired up about this project. I want the part of the servant to be played by a guy called Fela Lahbib. He's an African singer who's been creating a stir here. His fans want him to use the neurorch in his act, but he's been refusing. If I could persuade Lahbib to use the neurorch in *The Commission*, in the part of the servant, it would be the biggest thing to happen in New Venetian theatre for years. There could be one hell of a controversy. I talked to Synergise about it, and they're very happy for there to be an ethnic component in the piece. Since the opera's set in the eighteenth century, Lahbib could play an ex-slave or something like that. And of course, it would add an extra frisson to the flirtation between the pupil and the chambermaid. So all I have to do now is persuade Lahbib. I'm lunching him next week.

Over the past few days, your sister has been coming up to discuss things with Milstein and myself. I believe she's thinking of leaving New Venice. Well, she has my blessing if that's what she wants to do, and Milstein's too. God forbid that we would want to keep anybody in this city, seeing what it has become. But I can't pretend to approve of her motives, which seem to be mixed up with this neurorch contraption. She's incensed – with some reason – at this law that your mother's helped to get passed against it. But that hardly seems to me like a reason to leave. Supporters and defenders of the neurorch strike me as equally absurd. The thing is quite simply irrelevant to serious politics.

I had high hopes at one time of your sister. She was the only one of the family who showed a more than superficial interest in the city that has been my life's work. At one time I hoped she might become a political animal. I think she shares something of my dreams. When we went on our annual trips up into the hills, it was Jean, not yourself, who sat beside me on the grass and studied the emerging city. She would ask me all sorts of questions – silly childish questions, of course – about what it would be like to live in when it was finished. And when we were down in the city, when it was alive with labourers, craftsmen, designers – when it was alive with *hope* – Jean would spend hours wandering through the alleys, chatting to the workmen, exploring. More than once she was led back to the hotel by some irate foreman, who didn't appreciate a child strolling on to his site. Jean would regale me with tales of what she had seen. She loved the city then. It was hard to be cross with her. You, meanwhile, would be up in your room, practising your music.

Jean, I believe, has inherited my egalitarian instincts. I have made clear to her my scepticism concerning the neurorch, and I think she comes to see me to try and break down my resistance to it. Of course, it is flattering that she should take the trouble to do so. Milstein can see the falsity of her arguments from the start, and so he tends to have little patience with her visits. But while at the bottom I share his view, I do have some sympathy for Jean. She is my daughter, after all. Her heart is in the right place. Her fervent belief in the revolutionary potential of this machine is based on the soundest of egalitarian instincts. She wants to see the divisions between public and private destroyed, as does any good socialist. Unfortunately, she interprets this in terms of the private, the self-expressive, spilling out and taking the place of the public. Music is the most inward, the most private (the most 'spiritual', as I suppose you would put it) of the arts. To build a Utopia on the basis of that is to do away entirely with public, social life. That is not socialism.

I've been listening to Luisa Delaware. I never did do enough listening before. She's been talking to me about the place she went to college, in the west of America. Idaho City's new, like New Venice, but it sounds so different. The streets are wide. At sunset the skyscrapers are set on fire and the desert steals in down the highways. That's the kind of place where people could learn to listen to the neurorch. I could imagine a whole new civilisation being born in a place like that. New Venice is too cramped. People's thinking's too twisted. They spend too much time listening to themselves, not enough to each other. The neurorch needs space. I've been listening to the way people talk about it. There was one guy I met who said that when he was wearing his neurorch he felt like a tree – like one of those big old chestnut trees we used to see in the hills, with leaves as big as your face. He said he felt the neurorch drawing something up from deep in his roots. The electric currents flashing through his brain were like the sap seeping up, stretching towards the light. This guy was a junkie. There was a woman I listened to who told me how she'd put the neurorch on her six-month-old baby and heard a thin ribbon of sound, as quick and clear as a mountain stream. She compared it to birdsong. The neurorch needs light and space. And above all it needs time, time for people to listen to it and be with it. Already there are people here hurrying to use it for their own ends – like Cottimi, trying to turn it into a stage gimmick. That's just a way of making it safe.

Mother and father flatter themselves. Of course I was angry about that law, because it stops people listening to each other. But it wasn't mother's string-pulling that got it passed. The Municipal would have put restrictions on it anyway, just like governments all over the world are going to start doing. They see the neurorch as a threat, and they're right to. I'm getting out of New Venice before things go further. And I'm taking my neurorch with me.

Jean has been showing me your letters. I'm hardly surprised that your championship of the Wellfleet fishermen has ended in humiliation and failure. It was always a piece of romantic fantasy, bearing no relation to real politics. The notion of 'natural justice' that you cling to is entirely bogus. There is nothing natural about justice. It is a human, social creation that must be fought for. It is a matter of relations of power. The Coast itself only exists because certain relations of power have brought it into being. It was a product of that rage for regionalism, confederation and experimentation with new forms of local democracy that swept Europe some forty years ago. The Parti Turquoise rode that tiger with consummate skill. The Coast was their great achievement. So this problem of 'injustice' in Wellfleet about which you are so exercised is merely an artificial problem, a problem created by a larger problem. A sub-problem. How could one possibly solve it without looking at the constitution of the Coast itself? But you have decided to circumscribe everything you write and think by that artificial creation.

How ironic and fitting it is, therefore, that you should have compared your 'natural justice' with the waves and tides that batter the Coast. For there is nothing 'natural' about those, either. They too are man-made, the product of global warming. Those 'natural' forces, Paul, are created by the productive forces of man. The tides at Wellfleet are no more 'natural' than the tides that I have created here in New Venice.

The truth is that there is no longer any such thing as 'nature'. Man's control over the physical world is such that everything that happens in so-called 'nature' is the outcome of human decisions, and hence of relations of power between people. Any approach to politics, ecology or art that appeals to the notion of 'nature' (as in 'maintaining a balance between man and nature', or 'expressing the natural', or, of course, 'human nature') is mere mystification.

What's happening, Paul? Jean says she hasn't heard from you for a month now. I hope this doesn't mean you're staying out there on the Coast. As a friend, Paul, I have to tell you that it's doing you no good. Art is politics. It's about the message that you're sending out, and who you're sending it to. It's about context. It's about strategy. People are talking about you, Paul. To put it bluntly, they're laughing at you. Going out to the Coast, writing a symphony – by doing all that you're putting yourself on the most reactionary wing of the cultural field. Who writes symphonies now? Sure, ten years ago, maybe five years ago, you could get away with a pastiche symphony. But not now. You just can't *do* pastiche nowadays if you want to get taken seriously. People are looking ahead. They want the future. I've seen the future, and it's the neurorch. In ten years' time, any artist who has not absorbed the neurorch into his work will find it impossible to get taken seriously. Remember, Paul, you heard it here first.

A hundred years from now, I want people to look back and say, 'Yeah, Frank Cottimi and Paul Clearwater, it was them that started it. They were there first.' If you're an artist, Paul, you're an explorer. There's simply no point in what you're doing – pacing backwards and forwards over well-worn paths. Yes, I know, we've done that together in the past. All those operatic pastiches and parodies of yours. But that was then. This is now. Maybe in another ten years things'll be different again. *We* might have changed them. That backward-looking stuff might come back. But we're talking about *now*. Art has got to be for the moment. The artist has to catch it in flight. It's like a game. It's like a great ball-player leaping to catch a high ball, picking it out of the air. It's moving fast. It's moving faster all the time. Art isn't a monument, a rock of ages. The best that you can hope for is that a hundred years from now people'll look back and say, 'They kept their eyes on the ball.'

So sharpen up, Paul. Things are moving. I've reached an agreement with Synergise, and I'm working hard on your libretto. But the best news of all is that I've got Fela Lahbib aboard. I hooked him! Being a theatre director is ninety per cent seduction. You've got to believe in yourself. You're like a salesman. You're standing in front of someone and you're trying to get them to see things your way – not just to do what you want mechanically, but make it a part of themselves. If the person you're directing looks back into your eyes and sees a grain of doubt, then the whole thing's shot. It won't work. Everything's focused on that moment of commitment. That's what art's all about. That's what I live for.

I've assembled a truly mind-blowing cast for this production. The part of the old composer is going to be played by Bertrand Florial, the greatest character actor of the past thirty years. That was a mother of a lunch. I've got George Jerrold in a small part, and the kings's secretary is going to be Margaret McGrath. By the way, she said she'd just been to Wellfleet filming an episode of *The Discreet Dame*. You know, that interminable Victorian detective serial she stars in. She said she kept an eye out for you, but there was no sign. She's a terrific actress. And last but not least there's Zerlina Kousoulas. She has got to be the sexiest thing on the New Venetian scene in years. She's going to be the chambermaid.

So now there's just one piece of the puzzle missing. That's you, Paul. It was your baby originally. We may not need a composer, now that we've got the neurorch, but we do need you. You were always a great dramatist. You've got a feel for the stage. We need your energy. Come back where you belong, Paul. Be a part of it.

Frank Cottimi makes me laugh. He's so transparent. He let slip to me that the reason he wants to get you back is that he's scared you'll sue for breach of copyright if he goes ahead without you. Still, it's your decision. I remember when I first started this disk, I kept telling you you should come back to New Venice. I won't say that now. I've given up telling people what to do and how to be. We've just got to follow our paths and learn to listen. I wish I could hear you right now, Paul, like you can hear me. I wish I could hear that symphony of yours.

I'm going tomorrow. It was Luisa Delaware who made me think of going to America. Being with her on that yacht has given me space to think. There's no future for me here, or for the neurorch. At last I'm breaking out of that nest of stone and water that father pointed to when we were up in the hills. He'll keep his Olympian detachment when I'm gone, and mother'll adapt. She always does. I never get hurt by what she says, because she never really means anything. To mean something you say, you've got to have some core, some centre that's being expressed. But with mother, there's nothing underneath all that posturing and acting. That's all there is. I sometimes wonder what she'd sound like if she wore the neurorch. I think there'd just be silence.

*
181

So your sister has elected to leave New Venice too. On one level, of course, it is a sad personal commentary on the failure of the dreams that Milstein and I once had that both my children should leave the city we built. But even the judgement of history is provisional. One day, I'm sure, we shall be proved right. One day, New Venice shall be inhabited by the society which it truly deserves and for which it was built. Like all true socialists, I take the long view.

Of course, I do not deny the pain I feel at Jean's leaving. As I have said, I feel she was the closest to me of my two children. But one must look for causes and reasons. There is a purpose to everything. I have never believed in that bourgeois, liberal distinction between heart and head. As Milstein once remarked to me, 'We must be emotional in our analyses and analytical with our emotions.'

Yes, that is how we must be.

Jean departed yesterday. She was cold and unforgiving to the last towards me. She has her father's hardness. A mist of tears filled my eyes as we said farewell in the Piazzale Roma, for no matter what has been said and done, nothing can break that natural instinctive bond between mother and daughter. She may be thousands of miles away, but she is still in my heart. She can never really escape.

So both my chicks have flown the nest, dear Paul. In every parting, I sometimes think, there is an image of death. All our lives we slide slowly towards that twilight, even as a gondola drifts gracefully away into an evening mist. We are such fragile, transient things. When Jean had left me, rucksack bobbing up and down in the crowd, I turned to look down the Grand Canal. On either side of the water your father's noble edifices of steel and glass glinted in the sunlight. As the tears filled my eyes, the bustling scene seemed to freeze – or rather, it seemed to be suffused with a single elegiac tone. Life is so sad. Jean refused to tell me her plans in America, or even when she'd be in touch.

Her friend Luisa Delaware is waiting downstairs. She says she's setting out for the Coast in the morning. Paul, I do hope you listen to your friend Cottimi's advice and come home. I am quite distraught without you, and terribly worried now that we receive no letters.

Goodbye, sweet Paul.

III

The sun beat down from between mountains of high summer cloud. As he walked the empty shingle beach Paul felt himself to be entering an enormous, hallowed space. His feet were tired and hot. For over an hour now he had been unable to decide whether to cool them in the sea, a few paces to his left, or rest them on the bank of shingle that rose a few paces to his right. He'd been walking for several weeks. He'd lost count of how many. His experience of time moved in phases of emotion and purpose rather than days or weeks. Way back, there was the time of bitter elation just before leaving Wellfleet. He could remember writing a last long letter to Jean, in which he described the failed concert on the pier. He had enjoyed writing that letter. The letters were what had sustained him through the months in Wellfleet. But after that letter about the concert, things had closed around him and he hadn't been able to write any more. Every day there had been demands, invoices, threats from Hunter and Hawker. Then letters from Roland Hinchcliff, who was acting on their behalf. As well as the money he owed to them, there were the musicians to be paid. Of course, Paul had paid them first. But that had left him with little.

He had never had any head for dates, facts, occasions. His mind moved in headlong rushes – charging in one direction then suddenly stopping, turning, caught in an agony of indecision, and rushing off along a different path. It had been like that ever since he was a child – a never-ending series of pursuits, of enthusiasms and enchantments that seemed to turn themselves on and off at random. His mother, who liked this pattern of his life because it 'expressed the spontaneous

187

and creative side of his nature', would sometimes remind him, teasingly, of these enthusiasms. 'Do you remember the time when you were fascinated by the stars?' she would say. 'Father bought you some binoculars and you spent every evening for weeks complaining that your hand jiggled too much.' These reminders were intended to embarrass him. It was a game that mother and son played. Paul would smile back blandly, remembering something, a flicker, of his excitement at looking up into the darkness of the night sky through the dark tunnel of the binoculars. But of the externals of the thing, the occasion, he could remember nothing.

This forgetfulness worried him sometimes. It was as though he were an actor constantly switching roles, with no life of his own outside those roles. Like his old friend and collaborator Frank Cottimi, Paul adored masks, costumes, gestures. But unlike Cottimi, Paul had qualms about the theatre. To Paul it seemed too much a reflection of the pattern of his own life – the strutting and fretting, the dazzling moment of activity that extinguishes itself. Cottimi seemed to have a kind of steadiness through his single-minded belief in the theatre. Paul didn't even have that, and had always hankered after something more 'genuine', more 'real' than what he saw on the stage.

But it was only occasionally that Paul worried about his forgetfulness and his tendency to transform his own life. When he was in the middle of one of his enthusiasms, when he was charging at something, his head down, roaring to himself, he was completely absorbed in it. It was only when he raised his head, it was only when he looked around and saw that his quarry had eluded him, that this anxiety would seize him.

That was what had happened in Wellfleet. He had hurled himself into the life of the Coast, charged at it like an animal released from a trap. (He had come to think of New Venice as a trap.) And then when his plans to help the fishermen had failed, when his concert on the pier had failed, he had simply stopped. He had stopped writing his letters to Jean. He had stopped believing in the Coast. He had stopped, lifted his head and looked around him. That was when the old anxiety had taken hold of him. He recognised it immediately. Now he saw the archaism of the Coast not as an attempt to get back to something genuine and natural, but as another contemptible costume – a costume he had put on, paraded himself in, and was now discarding again. There was that familiar feeling of emptiness, of unravelling.

All this happened at the same time as the failure of the concert and his resulting financial problems. But in a way it was quite independent of those troubles. It had often been like that. Paul's internal changes of direction seemed to follow their own rhythm, their own logic. They happened independently of his circumstances. That was why he found it hard to remember dates, occasions – even people. Jean told him that he was only like that because circumstances had never really pressed on him. In a sense, Paul agreed: he was lucky. But Paul's sense of his own luck went deeper than that: he was untouchable. That was where Jean was different. She would never have thought of herself as untouchable, or even lucky.

Jean had always seemed involved, implicated in everything. Paul was detached. He had the knack of walking away from things. That is what he had done in Wellfleet. Hawker and Hunter had been closing in on him, most of his money had gone, and he'd got behind with his rent to Jacob Grindley. He paid Grindley, but when that was done there was nothing left. The situation was desperate. But already the period of anxiety – the 'in-between time', as he privately referred to it – was over. Just when his external circumstances had reached a crisis, he was internally over the worst. He had had an idea. He had seen a way out. He had seen *another way of living*. He would, literally, walk away.

The thing that he had realised, in those few days of crisis, was that Wellfleet had only been a kind of halfway house on his escape from New Venice. Now he had to escape from Wellfleet itself. He had to explore the Coast beyond. For Wellfleet was not the *real* Coast, not the *genuine* Coast. Wellfleet was a kind of 'New Venice-near-the-sea', with its empty aping of the past. Living in it had been like living in one of his own operas, living in his own past. No wonder he hadn't been able to make the break.

As soon as he conceived the idea of walking along the Coast, all the hopes and emotions that he had invested in Wellfleet and the fishermen fell away from him like so many discarded clothes. He bought a backpack and some boots, and set off. Standing on East HIll – where he had stood so many times before, buffeted by the wind, watching the sea-spray blow across the town – he looked back one last time. Now the town was quite still in the bright morning heat. The only movement was of hundreds of trippers pouring out of the railway station from the overnight train.

He had been told that there was a good coastal path, which had been popular in the old days when people had driven out here in cars to spend the day strolling along the cliffs. Now that access to the Coast was more difficult and there were no motor cars, the only people you were likely to meet were enthusiastic long-distance walkers and people on horseback.

For three weeks he walked slowly south and east, following the Coast up and down, in and out. Sometimes a whole day would pass as he walked to the mouth of a broad estuary, through a small town, and then out again to the cliffs. He was careful with his money, buying the cheapest bread and cheese he could find. There were olives too, and smoked and dried fish. He drank water. At night, for the most part, he slept out in the open. It was always warm and sultry. In the mid-afternoon the temperature would soar. Sometimes, at some spectacular headland – a 'beauty spot' – Paul would come upon what had once been a vast car park, where coaches had lined up and disgorged passengers dressed in neat brightly coloured clothes. Now the tarmac was cracked, sprinkled with shrubs and a film of grass. Crickets shrieked. In the heat of the mid-afternoon, the remaining patches of tarmac would be sticky under his boots, and the air rising off their black surfaces would swim in front of his eyes like water. Because he burnt easily, he would try to avoid the direct sun. When it was at its strongest, he would sit under a tree and try to work.

One strange aspect of the crisis, the 'change of direction' of those last days in Wellfleet, was that it seemed to have nothing to do with his own composing. Quite often in the past, the rhythm of these crises had followed that of his work. It was as though a particular composition, when it had been finished, when it had finished eating up his existence, would spit him out, expel him, and he would be left anchorless, anxious, free to invent himself again. But this time, it was different. The symphony he was writing – it was the first time he had attempted such a thing – remained unfinished, indeed barely started. The performance of the first movement on the pier had been a disaster, but this hadn't put Paul off or disenchanted him with the project in the way that it might have in the past. The success or failure of the performance of the movement had been something quite immaterial for him. The thing existed – if not on paper, then at least in his mind. The activity of having it performed was almost a distraction. The results didn't displease him, but neither could he get excited about them. The thing that struck him most was the gap between his conception and its realisation. It wasn't even that one was better than the other. They were just so different. They couldn't *be* compared. Of course, Paul was familiar with this gap. He had felt it at many first performances of his music. But somehow, with this symphony, the gap had become an abyss.

The coastal path was often overgrown, especially where it meandered away from the towns and villages. Few people used it now. Few had used it since the trippers had stopped coming, decades before. As he walked further into the heat, into the undergrowth, his sense of the abyss grew stronger. Once, when he stopped on the edge of a cliff at noon, looking out to sea, with a theme that he wanted to use in the second movement, the scherzo, weaving through his mind, he imagined himself to be the only person left on earth. And immediately it reminded him of a time (or had there been more than one? He couldn't remember;) when the family had gone up into the hills and Paul had run off across the sheep-cropped grass and put his head into the sky and really thought – as he spent much of his childhood thinking – that he was the only person in the world. That way of thinking was strongly connected in his mind with his music; he had started composing at about the time of that trip. Soon afterwards he had written a setting for four-part choir of the passage from *The Merchant of Venice* beginning:

> . . . in such a night as this,
> When the sweet wind did gently kiss the trees

He had set it with a simple scrap of melody in G minor, repeated in canon by all four parts. He thought he had written a fugue, but his piano teacher told him that for it to be fugal, rather than just a round, the parts must continue independently and not simply repeat the theme. This had come as a revelation to Paul. It had caught his imagination, had laid before him the whole rich field of musical composition. He had been eight years old.

Now, as he sat in the shade of a tree, out of the burning sun, with his manuscript on his lap, he felt the world as he had known it slip away from him. It became the world before he had known it. He had become a child again. From time to time he sketched a theme or figure, but for the most part he simply listened. He knew that one day, for his music to become music, he would have to relinquish it, write it down, let others appropriate it. He would have to let it become something else. But until then – and he wanted to put that time off as long as possible – he was happy just to sit and hear it, not to drag it back across that abyss that separated it from the world.

As he walked away along the Coast, Paul was quite aware that he was inhabiting a kind of limbo, and that he would have to return. He would have to come back down to earth, dragging his music back with him. He never lost touch with reality – even when he was living in Wellfleet, writing those letters to Jean. He knew that in the end he would have to return to New Venice. There was something hard at the centre of him. He was lucky. But he came close during that long, hot walk along the Coast.

The establishment of the Coast as a discrete zone for large-scale 'radical dedevelopment' had been part of a broader political tendency in the second quarter of the century – the experimentation with new forms of localised democracy and devolved decision-making. In some parts of the continent, where central control had a long history, the reforms were little more than cosmetic, a matter of changing a few ministerial addresses within what remained centrally controlled systems. In other areas, like the Coast itself, the principle of subsidiarity and autonomous development was taken to extremes. Throughout Europe there was fought a complex and multi-levelled battle, a Byzantine struggle between centralisers and localisers. It was fought out in a hundred constitutional courts, a thousand executive councils, in legislative assemblies that were so recently created and numerous that nobody knew what their jurisdiction was meant to be or why it was that they had been established. This was a period of internal upheaval in Europe, a period of introspection and uncertainty. It was the period when New Venice was built.

New Venice and the Coast remained the two most visible reminders of that period. Both, in their different ways, had clung to the principle of autonomous development. In the case of the Coast, this had gone much further. There was considerable devolution and local autonomy even within the autonomous area. Ecologically and economically, this meant considerable variations in how far dedevelopment was taken. Technology laws varied, and varied in the efficiency with which they were enforced. As the economic and ecological pressures of the outside world continued to be exerted, there were constant battles between the central Coastal Authorities on the one hand, and the towns and regions on the other, over what limits the central Authorities were allowed to set to the relaxation or tightening-up of technology laws. Wellfleet, closely connected to the interior by rail, was one of the least radically dedeveloped areas along the Coast. Technology laws were not as stringent as in some parts, nor were they as stringently enforced. Tourism – always the most important factor in reversing dedevelopment (or 'dededevelopment', as some wags had taken to calling it) – was a vital element in the town's economy.

Paul only really understood these facts about the Coast when he started walking south and came across towns and villages that truly had been plunged back into the past. Here, time did not so much stand still as move quietly backwards. On the roads, from which the metalled surface had long been worn (or, in the case of some enthusiastically radical places, torn) away, there were horses, mules, and occasionally bicycles. Cartwheels rutted the dirt and sent clouds of pale, chalky dust billowing into the still, hot summer air. The people were private, withdrawn into a somewhat self-righteous consciousness of their apartness from the outside world. They were a living statement, a living argument. To outsiders they were sometimes defensive, sometimes disdainful, and sometimes aggressive. Paul, of course, was enchanted by it all, by the harshness and simplicity of their lives. He loved watching the farmers and fishermen at work. He liked standing at the open doors of wheelwrights' and blacksmiths' workshops. But even towards a sympathetic outsider like

194

Paul Clearwater they were hostile. Their eyes, and the turn of their mouths, asked one question: 'If you like it so much here, why are you an outsider?' The rejection he experienced was like that he had experienced from the fishermen of Wellfleet, only it was more instantaneous and conclusive. Indeed, some of the fishing families of Wellfleet had originally come from these southerly towns and villages which had kept alive the radical tradition of dedevelopment. Though Paul had not realised it at the time, the battle between the fishermen and the council was only a skirmish in the wider and longer-running warfare between radical conservers and dededevelopers.

Despite the clean air, and the empty roads and paths of the seaside villages, Paul was aware as he moved south that this was probably a doomed world. His sense of isolation increased. He started avoiding those unfriendly locals, only venturing on to the streets to buy food. Now he just wanted to be alone with nature, with his symphony. Sometimes he would stop and look around him at the sunlight and realise that hours had passed in dreams of his symphony, in listening to non-existent music. Whole days would disappear. The beauty of the Coast – the cliffs and coves and wide sweeping beaches and hillsides cloaked in bracken – was so overpowering that at times it seemed to blot him out. Once, reaching the top of a steep climb, on a cliff top, he stopped as the path wound through tall undergrowth and was hit by the lemony smell – like fresh coriander, and as over-poweringly beautiful – of bracken at that particular season. For half an hour he hadn't moved, had hummed he didn't know what, had half-disappeared into the lemony smell and the endless glittering of sunlight on the blue sea.

By day he lost himself, and by night his anxiety returned. By night he thought again of his symphony, and in particular of that *Nachtmusik*, that second movement. That hardness at his core, that instinct for survival, would try to assert itself and he would tell himself that he had to go back, that this fantasy was getting out of control. But he hated the thought of going back. He was entering another crisis – or perhaps this was the same crisis as he had been in before he left Wellfleet, only a deeper phase of it. Lying at night in the darkness of bracken, kept awake by owls and rustlings in the undergrowth behind his head, Paul began to see the twists and turns of his inner life, the jump from one direction to another, not as the miraculous escapes of a born survivor, but as the twists and turns of a trapped animal.

In the past, Paul had believed that his life was progressing. There were difficult times, there were crises, there were obstacles. But these were things to be overcome and learnt from. They were passive things, and he was active. It had never occurred to him that one of these bad times might take control of him and that his life might pull itself apart from within. As he lay awake at night, in the heat, thinking this, he became aware that he was entering uncharted territory. He was frightened.

Some mornings he would swim in the sea. Perhaps he hoped that it would wash away his night-time thoughts, that it would enable him to lose himself in nature in the way that he wanted. But it didn't work. His head remained in darkness. His thoughts returned again and again to New Venice, as though he could discover in his past some point upon which he could put his finger and say, 'That was where I went wrong. That was where all this started.' Emerging from the water, he would return to his manuscript paper and make more notes for the second movement – the scherzo, the *Nachtmusik*. There was no continuity now. Different themes fought for supremacy, different voices chattered against each other, fighting to be heard. The music became part of his sense that things were now irretrievably falling apart, that all the old lines had petered out, that a whole world was being destroyed and a new one hadn't been created.

In the past he had made decisions. Now it was different.

About three weeks after leaving Wellfleet, he turned around and began retracing his steps. But he wouldn't have been able to say why. He couldn't comfort himself with the thought that he was walking away, because it felt more like walking further into something. Nothing had changed. The sun shone, the sea churned ceaselessly against the rocks beneath him, the path meandered up through the high bracken. But now he was retracing his steps. Places still came as a surprise to him, towns and villages that he had already passed through. Only now and then would he recognise something – a stretch of skyline, a tree, a rock – that he associated with his internal journey. Each one was a reminder of how far he had travelled, how isolated he was becoming.

He remembered this long, curving beach. It was about two days' walk from Wellfleet. When he had walked it on his journey out, he had been in the full flood of his enthusiasm for the *real* Coast, the *genuine* Coast. There was a village at the end of the beach, perched on cliffs that were being eroded by the sea. The village was poor and simple, and the inhabitants religiously committed to the principle of the Coast. All the twentieth-century buildings in the village had been pulled down. The inhabitants worked their patches of land or engaged in crude handicrafts. The economy operated at a low level. That was how they wanted it.

A woman from whom Paul bought some dried herring took him out to show him how the cliffs were being washed away. In perhaps a hundred years from now, she said, most of the present village would be gone. It was the same fear that the fishermen of Wellfleet shared. But the woman was fatalistic about it. To build sea defences would mean relaxing the technology laws, and the villagers would rather see their village fall into the sea than allow that. If it was nature's will, then it must be allowed to happen. It had happened before. The woman pointed out to sea and said that four hundred years ago there had been a town there, a thriving port with a dozen churches. She recited their names to Paul: St Aloysius, St Augustine with St Faith, St Giles-in-the-Fields, All Saints, St John the Baptist, St Mary and St Peter, St Barnabas, St Sepulchre's, St Michael and All Angels, St Benet, St George, St Mary Magdalene with St James. Now they were all gone, disappeared under the waves. The woman said that sometimes at night, she thought she could hear the sound of distant bells pealing.

Beyond this village the coast was flat and bleak as far as the hills that lay just to the south and east of Wellfleet. On the outward journey Paul had passed through this country quickly, keen to put distance between himself and the town. But now, coming back, not knowing why he was coming back, he moved slowly, seeing features in what had seemed a featureless wasteland. In some places behind the shingle there was lush freshwater marshland stretching back to the inland hills. In other places there were barren salt marshes, and in other places again there were just acres of shingle, with thin grass growing up in patches through the stones. This landscape was crisscrossed by tidal channels and lagoons, and many times Paul had to retrace his steps and make tortuous detours in order to find his way across them.

In one place the coast became a wide shingle promontory, and on this promontory, set back about a mile from the sea, was a vast power station that had been built some time in the second half of the twentieth century. The thing had been decommissioned and made safe even before the Coast had been established, but for some reason it had never been pulled down. Perhaps it would have been too big a job, for it was enormous and built like a medieval fortress. Paul had seen it on his outward journey across the waste of scrub and shingle, but hadn't gone close. Now he made that journey towards the looming silhouette on the flat horizon.

Much of the higher perimeter fencing had been pulled down, and a pair of large iron doors into the main structure stood ajar, allowing a shaft of light into the cavernous interior. It was cool inside, and for an hour or more Paul sat just inside the doors, recovering from the midday heat. He had grown used to the constant sound of the sea, so that the silence of this place made him feel lost. Birds flew in and out of the smashed windows high up in the exterior walls. The machinery that had filled this great chamber had long been removed, and the concrete floor was cracked and pitted down to bare earth. Even beneath the baking summer sun there was a trace of dampness in the air. Clumps of toadstools grew up in gaps in the concrete. One wall was streaked green and yellow with the growth of lichens and fungus where some broken guttering had poured water in. At the far end of the vast hall, whole sections of the roof had collapsed, creating pools of hot sunlight on the floor below. A lizard scuttled across one of these. Here, beneath the open sky, grass and small shrubs had grown up between the gaps in the concrete. A blackbird flew in from one of the windows, perched on the tallest of the shrubs, gave a burst of song, then broke into a chattering alarm call and flew upwards out of one of the holes in the roof. An irresistible tide of nature was filling the man-made structure. Paul sat gazing at it, motionless, thinking about the drowned town and its ghostly churches further up the coast.

He got up and walked slowly the length of the great hall, through the pools of sunlight. Here there was a door into another chamber. More fungus, more green vegetation where sunlight had penetrated through cracks and holes in the structure. He walked over a scattering of animal bones and feathers. He left that chamber and entered a complex of smaller rooms – offices, perhaps. Here there was more sunlight, more vegetation. He turned a corner and discovered a beech tree growing in the middle of a corridor. Beyond the tree was a door. With difficulty – the shingle had built up on the outside – Paul pushed it open and stepped out.

Sitting crosslegged on the shingle some ten yards away,

naked but for a pair of small grimy shorts, was a long-haired, bearded man. Paul blinked in the dazzling sunlight. Neither spoke or moved for a few seconds, then Paul stepped forward from the doorway.

'Shut the door behind you,' said the man irritably. 'I want everything left as it was.' He spoke English with an accent – Dutch perhaps, or Scandinavian.

Paul turned obediently and pushed the door shut, shovelling the shingle back against it with his foot.

Silence, but for the shrilling of the crickets. The man sat with a large drawing pad across his knees. In one hand he held a piece of charcoal. His skin had been tanned a tough brown.

'You're probably wondering what I'm doing,' he said.

Paul walked across the shingle and sat beside him.

'You're sketching.'

'I'm doing more than that. I'm recording. I'm a witness. I'm *celebrating*.' He said this firmly, a formula he had rehearsed many times before. 'This is *scientific*.'

'It's very good,' said Paul, looking at the drawing. And it was good – firm and sensitive. But Paul gave the compliment without enthusiasm. Paintings and drawings always bored him.

There was a long silence. The man continued with his work. Paul gazed at the tree which he had squeezed past in the corridor. From out here you could see the branches emerge from the offices in an explosion of greenery. It made a good subject for a drawing.

They sat for a long while without speaking. Paul listened to the shrilling of the crickets, the irregular rhythm of the man's charcoal scratching the paper. He could think of nothing to say. He was drowning in the heat. 'There,' said the man, 'I have finished. Now, if you wish, I will show you around this palace of vanities.'

He got up, and Paul followed him. He seemed to know a lot about the power station. He showed Paul where the reactors had once been housed, where great pipes had carried steam and water, where the turbines had been. None of it was there now. There was just the shell. The man grew more friendly as he led Paul around. He introduced himself. His name was Larsen. He described himself as a 'naturalist'. 'And this,' he added, 'is my wilderness.'

After the tour he took Paul to his home, the guardhouse protecting the entrance to the power station. On the walls there were dozens of drawings of the dilapidated buildings. They all featured the fecund vegetation of the place. There were detailed studies of grotesque fungi, and more distant perspectives of the whole site, from different angles.

'I make my own charcoal,' Larsen said proudly. 'I burn the driftwood from the beach. The paper is more difficult. I must buy that. I have tried matting together reeds from the marshes and bleaching them in the sun, but so far I have not been successful.'

He had been living there for three years. 'I was like you. I was walking the Coast. I found this place and I discovered my — ' He considered the right word, ' — vocation. I am recording the victory of nature over manufacture.'

Each of the drawings was dated and carried notes describing from where it had been drawn and under what weather conditions. There were sequences spread out over many months showing how a particular shrub had forced itself through a crack in a wall, how moss and lichen and ivy had spread out over a stretch of masonry, how yet another piece of concrete had cracked and given way to grass.

'This is my life's work,' he said happily. 'I also keep a journal of the plant and animal life. It keeps me busy. *This* is science,' he added. 'Not that.' He nodded in the direction of the power station. 'Science should celebrate nature, not conquer it.'

Paul shared an evening meal with him. They ate nettle soup, dipping hunks of old bread into it. After supper Larsen brought out a bottle of home-brewed calvados. 'There is a place a couple of miles from here where the farmer makes it. I help him at harvest, and he gives me his cider and calvados.'

Paul had not drunk alcohol for weeks. This calvados was a volatile, fiery liquid that evaporated off the tongue. He only remembered one thing that Larsen said to him: 'I think that one day, when this ruin has almost disappeared beneath the vegetation, a tribe of Coastal people will come upon it. They will see in this ruin evidence of a race of gods who had lived here once. They will use this ruin to worship those gods. And in this way, at last, they will turn it into something beautiful.'

Later in the evening Paul walked the ruins of the power station alone. He watched the sun glow red over the salt marshes, heard the distant piping of birds, stood in the fiery light between smashed walls. There was a time when Larsen's obsession, his daimon, would have set Paul Clearwater alight too. He returned to the guardhouse, where Larsen had fallen asleep on his bed. Paul laid his blanket out on the floor, took a last gulp of calvados, and slept.

Immediately to the south-east of Wellfleet, beginning at the East Hill that overlooked the town, was a country park that extended some four miles along the coast. Here Paul came to rest. He didn't dare go closer to Wellfleet – partly because of the money he owed there, partly because of a sense of shame. He didn't want to be seen in the town.

And yet he had been drawn back towards Wellfleet almost as if he needed to be forgiven, as if he were guilty. He hadn't been able to make the break. He felt poised between things – except that 'poise' suggested too much potential for action, for lightness and movement. He felt more as if he were dangling, in limbo.

There had been a golf course on these cliffs once. There had been many golf courses along the cliffs, before it was dedeveloped and golf courses became a symbol of everything bad about the bad old days. Here, the club house, built towards the end of the twentieth century, had long since been demolished. Only the lie of the land, the toy hills and sandy bunkers, betrayed where the course had been. The grass had grown, the neat clumps of bushes had spilled out on to the fairways. Tamed nature had taken its revenge.

Wandering the ruins of this golf course, Paul came across a hut that had escaped the attentions of the dedevelopers. Perhaps caddies had once used it to make tea, or groundsmen to store their lawnmowers and hedgeclippers. It was empty now, except for a couple of empty birds' nests and a yellowing, wrinkled copy of the *Wellfleet Observer*.

By day he wandered on to the cliffs and watched the trippers who had puffed and sweated their way up from Wellfleet, and by night he lay in the hut and listened to the sounds of the old golf course, the rustlings and sudden nightsounds of nature taking its revenge. When he watched the people coming up the path from the town, he was careful to stay out of sight himself, always ready to disappear back into the undergrowth if anybody he recognised from the town should see him. But they were all strangers. Paul could tell by their modern clothes that they weren't locals, that they weren't part of the make-believe of the Coast. Access to Wellfleet was liberalised in the summer months to allow in these trippers. They weren't so very different from the crowds you would see in San Marco in the summer.

Paul returned day after day to the same spot on the cliffs. Sometimes there would be a young family there. The children dashed across the cropped grass, screaming, stopping to examine things buried in the dirt of the footpath. They reminded Paul of himself and Jean at that age – only Jean would have been sitting next to her father, listening to him intently. He spent whole afternoons gazing at them, gazing out to sea. There was an elderly, raffish man – purple cravat, panama hat and a shooting stick – who took to greeting Paul with an awkward, slightly disdainful expression. There was a woman in her thirties, Paul's own age, whom he had noticed walking up from one of the coves and sunbathing on the cliff.

Days passed. The family disappeared. The old man stopped coming. The only thing that was the same every day was the breeze off the sea and the endless sunlight on the water. The space and light on the cliff top gave everything a feeling of inconsequentiality. People drifted past him where he sat, their voices tossed away by the breeze. The sunlight was dazzling, but the dark, knotted-up feeling inside him remained, undissolved. He brought manuscript paper with him on to the cliff top, but for the most part it stayed empty. Occasionally he would painstakingly transcribe something that had occurred to him, squinting into the glaring whiteness of the page, only to realise minutes later that it was a theme from one of his previous compositions. Later he'd discover that his pencil markings were so light and tentative as to be almost indecipherable.

One day, while he was bent over his manuscript paper, he felt someone staring at him. He turned around, and to his surprise there *was* someone watching him. Or at least he thought she was. She was wearing sunglasses, so she could have been staring past him at the sea. It was the woman he'd noticed walking up from the cove during his first couple of days on the cliff. She'd come back.

He turned back to face the sea. Somewhere far below him was the roar of the waves against the base of the cliff. It was difficult to disentangle that sound from the cries of children playing along the cliff and from the gentle swish of the gusting breeze brushing the grass.

He looked around again. The woman had moved. She was walking down the hill towards him. He turned back and watched a dog that was zigzagging quickly along the path, nose to the ground. With a sudden rush of movement beside him she came round the end of the bench and sat down.

'I hope you don't mind me interrupting. I saw your manuscript paper when I passed you before. Are you writing music?'

Paul hesitated. He suddenly realised how little he'd used

his voice in the last few weeks. Even when he was with Larsen in the power station he'd barely spoken half-a-dozen sentences. Larsen had done all the talking.

'Yes,' he said. 'Music.'

'I've always wondered how people can write music without trying it out on an instrument first. How do you know you've written the right thing?'

Paul looked at the manuscript paper on his lap, as though noticing it for the first time.

'I don't really know,' he said.

'That reminds me of something that happened to me the other day down in Wellfleet,' she said. She spoke slowly and earnestly, with a Spanish American accent. 'I was walking round the back streets and I found this blacksmith's. I watched him working for a while, then we got talking and I asked him why anvils are made that shape. You know what anvils are like, conical at one end and square at the other. Do you know what he said? He said "They just are." I liked that. 'They just are." He'd never even thought about it before.'

Paul listened, and when she'd finished he didn't know what to say. Sea, wind, voices poured in and filled the silence. He didn't know how many minutes it lasted. Then he remembered himself and said, 'I'm sorry, I can't explain.' But he'd forgotten what it was that he was meant to be explaining.

'That's okay,' she said. 'It's too hot for apologies.' She'd put her arm along the back of the bench, and she was looking out to sea. 'But you'd think they'd come up with something to help.'

'Come up with something?'

She nodded down at the manuscript paper. 'A gadget. Some kind of technical aid to make the whole thing easier. It looks a bit laborious.'

Paul gathered the papers together in his hands protectively. 'I don't need gadgets or "technical aids",' he said.

'Is that why you live on the Coast?'

'I suppose so.'

'I have to say, Wellfleet isn't quite what I was expecting. I don't feel plunged back into the past, like the brochures say.'

'It's different in winter.'

'Is that right? How long have you lived there?'

'Only ten months.'

'I see.' She fell silent. Paul noticed that she was playing nervously with the hem of her shorts. She stood up.

'I have to go now. Will you be here tomorrow?'

'Yes.'

'Maybe I'll see you.'

She turned and walked down the path towards the cove.

Paul stared out to sea. He couldn't remember much of the conversation. There was something about anvils, about gadgets, about Wellfleet. None of it seemed to make sense. He closed his eyes and watched an orange kaleidoscope of sunlight burn through his eyelids. He could remember the movement of her mouth, the way her chestnut-brown hair had been tucked back behind her ear, the brownness of her arms, the weight of her breasts as she'd turned slightly to speak to him.

He slept badly that night. The rustlings out on the old golf course disturbed him. His thoughts disturbed him. A few weeks before he'd left New Venice, his father had told him that the best thing about growing old was the gradual easing of sexual desire. He'd said it was like a painful weight being lifted from the body. Paul had been deeply hurt when his father had said this, suddenly aware that he owed his own existence to his father's sexual desire. He had cried when he was alone, and although – as was always the case – his tears were for himself, they were also for his father.

Paul had had affairs with women – mostly singers with whom he had worked – but none of these relationships had lasted. The sexual pleasure had been brief and awkward, and had left no trace of happiness. At some point he had decided that these adventures involved too much professional and personal complication. He realised, in the abstract, that for some fortunate people sexual love was possible. But he had come to accept that for him sexual need would remain a problem, a distraction, a burden. He had come to look forward to the time when, like his father, he could be released for ever.

It worried him sometimes that his lack of experience of sexual love created a gap in his work. Somewhere he had read that nobody who had not been in love could write a great slow movement. Once or twice, critics had remarked on how little the traditional romantic themes of opera appeared in his work. He was acutely aware of how he kept the erotic feelings that sometimes overwhelmed him separate from his activity of composition and music. When the two worlds collided – as had happened on that afternoon when he had made love to Madeleine Patrick in Grenier's apartment – he felt awkward, even ashamed.

He was awake at dawn, when a great band of rose-pink cloud arched across the sky from horizon to horizon. He was overwhelmed by misgiving. It was an extension of that fear, which had filled him on his journey back along the coast to Wellfleet, that he had lost the knack of escaping, that he was walking further and further into something he would do better to step clear of. He thought about walking away again along the Coast. But that too seemed like going further into something he already knew. He felt trapped.

These feelings didn't go away, but as the day went on they became suffused with something else. When he closed his eyes he saw that orange kaleidoscope again, and those vivid dissociated images of the woman. Towards noon he walked the quarter of a mile from the hut to his bench on the cliffs. He waited there an hour, and then he saw the woman walking up the path from the cove. This time she was wearing a thin, baggy dress. She was without her dark glasses.

She came up to him and in a voice that was slightly too

loud, as though rehearsed, she said, 'You are Paul Clear-water, aren't you? I mean, I haven't made a mistake?'

Paul nodded, unbelieving.

'I've been looking for you for three weeks. Nobody in Wellfleet knew where you'd gone.'

His first thought was to run away, to run across the old golf course to his hut, to take off again along the Coast. The woman had been sent by the Wellfleet burghers to track him down.

'I've come all the way from New Venice to find you.'

At this he changed tack. Perhaps she was some kind of operatic groupie? He'd come across such women in the past. That thread of sexual possibility that had dragged him through the night pulled taut again. His stomach clenched.

She was still standing over him, watching him. 'It was Jean who told me you were in Wellfleet.'

Silence. Paul's mind moved faster than it had done for months. In a moment, all the sexual projections and fantasies that had been raised in his mind by the appearance of this woman imploded. Along with everything else – the cliffs, the sun, the sea, the slow-moving train of thought that he had dragged with him along the coast – they disappeared, as though through a black hole, into a single point of fore-boding.

'What's happened?' he said. 'Is someone dead? Is Jean dead?'

She laughed quickly, a dry laugh that was lost immediately in the wide-open spaces of the cliff top. 'Nobody's dead. Jean's gone to America.'

'America?' Looking out to sea, he repeated the word as if he'd never heard it before. For a moment he saw cities, highways, canyons. In his present state, looking out from that tunnel of solipsistic unhappiness down which he'd been travelling, 'America' was too strange a concept for him to grasp. The woman might just as well have said, 'Jean's dead.'

'Did she give you a message for me?' he said.

'Yeah, she did. She sent a disk for you to listen to.'

The woman said it with false brightness, the kind of tone you'd use to cheer up a child.

A disk. America. Paul couldn't understand. He glanced at the woman as though he might read in her some explanation. She looked different today – more solid, somehow, and older than he remembered. Her presence grated on his nerves. He wished she wasn't standing so close. Her solemn grey-blue eyes intruded on him. He looked away.

'My name's Luisa Delaware,' she said. 'I got to know Jean quite well over the past few months. The tape's on my yacht, if you want to listen to it.' She waved a hand out to sea, in the direction of the cove.

Paul said nothing. In all that time walking along the Coast, speaking to no one for days on end, he'd never felt lonely. His own changes of mood had been company enough. And now, when someone was asking things of him, giving him things, he felt an emptiness inside that seemed as if it might swallow him up completely. He said nothing.

'Do you want to come aboard the yacht? I'll take you there now if you want.' She took a step back, half-turning to the path down to the cove as though to lead him. Then she hesitated and stepped back towards him again. There was something clumsily physical about her. He thought her tanned face tough and unintelligent. He didn't move.

'I've come a long way to give you this disk.'

Silence.

'Look, I know all this must be a bit of a shock. I guess you're upset about Jean. I've got to go down into Wellfleet to get some food. I'll be back in a couple of hours and we'll see how you feel then. Okay?'

Paul nodded unenthusiastically. She walked away over the hill towards Wellfleet. He'd wanted her to go, and as soon as she'd gone he felt worse. He didn't know what he felt towards this woman. Walking along the Coast, he'd felt as if he'd been carrying an unbearable load. And now this person had appeared, this strong person, and his first thought was that he might unload on to her some of whatever it was he'd been carrying all those weeks. He was grateful. But another part of him resented her toughness and hated her for the news she'd brought of Jean. His instinct, as always, was to comprehend what had happened by turning it into a part of his own internal journey.

So while Luisa Delaware was in Wellfleet, he sat on the bench and followed his thoughts, the same thoughts that he'd followed along the Coast. By the time she returned, he was so absorbed in them that he'd almost forgotten she existed. It was late afternoon.

She started talking about Jean. The words were coming too fast for Paul. His mind was still back on the curved shingle beach, moving slowly under the great arch of the sky. She was talking about a machine and trying to explain to him why Jean had gone to America. The tone of her voice was soft, but the words were like little hammers. Together they made no sense to him, but individually they chipped away at that world he'd constructed around himself during his journey along the Coast. The tunnel that had trapped and held him was beginning to crumble. He felt himself falling.

'Paul? I need a drink. I can't leave you here alone. Come back to the yacht with me. I'll put you up for the night.' She said it more as a statement of intent than an offer.

And Paul thought, 'She's right. I can't be left alone.'

They got up, and he followed her down towards the cove. The path was steep, winding down through woods. In places steps had been cut in the soft chalky soil. A bird flew away through the scrubby trees and undergrowth, chattering. They came out at some steep wooden steps. Below them was the cove.

210

Moonlight. The silver, inky sea, stretching out to the pale dark blue of the sky, licked at the rocks. Paul was in a dream. They reached the bottom of the steps and picked their way across the rocks. To their left was a small beach, and to the right a jetty. When they were standing on the jetty, Luisa Delaware nodded back at the beach and said, 'You get quite a crowd here by day.'

Paul looked at her in the moonlight as though she'd said something incomprehensible.

A rowing boat was chained to the jetty. She unlocked the padlock and indicated to Paul to get in. He obeyed. She rowed him out across the dark water, the rowing boat rocking from side to side, and Paul thought about going out with Reuben Grindley with the shingle cage balanced across the gunwales, about how perhaps he'd been happy then. He looked at Luisa through the semi-darkness while she rowed. She was looking past him, over his shoulder, not meeting his eyes. He was aware of blackness around him – the night sky above, the sea below, the emptiness on either side of the dinghy. Suddenly, he thought of throwing himself over the side and swimming downwards.

They reached the yacht, which was anchored a little way off the cove. Luisa guided Paul up a rope ladder. He sat on the deck – silent and absorbed – while Luisa switched on lights, opened cupboards, and brought out chairs. Vaguely, as though at a distance, he registered his surroundings: the liquid instability of the deck beneath his feet; the insects that had already begun to crowd around the lights; the breeze; the smell of the sea; the empty darkness all around, cut by the lights along the coast and by the great swathe of the Milky Way overhead.

'Here.' She guided him to a chair and pressed a glass into his hand. 'Whisky.'

He took a gulp. 'Can I have a cigarette?' he said.

She lit one for him, another for herself.

'I haven't smoked for a year,' he said.

211

'Do you want something to eat?'

He nodded. She went back into the cabin and came out again after a couple of minutes with some cheese and salad. He had finished his whisky. She fetched him another.

There was silence while they ate. The food felt gross in Paul's mouth.

'Will you be going back to New Venice now?' asked Luisa Delaware. She had sat opposite him on the deck.

Paul listened to the water slapping the side of the boat. The rhythm was irregular, unpredictable. Then it stopped.

'Why should I?'

He glanced at her face. She looked hurt and surprised.

Luisa said, 'She talked about you a lot. She was very close to you.'

The stars were spinning through the night sky. Paul drained his whisky and stood up again, with a decisiveness that evaporated immediately. His legs felt weak. There was something inside him that was like a physical force, but he couldn't have put a name to it. It unrolled upwards through his body and he fell to his knees on the deck, then heavily on to his side. His pain flowed out of him. His body heaved, then squeezed itself into a foetal ball. With every intake of breath there was a sound like a slow, low-pitched gasp of shock. He could feel his heart thudding against the deck of the yacht.

Luisa watched him without moving. All through the tedious journey up the canals from New Venice, she'd been wondering about this meeting with Jean's brother. Now that he was here, lying at her feet on the deck of the yacht, he was a thousand times stranger than she'd imagined even from those strange, dissociated letters Jean had shown her.

She wanted to kneel down and comfort him, but she didn't. She felt resentful. How many times, when she'd been sailing away from some place, had she wanted to break down like this? There'd never been any point. She'd never had an

212

audience. She'd moved nimbly around the boat, doing what was necessary, and inside she'd been frozen. She felt bitter as she watched Paul Clearwater's display of helpless emotion.

And there was another reason for not comforting him. She knew from experience that with men – and perhaps especially with this man – comfort was rarely innocent. It would be a leap in the dark. Luisa, drained by the anticipation and reality of meeting him, was not about to leap anywhere. And besides, she wasn't at all sure that she liked him.

The heavings on the deck continued for several minutes, then stopped. Luisa got up and stood over him. He was still. She nudged him with her foot, but there was no response. His cheek lay in a puddle of tears, saliva and vomit. He had passed out, or was asleep. He was tall and heavily built, but she was strong from years of working the boat. She lifted him under the arms and dragged him into the cabin. Then she came out again, swabbed down the deck, and lay down on some blankets to sleep.

Paul stumbled out of the cabin at noon the next day. He found the deck deserted. At first he thought that she must have been so disgusted by his exhibition of the night before that she had fled. Then he saw the dinghy still tied to the side of the boat. And then, squinting into the sunlight reflected off the sea, he saw her. She was swimming, her arms slicing the water in a steady, graceful crawl. He sat down and watched.

He had had a bad night. Several times he had been woken by the grinding headache that whisky always gave him. Each time he had lain awake for what seemed like hours, staring at the cabin roof, his mind shuffling obsessively through every single memory it held of Jean. There was Jean as a little girl, all dark impishness; there was Jean as an adolescent, when she had temporarily run to fat and indulged in long slanging matches with her mother. There was Jean as a young woman

– small, defiant, volcanic. Then there was Jean in America. That was a blank. Again it felt as if she were dead.

Several times he had been on the point of getting up and waking Luisa. Each time he had been immobilised by helplessness and headache. Now, watching her swim backwards and forwards through the dazzling water, he was thankful for her presence. Just to have this person here – this person who had been with Jean not long before – was a comfort. For a moment, as Luisa waved and started swimming back towards the yacht, Paul felt a surge of gratitude towards her.

She pulled herself up on deck, wrapped a towel around herself and looked at him warily, gauging his mood. 'How are you feeling?' she said.

'Okay. I'm sorry about last night.'

'Forget it. Come inside, you must be hungry.'

They went into the cabin, through the sleeping area into the galley beyond. Luisa made coffee and toast, fried eggs and mushrooms. They ate in silence, hungrily.

'So what about that disk?' she said. 'Do you want to hear it?'

'Have you heard it?' he said. He'd begun to flinch inside when the disk was mentioned.

'Only bits. Jean played me some of it now and then. I heard your father talking about New Venice. It's interesting.'

'I can imagine what it's like.'

'Well, there's a disk player in the cupboard. The disk's next to it. I'm going out in the dinghy. I'll be back in an hour.'

Paul watched her row away towards the shore, wishing he'd asked her to stay and listen to the disk with him. He got the machine out of the cupboard and put the disk in. Suddenly Jean was in the cabin. Then his mother, sounding stagey and not quite credible. As soon as Jean started speaking, he couldn't believe that she'd gone away. She was there. But he couldn't visualise her. All night long he'd been seeing snapshots of her – but now, with this live voice filling the cabin, those dead pictures were wiped out. For a second he could barely remember what she looked like.

Paul switched off the disk and went back out on to the deck. In the distance, on the beach, he could see people moving about. The sun was at its hottest. In his mind he was still in the cabin, still listening to the dark, closed-in sound of Jean talking to him. The sun seemed out of place, and it suddenly occurred to Paul that up to now he had never taken life seriously enough. He had only been playing at it. And life for Paul meant music. Now he could start writing *real* music. And again – as if in defiance of the sharp equalising light that stood like something solid in the afternoon heat – Paul's mind returned to the cabin. He listened to Jean's clear, hard voice. *There* lay the possibility of what the first scherzo could be. Yes, he was lucky He could turn anything to advantage. Paul realised this suddenly, and hated himself.

He had the sense of having been falling for a long time and now hitting bottom. The boat lay utterly still on the water. It was like an extraordinary imperfection, a speck, on the uniform and inhuman surface of the sea. Paul, inside the speck, sat down on the deck and squinted out into the light, waiting for Luisa to return.

When she did come back, Paul tried to reach out to her. She brought some drinks out on deck and they watched the sunset side by side, like a married couple.

Luisa broke the silence. 'Did you listen to the disk?'

'Only the beginning.'

There was another pause, then she said, 'Jean takes everything so seriously. That's why she couldn't stick to a career. She said that people who were a success had had to block out most of their lives in order to achieve it. Most of life passed them by without them knowing it was happening to them. She used to take the example of your father. She said there were vast areas of his life that were numb, that had been numb for years. She said she never wanted that to happen to her.'

Paul said, 'Do you think I'm like my father?'

She laughed. 'How would I know what you're like? I hardly know you.'

'You hadn't known Jean for long.'

Paul heard an aggression in his own voice. More appeasingly, he said, 'Do you think I'm like Jean?'

'You're a survivor.'

He said, 'I left New Venice because I could predict what people were going to say. When I listened to my friends, there was a little voice inside my head telling me what they were going to say before they said it. I wouldn't have minded that, it might even have given me a pleasant feeling of superiority. But a couple of things about this voice began to bother me. In the first place, it wasn't just anticipating what other people were going to say. It was anticipating what *I* was going to say. And I had the feeling that it wasn't just me that was hearing this voice. Everybody was hearing it, but they'd given up caring. Of course, we were terribly up to date. We were all well-meaning, well-informed people, the kind of people who went to all the new productions and saw all the new broadcasts. We were turning our lives into machines.

'So I came to the Coast. Believe it or not, those letters came to me more naturally than anything I'd said or written in New Venice. They were in the style of the Coast. That seemed natural to me.'

He hadn't spoken so much for weeks.

Softly, she said, 'So it wasn't really a joke?'

'No, I suppose not.'

'And now? Does it seem natural now?'

'I don't know. I'm not sure of anything now.'

There was a pause, then Luisa said, 'You know what you were saying about that little voice? It made me think that you're like Jean in some ways. She thought she could see through everything too.'

'You're laughing at me.'

'No, I'm not. I can understand wanting to leave New

Venice. I can't stand that place for more than a few weeks at a time. I find it claustrophobic.'

'Yes, that's it. Claustrophobic. And uncanny. When I was listening to that disk, it was like listening to ghosts.'

'Sure. I understand.'

And to Paul it seemed as though she did. 'I was wondering,' he said, 'would you listen to the disk with me?'

'If that's what you want.'

They went down into the cabin of the yacht, holding their whisky glasses. Luisa switched on a single dim light and started the disk where Paul had stopped it. They sat and listened.

They listened for what seemed like hours. When it was finished, Luisa got up and switched the disk-player off. The voices hung in the air.

'Another drink?' she said. His hand was shaking when she took the glass from him.

He said, 'Why is she so desperate that I plug myself into this *thing*, this *machine*?'

Pouring the whisky, her back to him, she said, 'But Jean wasn't telling you to do anything. She said it was your decision.'

But it was too late. When she turned back to him he was sobbing again. This time she had to fight harder not to comfort him. She put his glass down by the disk player and went out on deck. Leaning against the railings, she stared at the lights along the coast. For a few minutes there was only an occasional sniff from inside the cabin. Then there was a click. Paul had switched the disk back on.

The voices went on hour after hour, far into the night, disappearing into the darkness over the sea. Luisa heard everything again through the open hatchway. So much of her life seemed to have been spent like this, listening while other people's lives were carried on in a room next door. From time to time she would be invited in to adjudicate, or to dispense comfort, or simply to do a good deed, like bringing

217

this disk to Jean's brother. And then she would be ushered out of the room; she would sail away on her yacht, and the people would shut the door behind her and get on with their lives in the room. All she would take away with her was gratitude.

But there were times, when she was alone on the boat, when gratitude could seem like just a way of marking out distance. One day, she supposed, she could cash in on all that gratitude. But she wasn't at all sure what she would get in return, whether it wasn't in fact a worthless currency.

The Clearwaters had scared her to begin with. They had a hard intelligence. The first time Jean took her back to the hotel to meet her parents, her father had interrogated her and mocked her for her mystical views. Jean had made fun of her too, calling her an absurd relic of fin-de-millennium New Ageism. Jean's mother had just gazed at her with a bored expression. But Luisa hadn't been put off by this. Her optimism and good will could absorb almost anything. As her friendship with Jean developed, she became fascinated by the Clearwaters, by the way that the ties of family could hold together three such disparate individuals. It nourished her sense that the world was for the best.

She was in awe of Jean and her parents. She had intended to stay in New Venice only a fortnight, but meeting Jean at Frank Cottimi's party had changed that. She'd never lived family life so vicariously as she did during the weeks that followed. Only there'd been a missing element in the pattern – Paul. She'd spent a lot of time speculating about him. He was the one on to whom the others projected their strongest feelings. For his mother, he was simply the one who could do no wrong. Jean's feelings were more complex and intense, made up in equal parts of envy and love. And from his father came a strong sense of injury, a sense that in some way his son had betrayed him.

From these vivid but conflicting images, Luisa had composed a picture of the absent Paul. The mere fact that he seemed to have cut himself off from family life made her think that he might be something like herself. But now, as she looked out at the darkness from the deck and remembered his histrionics, she could see how he was different and how much he was a Clearwater. There was something in him that he shared with them, something that drew her to him and repelled her.

In the morning, Paul left. He said he had left some music in a hut up on the cliffs and needed to collect it. He thanked Luisa for all she had done. He took the disk. When she asked him again if he intended to return to New Venice, he looked at her blankly with his tear-reddened eyes and moved his head in a gesture that could have meant anything. She rowed him back to shore and watched while he climbed slowly up the steps from the cove. When he was gone, she took off all her clothes and walked into the sea. She needed to wash away the experience of the past forty-eight hours. The cold sea water gripped her skin with a thousand tiny pinches. Her body came to life. She swam away from the beach, thinking only about the rhythm with which she raised her head for air every fourth stroke. She enjoyed the feel of her arms bending in the air, slicing ahead into the water. She enjoyed the freedom of her legs kicking behind, and the feel of the sea water sluicing over her back, between her buttocks and down along her legs. When she had swum out almost as far as the yacht, she stopped and trod water. She turned and looked back up at the cliff. Paul was emerging from the woods. She watched his tall, heavily-built body stoop against the slope. He disappeared over the brow of the hill without looking back.

She swam slowly back to the cove and lay on the shingle. Her claustrophobic encounter with Paul had left her wanting to tend her body, to give it new life. She welcomed the warmth of the sun. She welcomed the warm ache of the muscles in her arms and shoulders. She tensed the muscles across her chest and felt for them with her fingers through the flesh of her breasts. There was nothing strange about this, she told herself. It was her life. She had always left the closed-in boxes of emotion, the cities, for the physical, for the freedom of the yacht and the feel of a sea breeze running across her body. She remembered when she had left China, after her affair with Cottimi, and the feeling of escape into the physical that she had experienced as she had set out into the East China Sea. When a summer monsoon had drifted across her path from the south-west, she had welcomed the feel of the warm tropical rain. She had moved about the boat naked, wearing only sneakers to stop herself slipping on the rain-washed deck. The yacht had always been there, her means of physical escape.

She spent the rest of the day sunbathing on the beach. Other people arrived down the steps that led to the cliff-top. They too took off their clothes and lay naked on the shingle, or swam in the slowly receding sea. The previous morning, when she had returned from Wellfleet and Paul had been relaxed and chatty for a while, she had mentioned the fact that nudists came to the cove, and been surprised at his expression of shock. He had said that he was surprised it was allowed so close to Wellfleet. He said that he had certainly never heard it mentioned in the town. Luisa merely shrugged and said that she couldn't imagine anything more appropriate to happen on the Coast, which was supposed to have returned to nature. She said she loved being naked and surrounded by people who were naked.

Towards evening she picked up her bundle of clothes and walked to the jetty. Without bothering to put them back on, she rowed out to the yacht. It was good to have the freedom of the yacht to herself again. She poured herself a drink and began thinking about where she would go now. She thought about the Baltic, about heading for Stockholm, where on one of the smaller of the ten thousand islands of the Stockholm archipelago there was a family with whom she had spent a long hot summer like this some eight or nine years before.

With every year that passed she felt more strongly this desire to go back to places she had already been. She was thirty-seven years old. She had been travelling for fifteen of those. When she went for a swim these days, she came back with a dull ache in her limbs that had not been there before. The skin on her face had tiny creases. Sometimes she looked down at her body with a terrible longing. She wanted a family of her own, before it was too late.

It was a warm night, with not a breath of wind. She went into the cabin and took out her telescope. She set up the tripod on the deck and pointed it into the night sky. First she looked at the moon, which was three-quarters full. The boat was utterly still in the water beneath her. She could see the shadows falling sharply across the basins of the craters. She shifted slightly on her seat and looked for the second brightest object in the sky. Venus was lower down, to the west. She looked into it, staring at it down the dark tunnel of the telescope. It was covered in cloud. She let her hand fall from the eyepiece, stroking down her chest, down her stomach. She shifted on her seat again and let her fingers wander between her legs, finding a centre, bringing comfort.

Paul took the disk back to his hut on the old golf course and stared at it for many hours. He felt at odds with the sensuous heat that was dragged through the hut by the sea breezes. Once he visited Wellfleet to buy food, but apart from that he remained on the old golf course. He was incapable of making decisions, of pointing his life in any direction. The idea of doing anything, of deciding to return to New Venice or deciding to stay, was distant. He felt as detached from his future as from the heat that surrounded his body.

There was a stretch of cliff to the east of the cove that had been fenced off because subsidence had made it dangerous. Several days after leaving the yacht, Paul went there. He didn't know why. He climbed the fence and followed a path that wound between gorse and bracken, then came out on to the open cliff top. Here the land had slipped towards the sea in wide, dramatic steps. Paul sat on one of the steps, where the earth had sheared under its own weight. There was a view from here of the stretch of sea just beyond the cove. The yacht was still there. The memory of Luisa came to him now not as a series of dissociated images, as it had done after their first encounter, but as a single presence. He felt a heavy tiredness and lay back on the grass. His legs dangled over the giant step where the broken land was slipping into the sea.

He woke suddenly, as though something had startled him. It was hours later. The sun hung low over the sea. He got up and walked purposefully back towards the old golf course. Once or twice he broke into a jog. When he got to the hut, he stuffed the disk and his few belongings into his backpack. He went back on to the cliff top, then took the path that plunged down through the wood to the cove. It was almost dark now. On the way down, he passed a few last bathers coming up after a day on the beach. The cove was deserted. He picked his way across the rocks to the jetty. He looked out to sea. There were lights on the yacht.

For the first time since waking on the cliff, Paul hesitated. For a moment he stood staring at the water. Then he started taking off his clothes. Dressed only in his underpants, he stuffed his clothes into the backpack and hid it among the rocks. He hesitated again, facing the water, then took off his underpants too and threw them aside. He walked slowly out into the sea. His scrotum and penis tightened against the cold. Then he launched himself out into the water, gasping. After the initial shock, the water was refreshing, even soothing. He did a slow, jerky breaststroke. He wasn't used to swimming.

It was dark now. The lights from the yacht slithered tantalisingly across the water towards him. The yacht itself seemed to move further off with every stroke. And the water became colder. He kept swimming, but his arms and legs were beginning to feel the same heavy tiredness he had experienced on the cliff. His thoughts were growing wild, vivid and disconnected. He was thinking back to his first days in Wellfleet. *I struck out boldly across the great ocean of poetry, caressed by the wild, sweet breeze of fancy . . . I felt within me the strength to reach the enchanted isle where the temple of pure art stands alone under a clear sky.* He looked out across the surface of the water. The light from the yacht was like the sun. The cold clung to him, dragging at him, and his thoughts dived, plumbing the black depths below him, measuring out each heavy yard of water. With a jolt he realised he was sinking. For a moment he had stopped moving forward. He grunted and began to exert himself, concentrating on each stroke.

'Paul Clearwater, is that you? What the hell are you doing?'

He found himself bobbing against the side of the yacht. There was a light shining in his eyes.

'Move to your right. Grab the ladder.'

He spluttered and splashed in the water. He tried to say something, but there was heavy weight pressing against his chest.

'Grab the ladder, you stupid man.'

He bumped against the side of the boat, and found a rung of the ladder. Near the top his strength failed, but Luisa's strong hands were under his arms, pulling him over on to the deck.

Paul experienced this from within a black coldness. It was only when he was lying in the cabin, wrapped in blankets, that he began to come to the surface. Luisa was holding his head up with one hand. In the other she held a mug of steaming liquid, which she held to his lips. It tasted of lemon and scalded his throat. The smell of the steam was wonderful, like the smell of the bracken high on the cliffs. She put it to his lips again and he took some more, finding it easier to drink this time, feeling the warmth trickle down into his shivering limbs. He had never tasted anything so good.

Her face was close to his, bending over him. It wore a detached frown of concern. He tried to say something, but his voice wouldn't work. He tried, experimentally, to cough, but his chest wouldn't move. She poured the last of the hot, lemony liquid down his throat.

With the strength that this gave him, he managed to say, in a hoarse whisper, 'In case you're wondering why I swam out here, I've fallen in love with you.'

There was no change in her expression, except perhaps a deepening of the frown, a look of greater concentration in the eyes that studied him. After a few seconds, the warming effect of the liquid began to wear off. He could feel that coldness stealing back up his legs and arms. Luisa, feeling him shiver, considered him for a moment or two, lips pursed, then stepped back and began taking off her clothes. She unwrapped him from the blanket, got in beside him, and tucked the blanket back in around the two of them.

At first the coldness of his body took her breath away. It was like hugging stone. She put her arms around his back and rubbed his buttocks. She spread her breasts against his chest. She put her cheek against his. She moved her legs around his.

'How long were you in the water?' she said.

'I don't know,' he said with a gasp, as though he were in danger of drowning again. 'I think I sort of passed out.'

'Well, let's hope you don't sort of get pneumonia. Lie flat on your back.'

He obeyed, and she lay on top of him.

'An old Eskimo trick,' she said.

Her own body was glowing hot from the sun. She began to move it up and down on top of him, trying to generate more heat by friction. Paul winced as her pubic hair scratched his penis.

'What was it you said to me just then?' she said. She began to massage his right thigh, which was seized with cramp.

'I said that I'd fallen in love with you.'

'That's what I thought you said.'

Her hand moved up and cupped his cold and shrivelled scrotum. He gasped. Softly she kneaded it, pulling at it gently until it was more pliable and she could feel the two balls inside. She held the icy penis in the palm of her hand and began massaging it. All the time she was moving her legs up and down against his, rubbing her breasts across his chest, squeezing his hand, rubbing her cheek against his, breathing hot air into his ears. She brought a leg up, pressed it up between his legs, and began working on his groin more vigorously. She grasped both his hands and pressed down on him with her whole body. Paul groaned, feeling himself poured into a furnace.

Hours later, when he had been heated through and drained dry, Paul fell into a deep sleep. He dreamt with theatrical vividness of the initiatory trials by fire and water of the lovers in the *The Magic Flute*. Luisa, curled up beside him, still holding his hand, dreamt of monsoons and bright starlit nights. They woke late the next morning and made love again more slowly, to the sound of seagulls screaming overhead. Over the past few days, when she had assumed that Paul had gone out of her life for good, she had wondered several times what it would have been like to make love with him, and remembered that months before in New Venice, something arrogantly performative in the tone of his letters ('raising the heroic key of E flat like a banner') had made her think that he would make an insensitive lover. But now, as the gulls screamed in celebration above the yacht, she was surprised. Yes, there was something self-conscious and performed about his love-making, something unabandoned. But it was performed with sympathy and care.

Later in the day they rowed to the jetty to collect Paul's clothes and backpack. Paul had wrapped a towel round his waist, and insisted on doing the rowing himself. Luisa had to explain to him how to use the oars. He felt a wonderful new

225

freedom in his body, a happiness that was physical, that was incarnated in the light that danced off the water, that bathed Luisa in its brightness. Sitting opposite him in the rowing boat, she stretched out her legs and smiled. He grinned back. The daylight filled his body, his brain. He stopped rowing and leaned over to kiss her. They embraced, laughing, rocking the boat from side to side. Paul was filled with the sensation of having broken through from a dark, enclosed world into bright daylight. It was a new sensation. For the first time in his life he had not run away. He'd broken through and found love.

They collected Paul's things and rowed back to the yacht. Neither of them wanted to see other people. She told him her life story. She had been born in Los Angeles, and brought up on the Pacific coast of the Baja California, about fifty miles from La Paz. Her grandfather, Emmanuel Montarco, had built a large ranch complex there, overlooking the sea, in the Thirties. He had been a computer wizard, trained at MIT and Harvard Business School, who had made his fortune in the Virtual Reality boom in the 2000s. He had secured patents for large parts of South America. He had built the ranch complex for the big family that he had planned, but in the event his wife – a fragile North American girl he had met while a student – died soon after giving birth to his only child, a son. He never married again. Joaquin Montarco, Luisa's father, was a wastrel. He had been through five marriages and drunk and drugged his way across the North American continent. Early on he had rebelled against his father and announced that he wanted to be a writer. He had been sent to the best universities in the north. But nothing he did had come to any good, and the only work of his that had been published was a collection of seven sketchy and self-indulgent short stories – *Amethyst Moments* – brought out by a small firm in San Francisco. They had disappeared without trace, and it later transpired that he had had to contribute to the costs of production to get them published at all.

For money he relied entirely on the goodwill of Luisa's grandfather, despite the fact that they were estranged. Luisa had been the product of the second marriage, a short-lived campus affair when her father had been working on a never-to-be-completed PhD on Malcolm Lowry at UCLA. Luisa was the only product of that marriage, but she had six half-siblings. Of these, the only one she saw when she was growing up was David, the oldest son of the first marriage. He, like Luisa, was brought up with the grandfather on the ranch near La Paz, and later followed his grandfather into the Virtual Reality business.

Luisa had been close to her grandfather. It was he, in a fit of disgust at his son, who had encouraged her to adopt her mother's maiden name, despite the fact that Mary Ann Delaware rarely ventured down to La Paz to see her daughter. She had moved on to a second marriage after the divorce, then a third. She travelled a lot.

When they explored this world that had suddenly opened up between them, Luisa and Paul discovered things that they had in common. They had both been brought up largely by paid servants, and in a place that was not quite home. Luisa had left the ranch at seventeen and, like her father, been sent to an expensive college in the north, where she had stayed on to do a Masters on 'The Idea of Order in the New Age'. If she had ever felt at home anywhere, it had been as a student.

'There was a famous library on the campus,' she said, 'where a lot of great scientists and philosophers worked. The college was rich, so it could get the best people on to the faculty from all over the world. There was an enormous reading room, which always echoed to the sound of papers being rustled and books being placed on desks. I used to love that sound. When I was meant to be writing my thesis, I used to sit there for hours — listening, wondering what would happen if one of those great thinkers sitting around me suddenly hit on the secret to everything, the idea that unlocked the whole mystery of existence. What would happen? You couldn't imagine something like that happening and there not being some sign of it, something to disturb that calm rustle of papers. I got it into my head that if someone did hit on the idea, then everything around me – all the chairs, the desks, the books, the library itself – would simply dissolve into nothingness. The universe would dissolve under the force of the knowledge. It sounds crazy, but I used to sit there waiting for it to happen.' She laughed, and kissed Paul. 'That's why I took so long to finish my Masters.'

Paul didn't understand, but he thought it was all wonderful – the kiss, the way she talked, the strange things she told him. It was all wonderful. They were lying side by side on the deck, and every hour or so they would dive into the sea and swim around the yacht to cool off. She was teaching him to do the crawl. When darkness came they would go down into the cabin and listen to the disk again. They were drawn back to it because it was what had brought them together, and because those cold, disembodied voices reminded them of the warmth and light of their own love.

At first love came in these long monologues. When Luisa listened to Paul she felt protective towards him. She was curious. She held everything he said carefully. She wanted to understand him, just as she wanted to understand everything. The way he talked about his father revealed a deep hurt. He was hurt by what his father said on the disk, by the way his father had rubbished his life, his music. And the hurt expressed itself as argument. Paul said he hated the way his father saw everything in terms of politics. It was so abstract, so Olympian, he said. This was what Jean had said too, but ironically it was also the kind of argument that his father himself would have used about others. Luisa could see father and son locked in a fight that neither could win, an antagonistic embrace without end or resolution.

'Your father's not necessarily a bad man,' she said. 'He's just a bad father. Maybe he wasn't meant to be a family man.' It was weak, but it was the only thing she could think of that might make him feel better. It didn't work. Paul stared back at her with incomprehension, unable to think of his father with any detachment.

Paul talked again about the reasons he had left New Venice. Each revealed to the other the precise moment when the possibility of love had come into existence. For Luisa it had been the moment in the cabin when, for the second time, Paul had curled up and sobbed. For Paul it had been a little while earlier, when he had felt able to talk to her about why he had come to the Coast. In that moment he had begun to break out of his tunnel of loneliness. And now, in the full freedom of love, he returned to it again – as though, it seemed to Luisa, he needed to justify himself.

'People admired me because I was a composer,' he said. 'What could be more fashionable and admirable in New Venice, of all places, than to be a composer? For a long time that was fine. But then something happened. I don't know why. Perhaps I began to take myself too seriously. My life, my composing, became detached from the world around me. I hated it. My father's wrong: I don't think art should be divorced from the rest of life. That was why I was becoming so unhappy. I used to look in the mirror and see this shadowy, wary face. There was so much self-reflection in it, so much doubt. My thoughts were hunting me down all the time. I couldn't think of anything without immediately thinking its opposite. I couldn't say anything without putting it in quotation marks in my mind. Everything became provisional. All I knew was that I had this passion for sound, for *sculpting* sound.'

It was at moments like this, when he spoke with such strange passion, in such strange tones, that Luisa felt most protective of him. His body looked so tensed and vulnerable in the hard sunlight. His long hair, matted by salt water, had flung itself about his head so wildly and forgetfully. She reached out to touch him, and he took her hand. They went

229

into the cabin together and he unrolled over her the way she had unrolled over him that first time. She taught him what gave her most pleasure, and he was attentive, performing each act with the care that she loved in him.

'What do you think?' he would say. 'You've got to tell me what you *think*.'

'When I was in New Venice,' she said, 'I went by myself to a piano recital. It was around the time those riots were going on. The woman played a piano sonata by Mozart. It was so completely beautiful, so simple and natural. This is going to sound crazy, but I thought about all the hate and violence in the world, and all at once I knew that the solution to it all was right there, in that music. God, I can hear your father laughing at that. But I swear, while I was listening to that music I was more certain of it than anything in my life before.'

Paul stared at her with tears in his eyes. After a few minutes, he managed to say, 'Did you tell Jean about that? What did she think?'

Jean always seemed to be there in their conversations.

'She laughed. She could be very cynical about that kind of thing. Not that she didn't believe in the power of music, in her own way. You've heard how she talked about the neurorch.'

'Yes.'

'She used to talk to me about it all the time, like she does on the disk. It was very important to her. She cared about how you would react to it. She thought of it as something she could share with you.'

Paul said nothing. Luisa was beginning to find that whenever she brought up the subject of the neurorch, he withdrew into himself. After a few minutes he would burst out with something different, changing the subject.

'Why do you live on a yacht?'

She told him about her grandfather and how when she was a girl he used to take her with him on his yacht up the Gulf of California. On their last expedition before Luisa had gone away to college, they had sailed out past the island of Espiritu Santo that guarded the approaches to La Paz, out into the Gulf, then onwards past the islands of San Jose and Santa Catalina. They had passed to their left the great mountain known as La Giganta, then crossed the Gulf and made for Guaymas, where her grandfather's mother's family had come from. With his usual efficiency and promptitude, her grandfather had paved the way for this voyage by letter. They were greeted at the quay by a motley army of cousins, by families whose connections to Luisa and her grandfather had long ago dissolved into genealogical abstraction. They had a wonderful week being fêted by these people. Luisa smoked cigarettes of the potent local marijuana that were pressed on her by eager, jokey young men, distantly related suitors who flirted with her by drawing family trees that proliferated across the table napkins like miniature jungles. Her grandfather had basked in familial affection, and in the vapours from the brandy glass that never seemed to leave his nose. They had returned to La Paz vowing to repeat the expedition on a future occasion, but Emmanuel Montarco's health deteriorated soon after that – he had contracted cancer of the throat – and within a year, Luisa, at college in the north, had received a letter from her older half-brother David informing her that her grandfather was dead. The two of them were the sole beneficiaries of his will and the sole inheritors of his considerable fortune. A trust fund had been set up in Luisa's name.

'I remember thinking when I returned with grandfather from that trip to Guaymas,' she said, 'that when I was older I would like a yacht of my own. My grandfather had taught me how to sail, and what was more important, had given me the hunger for it. So when I got bored with waiting at college for the universe to dissolve, I bought this yacht and named it the *Emmanuel* after him. I've spent most of the past fifteen years on it, travelling, seeing the world.'

Paul listened to this with amazement. His own childhood

231

had been spent entirely in New Venice, and he had hardly ever left the city since then. There were only the occasional trips to other European cities, where he spent his time closeted in other opera houses. He had led an indoor life. Now, listening to Luisa tell of her travels, it occurred to him with a pang of bitterness that his own life had been formed in the claustrophobia of New Venice. His only escape had been through the mind – through books and, above all, through the music that as he grew older seemed to open up wider and wider spaces inside his head. Real physical escape he had never known.

Each day was so long that it seemed to reach out and touch the next. It was August now, and Paul had been on the yacht with Luisa for almost a month. In the first days Luisa had once or twice asked Paul if he was going to return to New Venice, but she had had no reply. She learnt to avoid the subject. They talked of things that brought them together. They stretched out their bodies to fill the long hot days.

At night she took her telescope out on to the deck and taught him the names of the constellations. Orion. Ursa Major, the Great Bear. Scorpio. She told him about her most deeply held belief, which was that the universe was held together by a natural and cosmic order, capable of bringing peace to the human race if they would only attend to it. It was this that Luisa had written her thesis on, and she explained it to Paul with deep seriousness. He was impressed by her seriousness. He was always impressed by the manner and force with which someone said something, more than by the content of what they were saying. She explained, in an awed tone, how this deep order and balance manifested itself as the music of the spheres – a natural, cosmic harmony that men and women could hear if they were properly attuned. Notable individuals, such as Pythagoras, had managed to hear this music, but the vast majority of people through the ages had been deaf to it precisely because it was there all the time. If the human race were to save itself from extinction or from the misery of perpetual development, it could only be by attunement, by listening to what composed the cosmic silence: beautiful kaleidoscopic harmonies of vibration created by the swirling dance of planet, star, galaxy and universe.

'You know you're really lucky,' she said, tousling his hair. 'You're one of the chosen ones. You can hear that harmony.'

As she saw how much more respectfully Paul was listening to her than his father or sister had, she grew more confident and expansive, opening her heart to him. From a cupboard in the cabin she brought out her collection of special books – works by Plotinus and Iamblichus, by Werckmeister, Novalis, Rudolph Steiner and Karlheinz Stockhausen. She read passages to him. They all testified in one way or another to the music of the spheres, to the transcendence of cosmic music. Paul was open and receptive to what she said, and not just because of the quiet passion with which she said it. It also seemed so close to what he had come to believe himself in Wellfleet concerning the transcendence of music. Those unheard harmonies, the architecture of the universe. They were like the pillars of the temple that Paul dreamed about. Yes, he thought. That was what he was trying to articulate, what Luisa called the 'music of the spheres' – the universal and transcendent music that animated all visible matter.

Both were happy to be able to share this belief – Luisa because she had never been able to share it with a lover before, and Paul because it stopped him thinking about the neurorch. The neurorch frightened him.

One day, Paul asked, 'Did you mind what Jean said about you on the disk?'

Luisa smiled. 'I'd heard it all before. There wasn't anything on that disk that she hadn't said to my face. We're just different. She thinks that scepticism can help you see things more clearly. I think scepticism obscures things. There's nothing

233

strange about believing. It's not as if I believe in God. I just believe that there's an order to things, a sense to things.'

'Yes,' said Paul. 'So do I. I believe that too.' And when he said it, he did.

Inspired by the confidence that she had shown in him by telling him about her belief, one night he confessed to her his unhappy sexual past, the brief loveless relationships that had come to nothing. It was difficult for Paul to tell her all this, but she put her arm around his shoulders and consoled him until his sobbing had subsided. Then she took him into the cabin. It was the first time in his life that desire had become not a burden but an open door.

It was the only time that he hadn't had music around him. Even when he was walking along the Coast he had sung to himself, or had worked in his head on the symphony that he had originally come to Wellfleet to write. Listening to the disk had at first knocked Paul's mind into thinking of his symphony in new ways. But when he fell in love with Luisa, music seemed to lose its urgency. He was content with the slap of water against the side of the boat and the sound of Luisa's voice, groaning, when they made love in the cabin. In the dead of night they crept back on to the deck and sat listening in silence for the music of the spheres. This emptiness brought them together.

One afternoon when the air was particularly hot and heavy, and seagulls were bobbing on the water around the yacht, they talked about Frank Cottimi in the way that lovers sometimes talk with a sense of awe about people or places that might have brought them together earlier in their lives. They had both known him before either had known of the other's existence, and both were secretly hurt to discover that Cottimi had never mentioned the one to the other. They both felt inclined to denigrate him.

Paul told her how Cottimi had come to symbolise for him everything that he hated about New Venice – the tainting of art by fashion, the giddy work of self-promotion in a saturated cultural market. Luisa heard in the way he talked about Cottimi another trait she had come to recognise in Paul, which was his way of absorbing the outside world into a private demonology. But she agreed with what he said.

'Cottimi's the kind of person who thrives in cities,' she said. 'Especially in cities like New Venice. He's always doing something, without ever committing himself body and soul to any one thing. He's got push, confidence and charm. People like that get noticed. They fight their way to the front of the crowd. And in New Venice that's not just part of the battle, that *is* the battle. Remember how he talks about seduction on the disk? That's the highest compliment he can pay to women, that they make good seducers.'

She told him about her brief affair with Cottimi, ten years before, in Shanghai. She had gone to China because of her interest in Chinese music, which she had developed while researching her Masters thesis. In fact, her interest had been not so much in the music itself as in the theory that traditionally lay behind it, which held that the function of music was to imitate and sustain the harmony between heaven and earth, to achieve a concordance between the male yang and the female yin. In this theory she thought she had found that same connection between the musical, the natural and the social orders for which she had rummaged through western thought. Unfortunately, when she arrived in Shanghai, she had found little evidence of this austere theory being put into practice. The garish, iconoclastic and hi-tech revival of traditional Chinese opera – an irreverent, commercial cannibalisation of the glories of the Ming dynasty – was just beginning, and Shanghai was its epicentre. News of it had attracted Cottimi, and with his uncanny ability to make things happen, to slot singers, dancers, musicians and visual artists into a single dramatic machine, he was already beginning to make a name for himself there. Luisa allowed herself to be temporarily seduced from the ascetic theories of classical Chinese music by Cottimi's energy and confidence.

'But do you know what finally drove us apart?' she said. 'His fastidiousness. I've never trusted men who were too fastidious, either physically or mentally. There was one moment when I remember our relationship began to go wrong. It was only a little thing, but it marked the beginning of the end. We'd been out for a large and very rich meal – there were some spectacular restaurants in Shanghai at that time – and we were sitting in Cottimi's apartment. We were both drunk, and he was telling me a hilarious anecdote about how the two male leads in his company were trying to outdo each other in the traditional high-pitched falsetto of Chinese opera. He's a brilliant actor himself, as you know, and he had me in hysterics with his impressions of the desperate, prima-donna-ish screechings of the two men. Anyway, at one point I was so convulsed with laughter that I let out the most almighty fart. Well, I wasn't at all embarrassed about this at first, in fact it made me laugh even more. But I was amazed at Cottimi's reaction. He froze. Of course he couldn't admit to it, but I could tell immediately that he was shocked and disgusted. He pretended to laugh along with me, but it was an effort for him. That was the first night since we'd met that we didn't sleep together. The relationship continued after that, and the incident was more or less forgotten. But the seed was sown, and I think from that moment I began to see Cottimi as a bit of a phoney. I used to see the act that he put on with his theatre friends, who like all the rebellious Bohemian set in Shanghai at that time had pretty free and easy ways, and then I remembered his momentary expression of pained, prim disapproval that night. It didn't fit.

'Have you ever noticed that about people,' she continued, 'the way they often just don't seem to fit together? There's a roughness, a fault line running through them. It can show itself in hesitations, in all those little moments of awkwardness when a person doesn't quite know how to respond to a situation. Those tiny gaps tell you more about a person than anything they ever say. And sometimes, if events strike a person in the right way – or rather, in the wrong way – they can just fall apart, just like a rock falls apart if you hit it along the line of an existing fracture. Cottimi never fell apart, of course, because his fracture didn't go deep enough. When I left him he acted distraught, but it wasn't much more than wounded vanity. We've made it up since then. Now I always see him when I'm passing through New Venice. We're old friends. But we never sleep together now.'

Paul was thinking about how he'd cried when he first met Luisa. Was that what she was talking about? Had he cracked then? He thought he had. He hoped so. He was about to ask her, to be sure, but she had stood up. She walked to the side of the yacht and dived into the sea. He followed her. The cool water swallowed him instantly. In a second he was in a different world.

These long monologues stretched out over hours, over days. They might surface briefly when the two of them were lying in the cabin after making love, then disappear again for a while. Their pace was slow, and sometimes it might be a week before one of these lines of thought would be exhausted and disappear from the surface for ever. Some evenings they would sit on the deck and drink whisky until their heads were swimming, then make love without saying a word.

Each day began with the yawning whiteness of dawn across the water, then thickened with blue until even the sea breeze brought no freshness, just the accumulation of more heat. As August dragged on, the heat began to exert a kind of pressure, and the monologues began to break up and become the kind of conversation that ordinary people might have. (Like all lovers, they had thought of themselves as extraordinary.) There were long, comfortable silences now, and they took to drinking more often in the evenings. Luisa had put her telescope back in the cupboard in the cabin.

They took to going to the cove to lie on the beach. They

began venturing further afield. Sometimes they walked along the cliff top in the direction of Wellfleet, but Paul always insisted that they stop when they got as far as the top of the East Hill overlooking the town. This was the spot he used to come to in the winter, to experience the wind and to watch the rain and sea-spume sweep across the town. Luisa, who wanted to share it with him, reminded him of how he had described it in his letters to Jean. Paul didn't reply, thinking that she was trying to make fun of him. To change the subject, he pointed out the gulls tumbling and diving near the cliffs. He told her how he had tried to portray them in the first movement of his symphony.

'For a nature lover,' she said, 'you're not very observant. Those aren't gulls. They're called guillemots. They're nothing like gulls.'

There was a detachment in her voice that he hadn't heard before.

Why had Paul insisted that they stop there at the top of the East Hill? It was a question of money. He didn't want to be spotted by Hinchcliff or Hunter or any of the other people to whom he was in debt. Up here on the hill he donned Luisa's dark glasses. And money made him think of the future, and thinking of the future immediately broke the spell. What were they going to do? Were they going to stay on the yacht, anchored off the cove, for ever? Was he going to live off Luisa's fortune for the rest of his life? And what about his music? Was he never going to make music again? For a moment Paul had the same feeling as he had had before he had swum out to the yacht that night – a feeling that he was incapable of pointing himself in any particular direction, that he was facing a blank. He tried not to think about it.

'Let's go back,' he said. 'I don't like it here.'

Several days later, at sunset, they were sitting on the deck of the yacht. A mist was beginning to form over the water, through which the gas lamps of Wellfleet seafront were visible as a yellow glow in the distance. Paul was staring at them. He was slightly drunk.

'I wish you had a piano on board,' he said. 'I could do with a piano.'

'They don't make good ballast,' said Luisa. 'Perhaps I should have brought a neurorch from New Venice. They're more convenient.'

She'd been waiting to say this for a long time. It wasn't that she was curious as to what he thought of the neurorch, or why he avoided talking about it. She knew all that. In the weeks since she had met him, she had come to know Paul completely. She knew his exalted view of music, his exalted sense of himself as an artist. As Jean had pointed out on the disk, the neurorch threatened that. So much was straightforward and obvious. But even knowing that, Luisa wanted to confront him with it. She needed to smash something hard inside him.

'I don't know why you think I should need one of those things.'

It was so exactly what she was waiting for him to say, and in so exactly the irritable tone, that she couldn't help laughing. 'Do you know something?' she said. 'I can see right through you.'

He looked at her with a puzzled expression, then broke into a broad smile. For a moment he forgot his irritation. All he knew was that she was happy and that that was what he wanted. Then he remembered what they had been talking about.

'Do you know what it made me think of when Jean talked about that wretched neurorch thing?' he said. 'When I was living in Wellfleet, one of the fishermen gave me a fish that he'd just gutted. I put it in a basket and went for a walk along the beach. Half-an-hour later the thing starting flapping about, then jumped right out of the basket. It was leaping about on the shingle, stone dead with all its innards out. Jacob Grindley told me that it's the electrical impulses in the fish. I'm afraid that's what Jean's description of the neurorch made me think of – that slimy twitching fish. What's it got to do with music? Music is art, not instinctive twitchings.'

Luisa remembered the incident of the fish from Paul's letters, but she was surprised at how much he sounded like his father. They had the same tone of lofty disdain. Again she felt that need to smash something.

'I think you're wrong about the neurorch,' she said. 'It has possibilities. You're wrong just to dismiss it. It's there. It exists.'

He had been gazing at the distant glow of the gaslights of Wellfleet while telling her the story of the fish. When she said this about the neurorch, he turned and looked at her. Luisa, watching him, thought how strange it was that he knew her so little, that he was so blind to what was around him. He was like some strange creature that can recognise its environment only by beaming out emotion, and gauging when the emotion encountered resistance and was beamed back. In a way, he was quite stupid.

'But I thought you felt like me about it,' he said.

'How would you know? We've never talked about it.'

'We didn't need to. We felt the same way.' Paul frowned. Luisa watched him assimilate this, watched him groping. Suddenly she felt protective towards him again.

'Paul, don't dismiss the neurorch. I can see why you've reacted against it. You think it denigrates music. But it doesn't, not necessarily. It depends how it's used. It depends on the state of mind.'

She talked to him about how the neurorch could be another way of discovering the music of the spheres. That singing structure they'd talked about belonged not just to the cosmos, but the microcosm too. Their bodies were part of nature. Maybe they'd be able to hear the music of the spheres in the tiniest movement of their own brains. It could be there in the spinning of a single electron around its nucleus. But she wasn't getting through to him.

'Let's stop talking,' he said. 'Let's have a swim.'

'You know what happened to you last time you went swimming at night,' she said.

'I know.' He grinned. 'That's why I suggested it.'

They took off their clothes and dived into the dark water. The shock of the cold cleared their heads, and gave their drunkenness a light unreal quality. Luisa plunged underwater, kicking her legs in the air, then struck out in the direction of the soft lights of Wellfleet. Paul bobbed about near the yacht, waiting. In a couple of minutes she was back, and they clambered aboard and into the cabin to warm each other up.

They were both cold this time. They wrapped themselves in blankets and clung together, moving gently, forgetfully, like the water sliding along the sides of the boat.

'I'm tired of waiting. Let's go for a walk along the cliffs.'

'I'll stay here.'

'The sun'll have broken through by the time we get back to the beach.'

'You go. I'll be fine.'

She rowed away into the morning mist. There were mists now every night, and they were taking longer to clear in the mornings. The sun was still hot, but at night they were drinking more whisky to keep out the chill when they sat out on the deck. After she'd gone, Paul went into the cabin and poured himself a drink. He switched the disk on. He listened and felt the whisky begin to burn into his brain. He felt Jean's voice burn into his brain. He felt something soft and molten at the centre of himself stirring, needing to be poured out. Luisa Delaware's idea of the music of the spheres was too fixed, too hard. She didn't understand. He imagined himself as something liquid, continuous, without any of those cracks and disjunctures that she had talked about. Jean had talked about the trees they used to see on their family trips up into the hills. She understood. What if his nature and authenticity were something that could well up out of him, like sap, could pour up and become something beautiful? For a moment he saw his symphony as he had never seen it before. Each note of it was a single leaf. A thousand notes flickered and turned in the breeze, and light flooded down between them.

He stumbled out on to the deck and looked at the shore, feeling a long way from Luisa. He wished he hadn't let her go. He was missing her. He could feel the sun on the back of his neck. The mist had almost cleared. There was just a thin veil of it now, low over the water.

He went back into the cabin and ran the disk on to those parts where Jean described the neurorch. He listened to her, then switched the disk off. He poured himself another whisky, for the hell of it. He sat on the bunk and tried to hear his own mind. There was nothing, no music. He could visualise the brain cells, the electrical impulses fired from one cell to the next, but there was no sound. The only sound he could hear was the water against the side of the yacht, and a gull screeching overhead, mocking him.

He tried thinking about his symphony, but the only thoughts that would come to him were non-musical – a worry that he had not worked for a long time, a feeling of being drawn into a trap. There was no music in him. If he did put this neurorch thing on his head, then all it would discover would be a void. All his music had been artificial and un-rooted. To break the silence, he stood up and began to sing:

> A nightingale sings by starlight
> It regales the night with its song
> But when the stars give way to the sunlight
> We turn and the nightingale's gone.

He remembered how Priscilla Grindley had played it, stamping out the accompanying chords like barrelhouse blues. The tune came back to him easily, but his voice was quavery and uncertain. He strained to reach the high note of the phrase, then felt a catch as he settled to the sentimental feminine cadence. He stood for a moment, swaying, whisky glass in hand, then stumbled out again on to the deck and sang it across the water. It sounded flat and echoless in the open air. He wished Luisa would come back. He was lonely.

'I wish you'd tell me why you've been drinking.'

He looked at her. 'Drinking? We've both been drinking.'

'I mean by yourself, during the day. I smell it on your breath. When I came back from the cove the other day I heard you singing.'

'Why shouldn't I sing? I am a bloody composer, after all.'

'That's the first time you've done that,' she said.

'Done what?'

'Used your music against me. If you want to do your composing, go ahead. I'm not stopping you. I don't want to stop you doing anything.'

These words had the opposite of their intended effect. Paul felt trapped. He shifted in his seat and leant forward, avoiding her eyes.

'I wish you'd stop accusing me of things,' he said.

'I'm not accusing you of anything. I've got nothing against drinking. I do it myself. I just want us to be open. We love each other, don't we?'

'Yes.'

'Well then.'

Later, Luisa would look back at the long silence that followed and recognise in it the moment when things began to go wrong – or rather, the moment when a wrongness that was already there began to come to the surface. At the time she had only felt annoyed and ignored, but looking back she could recognise in her impatience for him to reply – then her disappointment when he didn't – an acknowledgement by a silent part of her that this was the beginning of the end. What had she wanted him to say? She didn't know. She wanted that hard shape inside him to break in her hands and reveal itself. But he didn't move. He was sitting stiffly, looking distractedly at the shore, thinking about music.

But when they went to bed that night she could still taste the salt on his arm and feel the thin wiry down. She could still claw at the hair on the nape of his neck when they made love. She could still hold him inside her and wrap him in her arms and legs, struggling between wanting to take him completely inside herself and wanting him out there where she could press her hands against his chest and then, in a flurry of desire, could slide her hands all around him to make absolutely sure that he was there: he was outside her, he was inside her. Then afterwards they could lie beside each other and Luisa could imagine that their vague, sinking, sleepward thoughts were looped around each other, barely distinguishable one from the other, like the idle thoughts of two people who had made a life together over a long period of time and for whom there was no hurry. She could imagine that, somehow, by a stroke of luck, she had there and then created a room of her own and that she was no longer a guest in other people's rooms but at home in the stability and order of her own. She could imagine that she no longer wanted to feel motion under her feet, but had found what she wanted right here, that she had resolved herself into a single overarching order. Then, deep in the night, when all this had overwhelmed her and she could hear his sleep-breathing beside her, she could sleep herself.

'We love each other, don't we?'

That she could even ask the question was a kind of rejection. He could feel her withdrawing from him. She didn't understand. He could see signs of her independence in everything she did. He watched her swimming and saw it in the graceful curve of her arms slicing the water. She had taken to bringing her telescope out on deck on nights that were free enough of mist to see the stars. She invited him to look with her, but he refused, seeing in it another sign of her independence. The music of the spheres had been something they'd shared. Now it separated them.

They still talked like lovers, but the subjects about which they could talk had narrowed, marked out by Paul's shifting sensitivity. They couldn't talk about the future, or the neurorch, or about whether Paul would go back to New Venice. When he felt things moving in these directions, Paul would dive off the yacht and swim away.

They stopped sleeping together. There was a bunk near the hatchway that could be folded down, and one night when she had stayed up late gazing at the stars, Luisa didn't join Paul. She pulled down this extra bunk and slept there. Neither of them said anything about it in the morning. Then it began to happen more often. Sometimes it would be Paul who would stay up late on the deck, drinking whisky, listening to the foghorns along the coast and gazing at the hazy lights of Wellfleet. And sometimes, on clear nights, it would be Luisa. It became usual for them to go to bed at different times, and in different places.

One day he surprised her by saying that he was thinking of going back to New Venice to work on the opera with Cottimi. He explained that the opera was about the patronage of those with money and power.

'Believe me,' he added with a bitter smile, 'we artists know about being patronised.' He had taken to using that bitter smile on her.

She was hurt. Perhaps he had no intention of returning to New Venice. She didn't know. It was as though all he'd wanted to do was let this drop of bitterness stain their relationship.

So a new phase opened. An atmosphere of dull sad stalemate settled on the yacht. Even when he sat huddled in the cabin, listening to the disk, she could feel waves of reproach coming through the hatchway. She felt besieged. To escape from him she took long walks along the cliffs into Wellfleet.

She swam. She lay on the beach in the cove and soaked up the last of the September sunshine. But when she returned to the yacht he would still be there, ostentatiously ignoring her, poring theatrically over a sheaf of manuscript paper, even though he wasn't really looking at it and his eyes were anyway too bleary to take much in because of the whisky he had been drinking to spite himself and her.

The sense of siege stretched into the nights. She was sure he no longer really wanted her, but he started coming to her when she was in her bunk and standing over her, making himself available to her. When she turned away he would go back to his bunk without a word. It was as though he wanted to register that it was she who was rejecting him.

This unhappy indecision, this stalemate, was as much because of her as him. She couldn't bring things to a head. She couldn't break their relationship with a final row and a demand that he should get off the boat and out of her life. It was what was expected of her – it was what he really *wanted* – but when she was on the point of doing it she always remembered the feel of him when she had pulled him up out of the water and warmed him in the cabin. She was scared of being alone now.

One morning Paul asked to go with her when she rowed ashore. He left her in the cove and climbed laboriously up the steep steps, through the wood, to the cliff top. He turned to the east, away from Wellfleet, and walked to the place where the cliffs had been eroded and were tumbling into the sea. He walked past the spot where he had stopped weeks earlier, before he had swum out to the yacht. He walked down the broad steps, each twenty yards wide, where the land was sliding into the sea. He walked as far as he could, to the cliff edge. Below him the soft brown sandstone fell away steeply, though not vertically. Spindly plants and saplings struggled up between rocks that seemed suspended in violent movement. It was an ugly place. Because of the incline of the bluff, he couldn't see the shore. He could only hear a distant noise of the sea, a noise that hung perpetually between a roar and a hiss.

Paul sat carelessly on the cliff edge, dangling his legs over. His whole past was clear in his mind now. New Venice had been a trap, a cold place of mirrors and illusions. Wellfleet had been a trap he'd constructed for himself. When all his projects there had collapsed, he'd walked away. But he'd only been walking further into a narrowing tunnel. Then he'd met Luisa, and after the crisis, the drink and the vomit, there had been transformation. There had been clarity and happiness. Now he could see through the happiness, as if he were seeing through the reflection on a pane of glass.

He still wanted to step clear. It would just be a matter of putting his weight on to his hands, leaning forward, and kicking off with his feet against the face of the cliff. Like this. For a moment he did actually lift himself on his hands and lean forward. But he didn't dive. His body was afraid of the pain. He remembered once reading about vertigo, about how it was a fear not of falling but of jumping, a fear that the will could not be trusted not to do in the next moment what it most feared in this: a fear of freedom, of the vertigo of consciousness. That was what Paul wanted now, the freedom to jump. But he couldn't. His body sat firmly on the cliff edge, refusing to budge.

That, he thought, was what the neurorch meant. All those ideas about the transcendence of music and the absolute freedom to create had been shadows cast on the walls of his brain by the only thing that was real: the simple, relentless switching on and off of ten billion cells. Now he understood.

He looked away from the cliff, towards the yacht lying at its mooring off the cove. He played over in his head Jean's descriptions of their family holidays, when they would go up into the hills and look down at New Venice from above, admiring father's beautiful blueprint for life. He could remember father and Jean sitting side by side on the grass, looking down at the lake and the city that was set in it. Paul would be running around, singing tunes in his head, apart from them, thinking he was different. But now he knew that he wasn't. He shared their genes. His father had laid out a blueprint for life not just in the alleys and canals of New Venice, but in his own son's brain. It was the limit of what his music could achieve. He remembered the way Jean had described it: looking down and seeing the claustrophobia of your own life.

He got up and walked away. He was inert now, not even wanting freedom. He was just a thing, a machine. He went down to the cove. Many hours must have past on the cliff top. It was late afternoon and most of the people had gone. Luisa's rowing boat had gone. He sat on the jetty and threw rocks into the water while it got dark. Lights appeared on the yacht. It crossed his mind to swim out there as he had done that first time, weeks before. Then he thought that this might be the moment to walk away. But he couldn't do that either. He sat on the jetty and kicked his legs, like a bored child. In the end Luisa came to fetch him and rowed him back to the yacht. Neither of them spoke. They were tired. They had nothing to say.

Luisa noticed a change in him after that time when he went up to the cliffs. For the first time she could imagine him as an old man. She had the sense of waiting for him to make the next move. She didn't know what it would be, because he was more mysterious to her now than he had ever been before. It was he who was pulling back now. Sometimes she would watch him while he sat on deck, staring at the shore, at Wellfleet, and she would realise that she could no longer even grasp the shape of him as she had been able to before. He was pursuing his own thoughts now, and she could hardly even guess at them.

She felt no anguish at what was happening. It had happened to her before, or something like it, but she always believed that things came right in the end. If a relationship collapsed, then that was because there was an imbalance in it, a wrongness that meant it had been doomed from the start. It was better that it should end.

'We love each other, don't we?' she had said.

Although he had quickly replied 'Yes', a silence had followed that seemed to go on for ever. It was a silence that she had hoped more than anything he would break. But he hadn't.

She had felt calm after that. Paul seemed exhausted. He was exhausted when she picked him up from the jetty that night, after he had been on the cliffs. Now the only connection between them was a thread as delicate and unspoken as the mists that wreathed the yacht during the chilly and windless nights. For Luisa an awareness of the beauty of the coast was beginning to fill this new vacuum. She loved the biting cold of the water when she went for her early morning swim, and the glow that it left on her skin. The light in the afternoon was both softer and sharper than it had been at the height of the summer. None of this she could share with Paul, who, when she glanced at him, seemed to have withdrawn into those private thoughts of his. They were like two strangers who had happened to go through some natural disaster together. It was a basis for mutual sympathy, but not necessarily for understanding.

Paul no longer knew what to think. At times he would listen to the disk and imagine himself as something organic and naturally expressive. At other times when he listened to Jean, the switching on and off of those brain cells would seem like an end to the artistic freedom he had sought on the Coast. He didn't know what to do. He didn't know whether to return to New Venice and confront the neurorch, or . . . but here his thoughts trailed away. He was looking at Luisa blankly.

Luisa felt a restlessness. It was autumn now, and she was

keen to be away from the Coast. It sounded like a description of bird migration, but that was almost how it felt to her – like some natural impulse telling her to go. Sometimes she had to control a feeling of resentment at the way he was eking out the end of the affair. It was like the resentment she had felt when he had broken down that second time they met. For all his theatricals, he would survive. Only his pride was hurt. He was only bruised on the soft surface.

It was during an early autumn day when the air was cold but the water as calm as it had been in July that Paul looked up and saw where he was. It was the old thing. It was as though he'd had his head down, charging at something, and now long after the quarry had eluded him, he'd slowed to a halt and raised his head out of that blackness, that fury, in which it had been stuck. This time the charge had been longer and blacker than ever before. It had left him drained. The first thing he saw when he lifted his head was Luisa. He saw her with complete detachment. He remembered with complete detachment her tanned, freckly body, and what it had been like to feel her legs wrapped around his hips, holding him inside her.

'What are you working on?'

He was sitting in the cabin, in the cone of light from the desk lamp, writing music on the staves of a piece of manuscript paper. The boat was rocking gently.

'Just some sketches for the symphony. I had some ideas for the slow movement.'

'Do you mind if I sit with you?'

He shook his head. She sat on the bunk and watched him work. His hand moved quickly, marking the notes then flicking up and across to form quavers, semiquavers, crotchets, minims. He scribbled time signatures and key signatures, drew sweeping arcs to signify phrasing. The only sound, other than the lazy, intermittent slap of the water on the hull of the yacht, was his pen scratching the paper. He used an old-fashioned pen – long and thin, almost like a quill – that he dipped from time to time into a bottle of ink he had extracted from his knapsack. It was probably a pen that he had acquired in Wellfleet. Luisa watched him with fascination. It was a mystery to her, this process whereby music could be created out of silence. For a moment she recovered in full the sense of his strangeness that she'd felt the first time she saw him on the cliff top.

'Which is the slow movement?' she asked softly, not wanting to disturb him.

'The third,' he said without looking up. 'After the opening Allegro there is a *Nachtmusik*, a scherzo.' He stopped writing for a moment, thinking. 'After the slow movement there will be another scherzo.'

After several more minutes, she asked: 'Do you think the neurorch will help you with it?'

Only a week before, the question would have been impossible. Now she could ask it.

He looked away from her. 'Sometimes I do think it might,' he said.

And there the conversation ended. He had withdrawn from her. Luisa went back on deck, knowing now that it really was over. A clear night. A three-quarter moon, and the white haze of the Milky Way racing across the heavens, reaching out beyond comprehension. She spun around. Orion. Ursa Major, the Great Bear. Scorpio. She didn't know, now of all times, why she should feel this sense of fulfilment.

They were both waiting. She was resting, her feet up on the rail of the deck. He was looking to shore, humming softly to himself.

'You know,' she said, 'just because things didn't work out, it doesn't mean we're bad people. I don't think you're a bad person. Sometimes things just don't work out.'

He looked at her for a moment, then nodded and looked away again, humming to himself.

Later he told her that he would be leaving next day. They sat together on the deck for the last time – dazed, abstracted, gentle with each other. He talked about his journey. When he had come to the Coast the previous September, he had come the fully authentic way – a two-day journey by coach-and-four. But going back he would take the steam train from Wellfleet inland. By the end of the day he would be in New Venice. He asked her where she would be going, out of politeness, and she told him she thought she might sail to Stockholm. She knew a family on one of the islands there. He didn't enquire further, and it was clear to Luisa that he wasn't interested. Later, when she was alone, she cried for a while. Paul was asleep in the spare bunk near the hatchway. Luisa switched on the radio for the first time in weeks and listened to the shipping forecast. With luck she would make it across the North Sea before the autumn gales.

They said goodbye on the jetty, where they had said goodbye before – where Luisa would from time to time, in moments of memory, say goodbye to him for the rest of her life. The shape and texture of his face was imprinted on her as deeply as was the shape and texture of the cliffs that guarded her place of anchor off the cove. She wanted to reach out and touch his hair, which hung loose and absurdly uneven around his ears. But she didn't. It didn't seem right.

'You'll have to get a haircut,' she said, 'if you're going to be on stage.'

He grinned, a boyish grin that she hadn't seen before. It caused her pain.

'Go on then,' she said.

He turned obediently and stamped away across the shingle towards the steps. She waited until he had gone, then she got back into the dinghy and started rowing back to the yacht.

The open cliff top above the woods came into view, but there was no sign of him. Either he was taking longer than she had anticipated to climb the steps, or – as seemed more likely – he was already gone. Whichever way, she had seen him for the last time.

Twenty years later, on another continent, Luisa would remember that moment when she got back to the *Emmanuel* and discovered that Paul had left his pen and ink. She would be sitting on the porch of an adobe-style house, looking out across a sea of rock and dirt that ended at the mountains in the distance. The sky would be livid. Her daughter would be playing her flute. Suddenly the memory would come back to her, and she'd find herself wondering – even now, after all those years – whether he had left them there deliberately, or whether he had just forgotten them. Perhaps it had been both. She had kept them, and when Paula had become passionate about music, she had given them to her so that she could use them to write her own music. But Paula hadn't used them. She said she was a performer, and although she could improvise beautifully, spreading a fountain of notes through the house, she never showed any interest in writing down her music. Luisa remembered feeling sad that she had never heard any of Paul's music. But perhaps in a way that was not quite true. And that would lead her to remember a discussion they had one time on the beach. They had been talking about the disk, of course. Paul had said that he didn't believe that anything was inherited – at least nothing important, like music. He was wrong about so many things.

Memory led to memory, like rooms that are so bathed in the white, blinding light of what has disappeared into the past that it is hard to tell where one has stopped and the next begins. She wondered if he had left anything else behind. The disk, perhaps? But it was gone. She went out on to the deck and looked through the telescope at the cliff top. He was gone. She sat down. Already inside her she could feel a change, a slight sickness. Happily, efficiently, she started making preparations to leave. In ten days she could be in Stockholm. The people there would look after her.

She picked up the bottle of ink and weighed it in her hand. The glass was cold against her skin. It reminded her of the coldness of his skin that first night. And twenty years later she would recall that memory. It would drop through the rest of her life like a stone through water. Like a gift.

IV

*The Teatro Miracoli in New Venice. The theatre is empty,
the stage set for the opening scenes of* The Commission: *a
large garret with a harpsichord and various pieces of old-
fashioned furniture. A large table piled high with a confusion
of books and manuscript paper. A cello is propped up in one
corner. Prominent at the back is a large casement window of
vaguely nautical design. It gives the audience the feeling of
being in the cabin of an old sailing ship.*

    *Frank Cottimi and Paul Clearwater enter. Cottimi is small,
dark-haired, energetic and handsome. Clearwater is tall,
heavily built and slow. His blond hair is still long and
uneven; it has not been cut. Cottimi wears black. Paul is
wearing his city clothes: purple silk shirt, puffed at the
sleeves; tight breeches; green woollen leggings; knee-
length brown boots with platform soles.*

COTTIMI

    Now *this* is where you belong. Home for the next few
    weeks. That tan of yours'll soon fade.

PAUL

    Where's my neurorch?

COTTIMI

    Give us a chance. Christ, what did that woman do to
    you? You've been a bundle of nerves ever since you
    got back.

PAUL

    I want to get down to work.

COTTIMI

> I'll get the neurorchs out in a minute. I have some other
> things to get ready for the rehearsal.

*Cottimi moves quickly downstage and begins arranging
some mats in a circle. Paul wanders upstage, sits at the harpsichord, and starts playing in a desultory fashion under the
following:*

COTTIMI

> How are your parents? Have they heard from Jean?

PAUL

> There's been nothing.

COTTIMI

> Still, they must have been pleased to see you back.

PAUL

> Mother was overjoyed.

COTTIMI

> (*Laughs*) How did they take Milstein's death? Was
> your father upset?

PAUL

> He didn't react at all. It was mother who organised the
> funeral. Now when can I try out this neurorch
> contraption?

COTTIMI

> I've already said: not until you've told me about Luisa
> Delaware. Who made the first moves? I want to hear
> all the details.

*Cottimi smiles knowingly at Paul, who doesn't reply. Paul
concentrates for a moment on what he's playing: a rolling
bass-line, like the opening of* Fingal's Cave, *and woven in on
top of a snatch of melody from* The Magic Flute.

COTTIMI

>Dull, dull. What's happened to the old Paul
>Clearwater? (*He moves upstage to join Paul at the
>harpsichord.*) Let's play the aria game.

PAUL

>I'm not in the mood.

COTTIMI

>Go on. For old times' sake.

PAUL

>I've forgotten how.

COTTIMI

>Don't be a bore. Give me an intro. I'll tell you about the
>cast.

*Reluctantly, Paul breaks off from what he has been playing
and launches into a vamping accompaniment. Cottimi listens
for a few bars – waving his hand, catching the rhythm – then
begins to sing in a confident stylish tenor voice.*

COTTIMI

>First there's Fela, the African I talked about.
>Black Bob Dylan, conscience of his continent,
>Icon, opportunist, spokesman and sell-out.
>Such names stick to the magnet of his talent,
>But now he's our dark star. Controversy's
>The aim of art: to goad and provoke, not please.
>And that's what Fela brings us. He'll play the servant
>Who gets the better of his master, the Figaro
>Who strains against his station – ardent, fervent,
>But a slave as well, despised for being a Negro.
>The old composer's taught him all he knows,
>But kindness has its flavours too; our Figaro's
>Thoughts are of revenge, of paying back
>The patronage that's marked him out as black.
>Through the neurorch and the old composer's
>>>>>>>>>>slackness,

This butler wins the commission and asserts his
                                                    blackness.

Cottimi smiles triumphantly and turns to Paul for a response.
Reluctantly, Paul joins in.

PAUL
     Okay, I've learnt about the colour of his hide.
     But what about the real man, the thing inside?

Paul slows the rhythm of the accompaniment.

COTTIMI
     Bravo!
     How does one describe Fela?
     A feline man, spinner of enigma,
     Shifty sometimes, sliding over
     What disagrees. A charmer.
     A rake, but shy. Like you, if I remember.

Despite himself, Paul smiles. He changes the rhythm of the
accompaniment again.

PAUL
     Like me? Like you, more like.
COTTIMI
                                   Whichever.
     The second in this catalogue's Zerlina
     Kousoulas, the most musky, sex-charged creature
     To have slinked the Venetian boards in years,
     A Greek, with black blowsy hair and eyes
     That tease out, taunt and inflame men's worst desires.
     She plays the maid, the sweetheart of the butler.
     I've known her spread her favours, but never fall
     In love before. It's happened now with Fela.
     Their stage flirtation's all too realistic.

PAUL
    You must be pleased with that.
COTTIMI
                                    Not at all.
    Life and art should be antagonistic.
    Drama needs the spurs of sexual friction –
    The frustrated hunt, the dangers of addiction.
    I'll stop this affair before things get too cosy.
    It won't be hard. To mess things up I'll use the
    Weaknesses of the others in the cast.

PAUL
    But all this manipulation –
COTTIMI
                                    Not so fast.
    I hope Luisa's not turned you pious and moral.
    Let me tell you about Bertrand Florial.
    The man's a queen of enviable notoriety,
    An ageing fruit who likes fruits of the same variety.
    He fell for Fela from the first, his eyes
    Following him in hopeful, hangdog circles,
    Lips gobbling with imaginary, lustful gurgles.
    He'd kill to have him, or at least tell shameless lies.

PAUL
    How wholesome. And what about the others?
COTTIMI
    Just as bad. George, who plays the composer's
    Colleague, the so-called friend who warns him about
    His servant, then tries to trick him too – George
    Jerrold's got a nose for sex, a snout
    That sticks firmly in the female gorge.
    He's a hanger-about outside the dressing-room door,
    A pathetic grunt in the trenches of the sexual war.
    He's also a terrible actor. I only picked him
    To secure the services of Margaret McGrath, who for
                                                years,
    God knows why, has longed to be his victim.
    She's followed that hog with touching, wistful tears

From stage to stage. A much better actor than he,
She plays the dignified part of the king's secretary.
Margaret, George and Bertrand: I'll use this old
But horny threesome like a wedge to force
The lovers apart. I'll douse hot passion in cold
Suspicion and spoil the smooth with the horribly
coarse.

Don't look so disapproving. Let's have some fun!
Watch and I'll show you how directing's done.
Bring up the lights! A roll of drums! Some trumpets!
I want action. Bring me my lechers and strumpets!

PAUL

(*With a hurried cadence, he stops playing.*) They're
here. I can hear someone coming.

COTTIMI

(*Laughing*) I won that aria. Now a bet. A hundred ecus
that I can muck things up between Fela and Zerlina.

PAUL

You're just jealous. You want to fuck her yourself.

COTTIMI

(*Laughing even louder and clasping Paul's hand.*)
Done.

The members of the cast enter – Bertrand Florial, Fela Lahbib, Zerlina Kousoulas, George Jerrold and Margaret McGrath. Florial (large, bearded) and Jerrold (thin, beardless) are voluble, greeting Cottimi with much cheek-kissing and thespian enthusiasm. Fela (black, beautiful) and Zerlina (Greek, beautiful) stand slightly apart from the others, close together. Once or twice they swap nervous smiles. They are on the brink of love.

COTTIMI

Folks, this is Paul Clearwater.

Everybody smiles at Paul, and he smiles back. Then Cottimi gives a signal, and the cast sit on the mats he has arranged in a circle downstage. It is clearly a routine ritual. They sit in silence. George Jerrold, rather ostentatiously, adopts a lotus position. The others are expressionless, gazing at the floor or into the middle distance. Cottimi walks into the middle of the circle, looks around at them, then leaves the circle again. They sit in silence for a couple more minutes. Cottimi walks back into the circle, looks round at them again, then speaks.

COTTIMI

Okay, have you all got the focus? Margaret? Good. Now I want you to imagine that you've been buried alive. You're in a coffin. Really be there. Now when I give the word, the lid of the coffin's going to be flung open and you'll be free. Okay? Stay with it. Now. You're free.

GEORGE

(*Leaping up*) Free! Thank God! Free at last!

COTTIMI

Thanks, George. Don't lose the focus.

George resumes his lotus position, smiling at Zerlina and patting her on the knee.

COTTIMI

That's how you're going to feel about your performance when you use your neurorch. It'll release your energy. Energy, but with focus. I've brought the neurorchs along today. I think you're ready to try them out in character.

He gets the neurorchs out of the boxes and hands them round. They look like Walkmans. The electrodes look like headphones, cushioned with purple foam rubber. Paul takes his greedily and puts it on straight away, fiddling with the knobs.

COTTIMI

These are the new top-of-the-range model. Synergise
only want the best for *Mindmusic*.

PAUL

(*Taking off his neurorch*) For what?

COTTIMI

Mindmusic. That's the new title. Synergise thought *The
Commission* was too dry, sent the wrong message.
What can you do? *Mindmusic*. I think we can live with
it. Don't lose the focus, Bertrand. We'll run the
opening scene and see how far we get. Put your
neurorchs on. Get to your positions. Remember:
focus, energy.

*Bertrand Florial sits at the table. Zerlina, George and
Margaret go offstage. Paul, at the side of the stage, turns his
attention to the neurorch again. Fela is just going offstage
when Cottimi calls him over.*

COTTIMI

Fela, I want us to try something different in this
opening scene. I'm worried about the relationship
between you and Bertrand. It needs fleshing out. Paul
and I have discussed it, and we thought it might add
something if the servant had a kind of sexual hold over
his master. It would emphasise your creativity and
power, and the old composer's impotence. So try
flirting with him. Demonstrate your sexual power.
Let's just see how it works.

Fela nods doubtfully and goes off stage.

COTTIMI

Bertrand, when you're ready.

BERTRAND

(*Writing at the table, and reading it out as he goes*)
June the fifteenth, 1792. Question: Where am I when
I dream? I lie on the bed, but I am not there. Question:
Where is music? We cannot see it. It is not the
harpsichord, for that is merely the thing that produces
it. It is not there, and yet it is present, just as I am
present here. But where am I? I am elsewhere.

Zerlina enters.

ZERLINA

Morning sir. We're all behind this morning. Let's get
some air in here, shall we?

*She opens the casement window at the back and starts
dusting.*

COTTIMI

Sound cue! Where is that blasted man? Zerlina, switch
on your neurorch.

ZERLINA

What for?

COTTIMI

Think church bells, street sounds.

*Zerlina flips the switch on her neurorch and there are some
feeble tinkling noises, interrupted by a wave of African-style
drumming and a loud moaning sound.*

ZERLINA

Sorry, Frank, I'm having problems with the focus.

COTTIMI

Never mind. Carry on, Bertrand.

BERTRAND

　　Shut it. For God's sake, shut it.

Zerlina shuts the window and turns her neurorch off.

BERTRAND

　　How many times must I tell you? The casement is to be
　　kept closed. I cannot tolerate that racket from the
　　street. It makes it impossible for me to work.

ZERLINA

　　But sir, it's so stuffy in here. It's unhealthy.

BERTRAND

　　Let me show you something.

*Bertrand goes over to the harpsichord and, clumsily, plays a
scale.*

COTTIMI

　　Bertrand, try using your neurorch for that. Just think
　　harpsichord.

*Bertrand flips the switch on his neurorch. There is a chaotic
chattering sound, like the dawn chorus played at the wrong
speed.*

BERTRAND

　　Oh hell. Frank darling, I told you this would be no
　　good. I am not a bloody musician. I am a verbal
　　person.

COTTIMI

　　That's all right, Bertrand. Use the anger. Keep the
　　energy. Just be the harpsichord.

BERTRAND

　　How can I be the bloody harpsichord? It doesn't say
　　anything. It doesn't do anything. I have not spent forty
　　years on the stage to end up as the bloody harpsichord.

COTTIMI
     Okay, Bertrand, don't force it. Paul, can you give me
     some harpsichord?

*Paul closes his eyes and concentrates. There is a rush of white
noise, which dissipates. Tentatively at first, a sound emerges
which is recognisably like a harpsichord. It plays a scale, then
a simple melody.*

COTTIMI
     Great. Let's carry on. Bertrand.
BERTRAND
     There. That was clear, was it not? Now open the
     casement again.

*Zerlina opens the window and switches her neurorch on
again. Tinkling bells. Drumming and moaning.*

COTTIMI
     Paul.

*While Zerlina's noise continues. Paul does his harpsichord
again.*

BERTRAND
     Please, shut it again.

*Zerlina shuts the window, and she and Paul switch off their
neurorchs.*

BERTRAND
     Did you hear it that time?
ZERLINA
     There was a bit of other noise, sir, but I could still hear
     it.

BERTRAND

Ah yes, you were listening for it. But did you really *hear* it?

ZERLINA

What's the difference?

BERTRAND

When you hear something it has a texture, like a word. It has a meaning. With that casement open, it's like having a conversation with everyone talking at once.

ZERLINA

Well, perhaps you could have the casement open when you're not playing the harpsichord, when you're composing at your writing desk.

BERTRAND

Ah, but the sounds are still there. It's just that when I compose, they're inside my head.

ZERLINA

You can't go round tied up in your own head all the time, sir. You can't live in this airy-fairy world. People have to breathe. You're not just a pair of ears. Look at the state of this room, sir. There's dust everywhere. It's so stuffy. It's like a tomb in here, sir. You could as well be dead. It's certainly not what I'd call living. (*Dreamily*) I like real things, things you can touch and feel.

BERTRAND

Ah, but how this room can be transfigured sometimes! When I'm sitting here playing at the harpsichord, this room becomes a palace, a gorgeous palace, a spacious apartment with acres of shiny floor. A scale in the treble becomes a fresh breeze rippling in through the window . . .

ZERLINA

And all the time you haven't budged an inch. That reminds me, sir, the harpsichord needs tuning.

BERTRAND

> Yes, it does. I'll do it now.

ZERLINA

> You'll be having a real lunch today will you, sir? Not an imaginary one? Not just one in your head?

BERTRAND

> No, a real one. The king's secretary is calling about the commission for the royal wedding. We must give her lunch.

ZERLINA

> Very well, sir.

BERTRAND

> And ask Joseph to come in.

ZERLINA

> Yes, sir.

COTTIMI

> That was wonderful. Feel the energy in it. Now let's have your duet with Fela, Bertrand. Ready Fela? Remember what we talked about. Thanks, Zerlina. Off you go.

She goes off. Fela enters.

COTTIMI

> Let's have you both with your neurorchs on, just to see what happens. I want some warmth in this scene. Bertrand, you can keep your volume down until you get the hang of it. Now go for it.

They switch on their neurorchs. The sound of them runs beneath the following – from Bertrand an unmusical chattering, and from Fela the elegant sound of a guitar-like instrument.

FELA

You wanted me, sir?

BERTRAND

Please fill up my inkwell and prepare
My manuscript paper. I must make a proposal
For what to compose for the king's secretary.
She's coming at noon. Are you ready?

Fela sits beside him at the harpsichord.

FELA

I could take your dictation.

COTTIMI

Great. Go with the flow, Bertrand.

BERTRAND

You certainly could. Let me dictate –

FELA

And I'll take down. Would you like
Me to sit over there, or perhaps
Over here would be cosier?

BERTRAND

Over here, please. Over here would be best.

FELA

There. Now we're ready to begin.

BERTRAND

Joseph, I think of you almost
As a son –

COTTIMI

Not too intimate, Bertrand. Keep something in reserve.
Remember: focus.

BERTRAND

You're the focus of my ambitions. I've taught you
Everything that I know.

FELA

                    I know. I wish I knew

How to repay you. I'd do anything
That you want. Is there anything?

BERTRAND

Only your love and loyalty.

FELA

Isn't it clear how I love you? Now tell me
The ideas that you have for the music
For the wedding.

BERTRAND

     Ideas, ideas.
I have so many ideas, and so little
Desire to fulfil them. Work bores me.
I'd rather just dream about music.

FELA

Love music would be good for a wedding.

BERTRAND

That's what I'll do. Take this down.

COTTIMI

Harpsichord! Still having problems, Bertrand? Paul,
can you give us some harpsichord.

*Paul, who has been absorbed in his neurorch all this time,
turns up his volume and produces some harpsichord again. It
plays a counter-melody to the rippling line of Fela's stringed
instrument. The two lines weave round and round each other
during the following.*

BERTRAND

Do you like it?

FELA

    Beautiful.

BERTRAND

      Sometimes
At night I feel giddy, with music
Swirling around in my head
And no chance of relieving it, no escape

271

From it.
I can't catch it. I can't capture it.

FELA

Don't fight it, release it. I'll take it
All down. I hang on your notes.

BERTRAND

My music's so private, like a dream.
They'll not understand it, they'll laugh –

FELA

Don't fight it, release it. I'll take it
All down. I hang on your notes
Like a kiss.

BERTRAND

       I'll share it with you,
Dear Joseph, but not with the others.
Write it all down, do with it
Whatever you need to. I leave it
With you. Delirious music –

FELA

Don't fight it, release it. I hang
On your lips with joy. Release it
To me. Leave it to me.
Let it flow, let it bleed, let it go –

The music stops

COTTIMI

Super. Stay with that. Stay with it. Great. Next scene.
Zerlina?

Zerlina enters.

ZERLINA

Sir, it's time for your nap.

BERTRAND

   Thank you. I'm feeling so sleepy.

Bertrand disengages himself from Fela and shuffles out, in a happy daze.

COTTIMI

   Neurorchs on!

Fela and Zerlina switch on their neurorchs, and there are chaotic sounds beneath the following: delicate kora; drumming; moaning; tinkling bells.

FELA

   Sleepy? Dozy more like. He's caught in my trap.

ZERLINA

   Mister Clever-Dick strikes again. Snap!
   And what's Clever-Dick done this time, eh?
   You two were looking friendly.

FELA

                              Not as much
   As I am with you.

ZERLINA

                    I've told you before: don't clutch
   Me so. You'll crumple my dress. Now tell me nicely
   How you've tricked him, and how you'll make it pay.

FELA

   He has a commission for the princess's wedding day.
   Fanfares, dances, music for dinner. It'll all
   Be worth a bit. But he'll complain and stall
   And tell me how it's prostituting art —
   While I steal in and fleece the ageing fart.
   He thinks he's dictating all the music to me;
   In fact I'll use my own and take the fee.
   I'm sick of kindly patronage. I'll stitch
   Him up once and for all. We'll be rich.

273

ZERLINA

You take a lot for granted. What's this 'we'?
I haven't said yes. I think I'll wait and see
If anything comes of your prank. Don't hold your
                                            breath.

FELA

But if I'm ever rich, promise me: 'Till death
Us do part.'

ZERLINA

                    Perhaps, perhaps not. I'm not deciding.
And besides, there are problems over which you're
                                            sliding.
How are you gong to get the music written?
He always wants you with him. You're his kitten.
You'll never get the time away to do it.
Admit, Clever-Dick, you haven't thought through it.

FELA

But I'm a kitten with a tiger's roar.
Don't fret – I'll get the commission done, and more.
A friend's given me this wonderful
Machine. He's servant to a master full
Of scientific tricks, an inventor.
This admirable contraption's a supplement or
Aid to the composer's clumsy craft,
Producing music without pain or graft.
You think what you would like to hear, and right
Away you hear it. No more the anxious fight
With quill or paper, orchestra or choir;
They're all consumed in one creative fire,
Burning from the individual soul
Through all the old distinctions, towards its goal
Of universal, natural self-expression.
Effaced will be those labels of oppression
Like teacher, pupil, master, servant, white
And black. The mind alone will burn with light.

Thus this age of revolutions raises
A level stage on which each actor blazes.

ZERLINA

What noble words! They might be more convincing
If you hadn't begun with all that talk of fleecing.
Mister Clever-Dick's put on political fashion
And tries to hid his crimes with righteous passion.
I like things clean and out in the open.
Who's this inventor that you've put your hope in?

FELA

Thanks to him, all may realise
Their dreams. His name's Nathaniel Synergise.

COTTIMI

Sorry about that line, Paul. The price of sponsorship.
Carry on, Zerlina.

ZERLINA

I want to hear this thing. I want to hear
What your passion sounds like. I begin to fear
You may prefer the body politic
To mine. So it'd better be erotic.

COTTIMI

Hold it there. Don't come on too strong, Zerlina. We
won't bother with your love song now, Fela. Let's
take a coffee break. Neurorchs off. George, can I have
a word with you?

George Jerrold comes out of the wings where he has been watching, and walks downstage to Cottimi. The other members of the cast, except for Fela, leave the stage. Fela wanders over to the harpsichord, sits down, and begins to play. Paul, listening intently, joins him beside the harpsichord and switches on his neurorch. He tries to reproduce, as closely as he can, the sound of the stringed instrument that Fela had produced on his neurorch during his dialogue with Bertrand. Their musical relationship is thus reversed, except that Fela is playing the real harpsichord instead of Paul's neurorch-

275

produced imitation. Their melodies weave around each other, as before. Their music forms a backdrop to the conversation, held downstage and sotto voce, between Cottimi and George Jerrold.

COTTIMI

George, a word in your ear. Have you been watching the rehearsal?

GEORGE

Oh yes, Frank. I haven't missed a moment. I want to understand how my character fits into the overall conception. It's going marvellously well, isn't it?

COTTIMI

What did you think of that scene between Bertrand and Fela? Notice anything strange about it?

GEORGE

It was very good. (*Pause*) Well, it was quite good. Of course there were things wrong with it. (*Pause*) Did you have anything particular in mind?

COTTIMI

Didn't you notice a sexual element creeping into it, a vague erotic frisson in the air?

GEORGE

Now that's funny, because I did notice that. I didn't like to say anything, but since you've mentioned it, I definitely did notice an element of frisson creeping into the thing. That's strange, I thought to myself. Isn't it funny that we should both notice it?

COTTIMI

I'm taking you into my confidence here, George. I know you're a man of the world. I'm worried that certain members of the cast are allowing their personal feelings to colour their work. I'm also worried that other members of the cast may get hurt. Do you understand what I'm saying?

GEORGE

Oh perfectly, Frank. (*Pause*) Well, almost perfectly.

COTTIMI

I'm talking about Fela. Did you know that he's having an affair with Bertrand?

GEORGE

Really? Well I always say, the theatre's full of surprises.

COTTIMI

You saw how they were acting up in that scene, flirting and petting each other. They can't keep their hands off each other.

GEORGE

Now that you mention it, that scene was getting a bit intimate by the end.

COTTIMI

It's colouring their work. They were all over each other.

GEORGE

I'd never have guessed that Fela was gay.

COTTIMI

He hasn't come out. But it's not really him that I'm worried about. It's Zerlina.

GEORGE

Zerlina?

COTTIMI

You know what a soft spot she has for Fela, like a schoolgirl crush.

GEORGE

Yes, I'd noticed that.

COTTIMI

She's so naive. So feminine and sensitive. I'm worried that she might get hurt. What she needs is a mature man to give her the loving attention she craves. I've noticed how you look at her, George.

GEORGE

You have?

COTTIMI

Like a father, a protector.

GEORGE

Yes that's it, like a father. Frank, just leave this to me.
Zerlina and I will have a cosy chat about things. She'll
trust me. I'll deal with it.

COTTIMI

I'm sure she does trust you, George. But I always think
that this kind of thing needs a woman's touch. I
thought we might enlist the help of Margaret.

GEORGE

Margaret? What's she got to do with it?

COTTIMI

Margaret's like a mother to Zerlina. I'm sure she'd be
the person to break the news to her. She'd do it if you
asked her. If she doesn't believe you, show her this. It's
a love note from Fela to Bertrand. Bertrand gave it to
me. He was boasting about his latest conquest. The
man's insatiable. You must recognise Fela's
handwriting.

GEORGE

I've never seen Fela's handwriting.

COTTIMI

Well you have now. Show it to Margaret, but don't let
her keep it. I don't want this spread around more than
necessary.

GEORGE

You can trust me absolutely, Frank.

COTTIMI

Of course. And I'm sure that Zerlina will be grateful to
you, when she learns that you've saved her from
making a fool of herself.

278

GEORGE

Yes, I suppose she will.

COTTIMI

Come on, then. You have to talk to Margaret.

They leave the stage. At the harpsichord, Fela and Paul are still making music. Their thin, delicate lines fill the empty theatre. They continue for a few minutes, then reach a cadence and stop.

FELA

You were trying to play the kora.

PAUL

Is that what it's called? I liked the sound of it when you played it – I mean when you made it with the neurorch.

FELA

The real thing is better. The neurorch can only produce a watered-down version. The kora is a very resonant instrument. Very physical. I'll play it for you sometime if you like.

PAUL

Yes, I'd like that. (*Pause*) What do you think of this thing, this neurorch? Do you perform with it?

FELA

I've tried it. I always try something new when it turns up. But this thing isn't such a big deal. People make a business of it, but it isn't so great.

PAUL

I find it unwieldy. I don't mean physically. I mean mentally unwieldy.

FELA

That's it. It might be possible to play it properly, but it would be very difficult. It would take a long time and for me it wouldn't be worth it. Everything that I want in music I can do with my voice, and with the kora or guitar, or balafon or halam. I like those sounds and I like singing. I like the feel of those instruments. If I think hard enough with the neurorch, I can reproduce those sounds quite closely. But what's the point, when you can have the real thing? Nothing you produce with this machine is going to be as real as that. I like the feel and texture of a string being plucked. Nothing can reproduce that. That is why I like playing this harpsichord, even though it isn't an African instrument. It is a powerful instrument. You touch a key and you can feel the string being plucked. A chord on this instrument is a very powerful, physical thing – much more so than the piano, which I don't like so much. Some day I'd like to sing songs to the accompaniment of the harpsichord. (*Pause*) I'm sorry. I always get carried away when I'm talking about music.

PAUL

No, it's fascinating. I haven't talked with another musician for so long. I've been living away from New Venice. Tell me more about the neurorch. I thought it was meant to make music easy to produce. It was just meant to happen when you put the thing on.

FELA

That was how it was sold in the first place. The music was meant to pour out of people naturally, out of their unconscious. People loved that idea. That's what Joseph, my character in the opera, hopes for. But it is all wrong. Music isn't an unconscious thing. Creating it isn't a matter of just letting it go, like having a shit. What I say is: if you think of music as being like shit, it will sound like shit! (*He laughs.*)

Often over the past months, people in the city, white people, have come up to me and said, 'You must be very excited about the neurorch.' 'Why?' I say. 'What has it got to do with me?' 'Well, you Africans are so intuitive,' they say. 'You are so spontaneous. You have such a natural sense of rhythm and melody. We Europeans are so constipated.' 'Have some respect, please,' I say. 'When I give a concert, I am not squatting over a toilet bowl and emptying my bowels. I come from a very old and noble tradition. My family have been singers, jalis, for generations. It took me many years to learn how to play these instruments and how to sing and to learn the many different songs that one is expected to know, and how to compose a praise song for a particular occasion.' The worst part is that these people who speak to me like this are my friends. They think they are being kind and paying me a compliment when they speak to me like that. When I answer them angrily, they are hurt.

PAUL

I understand.

FELA

Do you know what is happening in this city because of this machine? There is a lot of anger in New Venice. People are angry because the neurorch is not doing for them what they wanted it to do. I know. I have had that anger expressed against me. The people who are angriest are my fellow Africans, the ones who are on the streets selling trinkets. They were already angry because they saw how the Europeans despised them. In their anger they looked to me as a symbol and a leader, because I have been successful here in New Venice. Then the neurorch came, and everybody became very excited about it. It turned this city upside down. For many of my fellow Africans on the streets, the neurorch is very important. They are angry, desperate people, and the neurorch came to them as a kind of saviour. It was sold to them in that way. The only way for an African to get himself off the streets in New Venice is to become a musician or entertainer,

281

like myself. It makes Europeans feel good to patronise African artists. Perhaps many of my fellow Africans on the streets thought that now, with the neurorch, they could do what I have done.

Many of my fellow Africans, in their anger and frustration at being rejected in this white city, have come to believe that there is something special about themselves because of their race, as though their blackness was not just a matter of the colour of their skin, but ran all the way through them, penetrating to the core of their soul. Like my white friends who expected me to be excited by the neurorch, they thought that this machine would enable them to express this natural quality, this blackness.

I'm an honest man. I don't cut and trim according to who I am talking to. When my fellow Africans said all this to me about the neurorch, when they argued that I should wear the neurorch in solidarity with them and use it to express my blackness, I said the same to them as I had said to my white friends. I explained to them that my people, the Wolloff, are one of many peoples in Senegambia, my part of Africa. My music has many influences and many streams run into it. I hear things and put them into my songs. But at its origins my music is Wolloff music. It is African, and it is Wolloff. But it is not black. What does music care about the colour of skin? And I explain to them that although now I sing my songs for anyone who cares to listen, my forebears, the jalis, sang their songs for kings, and that hundreds of years ago these kings were men who sometimes enslaved their fellow Africans and sold them to the Europeans. Perhaps I am too honest, but I tell them that not everything that is black is good. Actually, in their hearts they know this already, from their own experience.

But sometimes, of course, people do not like the

282

truth. I began to lose the popularity I had had with my fellow Africans. They would stand up in my performances and demand that I use the neurorch. They said that I must have something to hide because I did not want to use it. They stopped coming to my performances. They started picketing my performances, to dissuade others from attending them. There were a lot of insults directed at me. Then when the news got round that I was to be in the cast of this opera, the anger became even greater. My crime now was that although I was using the neurorch, I was using it in this European opera house. I was betraying not just my blackness, but the neurorch itself.

PAUL

So why did you agree to be in the opera?

FELA

I had many reasons. These demonstrations and pickets outside my performances were destroying my career. The clubs and concert halls no longer wanted to hire me because it might cause trouble. I am as dependent upon patronage as my jalis forebears, who sang praise songs for kings. I am dependent on the patronage of money, of the market.

But I had other reasons. I had always been fascinated by opera and musicals. It was the first thing that struck me when I came to Europe. We have no equivalent in my part of Africa. It became my ambition one day to take part in an opera. I had seen one of your operas, *The Crooked Timber of Humanity*. So when Cottimi invited me to take part in this production, I accepted. I was not going to let these demonstrators intimidate me. I am stubborn. And I am happy, because I have met Zerlina. Life is complicated, but it is good.

PAUL

(*Pause*) Cottimi told me that you were an enigma.

FELA

Cottimi is a good director. He is good at persuading people to do what he wants. He is cunning. But he is not so good at listening. Cottimi says I am an enigma because he likes to think of me as exotic. He is like my white friends who think I should use this neurorch machine. Which reminds me, I was going to play you the real kora. I keep it in my dressing-room. Cottimi won't allow it on stage. Only the neurorch is allowed on stage. Come. I'll play it to you.

They leave the stage. Then Zerlina and Margaret come on.

ZERLINA

Fela and Bertrand? It's ridiculous. I can't believe it.

MARGARET

I didn't believe it myself at first. I still don't want to believe it, for your sake.

ZERLINA

Who told you this?

MARGARET

George.

ZERLINA

Him. Well, I certainly don't believe it then.

MARGARET

He's a good man, basically. I know he acts stupidly sometimes. But name me one man who doesn't.

ZERLINA

Fela.

MARGARET

Zerlina, I don't like doing this. It's just that I'm fond of you and I don't want to see you end up like me.

ZERLINA

What do you mean?

MARGARET

I know what people say about me and George. Maybe
I'm stupid to keep faith with him like I have. You
develop a kind of blindness as the years go by. I'm too
old to change now. That's why I think you should
make the break now, before it's too late.

ZERLINA

But I just don't believe it. Fela would have told me if he
was gay. Why would he pretend to be interested in
me?

MARGARET

Perhaps he didn't want to accept the fact himself. Not
everyone likes to face up to what they really are. But
you can't deny your own nature. You can't pretend for
ever. You mustn't be angry with him. Zerlina, I've
seen definite proof of this. A letter to Bertrand from
Fela.

ZERLINA

Let me see it.

MARGARET

I can't. George had to return it to the person who'd lent
it to him. I don't know who that was. I suppose it was
Bertrand. I can imagine him boasting about his
'conquest'.

ZERLINA

And did George say why he was telling you?

MARGARET

He's fond of you. He wanted me to warn you, to stop
you getting hurt. He sees himself as a kind of father to
you –

ZERLINA

That's a joke.

MARGARET

– like I think of myself as almost a mother to you.

ZERLINA

Margaret, I know you're only doing this for my sake –

MARGARET

Look, you saw with your own eyes what they were up to this morning, kissing and petting each other during their scene. Well? Did you see it?

ZERLINA

Yes. But I thought they were just acting.

MARGARET

I don't think so. Apparently Cottimi's worried that they're letting their personal feelings colour their work.

ZERLINA

Cottimi? You mean everybody's talking about this? Everybody's known about this but me. My God.

She starts weeping, and Margaret, comforting her, leads her offstage. The rest of the cast enter. Cottimi rehearses Bertrand and George in the scene where the old composer is warned by his old friend and colleague against the machinations of his servant. But the old composer doesn't listen. Bertrand and George are both cheerful and boisterous, and perform with great gusto. When they've finished, Cottimi calls into the wings for Margaret.

MARGARET

(*Coming on stage*) Sorry, Frank. I was just looking after Zerlina. She's in her dressing-room.

FELA

What's the matter with her?

MARGARET

It's something she ate. Nothing serious.

FELA

I'll go and see her.

COTTIMI

No need for that. She's best left alone. That's right, isn't it, Margaret? Besides, we need you here with your neurorch. Remember: focus and energy.

Now Margaret, we'll run your recitative with Bertrand. Bertrand, you're tuning the harpsichord when she comes in. Paul, can you give us some harpsichord tuning.

Paul switches on his neurorch and makes harpsichord-tuning sounds.

MARGARET

(*Clearing her throat*) The king sends his apologies.

BERTRAND

Quite so. Come and make yourself comfortable. I hope you'll stay for lunch.

MARGARET

Thank you. It's rather warm in here, if you don't mind my saying. Do you mind if I open the casement?

BERTRAND

I – No, of course I don't mind. Go ahead.

Margaret opens the casement.

COTTIMI

Paul. Street sounds.

Paul switches from harpsichord-tuning to street sounds.

MARGARET

There. That's better. Now. Business. (*Rattled off, quickly*) I have here a memorandum, sir, dictated to me by the king concerning the entertainments for his daughter's wedding on October the seventeenth, the year of our Lord seventeen hundred and ninety-two –

BERTRAND

What day was that? How much time do I have?

MARGARET

Well it's June the fifteenth today, sir. So that leaves just over four months.

BERTRAND

Four, of course.

MARGARET

Including time to rehearse the musicians. (*Rattled off*) The music required for the entertainments falls under four heads: fanfares and flourishes; dances; dinner music; and a short dramatic scene to be performed after dinner.

BERTRAND

Fanfares – that means trumpets. I hate trumpets. And you can't use trumpets for dinner music. With just four musicians it's quite impossible –

MARGARET

No, sir. Four months. And four heads. You may have more musicians than that. (*Rattled off*) The king has appendixed to the memorandum a budget for expenditure on the hiring –

BERTRAND

Sorry, I'm rather flustered this morning. It's all the noise. The casement's open – the maid's always opening the casement. Would you mind if I shut it?

Bertrand rushes over to the casement and closes it. Paul switches off his neurorch.

BERTRAND

There. That's better. I can hear now. What was going on? What were we talking about?

MARGARET

(*Rattled off, rather more impatiently*) The king will require six different fanfares, for the entrance of important personages, and two different flourishes to announce the commencement and conclusion of dinner. All the fanfares and flourishes will be joyful in spirit, and they will be performed by a chorus of (*with emphasis*) trumpets.

BERTRAND

(*Going over to the harpsichord*) There was something that occurred to me the other day that could be used for a fanfare or flourish. Perhaps you'd like to hear it and tell me whether the king might approve? Now, how did it go? You'll have to imagine the trumpets, of course.

COTTIMI

Paul, we need some more harpsichord here. Let's see. Imagine Shostakovich had written a fanfare for an out-of-tune harpsichord.

PAUL

Christ.

He switches on his neurorch and, after some effort, produces a bitter, ironic fanfare on an out-of-tune harpsichord. Then silence.

MARGARET

(*Clears her throat*) I think the instrument is out of temper, sir.

BERTRAND

Oh yes. I was tuning the instrument and someone disturbed me. You can't get a moment's peace in this place. And someone keeps opening the casement.

MARGARET

Quite so.

BERTRAND

Now, what were we talking about? Ah yes, the fanfare. Did you like it?

MARGARET

To be honest, sir, I did not.

BERTRAND

But perhaps you could imagine, in your head, what it might sound like played properly. On trumpets.

MARGARET

I'm not qualified to judge, sir. But perhaps I could direct your attention back to the king's directive that the fanfares should be 'joyful in spirit'.

BERTRAND

Joyful. Joyful trumpets. I can't imagine it.

MARGARET

Yes, sir, joyful. (*Rattled off*) The dances should last approximately one hour. The king is particularly fond of the gavotte and minuet, though he says you may include others of your own choosing, including quicker ones such as the gigue, so long as they don't sound common. The dinner music will last for approximately an hour and a half, or until it is ordered to cease. It should be soothing and quiet, so as not to disturb the conversation at table, and may for short periods be of a melancholy character. The *scena* will last for approximately half an hour and will be on the theme of wedded bliss. Some dramatic tension is permissible before the final reconciliation and ecstasy of the lovers, but not so as to upset the digestion of the guests.

BERTRAND

Do I have to have trumpets in the *scena*?

MARGARET

Apart from his stipulation concerning the fanfares, the king has left all such matters to your discretion.

BERTRAND

Thank you.

MARGARET

The king will pay you a retainer of twenty-five pounds
in instalments on delivery of the manuscripts. This
covers the cost of copying the parts, but not the hiring
of musicians and singers. I shall leave you a copy of
the memorandum and ask you to sign this contract.

BERTRAND

Thank you. You're most kind.

COTTIMI

Love it. Hold it there. Margaret, you're a marvel. And
you, Bertrand. Let's call it a day. You're all little
miracles. Remember, early nights and plenty of beauty
sleep. Now off you go.

*They all troop off the stage — all except Paul, who wanders
over to the harpsichord as though magnetically drawn to it.
He begins to play, improvising a slow, thoughtful melody
with an accompaniment that rocks up and down in triplets.
He hesitates for a moment, then puts on his neurorch, which
has been hanging slackly around his neck. He switches on the
neurorch and resumes his improvisation. At first there are
some wild, unfocused sounds and blurred, smudged harmonies. Then the music coming from the neurorch begins to
grow into a more definite shape, rooting itself in the harpsichord improvisation. The neurorch forms strange shimmering chords that hang like rich tapestries behind the simple
wandering melody he plays on the harpsichord.*

*Paul is utterly absorbed in what he is doing, in what he is
thinking and hearing. His eyes are open, but his mind doesn't
register what they see. He doesn't notice Zerlina crossing the
bottom of the stage, making for the exit to the street, and
Fela hurrying to intercept her.*

FELA

(*Jokey and exuberant, but in a half-whisper so that
Paul won't hear*) Zerlina! Don't think you can escape

291

from me that easily. You're having dinner with me, remember? If I can't have dinner with you, I'll eat *you* for dinner.

Zerlina turns and faces him. Her eyes are red.

ZERLINA
Is there something you wanted to tell me?
FELA
(*Still half-joking, but the joke dying on his lips*) Only that I think you're the most delicious – What's the matter?
ZERLINA
I think *you* should answer that question. You don't have to pretend. I'm not angry. Well, I am, but with myself. I've been such a fool. I don't want to see you again until you can talk about it and stop all this pretending and play-acting. Now leave me alone.

She runs off in tears, leaving Fela dumbfounded at the bottom of the stage. He stands there for two or three minutes, staring after her, then gazes abstractedly up the stage at Paul, who is absorbed in his music. Then he walks slowly off, following Zerlina. As soon as the door has closed behind him, Cottimi rushes out from the wings, laughing.

COTTIMI
Did you see that?

Paul stops, as though woken from sleep. He takes off his neurorch.

PAUL
See what?

COTTIMI

    Fela and Zerlina.

PAUL

    What were they doing?

COTTIMI

    Arguing. Doing what I'd directed them to do. I've won
    our bet. Sometimes, Paul, I feel like I could do
    anything. Come on, you dozy thing, play an
    introduction and we'll have a return match. You lost
    the last aria fair and square.

*Paul frowns, and plays an introduction. This time it has a
bitter, even sinister edge. Cottimi, beating time with his
hand, begins to sing.*

COTTIMI

    I sing and celebrate the sacrifice
    Demanded by this strange hungry device:
    A waiting stage, an empty still-lit space
    Where everything that matters takes place.
    There's no warm dark corner here in which
    To hide, and now there's not one tiny stitch
    In the fabric of the actor's brain
    That's not subject to unbearable strain.
    Total dedication to the part
    And negation of the self for Art:
    From the start, that was what I asked
    Of them. Nothing secret could be masked,
    Self-indulgence would be reprimanded.
    Nakedness was what the work demanded.
    Hence my anger when I saw those two
    Slinking off alone to bill and coo.
    Well now that's over. Pay up, I've won our bet.

PAUL

    It frightens me to see your mind so set,
    So single-minded and directed. Relax.
    You seem to think the neurorch's like a test

To stiffen the actor when he's lax,
A machine that gives the brain no rest
But acts upon it, probing and dissecting.
It's not like that. I've seen another way.
You'll never find the musical effect in
Static states of mind. It's in the play
And movement of the mind as it acts,
Not as it's acted on. An instrument
Is what the neurorch is.

COTTIMI

Bravo! You've lent
Your words such beauty, their sense barely detracts
From them. I don't agree with what you sing,
But like the way you sing it.

Paul suddenly changes the mood and rhythm of the accompaniment. Now it is slower and sadder.

PAUL

It's distressing
To feel we're moving in opposite directions,
Like distant trains heading for distant stations.
The knack's still there, but nothing feels the same.
I'm tired of our old operatic game.

Paul's harpsichord accompaniment peters out and reaches a half-hearted cadence. There is silence for a few moments, then Cottimi speaks, softly.

COTTIMI

Well, I think you won that one. You haven't lost the knack. I have work to do. I'll see you tomorrow. Cast notes at ten.

He walks slowly downstage to the exit. Paul watches him leave, then puts his neurorch back on and flips the switch. A strange incandescent music fills the empty theatre.

*

294

A couple of weeks pass. The rehearsals progress. Outside in the city, the controversy surrounding the new opera intensifies. Some Africans, former fans of Fela, start picketing the theatre. They are joined by other young people. Passionately committed to the neurorch, they object to its being taken inside the opera house. Their slogans echo across the campo: 'Brain music, people music.' 'Keep the neurorchs on the campos.' Emblazoned on a long banner that the demonstrators hold up is this message: NATURAL NEUROMUSIC FREES US ALL FROM THE PRISON OF TRADITIONAL ART. At first these demonstrations outside the Teatro Miracoli are good-humoured. But as more people join them – and carabinieri are posted in small defensive groups to keep watch over them – the demonstrations grow more noisy. The mood sours. The actors and theatre technicians are jeered as they come in and out of the stage door.

The chanting of the demonstrators can be heard from the stage as a distant roar. This constant pressure is beginning to take its toll on the actors. Fela and Zerlina have hardly spoken to each other since that night when she ran off. Fela, proud and stubborn, withdraws into himself and sulks. The rift between Fela and Zerlina, and the mounting demonstrations outside, have spread a kind of poison through the company. The atmosphere is strained. The neurorch is not proving a success. Nobody but Fela and Paul is producing anything approaching coherent music. Fela sullenly produces a watered-down version of the music he plays on the kora. Paul does what Cottimi asks of him, but his mind is clearly not on the opera. He spends hours by himself, experimenting with his neurorch. He had been staying in the hotel with his parents, but for the past week he has not left the theatre, and sleeps on a sofa in one of the greenrooms. The old friendship between Paul and Cottimi shows signs of cracking.

Cottimi has been unrelenting in his pressures on the cast, putting them through every improvisational exercise in the Method book to get them to 'be' their characters completely

*and thus, through the neurorch, produce their characters'
internal music. He makes them go around with their neurorchs switched on all the time, so that at meals — which they
take together in the theatre to avoid running the gauntlet of
the demonstrators more than is necessary — the air is filled
with an atrocious cacophony of noises. Cottimi tries every
trick, every manipulation and sleight of mind that he has
learnt in his years as a director. But nothing seems to work.
Then one morning, when the cast are sitting on the stage for
their usual pre-rehearsal focusing and attunement session, he
decides to tackle the problem in a more direct way.*

COTTIMI

(*Walking hesitantly into the centre of the circle and
looking round at them*) Would you mind if I said a few
words? I know you've all got a lot on your minds.
You're all important people and I hesitate to impose
on you like this. I'll be as brief as I can. I'd just like to
say (*raising his voice*) that if you don't start trying a
bit harder, and getting some results (*he pulls a handgun
out from his jacket*) I'm going to shoot the lot of you.
And after I've shot you lot, I'll shoot myself.

BERTRAND

Just one request, Frank. Could you shoot me in front of
an audience? It's how I'd like to be remembered.

COTTIMI

(*Fiercely, pointing the gun at Bertrand*) You think I'm
joking, don't you, you complacent old hack? I'm
telling you, if you don't start producing something with
the neurorch, I'm going to put a bullet through that
over-extended gut of yours.

GEORGE

My God, he means it. He's gone mad.

COTTIMI

I will not stand for mediocrity. Mediocrity is out of the
question. Mediocrity is unacceptable. I'd sooner die

296

than accept mediocrity. Right. Bertrand, switch on
your neurorch and let's see if the prospect of
execution can't concentrate your mind.

*Cottimi is still pointing the gun at Bertrand. Bertrand, who
has begun to appreciate the seriousness of the situation,
shakily puts on his neurorch and flips the switch. At that
moment there is a roar from outside and a loud chant: 'Brain
music, people music. Brain music, people music.'*

COTTIMI

Christ. Some fool must have left a window open. We
can't work with that racket going on. Zerlina, will
you be an angel and find that bloody window and close
it. As if we didn't have enough problems as it is. I like
a bit of controversy, but this is getting out of hand.
We're on their side, aren't we? Isn't *Mindmusic*
precisely about how the stale old walls of traditional
European art are brought down by the natural force
of the black slave's music? If those bloody people
shouting outside really understood what it is we're
doing, they'd be cheering us on. They're criticising an
opera without having seen it.

FELA

Then why don't you ask them in?

COTTIMI

We can't let them in here. They'd wreck the place.

FELA

Ask a few of them in so that you can explain to them
what it is we're doing. Tell them what you've just told
us. You must do something to calm this situation
down. Frank, I don't think you understand the anger
that is building up out there. I know. I have been on the
receiving end of this anger for some time now. I know
what I am talking about. We must do something about
it soon.

297

The noise of the crowd has become quieter. Zerlina rejoins the circle.

COTTIMI

Thank you, Zerlina. Fela, I hear what you're saying. Okay? Now, can we please do some work? I want the second scene. And Bertrand, I'm not joking, you know. I'll shoot you if you don't start trying harder. Now get to your position.

Cottimi holds his gun pointedly, for Bertrand to look at, then tucks it back into his jacket. Bertrand smiles feebly, still unsure whether to take the whole thing as a joke, then walks upstage to take his place at the writing table. The others disperse to the wings.

BERTRAND

(*Writing at the table, and reading it out as he goes*) August the second, 1792. It is becoming clearer to me now. All music is a gesture, and like all gestures it points to something beyond itself. All music points to that from which it has come, and to which it eventually returns: silence.

He sits in silence for a few moments, contemplating this. Then Zerlina comes bustling in.

ZERLINA

Morning, sir. All behind again this morning, sir. (*She goes to open the casement at the back.*)

BERTRAND

No! How many times must I tell you, you stupid girl? I must have silence.

ZERLINA

All right, there's no need to talk like that. If you want

298

to roast in this oven, that's your business. The king's
secretary is here to see you about the commission.

BERTRAND

Send her in.

COTTIMI

Good. Straight on with the duet. Neurorchs on.

*Zerlina exits. Margaret enters. There is a hazy grumble and
clatter of neurorchs during the following.*

BERTRAND

My good lady, how kind of you to come.

MARGARET

Were you expecting me?

BERTRAND

                       Well no, but welcome
Anyway. You honour a humble musician.

MARGARET

I've come to talk about the king's commission.
We'd hoped to receive some manuscripts by now,
But there's been nothing.

BERTRAND

                      Some tea? I won't allow
My maid to open the casement. I hope you're not
Too hot?

MARGARET

           Please, don't change the subject. What
Has that to do with the commission?

BERTRAND

                          A lot,
As it happens. You see, I must have silence
To achieve my goal of music without contrivance,
A music that spurns the passing fashions,
Expressing only the essence of our passions.

MARGARET

And how does this essential music sound?

BERTRAND

Like this. Listen.

MARGARET

I can't hear anything.

BERTRAND

Precisely. That,
To use a passé phrase, is where it's at:
Sound boiled down to its bones; the birth and death
Of music in one moment. The purest breath
Of the musician's art is so slender,
So wisp-like and without vibrato, the sender
Of that breath ends up remaining silent.
The best music lies in mute refinement.

MARGARET

You're being most obscure. Do I take it
You intend not to compose, but merely to fake it?
That was once tried by a colonial called John Cage;
It caused a stir but never became the rage.
The fashion now's for something more substantial,
Something less austere and more financial.
The king is not prepared to pay for nothing;
He'll expect a dish that comes with stuffing.
So get to work. Silence isn't golden
But merely dull. Remember to whom you're beholden.

BERTRAND

But silence can come in many different varieties,
Encompassing joy and sorrow, jokes and pieties.
Silence can be –

MARGARET

I've had enough of this.
You can either come up with the goods, or kiss
Goodbye to this commission. On behalf of the king
I deliver this ultimatum: compose or sling
Your hook.

BERTRAND

        All right, all right. I've got the message.
I was only testing the waters. It seems that age
And wisdom don't count for much any more.
The king'll get his modern noises – four
Heads, four trumpets, whatever else he needs.
I've given my servant some ideas, some seeds
That he can nurture and grow. I have no time
For details. My mind's tuned into the sublime.

MARGARET

I'll tell the king. God knows how he'll react;
We weren't expecting you to sub-contract.

BERTRAND

I knew there'd be no problem. Talk to Joseph
About it all. I'm tired, I need to doze –

MARGARET

                              If
The king's not agreeable, we'll have to talk again.

BERTRAND

Leave me. Talk to Joseph. I can't stand strain
Of any kind. (*He shuffles off.*)

FELA

                (*Entering*) All all right, my lady?

MARGARET

Is your master well? I'm afraid he
Might be getting slightly out of touch.
Is he finding work a bit too much?
I understand that you've been helping him.

FELA

I have, but his ideas are rather dim
And nebulous. They're hard to realise.
I'm afraid I've had to improvise.

MARGARET

But that's all wrong. It's him we're going to pay –

FELA

Forget I spoke. A slave should not betray

His master. I don't want to cause him trouble,
Or see his silent dreams reduced to rubble.

MARGARET

You're much too loyal. The whole thing's far from fair.
Why should we pay for castles in the air,
When it's you that's doing all the work?
He must think the king's a gullible berk.
Already rumours have been circulating.
They're put about by so-called friends who hate him,
Musicians who for work will do him down,
And don't mind getting their treacherous noses brown
By crawling to me with unctuous tittle-tattle.
I came along today merely to rattle
Your master's cage a bit. But now I find
He flouts the very contract that he signed.
It's insupportable. If it's you
That writes the music, things would be askew
If your master got the fee. It's yours –
Both the money and the royal applause.

FELA

Thank you, madam.

MARGARET

Show me your manuscripts.
We have to work out how the music fits.

FELA

There are no manuscripts. It's all up here.
It's in my head.

MARGARET

What, you as well? Dear
God! Is everyone in this town quite mad?
Has every musician decided that sounds are bad?

FELA

It's not like that with me. Let me explain.
I have here a machine that takes the strain
Out of musical composition. It listens
To the soul, then prints, like first editions,

302

The patterns it has found on to the pristine
Pages of the air. Not even the Sistine
Chapel has heard such celestial music.
No ear can hear it once and then refuse it.
Listen.

*Fela switches on his neurorch and produces the sound of the
kora, the delicate lines weaving around each other.*

COTTIMI

That's very nice, Fela, but can't we have something a
bit more, you know, *African?*

FELA

That is African.

COTTIMI

I know, Fela, of course it is. But can't we have a bit
more drumming with it, something a bit funkier? Just
see what you can do.

*The sound of the kora dissolves, then recoheres, this time
accompanied by the light drumming of an Indian tabla.*

COTTIMI

Better. Carry on, Margaret.

MARGARET

That's not bad. It has a certain something.
It's different. It could even bring
To the celebrations a kind of wild
Spirit. Weddings can be so meek and mild.
They should perhaps be more like festivals
Of instinct, dedicated to conjuring devils
And summoning up people's natural urges.
The marriage bed's no place for dusty dirges.
A round of royal pleasure's what I have in view,
A vision of dancers dancing till they're black and blue.

Come to the palace today at four;
Your performance leaves me wanting more.

Margaret leaves the stage, and Fela does a little dance of victory around the harpsichord. Zerlina enters.

ZERLINA

What are you up to now, you shameless trickster?

FELA

I can't believe I've done it. I've convinced her;
The commission's mine. She said they'd dance
Till they're black and blue; well, now's our chance
For marriage too. Now's our chance for frolics
In the wedding bed. We'll get our kicks
Till we're black and blue, too.

ZERLINA

                        But what
About our master? Do we want a blot
Of guilt to stain our virginal liaison?
The edifice of marriage should not be based on
Trickery, lies and starving old men.
Look to firmer foundations, my lover – then
I might reconsider. (*Exit*)

FELA

                      Give me strength.
A woman will go to any tortuous length
To twist you around her faithless little finger.
Firmer foundations, my foot! I can't help watching her
Eyes, and seeing the way they laugh at me.
I'm hopelessly in love. I wish I were free
To throw her out of my life and keep the money
For myself. She wouldn't find that so funny;
She likes *la dolce vita* as much as I do.
I'd leave, play Aeneas to her Dido,
If I only thought she'd rather take her life
Than live without the joy of being my wife.

Bertrand shuffles back on.

BERTRAND

    The king's secretary was here just now.
    That stupid woman will never grasp quite how
    Difficult it is to make art.
    I explained to her the minor part
    That you are playing in the realisation
    Of my ideas. It's beneath my station
    To talk about my work with that lackey.
    She'd probably like something light and tacky
    For her wretched wedding. Did she say
    Anything to you?

FELA

                    She made great play
    Of how the elevation of your thought
    Made her weak with wonder. You've got her support.

BERTRAND

    Did she really say that? How surprising.
    There were no complaints? No matters arising?

FELA

    None whatsoever. She sang your praises.
    Your name will come up at court smelling of daisies.

BERTRAND

    Excellent. Now get back to transcribing
    Those thoughts of mine that you've been imbibing.
    Art and commerce make a noxious mélange.
    But we must hold our noses and take the plunge.

FELA

    Yes, master. I think you'll be amazed
    At how your melodies have been rephrased.
    (*Aside*) Before the end of this artistic farce
    I'll make this stupid codger kiss my arse. (*Exit*)

BERTRAND

    Oh dear, reality and real life –
    What pointless and unnecessary noise and strife.

My world of art lives in a world of its own;
Brute facts are things that dreams disown.
I'd rather dream of music than have to hear it;
It's when it's far away I feel most near it.

COTTIMI

Right, Bertrand, neurorch on. I want wisps of ethereal
mind music. Now, be the part.

*Bertrand switches on his neurorch, and there is some raucous
chattering.*

COTTIMI

(*Advancing towards him and pulling the gun from his
jacket*) I've had enough of this. I said ethereal. (*He puts
the gun to Bertrand's temple. Bertrand closes his eyes
and screws up his face in an agony of concentration.
The rest of the cast edge on to the stage from the wings,
watching with horrified fascination.*) Now. Ethereal.
This is your last chance.

BERTRAND'S NEURORCH

—bluchkafadadomumophodlindrontdozoowafeluprrrah
blopmmdontdoitaguaguamifelahuhuwantyouyayea
dontwantdiefelahuhdontshoot—

MARGARET

What's happening? His lips aren't moving.

BERTRAND'S NEURORCH

—namafelagoowantyourbutt—

GEORGE

They aren't even open.

BERTRAND'S NEURORCH

—dodontshoothahameflop—

COTTIMI

It's not him, it's the neurorch. He's made the neurorch
talk.

BERTRAND'S NEURORCH

    –gobblegobblefela–

ZERLINA

    It's disgusting. You're all disgusting. (*She runs weeping from the stage.*)

BERTRAND'S NEURORCH

    –blagobblewawantoliveoojawop–

COTTIMI

    He's done it. Did you hear that? He's done it. This changes everything.

In an ecstasy of enthusiasm, Cottimi fires the gun in the air. It goes off with a deafening report and Bertrand collapses in a faint. The bullet passes through a rope in the flies, causing the curtain to fall.

It is later the same day. The curtain has been opened again. Cottimi, Fela, Bertrand and Paul are sitting on stage. Bertrand is lying on a chaise longue, with a damp towel across his forehead.

GEORGE

    (*Entering*) She's still resting. Margaret's looking after her.

FELA

    I want to talk to her.

COTTIMI

    Best not, Fela. Let her calm down.

BERTRAND

    Calm down? I don't think I'll ever calm down. My nerves are shattered. You weren't really going to shoot me, were you?

COTTIMI

    Let's just stay I'm glad I didn't. You, Bertrand, have managed to do what they said could never be done. But why shouldn't it? If the neurorch can produce music at the moment you think of it, why shouldn't it

do the same with language? Synergise Corporation said
it would never happen. It *could* never happen. It's
taken you to make the breakthrough, Bertrand. You're
a genius.

BERTRAND

One tries one's best.

COTTIMI

This will revolutionise the theatre. Nothing's going to
be the same again. Think of it. Entire plays with the
cast never opening their mouths, communicating
through only their neurorchs. One subconscious
talking to another. Think of the depth. And think of
the mental discipline it'll need.

FELA

Don't you think all this is a bit dangerous?

COTTIMI

Dangerous? Of course it's dangerous. This is the
theatre.

FELA

No, I mean when people out there get to hear about
this. Have you thought about the political
implications? The neurorch makes it possible to listen
to what people are thinking. You can force people to
say what they're thinking. Have you thought about
how it could be used as an instrument of political
control?

COTTIMI

Don't be boring.

*There is a sound of breaking glass and a roar from the crowd
outside.*

COTTIMI

What the hell's happening out there? See? I've got
enough to think about without your fantasies, Fela.
Go and have a look what's going on. (*Exit Fela.*) How

are you feeling, Bertrand? Ready for another go with the neurorch? You've got to work on this. We've all got to work on it.

PAUL

Do I take it that there's no longer going to be music in this production, that it's going to be some sort of play rather than an opera? If so, I might as well leave now.

COTTIMI

Paul, what are you talking about? Opera? Play? What does it matter what you call it? Who needs categories? This is theatre.

FELA

(*Entering*) The carabinieri are trying to clear the piazza. The crowd's throwing stones at the theatre.

COTTIMI

Now what?

FELA

Ask some of them in here. Talk to them.

COTTIMI

Okay. Can you arrange it?

FELA

I'll try. Some of them used to be my friends.

Fela goes offstage and the others wait. Cottimi paces up and down; Bertrand lies back on the chaise longue, sighing occasionally; George tries once or twice to strike up a conversation with Cottimi, unsuccessfully. Paul retreats into a corner of the stage and puts on his neurorch. He wears headphones, so that nobody else can hear the mind music that he is making and playing to himself.

At the end of about twenty minutes, Fela returns. With him come a group of about thirty young people. They stand at the back of the stage, rather like an opera chorus, looking around them with varying mixtures of antagonism and curiosity. About half of them are African, Afro-Caribbean or Afro-European. The others are white, Arab and Indian.

309

Overlaid upon this, and expressed in clothes, hairstyles and body language, a number of cultural tribes are represented: soul-boys, skin-sisters, white-rastas, bhangra-victims.

The members of the cast stare back at them. Paul has taken off his neurorch, and Bertrand has lifted the towel from his face and is sitting up on the chaise longue to look at the new arrivals.

A copper-coloured woman — tall, with a round face, cropped hair, black-rimmed glasses and chic black clothes — steps forward from the group. She reads from a piece of paper.

AMA

> My name is Ama. I have been elected by the People's Forum for Free Access to the Neurorch to read this prepared statement of our positions and demands.

She looks up from the paper for a moment, to check that the members of the cast have registered this. She is nervous, which serves to highlight the tone of defiance in her voice. Bertrand, sitting regally on the chaise longue, is stroking his chin meditatively with his hand and looking at Ama in a superior manner, as though assessing the performance of a rival actor.

AMA

> One. The neurorch is an instrument of liberation for all peoples — black and white, male and female, gay and straight. The neurorch is an instrument for celebrating our diverse identities. Let the rainbow shine forth.
>
> Two. The neurorch has been the target of attacks and manipulation by those who wish to stem or tame the tide of liberationist energy that it has unleashed. The racist and repressive European authorities have tried to ban its use on the streets. The racist European art establishment has attempted to imprison it within the context of the discourses of traditional hierarchical

and linear European art forms. They have thus attempted to reify it and turn it into an art-object that is fixed by the gaze of an audience. It is thus alienated from the people to whom it rightfully belongs.

Three. We the people refuse to play the role of Other in racist and patronising aesthetic mind-games.

Four. The neurorch is the intellectual property of all peoples. The Synergise Corporation have no right to exploit it for profit. Neurorchs should be manufactured by the public authorities and be available free and on demand.

Five. All laws restricting the use of neurorchs should be withdrawn.

Six. The sole exception to this is that the use of neurorchs should be banned in circumstances where it is treated as an object of paid-for entertainment. The neurorch should not be imprisoned within the dualities of spectator and spectacle, nor must it become just another item on the shelves of that consumerist supermarket called Western Culture.

Seven. Production of the opera *Mindmusic* should cease immediately. Instead, the theatre should be given over to an ongoing festival of popular vibrations and people's music. This festival will have no structure or goal.

Eight. We the people note the participation in the production of the opera *Mindmusic* of the singer Fela Lahbib, and express our sadness and anger that a brother has allowed himself to be seduced by the European art establishment into cutting off his roots and betraying his brothers and sisters.

Nine. We the people note the leading part played in the production of the opera *Mindmusic* by the theatre director Frank Cottimi. This man is a pillar of the European art establishment. We demand that Cottimi apologise to the people for his abuse of the neurorch.

Ten. We the people also note the part played in the production of the opera *Mindmusic* by the composer Paul Clearwater. This man is a composer of European art music. We also note that he is the son of Daniel Clearwater, who assisted the notorious European architect Miles Milstein in the designing of this city. We demand that Paul Clearwater brings his father here to answer to the people for his actions in helping to build this Eurocentric, racist city.

These are the ten positions and demands of the People's Forum for Free Access to the Neurorch.

BERTRAND

(*Applauding*) Bravo!

FELA

(*Angrily*) Is there anything else you'd like, Ama? Perhaps you'd like us to line up and kiss your arse?

AMA

(*Smiling at him*) You're getting the right idea, Fela.

Cottimi strides into the space between the demonstrators and the members of the cast. Attention focuses on him. He paces up and down, looking at the demonstrators, sizing them up as though blocking a crowd scene in one of his productions. Then he stops in front of the demonstrators, holding their attention, and, in a dramatic gesture, flings his arms wide open, as though embracing them.

COTTIMI

I accept all your demands. Paul, could you persuade your father to come here tonight to talk to these good people?

PAUL

Maybe. He likes an argument.

COTTIMI

Good. People, come back here tonight at nine, and

we'll hear some recantations. What you've said has
made me think.

*The demonstrators are surprised by this. They look
uncomfortable, uncertain how to respond. They whisper
together, then Ama steps forward again.*

AMA

Okay. We'll come back tonight to hear what you have
to say. But the picket remains. And Fela Lahbib had
better be here to answer the charges against him.

COTTIMI

He'll be here.

AMA

Okay then.

The demonstrators leave.

FELA

What the fuck is going on? Are you just giving in to
these people?

COTTIMI

I'm thinking, okay? I need time to think. And while I
think, you people have work to do. Where have those
women got to? George, go and fetch them. (*Exit
George.*)

FELA

You mean we're going to rehearse? But you told them
that you'd agreed to their demands.

COTTIMI

Fela, why must you create problems all the time? The
show must go on.

*George returns with Margaret and a red-eyed subdued Zer-
lina.*

313

COTTIMI

Right, ladies, now that the excitement's over, let's do
some work. Zerlina, Bertrand, I want the duet at the
beginning of Act II. Bertrand, put your neurorch on. I
want more mind-language.

BERTRAND

On condition that there are no guns this time. My
nerves are shot to pieces. Never in all my years in the
theatre –

COTTIMI

Shut up and get to your position. Paul, give us some
harpsichord.

*Bertrand sighs and takes up his position at the writing table.
Zerlina goes into the wings.*

COTTIMI

When you're ready. Neurorch on, Bertrand.

BERTRAND'S NEURORCH

–huhusixteenthojawooseventeeninety
wohulakingsaplonooweddingoobablngng–

BERTRAND

It's no good. This is impossible.

BERTRAND'S NEURORCH

–ngwhaxupokuchajuji–

Cottimi, deep in thought, merely waves him on impatiently.

BERTRAND'S NEURORCH

–boopoomusicagagazupsilencedong
jabbafelagrriimoneyheaholooxiahungrybangbang–

ZERLINA

(*Entering tentatively, unsure of her cue*)
Are you all right? You're looking tired, sir –
So thin and drawn. I wouldn't want to stir

Trouble, sir, but perhaps you ought to know
That Joseph's got designs upon your dough.

BERTRAND'S NEURORCH

—gobblegrrrangangchuchutrustservant—

ZERLINA

The man's not worth such naive affection.

BERTRAND'S NEURORCH

—whrummplablaherection—

ZERLINA

(*To Cottimi*) I'm not carrying on with this.

COTTIMI

(*Distractedly, angrily*) Damn it, just get on with it.

ZERLINA

(*Delivering the lines sullenly, mechanically*)
He's been seeing the king's secretary
About the king's commission. Oh, he's been very
Fly about fleecing you on the sly,
And now his finger's firmly in the pie.

BERTRAND'S NEURORCH

—pilizwukudoknowharmeebee—

ZERLINA

I too was briefly captured by his charm —
But no more. I'm free, and now the time
Has come to raise the curtain on his crime.

BERTRAND'S NEURORCH

—yafladontcaremommisilencekakaka—

ZERLINA

It's hopeless. You won't listen to a thing.
I'll have to take the matter to the king.

COTTIMI

(*Leaping up dramatically*) That's it! That's the answer.
Right, rehearsal over. I've got things to do. I want
everyone back here at eight. Paul, you go and see your
father. Get him to come this evening. It should be
quite a party.

315

PAUL

What are you doing, Frank?

COTTIMI

What do you think I'm doing, Paul? I'm doing what I
always do. I'm riding the tiger. (*Exit*)

*Zerlina goes offstage with Margaret. George follows them.
Only Paul and Fela are left onstage. Paul sits down at the
harpsichord, switches on his neurorch, and begins to play
both harpsichord and neurorch. Fela listens for a minute or
two, then interrupts him.*

FELA

You're beginning to like this neurorch machine.

PAUL

(*He stops playing*) I was very struck by what you said
about it, about how it might be possible to play it, but
it would take a long time to learn how.

FELA

You think you'd like to learn?

PAUL

Yes.

FELA

Good luck. And what about *Mindmusic*? Did you
mean what you said to Cottimi about leaving?

PAUL

Yes. I don't know what's going to happen with the
production now – but whatever it is, I don't think it'll
have much to do with music. There's no reason for me
to stay.

FELA

I think Cottimi's playing a dangerous game. That's
how he likes to operate. You're right, it has nothing to
do with music. I think I may leave the production too.
There's no place for me here now. I only carried on

because I was in love with Zerlina. Now that's all gone wrong.

PAUL

There's something I ought to tell you –

FELA

What?

PAUL

It's about Zerlina.

FELA

What about her?

PAUL

I think I know why things have been strained between you and her.

FELA

Tell me. What is it?

PAUL

Cottimi spread a rumour that you were having an affair with Bertrand.

FELA

That's ridiculous. Zerlina would never believe that.

PAUL

He got Margaret to convince her. He forged a letter. He's manipulated everyone very cleverly. He didn't want you and Zerlina getting too intimate. He said he didn't want you to be distracted from the production, but I think he really wanted Zerlina for himself.

FELA

Distracted? I'll distract him. The man's a devil. Thank you for telling me, Paul. I must find Zerlina.

PAUL

And I suppose I'd better see if my father will come down here.

It is eight o'clock that evening. A large television screen has been wheeled onstage. Cottimi, Paul, Fela, Zerlina, Margaret, George and Bertrand, along with Paul's mother

317

and father, are watching it intently. Fela and Zerlina are standing together, slightly apart from the others, holding hands. Paul's mother — tall, with bird-like features — is dressed, daringly, in a full-length fur coat. Paul's father, who is hunched, small-featured and wild-haired, has been given a chair, and rattles his walking stick between his knobbly knees as he watches the television.

It is the news.

NEWSCASTER

The New Venetian Municipal has banned use of the neurorch and ordered that all the machines should be handed in. The decision follows reports reaching the Municipal of an incident in which a neurorch produced words rather than just sounds. A spokesperson for the Municipal, explaining the decision, said that it was being made in the interests of civil liberties. She said that the development had important implications for the freedom and privacy of the individual. A spokesperson for Synergise Corporation has said that the company plans to contest the Municipal's decision in the European court at the earliest opportunity.

The European parliament is meeting at this moment to consider calls for a European-wide ban on the neurorch. The Speaker's Committee is meeting with representatives of the devolved regions to see if the ban could be implemented under existing Movement of Technology statutes.

The General Assembly of the United Nations has gone into emergency session to discuss the matter —

Cottimi switches off the television, and there is a buzz of conversation around the group. Banging is heard outside. Cottimi goes offstage, and returns with Ama and the other

318

demonstrators. There are more of them this time, about fifty.
They almost fill the stage.

COTTIMI

This is your meeting, Ama. Who do you want to speak
first?

AMA

(*She looks around, and her eyes fix on Paul's father*)
Daniel Clearwater, architect of this Eurocentric, racist
city. Let him speak first and explain himself.

PAUL'S MOTHER

Before my husband speaks, I'd like to say a few words
on his behalf. My husband and Milstein have come in
for an awful lot of very unfair criticism over New
Venice. May I remind you people that elitism is
merely the acknowledgement of that which is best. You
people are just jealous because you are mediocre. You
want to pull everyone down to your own pathetic level.
That's all I have to say.

AMA

Is that your view as well, Daniel Clearwater?

PAUL'S FATHER

No, it most certainly is not. (*He rises painfully from his
chair and hobbles to the centre of the stage.*) Six
months ago my daughter Jean went off to America. I
think some of you young people knew her. (*He looks
at the demonstrators, and some of them nod.*) I have
not been a good father, and I have not been a good
socialist. Jean is a great believer in the neurorch. Like
you, she thinks it is an instrument of liberation and
revolution. We had many arguments on the subject.
When she left us, I tried to make sense of what she
believed. I did so both as a father and a socialist. My
colleague Miles Milstein died recently. He will be
regarded as an enemy by many of you. But for all the
faults in his thinking – faults that I have come to

319

recognise – he was a socialist to the end. He kept the faith. Milstein once said to me. 'We must be emotional in our analyses and analytical with our emotions.' It was in that spirit that I tried to make sense of Jean's departure.

I have come to understand more clearly what it was she believed in. And through that understanding, I came to question my own socialism. The mistake that Milstein and I made was in believing that socialism could be built from above, that the revolution could be set in motion from above. We had lost sight of the vital fact that socialism must be built on faith in the people, and that revolution must be set in motion from below, by the people. In our defence, I can only say that, having grown up in the darkest days of socialism, we had become cynical and impatient. We had lost faith in the people's capacities. In that respect we were not good socialists.

We thought we were building the city of the future here. But it was just another prison, another restriction on the natural capacities of the people. To you young people I say, 'Tear it down! Have done with it.' I'm on your side. The history of socialism is littered with missed opportunities, with old campaigners like myself who have looked the other way when something happens to bring society to the brink. Up the neurorch, I say. Up the revolution!

There is an embarrassed silence at the end of Daniel Clear-water's speech. The old man is still waving his walking stick defiantly. There is some whispered conversation among the demonstrators, then Ama steps forward.

AMA

We accept Daniel Clearwater's recantation. We call on Fela Lahbib to speak next. We demand that he answer the charge that he has been seduced by the racist European art establishment into betraying his brothers and sisters.

FELA

(*Stepping forward to face the demonstrators*) You won't get any apologies or recantations from me, (*sarcastically*) 'brothers and sisters'. The game you're playing has nothing to do with liberation and everything to do with control. But look around and ask yourselves who is controlling who in this game. It's not me who's the victim here. I want nothing to do with your skin-colour games. This neurorch machine is ugly and dangerous. They're right to want to do away with it. As a musician, I have no use for it. This is all I need. (*He holds up the case that contains his kora.*)

COTTIMI

So what are you going to do?

FELA

I'm going home.

ZERLINA

And I'm going with him. You're a cruel, clever man, Cottimi. You can go to hell.

They leave the stage together. One or two of the demonstrators make to stop them, but Ama waves them away.

COTTIMI

May I speak now, Ama?

AMA

Go ahead.

COTTIMI

You've heard from Daniel Clearwater how he's changed his views. Well, I've changed mine. I acknowledge that I've misused the neurorch. I renounce opera. It's a racist, Eurocentric art form. I

321

can see now that the neurorch should be an instrument of revolution and liberation, not a means of propping up clapped-out, archaic art forms.

We have reached a turning point, friends. An historic moment. The revolution starts here, in this theatre. What could be more appropriate? Revolution is the highest form of political theatre. We're on the same side, you people of the street and we people of the theatre. Together we can be historical actors. We can make street theatre.

You've all heard the news. The authorities want to take the neurorch away from us. They're scared of it. They're scared because it's talking, it's telling the truth. These people are scared of the truth. We've got to fight them. They'll be here soon to try to take our neurorchs away from us. Will we resist? (*Stirrings among the crowd; shouts of 'Yes', 'Resist'.*) Let's do it then. Put up the barricades!

The stage explodes into activity. People are running about, gathering material to form barricades. The harpsichord is kicked over with a resonant crash and pushed offstage. Bertrand's chaise longue is swept off into the wings. The crowd spills off the stage into the stalls and begins ripping up the seating. The wooden armrests make clubs which they test by smacking them against their palms.

Cottimi seems to be everywhere at once – helping to heave a trunk of props against a door, yelling orders, organising a team to secure the front of house. As he runs downstage, he bumps into Paul, who is making his way offstage.

COTTIMI

Where are you going?

PAUL

I'm leaving. Fela's right – this is no place for a musician.

COTTIMI
     Your choice. What's that under your jacket?
PAUL
     My neurorch.
COTTIMI
     (*He laughs*) You'll never get it out of here.

At that moment, there is a squeal of carabinieri sirens and whistles outside. Shouting. Glass breaking.

PAUL
     It was you that told the Municipal about the neurorch, wasn't it?
COTTIMI
     (*Smiling*) Like I said, I'm riding the tiger.

They look into each other's eyes for a moment, then there is a surge of noise from outside. Paul runs off, clutching the neurorch under his jacket. Cottimi returns to directing the erection of the barricades. Suddenly, the lights go out. Mayhem. The sound of breaking glass, and a rush of flame across the stage. The curtain comes crashing down.

V

Paul Daniel Clearwater b.15/5/2030 d.19/9/2099. Composer. Came to public attention at an early age with his operas *Ulysses* (2059) and *The Crooked Timber of Humanity* (2063). Also composed vocal, choral and orchestral music. He was Musical Director for the projected New Venetian stage show *Mindmusic*, which was at the heart of the 'Neurorch Affair' in 2065. He disappeared from public view in that year, and is not thought to have composed again.

I'd never have known about it if Sally hadn't brought the *New York Times* when she came over with the baby. When she'd gone, I spent a long time just thinking, remembering people and places. I told Helen about the obituary notice, but she wasn't very interested, which I suppose wasn't too surprising. It was a long time ago and she never even met the guy.

There's a big chest of drawers in my studio where I keep old sketches. I began going through one of the drawers, but it was in a hopeless muddle. There was one drawing in particular that I wanted to find. The best drawing I ever did. I thought I was getting close to it when I found a little scrap, a pencil drawing of a man leaning against a mantelpiece. It was a bit hasty – the body was just a couple of suggestions – but I'd gone to particular trouble to try and get a likeness of the face, a long-jawed face with a moustache that looked like a pair of thin gull's wings trying to take off from it. Underneath it I'd written: 'Freeman Du Cros. Patricks' soirée 6/8/75.' I thought the drawing I was looking for might be underneath it, but there were only some things from a student life class. I'll just have to keep looking.

A first memory of Wellfleet: we're standing in a group on the pier. Below us a body hangs from a rope. The wind that's blowing off the sea catches the corpse's coat, causing it to flap wildly. The body swings backwards and forwards, and every four seconds or so its shoes strike one of the pillars and there's a hollow BOOM BOOM. The noise is loud, as though the corpse is kicking the pillar in annoyance and frustration. The mood among the group of people above is jocular and breezy, the mood of people who know they are being paid good money to stand around in the sunshine doing nothing. Helen's going through some papers with the director, a handsome man with a clipped moustache and camel-hair coat. She's new to the job, a bit nervous, and he keeps cracking jokes and putting his hand on her shoulder. Standing with them is a stocky man wearing a straw boater. He's got no neck. This is Johnny Hunter, the manager of the pier. He's chuckling at the director's jokes at the same time as keeping a sharp eye on what Helen's making of the papers. The camera crew have started fooling about with the body, pulling on the rope to make it kick the pillar some more.

A second glance and you can tell the body's not real. For a start, the wide-brimmed hat that it's wearing to hide the face would have blown off by now if it hadn't been glued on. They're filming another costume drama, another whodunnit as stuffed with ridiculous plot complications and 'period detail' as a horsehair sofa. It's Helen's first week in the job, and already this is the second crew she's had to deal with. The town relied so much on the income from filming that an application was never turned down, but still Helen had to go through the paperwork on behalf of the authorities, checking that each Transfer of Technology Permit was in order and counting up generators, lights, cameras, microphones. That was how she spent most of her summer.

It was May '75. A career opportunity for Helen. 'Coastal Authorities. Department of Technology Transfer' read the sign on the frosted glass door of her poky seafront offices. Paperwork. Regulations. I think she was already bored with being a civil servant, already scared of going stale and becoming a bureaucrat. And this was the worst kind of civil servant's job, because the only positive thing you could do in it was to say no to people. She did say 'no' to begin with, but less as time went on. The political pressures from the town, and from higher up in the Coastal Authorities, were too great. She was there to enforce a set of regulations that no one believed in. The Transfer of Technology laws were fast becoming a fiction in Wellfleet, a legal net with so many loopholes that it was more hole than fabric. No wonder she was quickly disillusioned. Nobody really wanted her to do her job.

The decision to go to Wellfleet was something that happened slowly, from talking around the subject. I suppose there was an element of political idealism in it. For us, like most people of our generation, the Coast was a Good Thing. Even if you didn't actually live there and become a part of it, it was one of the things you believed in, the way once upon a time young idealistic people might have vaguely believed in socialism. Our friends envied Helen her new job. But that was politics, and politics has never interested me. As soon as I hear someone talk about politics, I hear a part of their brain switch off. Then the same part of my brain switches off. I don't like that.

I wanted to go to Wellfleet because of the light, and because of the things I'd heard about the town. It had a reputation as a rich, sealed-off kind of place, a place that had become so inbred and insular as to be above snobbery. The 'burghers of Wellfleet', as I'd heard them referred to, were said to surround themselves with a cocoon of Art, as a consolation and protection against the onslaughts of the modern world. Light and patronage. Though I wouldn't have admitted it to our politically correct friends (I don't think I admitted it in so many words to Helen), those were the reasons that I wanted to go to Wellfleet. Although I was supposedly just along for the ride, I think it was me that nudged us into deciding to go. I was only two years out of college then, and crazy about painting. At college I'd done mostly abstract work. I had a sense of form and colour, and my teachers tried to push me into design. But I didn't want to spend my life producing corporate logos. I wanted to paint, and I wanted to paint from life. When the possibility of moving to Wellfleet came up, something clicked in my mind and I thought of portraiture. Surely, I thought, there'd be a market for portraits among the 'burghers of Wellfleet'.

We had rooms on the seafront, above Mother Maria's Teashop. It was just like a dozen other places in the town – bulbous mahogany furniture, polished brass tea urns, and an impression of lace everywhere. The steam from the urns mixed with sea salt and gave everything a feel of matted dampness. The husband of the owner was a drunk, and he'd come home late at night to be greeted by her rapidly whispered protests. The food in Mother Maria's was exactly the kind of doughy stodge that you don't want to eat on a hot summer's day, but there was never any shortage of customers. At first, because of their costumes, I thought they were townspeople, genuine Wellfleet burghers. It was only later I realised that they were just visitors entering into the spirit of the place. The costumes were hired. The women were unused to the flounces, festoons and bustles on their dresses, and quite often from our flat above you'd hear the crash of falling crockery as they tried to manoeuvre between the closely packed tables. (In *A Guide to the Pleasures of Wellfleet Life* by Madeleine Patrick, I read that crinolines could be dangerous in high winds, because they could cause the unfortunate woman to spin round and round like a top. I always hoped to see this happen, and once or twice when it was breezy I followed groups of women from the teashop up on to West Hill. But I never got lucky.)

I have to think myself back into a different world to imagine what it was like when we first went to Wellfleet. This was before the children, before we emigrated. In retrospect it seems like an era of pure irresponsibility. I remember the good times we had in that flat above the teashop. There were big picture windows looking out on to the sea. When you flung them wide open, the whole flat would swim with the sound of the surf on the shingle and the clatter of horses' hooves and carriage wheels on the road below. The pier was right opposite our window, and all through the day the noise of the crowds would drift through the flat. Sometimes if things were slack in the afternoon Helen would shut up the office and come home for a while. Our bed was by the window, and when we made love there in the afternoon it was like making love in a crowd, in the open air.

I'd had cards printed before we got there – 'Malcolm Abrahams, Portrait Painter' – and I wrote the address of our flat on the back of them. I had them put up in shops and restaurants and left them lying about in the lobbies of the cavernous seafront hotels. I waited. Nothing happened. Two weeks passed without any response. I kept myself busy by sketching along the seafront. I particularly loved the view of the front below West Hill, from the beach. The light was unpolluted and brilliantly clear. The changes in tone were magnified by the sea. In fine weather, at noon, the rocks of the cliff were yellow ochre, and the grass on the ledges and overhangs vibrated against them in yellow-green. The whole scene was awash with light. Backed up against the cliffs, in contrast, were the whites and blacks of the villas and hotels. At sunset, with the low light across the water casting deep shadows, everything would be thrown across the spectrum. The rocks would shift to raw sienna, touched with yellow-orange, and the grass would intensify to blue-green. And then in dull or rainy weather it was different again, the colours neutralised with a wash of grey-blue. I made these notes in watercolour, then took them up to the flat to work on them in oils. I'd turned the kitchen into a studio. It was at the back of the flat, the window looking out on to a terrace of houses and above them the cliff. Light flooded through the flat from the front. I had some of my happiest hours painting in that back kitchen. Every now and then I'd wander through to the front and lean out of the window to breathe in the sea air, the light, the kaleidoscope of sound from the seafront crowds. I later sold those paintings for a lot of money. They were some of the best of my early works. But at the time I was just having fun. I had no hopes of selling them in Wellfleet, which was already saturated with scenic views of itself.

I did a portrait of Helen and showed it around the customers in the teashop, but without success. It was about that time that I realised that the burghers of Wellfleet weren't in the habit of dining at Mother Maria's. Then one afternoon I walked up the winding street away from the seafront to the streets where I'd been told they lived. The wealthiest houses were on the tops of the two hills, at the back of the Old Town. High up on the slopes of West Hill and East Hill were streets of free-standing villas commanding views of the sea, of the town below, of the pier, and of the coast stretching away in either direction. They were curiously still and quiet, these houses. Even on this warm day in early summer there were no doors or windows open, no children playing on the lawns, no comings or goings. The curtains were drawn. I'd brought some cards with me, to push through letterboxes, but once I was up there I thought better of it. Something made me think that the burghers of Wellfleet wouldn't take kindly to that kind of impertinence.

The only resident of Wellfleet whom I'd met to date — apart from the long-suffering owner of Mother Maria's — was Johnny Hunter, the manager of the pier. Helen had already had a few dealings with him over the film crews. As well as charging fees for filming on the pier itself, he acted as an agent for Wellfleet Corporation, negotiating the fees that were paid by the crews for working anywhere within the town limits. These fees were pretty steep, so Hunter worked hard at keeping the film companies happy. That meant putting pressure on Helen to speed up the Technology Transfer Permits. According to her, there was a ruthless brain at work underneath that straw boater.

From everything I'd heard about Johnny Hunter, he didn't seem a likely art-lover. But he was the only chance I had of getting a foot in the door of that closed Wellfleet world. So I called on him in his office at the end of the pier. I placed my portrait of Helen on his desk and asked him if he'd be interested in one of himself.

'I've always wanted to ask one of you fellows,' he said, with the air of a man who believes in getting straight down to business, 'what makes you think you can do better than a photograph? We've got a first-class photography booth here on the pier. Choice of backdrops, sepia prints. It took a hell of a job getting *that* past your wife's predecessor. Now if I wanted a picture of myself, I'd go there. What have you got to offer that a photographer hasn't got?'

'Isn't it obvious?' I said. 'The camera's just a machine. It's got no intelligence or imagination. The human eye can see things that the camera can't.'

Johnny Hunter gave me a sceptical smile. 'That's all very well,' he said. 'But the camera never lies.'

It was clear that I was going to get nowhere with him. I picked up my picture and was about to go, when he said, 'Hold on a moment. My assistant might be interested. Charlie Hawker's much more cultured than me.' He grinned, then shouted through to the office next door: 'Charlie? Can you spare a minute?'

The man who appeared in the doorway was extraordinary. He was well over six foot tall, slightly built, with a head that was vastly out of proportion to the rest of his body. His large moon-face was almost white, with faint rings of bluish grey under each eye. The hair was jet black and slicked down on to his scalp. The nose was long and slightly bulbous at the end. The mouth was tiny by comparison, and twisted into a pained, fastidious smile. He was quite beautiful, in a strange way. I knew immediately that I had to paint him, whether he'd pay me or not.

Hunter explained what it was all about. Charlie Hawker nodded at me, came forward from the doorway and looked down at my picture. 'Exquisite,' he said quietly. He had a high-pitched voice. 'Quite delightful.'

I think at first I saw Hunter and Hawker as some sort of eccentric double-act. It was easy to treat everything as a stage show in Wellfleet. Johnny Hunter played the blunt, bluff businessman, while Charles Hawker impersonated the half-reluctant acolyte, pained by his employer's crassness. But Wellfleet wasn't just a film set – it was a place made and inhabited by real people. The eccentricities of Hunter and Hawker were stagey, like those of the other Wellfleet people I came to meet. But that visible surface was animated by a depth, an invisible reality that was causing it to surge into being. It was like light, which is invisible except through the material surfaces that it brings to visibility. As my own painting progressed, and I learnt to read the shifting light that played across the town, I felt myself enter another world, a world of light and shadow, the world behind the costumes and the curtained windows of the hilltop villas.

Yesterday I went through the second drawer and found two sketches of Charlie Hawker. Neither of them pay much attention to that strange face. I remember that when I did those sketches I was more concerned with finding the right setting. One of the sketches has him sitting in his office, one long leg folded over the other, holding a piece of paper in his hands. A conventional businessman's pose. The other sketch shows how I finally had him. There was a conservatory in one of the seafront hotels, and it's there that Charles Hawker stands, against a jungle of ferns, rubber plants and palm fronds. He's wearing his top hat and black leather gloves. His black woollen overcoat is buttoned to the chest, and he leans elegantly on his cane-topped umbrella. The swirls of green behind set off the black outlines of hat, umbrella and coat, edged with brilliant white at collar and cuff. Between these rigid forms, and against the vegetation, the pale oval of his face floats like something unreal, a ghost peering out from between brilliant greens and brilliant blacks. Of course there was humour in it too. Hawker always looked like a hothouse flower, and I liked the idea of having him buttoned up against that tropical vegetation.

The thing about portrait painting is that people tell you things. It doesn't take them long to get over that first self-consciousness, and then something strange happens. You, the painter, disappear. They think they're in front of a mirror. They start talking to themselves. Perhaps it's different for other painters — I never chat to my sitters to make them feel comfortable. I've noticed that if I do say anything, it only serves to remind them that I'm there. From my point of view, I'd just as soon work in silence. But I guess it's boring for them to sit in silence, doing nothing. So they start telling you things.

Charlie Hawker started with his boss. He had a wife and children, but Johnny Hunter was the beginning of his world, the surface that he presented me with as I pencilled in my first outlines. He talked about Hunter eagerly, in that role of respectfully disapproving acolyte that I had already given him. By our second sitting he was taking me into his confidence, telling me about Hunter's sharp business practices. His voice had the kind of delighted disbelief that children have when they're describing adults misbehaving. He began telling me things that he shouldn't have done, shattering that impregnable double-act. It was then that I first heard the name Paul Clearwater.

335

There had been a long silence, and Charlie Hawker had broken it in that abrupt, quick way of his, his tiny mouth flicking open and shut, twitching sideways into nervous, appeasing smiles.

'Do you remember that film crew we had on the pier a couple of weeks ago?' he said.

I grunted my assent, not wanting to shatter the mirror into which he gazed with just a hint of arrogant confidence, leaning on his cane-topped umbrella.

'It reminded me of one of Johnny's escapades.' He gave a light, gunfire laugh. 'I probably shouldn't be telling you this.'

I said nothing.

'It was the noise of that dummy swinging against the pier. About ten years ago, we had a composer living in the town, name of Clearwater. Pushy kind of fellow. He tried to organise a series of concerts on the pier – something to do with raising money for the fishermen. Johnny took against him right from the start. Dear me, did he have that fellow Clearwater's balls for breakfast! Like a fool, Clearwater signed a contract agreeing to pay two-thirds of the rental for the series up front. Then I discovered that Johnny had double-booked. "Look here," I said. "If that fellow Clearwater gets his subscriptions, we're going to be in hot water." "Don't you worry, Charlie," he says, cool as a cucumber. "He won't get the subscriptions." I knew he was plotting something, the old fox. The first night of Clearwater's concert series it was blowing a gale. Of course not even Johnny could have planned that, but he sure as hell knew how to use it. Early in the evening, before anybody arrived, he got one of those decorator's platforms and dropped it over the edge of the pier, right under the ballroom. The wind got stronger. The concert had hardly got going when that thing starts swinging backwards and forwards against one of the pillars. Boom! Boom! The whole pier shook. We were sitting in the office and Johnny was practically wetting himself with laughing so much.

336

'In the interval of the concert this Clearwater fellow comes dashing into the office to complain about the noise. Johnny quickly pulls himself together and starts cursing the decorators and saying he'll do something about it. Clearwater goes back to his concert and Johnny does something about it all right. He was worried that the wind was dropping, so he goes out there and starts swinging the bloody thing by hand! That Clearwater fellow didn't get his subscriptions.'

'What happened to him?' I asked.

'He did a runner. But old Johnny still came out on top. The Corporation was so pleased to get rid of this Clearwater fellow, who'd been causing a bit of trouble in the town, that they agreed to pay Johnny compensation for what Clearwater owed him, plus money "for the inconvenience caused". No flies on Johnny Hunter. "For the inconvenience caused"!' Hawker laughed again at the memory.

He talked with a mixture of crudity and refinement that was typical of Wellfleet. The town was built on polite brutality. There was something authentically pre-twentieth century about that. There was no liberal guilt, no ideological anxiety, no moral self-consciousness. A man could kick his servant, then sit down at his piano to play a sonata. The contradictions and bad faith of the place were so transparent that they could scarcely be repressed. Instead they had been ingested, had entered the fabric of the town. True cynicism requires a sense of strangeness, a self-consciousness and distancing of oneself from oneself. Here it was so commonplace that it had become a kind of naivety. The elite of Wellfleet looked down from their villas and sneered at the visiting crowds who both spoilt the view and made the town possible. They could complain about them without a hint of a smile. Irony was so debased a currency in Wellfleet that it had fallen out of use.

Hawker was at the hinge of the town's bad faith. He faced two ways. One side of him looked out at the pier, at Johnny Hunter, and at the summer crowds streaming through the turnstiles. The other faced inward, towards the villas on the

337

hills. He liked talking about the burghers, about parties and balls and soirées to which he hadn't been invited. He tossed names about. I was keen to get introductions and commissions, but when I asked Hawker for his help, he became evasive. He didn't know those people as well as he made out. On the other hand, even when he talked about the people in the villas there was a laugh and sneer in his voice, just like the laugh and sneer when he talked about Hunter. He faced both ways. He and Hunter, after all, made their money as much from the burghers as they did from the tourists. They were gatekeepers between two worlds.

As my portrait of Hawker progressed, that impregnable double-act that he and Hunter had seemed to present gradually broke down. I began to see shadows, differences of tone, patterns of contrasting colour. Without losing his stagey quality, Hawker had become three-dimensional, almost tactile. It was as though an actor had invited you up onstage and allowed you to walk around him and touch him while he worked, to appreciate the reality of his falseness. I felt myself enter the world of Wellfleet.

But I'm jumping ahead. During those first weeks the portrait painting was still only a small part of our life there on the Coast. Above all we were having fun. It was hard to be serious about anything in that summer sunlight. We swam from Wellfleet's unpolluted beaches. At night we'd walk up through the narrow streets and eat by candlelight at one of the town's small restaurants. Outside it was incredibly peaceful. There was no traffic, of course. The only sound was of people walking, and now and then a horse going by. We succumbed to the magic of the Coast.

'We succumbed to the magic of the Coast.' You see, already I start sounding like an article in a travel magazine. But that was what it was really like. One night, I remember, Helen looked out of the window of the restaurant and said, 'Everywhere ought to be like this.' I remember agreeing with her. We believed in the Coast and we were happy.

Helen had gone through a kind of transformation since we'd arrived. She'd unwound. Ever since I'd known her she'd worried about things – intensely, fiercely. Nothing passed through her life without her pouncing on it and worrying about it. Sometimes she seemed to me like some small nervous animal – watching, waiting, ready to jump, giving herself no rest. And I loved her for it. I've always been scared of sloppy people (of sloppy *women*). I don't like people who slop on to you and slop off you again without caring or remembering, without *worrying*. Helen cared, tenaciously. And it wasn't that she lost that when we went to Wellfleet. It was just that the world seemed to relax around us, to fall back and open like a flower. Our horizons were wider.

Her job helped. Her first reaction when she realised that nobody really cared whether or not she did it properly was to worry about that. We sat up late one night discussing it. Perhaps we should never have come to Wellfleet. Perhaps she should try to change things, shake things up a bit, maybe start a campaign to get the Movement of Technology laws tightened. How long would the Coast keep its special magic without their proper enforcement? It was bad if you let things slip.

But in the morning we dropped the subject. Like I said, it was hard to be serious about things with that sunlight breaking on you. Helen began to accept that her job was a bit of a joke. She stopped worrying and started enjoying the fact that she could shut up the office in the afternoon and go swimming. I began to see a new side to her. Together we began to think that we'd discovered the good life. The simple life.

Things were turning out strangely. Before we went to Wellfleet, we'd joked about how she'd be doing the work and I'd just be along for the ride. Secretly we were both worried that I wouldn't be able to get work painting in Wellfleet. I felt guilty about it. But my portrait painting began to take off. Charles Hawker may not have been intimate with the *haute bourgeoisie* of Wellfleet, but he was able to give me a few names and make a few recommendations. I began to get work.

Hawker's friends came from a distinct strand of Wellfleet life. They were far enough up the social ladder to aspire to get further, yet far enough down to know what it would be like to fall. They were anxious people, gnawed by restlessness. Like Hawker, they tended to do jobs that faced both ways – to the inner world of Wellfleet and to the outside world beyond the Coast, the world that kept Wellfleet going and also threatened to ruin it. There was James Dunwoody, the assistant manager of the railway station. (The general manager himself was a part of Wellfleet's inner world.) Dunwoody was in charge of the daily running of the station, juggling the demands of visitors from beyond the Coast with the requirement to maintain the illusion of a nineteenth-century transport system. Then there was Mr Paul O'Casey, the Corporation's Chief Executive for Technology Transfer. You'd have thought that a man like that, holding the key to Wellfleet's very existence, would have been at the top of the social pyramid. But O'Casey was nowhere near the top. He got his hands dirty. He was the one who had to negotiate with water companies and gas companies, who had to know the specifications of generators and the length of time that an outside, non-Coastal construction unit would need to lay a new pipe. For the inner society of Wellfleet, all this stuff was necessary but unsavoury. Whoever did it would be well rewarded but openly despised.

Most of Hawker's other friends were the sergeant-majors of the hotel trade – assistant managers, catering managers and accountants – who took their orders from the hill-top villas. I went through another drawer in my studio today and found some sketches of them: Wilson Eddington of the Excelsior, a haughty underling who wore a permanent frown of dissatisfaction. I painted him in bold colours, staring out of the canvas with truculent scarlet-rimmed eyes. Lorraine

Griffiths, wife of the catering manager of the Astor, and a woman who had come to know her place. She was done in washed-out neutral tones. The list goes on. It was, of course, a man's world. That was another of those authentically pre-twentieth-century states to which they had returned.

It's a strange experience to look through those sketches now, to look back at Wellfleet from the madhouse of New York. Nobody knows their place here, or if they do it's only at the level of ideology and words – 'white liberal pluralist', 'radical lesbian separatist', 'black progressive integrationist', 'native American cultural conservative'. Abstractions float from mouth to mouth like enormous balloons. I suppose it was that kind of thing that Wellfleet was rebelling against. And I have a sneaking sympathy with that. After all, I have reason to be grateful to the place. I learnt to be a painter there.

To begin with, at least, I was the beneficiary of Wellfleet's concrete social codes. As my portraits began to appear on drawing-room walls, it became *de rigueur* for all Hawker's peers to acquire one. The difference between social success and social failure in Wellfleet could be that small. Work began to roll in. And that was how things began to pan out in a way we hadn't expected. It was Helen who began to have the holiday, and it was me who found myself working my way into the fabric of the town.

A family group. I found it yesterday in among some studies of skyscrapers I did when we first arrived in Manhattan. The little boy stands in front of his father, the girl sits on her mother's lap. The figures are strong but not well integrated. The mother-daughter and father-son pairs seem to form separate compositions. The relationship between them isn't clear. The father was Matthew Rimmer, who owned the stage-coach company. He was the most interesting of Hawker's circle of friends; if most of them faced two ways, Rimmer faced three. He was a reminder of a different older side to the Coast. The stage-coach company was not a thriving business.

*

A five-hour journey in a jolting draughty carriage was a bit too authentic for all but the most ardent enthusiasts of Coastal life. Rimmer lived with his wife and children in a house on the lower slopes of West Hill, not far from the Old Town cottages of the remaining fishermen. His house had some of the authentic privations that those further up the hill avoided by technical subterfuge and cosmetic architecture.

Rimmer was a true believer in the Coast. He was better educated than Hawker's other friends, but seemed to go along with their snobberies. Like everybody else in Wellfleet he was a troubled mixture, as changeable as the weather that moved swiftly off the sea and disappeared across the hills beyond. He was about fifty, older than Hawker and his friends, but he had a young wife and a young family. His gaunt, lined face wore a clipped goatee and round glasses. He always spoke with an impatient *emphasis*, as though he were forever having to contradict the world. He also suffered from melancholy. ('Melancholy.' It seems bizarre even to think of that word here. Has anyone ever suffered from melancholy in New York? Depression, yes. Suicidal desperation, for sure. But *melancholy*?) He made me think of some character from an old play – an embittered 'provincial' intellectual who has always longed to escape into the wider world but has never succeeded, and still rattles gloomily around the old town. But none of that was really true of Rimmer. He'd come to Wellfleet by choice when he was a young man. There was nothing stopping him leaving again for that wider world. If there was a small claustrophobic town, it was inside his head. He had a fine collection of books – William Morris, Edward Carpenter, Patrick Geddes, Paul Goodman – books that offered alternatives to what they saw as the madness of modern living. These were the books that he'd brought to Wellfleet – or rather, that had brought him to Wellfleet. He'd turned his book collection into an unofficial lending library for the fishermen, encouraging them to absorb the ideas that had helped inspire the original creation of the Coast. In his time he'd been something of a teacher and prophet in the Old Town, helping to keep the spirit of the Coast alive along the fishing beach. But at the same time he was the owner of a commercial enterprise that brought visitors into the town. That position made him different from the other true believers, the vascular old men who shuffled abstractedly through the streets of the Old Town and wore woollen socks under their sandals. Part of him faced the Old Town, but he also had two other faces – one turned towards the other owners, the burghers, and the other towards the world beyond that kept his coaches on the road.

Rimmer told me about the fishing community. A few years earlier, the Corporation had decided to build new sea defences. These extended the groynes in front of the main seafront, but not along the fishing beach. The beach in front of the hotels was built up and protected, but the fishing beach was being eroded. There had been a lot of opposition to this scheme at first, but in the end the Corporation had bought off the fishermen with cash compensation. Rimmer was still bitter at the way the fishermen had taken the money and sold out on their way of life. A few die-hards had moved to the small pockets along the Coast where life remained as it had once been envisaged. But most had left the Coast entirely. Only a handful were left on the dwindling beach, maintaining a token presence for the tourists and living off subsidies handed down by the burghers. Rimmer didn't lend his books out any more.

He was a businessman, a man of action. Mixed with his bitterness at the defeat of the fishermen was admiration for the way that the burghers had defeated them. And mixed with this admiration was a worry that he was a victim too. The kind of visitors who braved his stage coach were the kind who were attracted by the fishing beach. Now they might stop coming. Everything was twisted for Matthew Rimmer, pulled in three directions at once.

*

'You remember that dog of theirs?'

'What about it?'

'Bit through the wire of their videophone.'

'Christ. What happened?'

'It exploded. All its teeth came out, flew out the sides of its mouth.'

'Christ.'

'They had to have it put down. Vet said it'd need plastic surgery. Only they don't do plastic surgery on dogs.'

'Remember that dog when it was teething? Put your finger in its mouth and it'd practically have your arm off.'

I remember that scene vividly. Two young women sitting on the front, gazing out to sea. I walked on, drifting through the summer crowd, catching scraps from the sea of people that rose and fell around me. The crowd eddied along the front, gathered in a great swirl around the entrance to the pier. Sometimes I stopped and flicked open my sketchpad, seized for a moment by an old man's face, or by the stiffness of a woman's back as she leant over some railings, or the billow of a shirt open to the breeze.

'Be serious. They don't stand a cat's chance in hell.'

'I'm telling you. They're gonna win.'

'Come back Thursday morning. Look me in the face.'

Two men this time, eating fish from paper bags. They parted to let a stream of children through. I found it cleansing, after sessions with Hawker's friends, to plunge into the seafront crowds and swim aimlessly, watching splashes of colour surface and disappear as the people revolved endlessly. I'd heard that the Coastal Authorities had once been strict about things like dress. Now anything was allowed, no matter how modern. A clashing of styles and cultures. A clashing of purple T-shirt against the turquoise sea. A thousand voices flying round and round as though stirred up by the bars of hot hard sunlight. Children squinting upwards, holding their hands over their eyes until they could see their bones through their burning orange flesh. Someone jumped. A crash of shingle.

I felt a sense of relief when I left those stuffy sittings in the stuffy upholstered sitting rooms and went out into the seafront crowd. Sometimes I'd meet Helen coming out of her office, heading for the beach. I'd see Hawker, moving through the crowd like a black shark, a black shark with a white face under a black top hat. Then after a moment I'd see Hunter at his side, swaggering easily in white flannels that flapped around his ankles. Years ago, I'd been told, Johnny Hunter had been on the stage, a song-and-dance man. You could see it in the way he walked. They didn't notice me as they moved swiftly through the crowd towards their destination. A couple of sharks.

Once I was sitting further along the front in the late afternoon when two small boys, both about four or five, came wandering towards me, licking ice creams. They were lagging behind their parents.

'John?' said one of them, contemplating his ice cream. 'Are you a human being?'

There was a pause before the other answered. 'Nah,' he said. 'Don't be daft.'

In among dozens of etchings I did when we first came to New York – surreal, intricate cityscapes; Escher-like antheaps – I've come across two more Wellfleet sketches. They're both charcoal nudes. One is of an elderly couple, the other of Helen. In both cases they sit against some rocks, which fall against their backs in frozen jagged motion. Neither is very good. I'd tried to make the solidity of the bodies echo that of the rocks behind. They were bad imitations of Cezanne. But one of the sketches still has glue and scraps of binding along the top edge where I'd torn it quickly from the pad. Still stuck to the glue I found three grains of sand. Three grains of Wellfleet sand from twenty-four years ago. I'll put them in an eggcup to show Helen.

I remember doing those sketches at the beach beyond the East Hill cliffs. We'd been in Wellfleet for six weeks or so before we got to hear about that place. Because it was a nudist beach, most of Hawker's friends would pretend that it didn't exist. In the end it was Matthew Rimmer who told me about it. Nothing epitomised better the conflict between the 'old' and 'new' towns, between the original ideals of the Coast and the claustrophobic costume-drama that it had become.

The beach was in a wooded cove, at the bottom of a steep path. There were no roads nearby, so that anybody visiting it had a five- or six-mile round trip on foot. This deterred sightseers. The people who came to the cove were true believers. There were old men with nut-brown scrotums hanging slackly between their legs and leathery belly skin that folded thinly when they sat on the rocks, their knees drawn up, gazing with blue eyes at the blue sea. I saw an elderly woman run across the shingle like a child, lifting her legs with awkward, jerky movements. It was a good place to sketch.

For many years the Wellfleet Corporation had tried to have the cove fenced off and nude bathing banned on grounds of 'public decency'. There was opposition from the true believers in the Old Town, but the Corporation's defeat came when the Coastal Authorities determined that the Corporation didn't have jurisdiction that far along the coast. It fell within the neighbouring district, which encompassed several fundamentalist Coastal Villages that had a different political outlook. The nudist beach remained.

We grew to love the place that summer, and walked there three or four times a week. I was fit. I could swim for half-an-hour in the sea without stopping and then get out and feel the capacity of my lungs when I breathed, swing my arms back and feel the tension of my muscles. Like the couples from the Old Town, we lay in the long afternoon sun till we felt our bodies merge with the rocks, our eyes melt into the blueness of the sky. At sunset when we walked back to the town our minds were full of the emptiness of the waves pounding the shore. We were happy.

But there came a point where happiness became bliss, and bliss became a kind of void. We were stepping into a blue emptiness. And through all that emptiness, I found myself thinking about those villas up on the hills, and those rooms that I wanted to get into.

I was being frustrated. While commissions had come in from Hawker's circle, I'd been a beneficiary of Wellfleet's social codes. Now I began to be their victim. The commissions started to dry up. I'd done a couple of dozen portraits, been through most of Wellfleet's middle stratum. My name was known and people had seen my pictures on parlour walls. But to get more work I'd have to move up to the higher echelons. That was the problem. My name was associated with Hawker's circle. For anyone higher up to commission me would be to associate themselves with that lower level. It would be to take a deliberate step down the ladder. Here and now that may sound incredible. But then, in that place, these things were real. Style and distinction were the stuff of life. And I'd immersed myself in it, I'd become part of it. When we lay on the rocks – Helen beside me gazing out to sea, humming to herself some long blissed-out melody – my mind explored people and possibilities, unpicking Wellfleet's finely-tuned social mechanisms, trying to find a weak link, a point of entry. Perhaps Matthew Rimmer might be able to help? As an owner and employer he must have some connections. Then there was Wilson Eddington of the Excelsior. I'd heard it said that he was a trusted confidant of the Excelsior's owner, and had started his career as his butler. Or perhaps I should go back to Johnny Hunter and see if he could help.

I tried all these avenues, but none of them led anywhere. For two weeks, in July, I had no work. Then I got my break, and from an unexpected source. I received a letter, an excited, jubilant letter, from James Dunwoody, the assistant manager of the railway station. His boss, Stanley Blair, was leaving Wellfleet, and Dunwoody had been promoted. As a leaving present from the staff at the station, Dunwoody thought it would be 'delightful' (a favourite word in Hawker's circle) if I could paint Mr Blair's portrait. It would be a souvenir for him to take away from the Coast. I remembered Dunwoody. He'd struck me as one of the more unpleasant and snobbish of Hawker's friends. It crossed my mind that in hitting on this idea Dunwoody was having a malicious dig at his former boss, subtly suggesting that by giving up his post he had slipped down the social ladder.

An appointment was made, and I hauled my easel and paints up the hill to the station. I was to paint Stanley Blair in his office. There are no sketches from that commission in the drawers I've been through. But I do remember that the job posed particular problems, and that I solved them in unusual ways. The main difficulty was Stanley Blair himself. His face was squashy, with ill-defined features hidden behind a pair of large black-framed spectacles. I tried to persuade him to take these off, but he was having none of that. His only interesting point was a slightly protruding upper lip, which gave his mouth a permanent pouting curve. His large torso slumped inside a baggy morning suit.

I solved the problem of Stanley Blair by submerging him in his surroundings. Instead of painting him face on, like I'd done my other portraits. I had him in profile. The angle was just right to catch the tip of his lip. It was the most well-defined point of his body. He sat at his desk, and behind him was a window looking on to the station platform. People waiting for trains peered in through the grimy window to see what was going on. At first I found this distracting and irritating, but then I began to incorporate those disembodied, inquisitive faces into the painting. On the wall beside the window were maps of the Coast, and those 'olde' prints that you found everywhere in Wellfleet. I put those into the painting too.

Of course, I explained to Blair what I was doing, suggesting that it would be nice to have a reminder of where he had worked. He agreed without expressing any interest. For him, it seemed, the whole process was an irritation. He created all sorts of problems about sittings. He said his time was taken up with arrangements for his family's departure. He seemed to be in a hurry to leave Wellfleet.

Our first couple of sittings were conducted in complete silence. Blair had none of that nervous self-consciousness that my other subjects had had, and he showed no desire to chat. I, meanwhile, was thinking about colour. I've always preferred strong colours to pastel or neutral tones. That portrait of Blair is the only 'brown soup' painting that I've ever done. But there were special reasons for that. It was August and the temperature was in the high eighties. The windows of Blair's office were kept open, and when a train came into the station a cloud of steam and soot would billow down the platform and in through the windows. My palette was soon covered with a thin film of grey-black particles that were impossible to pick out. The soot dissolved quickly and muddied my oils. This drove me mad to begin with, but as with the faces at the window, I began to accept it and incorporate it into the painting. I began using the muddied neutralised pigments to represent the grimy steam of the trains. As the painting developed, Stanley Blair's unremarkable face began to be swallowed up by its setting, by the smoke, the faces at the window, the clutter of objects in the office. Only the small silhouette of his upper lip remained as a point of clarity.

Blair himself, meanwhile, was beginning to talk. I was happy to work in silence, but I was also keen that he should give me some contacts. After a couple of silent sittings I had given up on him talking of his own accord. I began to prod him with questions. I asked him how long he'd been living in

Wellfleet, whether he liked the place, what his plans were now. Normally, like I've said, whenever I speak it has the effect of making the sitter clam up. But with Blair it was different. He didn't exactly confide in me, but it was as though he was looking for the chance to talk. I got the feeling he had something he wanted to get off his chest.

He only really loosened up when I asked him why he'd come to the Coast. He'd brought his family to Wellfleet fifteen years before, he said. Before that he'd managed one of the Railway Heritage Lines. 'But I didn't just come here because of the steam trains. I also came here for the sake of the family. I wanted a decent, clean, old-fashioned place to bring up the children. I'm afraid I'm that kind of person – decent, clean and old-fashioned.'

'I don't see why that's anything to apologise for,' I said. (Well, you have to humour your clients.)

'You'd be surprised,' he said.

Later I got him to tell me more about what had attracted him to Wellfleet. 'I'm not a fan of the modern world,' he said. 'No values. No respect for what's good and beautiful. Everyone out for themselves and the devil take the hindmost.' He spoke in that stilted, stiff manner that I'd noticed Wellfleet people use. 'No sense of community. No sense of where people belong. Just anarchy and fashion. People making life up as they go along.' There was a controlled, explosive rage in his voice, a real bitterness that went beyond the sneering snobbishness that I'd heard from Hawker's friends when they talked about the summer crowds.

'So why are you going back there?' I asked. 'Why are you leaving Wellfleet?'

It was a question too far. He gazed fixedly out of the window at the faces bobbing about on the platform. 'I'd prefer not to talk about that,' he said.

This intrigued me. I wanted to keep him talking. I changed the subject and told him how Helen and I were enjoying swimming at the cove beyond East Hill. I asked him what he thought of the Coastal true believers in the Old Town.

'I don't go along with all that nudism and back-to-nature stuff,' he said. 'It's going too far. That's the trouble with people,' he said. 'They don't know when to stop. They go too far. They lack self-control.' Again that anger detonated under the surface.

Still hoping to get some contacts or introductions out of him, I asked him about the burghers. Du Cros, a former mayor of the Corporation, was one name I'd heard. It struck the right note with Blair.

'He was made mayor shortly after we came to the Coast,' he said. 'He was a decent enough chap then. Now, his wife I have a lot of time for. She has her head screwed on right. The town was quite a decent place when he was mayor. We used to have very nice concerts in the Everyman Theatre. Everyone used to come. They were family occasions. And concerts in the pier ballroom. But that was before the hoi polloi took over' – he nodded towards the station platform – 'thanks to the good offices of Mr Hunter. There were dances, balls, family entertainments – '

'It must have been a very cultured place,' I said.

'Yes, well you can have too much of a good thing, including culture.'

'I haven't noticed anything advertised at the Everyman,' I said. 'Are there still any concerts?'

Again it was a question too far. 'There have been changes in Wellfleet,' was all he would say, and then he clammed up.

I was enjoying the painting. I was beginning to find a kind of spontaneity. The oils were going on thickly, in grimy energetic swirls. The form of Blair's face could just be made out, peering defensively and uncertainly through the ever-moving murk. And all the time I led him gently back to the question that intrigued me. What had happened to make him want to leave?

But his desire to get whatever it was off his chest wasn't

strong enough. He saw my game. 'Is it usual,' he asked, 'for a painter to interrogate his subject?'

I said I was curious about the town.

'There are some things best left alone,' he said. 'People can go too far.'

And that was all I got out of him. Except that I did get an introduction. To my surprise, he liked the finished painting. 'Bit unusual,' he said. In his enthusiasm, he wrote a letter of recommendation that he said I could present to Mrs Barbara Du Cros, wife of former Mayor Freeman Du Cros. At last I'd broken through. I had a foot in the door.

There's a moment of doubt that a painter feels when his brush touches the canvas. What speed should his stroke be? How long should it be? How much pressure should he apply? This is the moment of creativity, the moment of doubt. The more doubt there is, the more creativity. (That's why I don't like politics. Politics is about certainties. Painting is about doubt.) At that point in Wellfleet, for the first time, I began to feel the excitement of that abyss opening up below me. It's hard to put into words. It's as though each stroke were opening up canyons ahead, throwing lines across that kept you going but never let you rest. To put it another way, I was beginning to realise what can be done with a paintbrush.

It was a time of discovery for Helen too. We'd met when I was at art college and she was at university. We moved in together. Three years later I was still bumming around, half-heartedly applying for design jobs, and Helen was in the civil service fast track. I used to tell her that 'fast track' was a good name for it – a moving walkway that was hurtling you forward into a future without giving you the chance to stop and think about it. It looked as though our lives were going in different directions and at different speeds. Helen was working twelve high-pressure hours a day, and I was sitting at home wishing I could be a painter and nurturing my resentment against that big wide world out there that didn't want anything of me. We had rows. I said she was becoming hard and conventional. She said I was being adolescent. I began to suspect that she suspected I was scrounging off her. It was that kind of situation.

Maybe if Wellfleet hadn't happened we'd have gone our separate ways. For Helen it was supposed to be a little loop on the fast track, something to give her hands-on experience of the Movement of Technology laws before being put back into the centre of things. Only in the case of Wellfleet, like I've said, it was mostly hands-off. Helen found herself bobbing about for a few months in this backwater of the European civil service, and it gave her time to think. Slowly she began to sort out her priorities. She began to realise that she'd taken a wrong turn.

But I'm jumping ahead again. Those things didn't crystallise until after I'd met Paul Clearwater. In August she was still unwinding, and I was taking my first steps into that enormous world that opens up when the tip of your brush touches a canvas. At the same time, I was beginning to access that closed world of Wellfleet society. The two things were inextricably connected in my mind. In both cases I felt like an explorer. And they were both private expeditions. I've never been good at talking about painting, and I found it hard to interest Helen in the Wellfleet burghers. They reminded her of her own work, and she was losing interest in that. So I kept my projects to myself. It seemed that once again we were moving in opposite directions. But as it turned out, that was because we were coming together again.

Stanley Blair left town and James Dunwoody took his place in that hot and sooty office in the station. I lost no time in presenting my card and Blair's letter of recommendation at the villa on West Hill where the Du Cros couple lived. Within a week I had a commission.

I knew right away that the Du Cros were the real thing. A servant let me in and left me to wait in the entrance hall. To my right was a stained-glass window in art nouveau style, showing a girl in a white dress beside a waterfall. Her head was bent and her hair cascaded like the water of the waterfall. Behind her a weeping willow continued the motif in green. To my left was a large and impressive hall stand made from cast iron. At the base, incongruously, four animal claws extended from under what looked like a large lily pad. Above this was the stand itself, a fantasy of iron vines and bunches of iron grapes. In among the foliage was a mirror and various hooks for hats and coats, and below these a rack for umbrellas and walking sticks. Beside the stand was a pair of lady's walking boots.

The servant came back and led me into a pannelled study. For a moment I could hardly see anything after the bright sunlight outside. The shutters had been half-closed, casting the room in darkness. Mr Du Cros was sitting in a dark-blue balloon-backed chair and reading by the light of a tall, elegant oil lamp. When I entered, he unfolded himself and approached me on his long, spindly legs.

'The profession of painter must be a deeply fascinating one,' he said.

His low voice made everything he said seem profound. Like Hawker he was strange-looking, but in his own way he was even stranger. He was as tall as Hawker, but his torso was stouter. He had green eyes, set deep in their sockets, and his moustache looked as though it had been stuck on by a make-up artist. What made me want to paint him above all was an atmosphere of pain that hung about him. My portrait painting had made me sensitive to these atmospheres. If you can capture an atmosphere, you have a likeness. Freeman Du Cros seemed to have some private burden inside him that was sucking him inwards. There was that deep breaking voice, the long-jawed face, the heavy eyelids, the sunken eyes. He looked like a man going through a kind of inner meltdown. But it was a subtle thing, this atmosphere. A shadow cast by a shadow. It wasn't as if he sounded depressed or unsure of himself. His voice was loud, arrogant and bored. It was that thing in his eyes that I wanted to get at.

'Could you tell me,' he said wearily, 'something about your methods of work?'

It took me a few minutes to understand the purpose of our conversation. He was checking me out, to see if I was a suitable person to be painting his wife's portrait. He didn't relish the task. More than once, as I answered his questions, I saw him glance impatiently at his discarded book. It was called *Victorian Banking*. Eventually he decided that I wasn't going to disgrace his house or assault his wife. He went to fetch her, and as soon as Barbara Du Cros came into the room she took charge of things. Her husband retreated gratefully to his Victorian banking. The painful necessity of the interview was over.

I had the same kind of problem with Barbara Du Cros as I'd had with Stanley Blair. She had squashy pudding-like features. But she had an atmosphere about her, a strength of character in the way she held her head and set her shoulders. Her response to just about everything was that 'she couldn't understand it' or that 'she knew nothing about it'. From her they sounded like statements of principle. Along with just about everybody else in Wellfleet, of course, Barbara Du Cros showed no interest in what was going on in the world beyond the Coast. (Johnny Hunter and Matthew Rimmer were the only two exceptions that I'd met.) But her ignorance went beyond the usual nervous insularity of the Coast. She seemed to have a cheerful blindness to everything – to Wellfleet, the burghers, her husband. To make conversation, while I set my easel up, I asked her about her husband's interest in Victorian banking.

'Really, I can't be expected to account for every silly book he may decide to read. I don't understand why you ask me these questions.'

She was cheerful. It seemed as though nothing would offend her or put her off her stride. She spent her life setting her face against things, and her world had become dense and solid as a result. I couldn't help feeling a sense of exhilaration. Here was that Wellfleet world that I'd heard about, a world that was so snobbish that it had risen above snobbery, a world of cultivated naturalness and learnt ignorance. Barbara Du Cros didn't need to look over her shoulder, like Hawker and his friends. It wouldn't have occurred to her to sneer at the summer crowds that surged backwards and forwards along the seafront. I felt like an anthropologist who'd found one of a dying tribe.

I'd learnt from painting Stanley Blair how to deal with Barbara Du Cros' plainness. As soon as we entered the sumptuous sitting room I saw how I would have her sitting. Against a wall was an enormous chesterfield – ugly and heavily upholstered in an incongruous salmon pink. ('I have no knowledge of things visual,' she told me. 'I find that kind of thing terribly irksome.') Beside the chesterfield, also against the wall, was a marble-topped table with lyre-shaped supports in walnut. And sitting heavily on the table were two objects under separate glass domes. The first was a bulbous clock, in white and black marble and mounted with ormolu. The second, nearly two feet high, looked from a distance like a multi-coloured headless and armless figure, with a model ship passing between its two legs. It was painted in blues, purples, scarlets, oranges, yellows, splashes of olive green. No thought or imagination had gone into the colouring. It was without doubt the most disgusting thing I'd ever seen.

'I see you're admiring our archway,' she said. 'I know nothing about shellwork myself. It was presented to Freeman by the fishermen in the Old Town when he became mayor. I painted it myself.'

Up close you could see that the thing was made from hundreds of shells – limpets, clams, barnacles, oysters, cockles, sea snails, whelks, sea acorns. A graveyard of molluscs. It looked as though the refuse from some gargantuan *fruits de mer* feast had been swept up and glued together into a single ugly memorial. A good deal of care had gone into its construction, with the shells arranged into flowers and spirals. But why? I liked the shells that you could pick up along the shore. Why put them together like this under a glass dome? And above all, why paint them? I asked Mrs Du Cros.

'Oh, I don't know,' she said. 'I read in some silly book that that's what one does with shellwork.'

I sat her at the end of that salmon-pink chesterfield, with the marble clock and shellwork archway at her shoulder. The wallpaper behind her head was crimson and Prussian blue in a floral pattern. Her dress, with leg-of-mutton sleeves at least twenty inches round at the shoulders, was mauve taffeta, spotted with silver, and with the matching jacket turned back on each side of the bodice to show the violet velvet revers. There was no way that this was going to be another 'brown soup' job. I squeezed the oils on to my pallet with relish and anticipation. I'd sink Mrs Du Cros with colour. I'd stuff her with colour. I'd shout the disgusting stolid solidity of those objects – the woman included – with the loudness of colour. A raging appetite for the job took hold of me. I manoeuvred her head so that it was next to that gaudy grotesque shell thing. I moved the clock closer to the shell thing. Already I had a rhythm in mind: the clock, the shell thing, Barbara Du Cros's head. She didn't mind in the least being manhandled and ordered about by me. She talked purposefully about how she knew nothing of this, was ignorant of that, had no desire to know about something else. I was manic, eaten up by a hunger to construct her and smother her in colour, a hunger to prise open Wellfleet itself and smother it in colour.

Her face had scarlet weather burns on each cheek. It was an outdoor kind of face, and made me think of the lady's walking boots I'd seen in the entrance hall. I'd noticed that when we came into the sitting room the first thing she'd done was pull apart the damask curtains and open a window.

'Your husband likes to keep the house shaded,' I commented as I began to make a pencil sketch.

'He claims the sunlight makes the fabrics fade. He's probably right. I know nothing about these matters.'

'But you like a breath of fresh air?'

'It can get so stuffy sometimes.'

'My wife and I like walking on the cliffs beyond East Hill.'

'You do get a welcome breeze up there.'

'We go swimming at the cove along that way. The nudist beach.'

'Ah yes. I've often felt like popping down there myself for a dip. But discretion is the better part of valour.'

'Most people in the New Town seem to disapprove of it.'

'Do they? I suppose you must know. Some people have the silliest notions.'

I stepped forward to change slightly the way in which she was sitting. 'And what does your husband think?' I asked.

'About that beach? I haven't the faintest idea. We've never discussed it.'

'I get the impression that he's not a man for the great outdoors.'

'Perhaps you're right. I haven't thought about it before. I'm not a very observant person. I suppose you have to be observant for your trade?'

'It helps.'

'Well, I'm glad I don't have to do it. It must be very tiresome to go around being observant all the time.'

'What *do* you do all the time, Mrs Du Cros?'

'Do? Nothing. We used to have a lot of social engagements, but thank God there are fewer of those nowadays. Freeman feels he has to put in an appearance sometimes.'

'He used to be mayor, didn't he?'

'You're very well-informed, Mr Abrahams. I suppose it comes of being so observant.'

'Stanley Blair told me.'

'It was a shame to lose Mr Blair. He was an asset to the town. A very level-headed, sensible sort of man.'

'Why did he leave?'

'How should I know? I think you'd better ask him that.'

'I did. He wouldn't say.'

'There's your answer then. Perhaps you were being a bit over-observant.'

'He seemed a bit upset about something.'

'People get upset for lots of silly reasons.'

'Was he unpopular in Wellfleet?'

'Some people may have thought him a trifle dull. There is what you might call a "fast set" in town society. No, "fast" is the wrong word.'

'Racy?'

'You're a very persistent young man, aren't you? Persistent and observant. What a tiresome combination.'

This didn't shut me up for long. I was working with my pencil on the canvas now, roughing in shapes. For once I felt like talking while I worked. I was getting the feeling that there was something going on in Wellfleet, something that had caused Stanley Blair's departure.

'When did your husband stop being mayor?' I asked.

'Six years ago. He was replaced by Roland Hinchcliff.'

I'd heard about Hinchcliff. He was a lawyer, and had only been mayor for a short time.

'Do you think he or his wife would be interested in a portrait?' I said.

'Perhaps.' She allowed herself a smile. 'Hinchcliff's always talking about what a connoisseur of the arts he is.'

'And what about your husband?'

Her laugh came from deep below the rolling acres of mauve taffeta. 'Freeman? I can't see Freeman wanting to have his picture painted.'

'How about you? Don't you like having your picture painted?'

'To tell you the truth, young man, I'm only doing this because Freeman wants me to. My husband's a great one for keeping up appearances. As far as I'm concerned, I don't want to have to look at a bloody picture of myself every time

359

I come into the room. I know I'm no beauty. Never pretended to be. I hope you're going to make me as inconspicuous as possible.'

'I think you'll like it.'

'What you want are some young, vain women.'

'Any suggestions?'

'There are plenty who are vain, but not many young ones.'

'Do you and Mr Du Cros have any children?'

'We were not favoured.'

'I've noticed there aren't many children in Wellfleet.'

'We're not known as a town of breeders.'

That was another thing I'd noticed about Wellfleet people. They talked about themselves collectively. 'So you don't think your husband would like his portrait painted?'

'Oh, I don't know. Why don't you ask him? You seem to think I'm omniscient.'

'It's just that he's got an interesting face.'

'Has he? I must observe him more closely in future.'

'He's got a sad face. I don't mean to imply that he's unhappy. He's just got a sad face.'

'Mr Abrahams, I have the greatest difficulty sometimes in understanding what you are talking about.'

Conversation used to meander like that with Barbara Du Cros, moving lazily from topic to topic, getting silted up all the time by her refusal to give anything away. Her atmosphere was different from Stanley Blair's. She wasn't hiding or repressing anything; it was more that if there was anything she hadn't liked or approved of, she'd just turned away and ignored it. She genuinely didn't know. Once, after one of our sittings, I saw her marching along the beach. She'd put her walking boots on and changed out of her mauve taffeta dress into something plainer. Her face was turned away from the town into what little breeze blew off the sea in those hot summer days. She must have changed her clothes quickly, as soon as I'd gone, and rushed out of the house and down the hill to the beach as though she couldn't wait to cleanse herself in the breeze.

She didn't resent my questions. In fact I think she enjoyed stonewalling me. We were playing a game. I wanted to know more about why her husband had been replaced as mayor by Hinchcliff. I had the feeling there'd been some kind of unpleasantness behind it.

'It was so long ago,' she said, 'that I've forgotten the details of what it was all about. And besides, it's all forgiven now. We live in a small town, Mr Abrahams. Where would one be if one bore grudges? My husband and I have a system. At the end of every year we mentally pack things away and start afresh. Don't you think that's a sensible way of proceeding?'

I felt sorry for Barbara Du Cros. There was something sad about this couple packing away their lives year by year like old crockery. It made me think again about that look in Freeman Du Cros's eyes.

When the painting was finished I had to have a private viewing with him, a formal debriefing to balance the formal interview I'd had before the first sitting. I'd thought he might guess that I was using his wife for my own experiments in colour. I'd wanted to see just how far I could push brilliance and keep the picture holding together. Just about every colour was as bright as I dared, and pushed right up against its complementary. I'd even scintillated the mauve of her dress with tiny traces of violet and crimson. I'd had fun with that shellwork archway. But he liked the picture. He agreed to write a letter of recommendation that I could send to Roland Hinchcliff.

So a few days later I had an invitation to the Hinchcliff villa. I was greeted there by another interview. Roland Hinchcliff inhabited another shuttered study, weighed down by leather-bound books and leather furniture. The place felt heavy with comfort. As soon as I walked in I felt my lunch settling at the bottom of my stomach.

Hinchcliff larded his questions with the kind of flattery

that sets you firmly in your place. Again I was experiencing that way that Wellfleet people had of keeping things at arm's length. (It was the kind of place where the most important things were kept hidden. They liked tossing words like 'spiritual' and 'sublime' into conversations.) He said that he'd seen quite a few of my portraits ('My work brings me into contact with all manner of people,' he added), and he found my work 'odd and interesting'. Was I available for commissions at the moment?

I said I'd love to paint his portrait.

He laughed. 'Not me. I hardly think that my appearance is worth memorialising.'

That was a pity. I'd been studying his face since I came in the room. There was something interestingly simian about it. The skull was prominent, and when you first saw him you thought his lips swelled into a kind of creamy pout. But then you realised that the forward thrust of his mouth was because of his teeth – thin, nipping teeth that jutted forward and met in a perfect line. In fact his lips were thin. They slid over his teeth like eyelids over an eyeball.

'You've aroused interest in some high places,' he said. 'If you were interested, I might be able to get you an introduction to Madeleine Patrick. She's a great lover of fine art. And I know Clifford has been wanting a portrait of her.'

Clifford Patrick was the present mayor, and his wife was the author of the *Guide to the Pleasures of Wellfleet Life* that I'd read. I'd first heard their names from Charlie Hawker, and they'd come up again in the context of Barbara Du Cros's 'fast set'.

'That's very kind of you,' I said. 'But I don't know why you're going to this trouble for my sake.'

He looked embarrassed. His bony jaw readjusted itself behind its membranous lips. 'I'll do anything to help an artist,' he said.

Helen was in the apartment when I got back from seeing Hinchcliff. She was lying on the bed reading one of those

362

pinched, polite detective novels that the shops in Wellfleet sold.

'Nothing to do at the office?' I asked.

'EuroTV were meant to be sending a crew down to film the fishing beach,' she said, without putting down the book. 'But they've pulled out. They wanted something a bit more "authentic". They've gone for one of the villages further along the Coast.'

'That's a pity.'

'Is it? Quite honestly, I couldn't give a fuck.'

I leant out of the window, breathing in the sea air. The noise of the crowd rose in a blue bubble from the road below. I looked along the shore from one side to the other: the distant fishing beach; the groynes jutting out into the water; the speckled grey and brown of the long stretch of shingle curving towards me; people everywhere, swarming over everything; the pier, like the beginnings of some baroque, *fin-de-siècle* bridge across the sea; then more shingle, more people, and a white-blue heat haze at the horizon. It felt good to be away from Hinchcliff's office.

'Do you find this place weird?' I said.

She said, 'I guess it's what people want.' She wasn't paying attention. I sneaked a look at her. Her eyes were on the book and her forehead was creased with concentration. The only thing she was worrying about at that moment was the solution to a detective mystery.

'Hinchcliff said he might get me a commission from Madeleine Patrick.'

'Who's Hinchcliff? Who's Madeleine Patrick?'

'Hinchcliff's the guy I told you about. Madeleine Patrick wrote that book you haven't read. She's the mayor's wife.'

'That's one thing I don't like about this town. The creepy people who run it.'

'You've never met them. You always deal with O'Casey.'

'Well, don't you find them creepy?'

Something made me want to defend the Wellfleet burghers.

363

'They're just trying to hang on to something,' I said. 'That often makes people act strangely.'

My generalisation stood stiffly in the middle of the room, a large, comically incongruous object. There was silence from the bed. I looked over at Helen. She glanced up from her book. 'Come here,' she said.

I slid up the bed and rested my head on her chest. Between her breasts I could feel the hardness of her ribcage. Her breathing was slow, like someone sleeping. I could feel the soft rush of it over my head.

'Aren't you happy here?' I said.

She shifted the weight of her body slightly. 'Yeah,' she said, 'I'm happy.'

There was a reluctance in her voice, but it was more a kind of laziness than doubt. She didn't want to talk. Her T-shirt smelt faintly of brine. She must have come from swimming. I turned my head and kissed her. I could feel her nipples hardening between my lips, her breathing getting deeper, moving down her chest. For a moment we held still, like we always did, letting the blood rush. She pulled a leg up. Through my thin cotton trousers I could feel the stiff roughness of the stitching on her jeans against my thigh. We got undressed. When we were back on the bed again, we seemed to be surrounded more than ever by the sea of light and chopped-up sounds that flooded over us through the window. Screams, laughter, shouting, scraps of singing. I rolled on to my side, inside her, her thighs around me, and gazed at a watery reflection of sunlight on the wall.

Afterwards we lay for a long time, hearing the crowd, listening to our blood slow down again. Helen said, 'Do you know what I really miss here? Music. I wish we could have a radio.'

That could have been any afternoon. We were making love more often now that we were in Wellfleet. In the city we'd come from, sex had been killed off by over-familiarity. It was something you watched and read and talked about. And even

364

that's not quite right. You didn't talk about sex. You talked about *sexuality*, which was something different. I always switch off when I hear those -ity words.

I remember that particular afternoon because of our brief exchange about the Wellfleet burghers. There'd been something unsaid, a tension or potential disagreement that we'd turned away from. Instead of arguing we'd made love. Sex had begun to feel like that – a beautiful blue escape that we'd dive into together. Later when we had a family in America, it was different again. Behind a closed door, trying not to make too much noise in case the kids heard. It was more private, more personal – less objective and overwhelming. Helen was gazing sideways out at the sea when she said that about music, knocking her hand against the sill. I was already thinking about the burghers. It was pompous but true, what I'd said to Helen about the people in Wellfleet trying to hold on to things. Some big wind was trying to blow them on into the future, and they were holding on for dear life to what was fixed for them. Some had a firm hold, some were losing their grip, and some had lost it completely.

Helen went out to the bathroom. I was thinking about Matthew Rimmer. He was another one who was hanging on to something, only he'd lost his grip even more than Du Cros and Hinchcliff and the others. When I first met him he'd told me about the ideals that had inspired the founding of the Coast. It was going to be grassroots local democracy. The economy would run at a low level, ideally without money. He read me passages out of William Morris's *News from Nowhere* to show me what kind of a world it would be. (I thought it sounded ghastly. Morris's book reminded me of those chocolate-box pictures of heaven that you get on the covers of Jehovah's Witnesses' pamphlets.) But as time went on, that wind began to blow along the Coast, and the Coast began to develop its own internal momentum of development. The ideal of Rimmer and the other true believers of the Coast had been pre-industrial, even medieval. Guilds and artisans. But other people with other ideas moved on to the Coast. For them, the purpose of the Coast was to present a *style* of life, an affluent, *gemütlich* style of life. They brought money. They began to buy influence. (The grassroots democracy of the true believers − open ballots, vote by town meeting − was particularly susceptible to corruption.) Rule by town meeting was gradually replaced by rule by Wellfleet Corporation. And these internal winds of change were fanned in turn by the winds of the outside world from which the Coast could never isolate itself. The Corporation, which had destroyed the original project of the Old Town, was threatened by those very outside forces that also sustained it. Part of the problem for the people of Wellfleet was not just that the wind was strong, but that the things they were holding on to were so flimsy and phoney. Even if you kept your grip they might crumble to nothing in your hands.

It might have been better if we had argued instead of making love. We stopped sharing something that afternoon. From then on I came back to our seafront apartment from painting the Wellfleet burghers the way someone else might come home from an office job, telling the wife about it in brief bland bulletins. Only, of course, it wasn't like that for me. For me, it was like an expedition into unknown territory.

It was hot the afternoon I first met Madeleine Patrick. I had to carry my easel and paints nearly two miles − along the front, up through the Old Town, then way up to the top at the back of East Hill. There was a breeze on the front, but once you turned up into the Old Town you could feel the heat begin to press in around you. The winding street felt like something being squeezed out from between the gabled cottages. Narrow steps and alleys led off it to more cottages perched on the side of the hill. I was wearing rope-bottomed beach shoes that kept slipping and wedging in the cobbles. The easel was a bastard to carry. I was getting sick of lugging it around the town. I had it hooked over one shoulder, with my bag of paints in the other hand. But that way it banged against my side, so then I carried it lengthways in my hand and my arm began to ache with the weight of it and I knew I'd have to stop and rest.

At the back of the Old Town, where the road curved round to the right up the side of East Hill, there was a church. It was an old church and nobody had used it in a long time. A tree grew in the porch and there were birds flying in and out of the broken windows. I sat on the side of the road. There'd been crowds on the front, but as soon as you turned up these backstreets you were walking into a picture postcard. Nothing moved. Wellfleet people weren't much into religion. I suppose some of the Wellfleet true believers might have had leanings that way, but their gods would have been too private or quirky to be accommodated by a church. As for the Wellfleet burghers, I could imagine incense and cassocks, evensong and candles all right. But I couldn't imagine them doing anything as crass and vulgar as getting down on their knees and praying.

The cobbles stopped at the church and for a little way the road was just a dirt track going up the side of the hill. The hill banked up steeply, high bracken and gorse spilling down its side. The yellow gorse flowers had wilted in the heat. I had to stop and put the easel down a couple more times before I'd reached the top. East Hill was bigger than West Hill, and as you got near the top you could see right over to the New Town, with its Georgian crescents, its shops and its crowds that flowed out from the railway station in streams, down the brightly coloured streets that slid in and out of view between the houses, down to the sea. You could see the row of groynes along the front, the sea shuffling between them, sliding white-nosed waves flat up the banks of shingle. Tiny dots swarmed over the beach. I found a picture postcard of that view the other day in among my sketches, an arty, sepia-tinted photograph taken in an artfully chosen moment, with rays of sunshine slicing on to the town from between ominous grey clouds. Or perhaps it was just touched up. In white letters at the bottom – the way it's usually done in 'olde' photographs – there's written 'Olde Glory. Wellfleet'. I don't know what it means, but it makes me laugh when I look at it. It just seems right for Wellfleet. Olde Glory.

The paving began just before you got to the first villas, sweeping round in front of them like a smooth brown carpet. I'd heard down in the town how this street at the top of East Hill housed the elite of Wellfleet. They were big white-painted villas with black shutters, proudly riding the top of the hill as though they'd caught the crest of a wave. When you looked back down you could see how far people like Hinchcliff and Du Cros had fallen from grace, clinging on down there on the lower slopes of the hills. Any moment they could slip even further, down into the sea itself.

I struggled up some steps on to a terrace which was decorated with urns and white wrought-iron garden furniture. Sweat was trickling down the small of my back and creating an unpleasant oily sensation in my backside. I rang the bell. Silence from the house. I turned back and looked at the view, breathing deeply. Profound blueness in the sea and upper sky. Flashes of brilliance towards the horizon. The town far below giving an impression of whites and browns being shovelled unceremoniously off the land. And then, from up here, there seemed to be something else that I couldn't identify hanging over the whole scene – veiling it, completing it.

'Can I help you?'

The door had been opened wide without any noise and a woman stood there, hanging on the door-handle, her weight on one foot, as though she was caught in midflight and might overbalance.

'My name's Abrahams,' I said. 'Mrs Patrick's expecting me.'

She stepped forward and put out a hand. 'I'm Madeleine. You look exhausted, Mr Abrahams. I'm afraid it's a long climb.'

I put down my easel and bag and sat gratefully on one of the garden chairs.

'You'd think I'd be used to it by now,' I said. 'I've dragged this damned easel all over the town.'

'I know,' she said. 'We've been following your progress, Mr Abrahams. But you've never been up here before, have you? I'll get you some lemonade.'

She went back into the house. That comment about 'following your progress' would have sounded a little creepy if it wasn't for the childish zest and freshness in her voice. She was younger than I'd expected and, unlike the other Wellfleet burghers that I'd met, she seemed at first almost ordinary – an ordinary, youngish woman you might see walking down a city street. Her clothes had only a couple of suggestions of the usual Wellfleet Victoriana – some lace decoration on her white sleeveless blouse, and a pair of lace-up ankle boots. Her wrap-around floral skirt, hugging her thighs, came down just below her knees. She was well-built, with large breasts and plump tanned forearms. Her clothes gave the impression of being too small for her – or perhaps too *young* for her, like that young, childish voice. She had full jet-black hair and a round pretty face.

She came back out on to the terrace carrying a tray with two glasses of lemonade.

'I'd like my picture painted out here,' she said, 'on the terrace.'

The lemonade was refreshing. I fished an ice cube out of the glass and ran it over my face before unpacking my brushes and paints and setting up the easel.

'This'll be my first outdoor portrait,' I said, to make conversation. 'Everybody else seems to want to be done in their drawing rooms – '

'They're all so stuffy,' she interrupted crossly. She stood up and walked to the edge of the terrace, looking down at the town as though she were looking down at an ill-behaved child. 'They drive me mad sometimes.' Then she whisked round and said, 'I want my portrait to be something special, Mr Abrahams. I don't want to be just "done". I want – oh, I almost forgot – '

She ran past me into the house, her boots clattering on the tiles of the terrace. She left behind her in the warm afternoon air that same atmosphere of outgrown girlishness.

'You must put Charlie in.'

She'd come out again carrying a domed cage, about nine inches high, with gilded brass bars rising from a base of dark wood. She carried it by a small brass ring at the top of the dome. Inside the cage was a black and yellow stuffed bird about the size of a thrush.

'Mr Abrahams, meet Charlie. Charlie, meet Mr Abrahams. Charlie's a golden oriole. He sings.'

She placed the cage on the white wrought-iron table, put her hand in a small door at the side, and turned something in the bird's back. The beak opened and closed jerkily, and a moment later the thing began to tweet. It was pure kitsch. The sound was dead and mechanical. Charlie opened and closed his beak. 'Tweet tweet tweet.' It was a grating noise, like something brittle and metallic being poked through the soft, warm air.

'Doesn't Charlie sing beautifully? And I can make Charlie sing all day for me if I like.'

Just as I was beginning to find this girlishness embarrassing, she changed back to the woman I'd met when I arrived. Charlie was forgotten. Where did I want her to sit? Some more lemonade? Was the sun too bright out here? She sat at one end of the terrace with her back to the white balustrade. On the table beside her sat Charlie, who gazed blankly past me at the vegetation billowing down the side of East Hill. Her bare arm rested close to the cage on the white table, establishing a proprietorial relationship to it. I'd suggested that she let her left hand rest in her lap, but after a while she said she didn't feel comfortable with this. She stretched out her left arm and rested it along the balustrade behind her. It was a masculine gesture, seeming to indicate proprietorship not just over Charlie but over the house as well.

A couple of days ago I found my first paper sketches for that portrait. In the first of them her legs are crossed demurely, but then I remember she complained of feeling cramped, and stretched them out in front of her. It was a casual pose, a strange mixture of girlishness and virility. I could tell she was going to be a fidgety subject.

I moved around, trying to find the best angle and distance for the composition. I wanted to include the view behind her of the town tumbling into the sea.

'It was good of Mr Hinchcliff to recommend me,' I said. I wanted to keep her talking. I didn't want her to wind up that damned bird again.

'Hinchcliff?' she said. 'He's got nothing to do with it. The man's a creep. I don't need his recommendations.'

'So why was he so helpful?'

She laughed. 'I'm sorry, Mr Abrahams. There's no reason why you should know anything of our petty affairs. Hinchcliff's always trying to suck up to us. He probably heard we were going to commission you and wrote that letter to get credit for himself.'

It was refreshing to hear a Wellfleet person talk so bluntly. It was also flattering to be the object of intrigue.

'How did you hear about my portraits then?'

'Nothing happens here without Clifford and me knowing about it,' she said matter-of-factly.

By now I was beginning to get the composition. The town tumbled past her right arm. The roundness of her bare shoulder was echoed in the slope of West Hill, at the base of which the pier could just be seen poking out into the sea. But the light was casting shadows from behind her, sucking the natural vitality from her face. It wasn't right. I thought of coming back and doing the sittings in the morning. But for this picture I wanted softer, afternoon light.

371

'You're looking terribly irritable, Mr Abrahams. Perhaps Charlie can soothe you.'

She set the bird singing again. That hard, uncanny tweeting began mixing itself up in my mind with this stupid problem that I couldn't see a way round. 'You can't *do* it, you can't *do* it,' it seemed to say.

And then suddenly I *could* do it. The solution to an artistic problem may take a long time to achieve, but when it happens it happens quickly. It's like mixing colours. When you mix a blue and a yellow, it doesn't gradually turn to a green. The new colour's there immediately. It's a tiny miracle that I see a thousand times a day on my palette. With an artistic problem, the solution happens in the same way. What had been a problem dissolves instantaneously and becomes something else: an opportunity.

In the case of Madeleine Patrick's portrait, that moment came at sunset. Suddenly the light turned burnished gold. The shadows softened and gained depth. Even Charlie's dowdy feathers were warmed. The sun was falling precisely into that point where the shoulder of West Hill met the horizon of the sea. Here was a new focus, a new light. I got out some watercolours and began making some notes.

'What is it, Mr Abrahams?' She'd sensed my change of mood immediately.

I explained what I was doing.

'That's wonderful, Mr Abrahams. How exciting.' There was the slightest sneer in her voice.

I heard the door of the house open behind me.

'Aren't you changed yet? The guests'll be here soon.'

A heavy-set man in tails and bow-tie marched past me and stood in front of Madeleine Patrick, his hands thrust into his pockets. I couldn't tell from the way he stood before her whether he was used to giving her orders, or to taking them.

'Shut up, Clifford,' she said, waving him aside. 'You're in Mr Abrahams's way. The sunset's giving him inspiration.'

Clifford Patrick sighed heavily, but obeyed. He stood at

the balustrade with his back to me, lighting a cigar and looking out over the town. After a long silence, remembering that
she hadn't introduced me, Madeleine Patrick flopped a hand
in her husband's direction and said quickly, sulkily, 'Mr
Abrahams, my husband Clifford. Clifford, Mr Abrahams.'

Clifford Patrick turned his head so that it was in profile
and nodded. His bushy eyebrows were like tiny, wispy horns.

Twenty minutes passed. Clifford Patrick finished his cigar
and ground it into the terrace with his shiny black shoe. His
wife watched me while I worked with the watercolours, self-
consciously holding her pose. Every few seconds she'd glance
over at the large black figure standing at the balustrade, and
each time she did, a flicker of internal laughter caused her lips
to tremble slightly. Clifford Patrick had introduced a kind of
electricity into the air. I could feel them both getting restless.

'There,' he announced triumphantly. 'I can see them
coming. Now you've *got* to get dressed.'

Madeleine Patrick got up from her seat and stretched,
arching her back. Her blouse rode up from her skirt, showing
bare midriff. 'I'm sorry, Mr Abrahams,' she said when her
shoulders had slumped back again, 'but duty calls. Clifford
and I find that we have to do a lot of entertaining. It's terribly
tiresome, isn't it, Clifford?'

'I'll be in the drawing room,' he said. 'Don't be long.' He
marched back inside.

'Well, Mr Abrahams, what do you think? Have I married
an ugly foul-tempered man?'

I ignored the question. 'Can I leave my stuff up here overnight?' I said.

'Of course.' She smiled. 'It must be such a sweat to carry it
all the way up the hill.' She put a hand on my arm. 'Leave
everything over there in the corner of the terrace. Nobody'll
steal it.'

She was standing close to me. 'Yes,' I said, flustered. 'Well,
there's not much crime in Wellfleet, is there?'

'No crime,' she said, 'but plenty of wickedness.' She

rubbed my arm gently, then suddenly stepped back, girlish again. 'Till tomorrow, Mr Abrahams.' She took another step back. 'Till tomorrow afternoon.' And then she turned and ran into the house.

While I was gathering my paints together, I looked down the hill and saw what Clifford Patrick had been referring to. Down in the distance, near the church, there were groups of figures in evening dress making their way slowly up the dusty road. I put my easel and paints in a corner of the terrace and set off down the hill. I met the first of them about halfway down. The men were in tails, like Clifford, and the women in gowns and tiaras. They smiled distantly at me as I passed, looking flushed and dusty. They kept coming, moving up the hill in faltering groups as the shadows deepened into night. The women lifted their gowns to keep them out of the dust. Murmured breathless conversations drifted up the hill, over the still rolling waves of dark vegetation. Watching this line of pilgrims, I wished Madeleine Patrick had asked me to stay. It seemed there was going to be quite a party in the villa that night.

When I arrived next afternoon Madeleine Patrick was quiet and morose. While I sketched on canvas, she spoke only to complain about the light and the heat. It must have been a good party. As I worked, I kept seeing out of the corner of my eye flashes of sunlight on the sea. I wished I was down there. Up here it was hot and claustrophobic.

I must have been working about an hour, concentrating hard on the relationship between the curves of Madeleine Patrick's torso and the white table that partially hid them. I'd just stepped back, screwing up my eyes to get a different view, when I heard a noise. Or rather, I suddenly became aware that I'd been hearing a noise for some time. It was very quiet, very subtle. Earlier there'd been crickets shrilling in the bracken beyond the terrace, but this wasn't crickets. It was more human, almost like music. Impossible to tell where it came from. It didn't seem to have any one source. It was more like a force-field, a feeling of vibration.

'Is there anything the matter, Mr Abrahams?' Madeleine Patrick was slumped in her chair. There were tiny beads of sweat on her upper lip.

'Can you hear something?' I said.

She sat up. There was no mistaking it now: a strange kind of music that wasn't either low or high in pitch, but seemed to oscillate very quickly between the two. And it wasn't so much quiet as distant – though, as I've said, it was impossible to tell which direction it was coming from. There was something about it. I'd have liked to sit down and listen. But Madeleine Patrick stood up.

'Oh, for goodness sake – '

She ran past me into the house. A couple of minutes later I heard angry voices from an upper storey, and a window being slammed shut. Then Madeleine Patrick came out again. The noise had stopped. She flopped back into her chair and began fanning her face.

'I hope you didn't mind me asking,' I said.

'As a matter of fact I did mind you asking. Perhaps you should concentrate on your painting. That's what you're being paid for.'

Well, that put me in my place. Our sitting settled into sullen silence. From time to time Madeleine Patrick stuck out her lip and blew up on to her face. The crickets were screaming again in the bracken. But at least she didn't wind up Charlie. And the lack of conversation gave me time to think about that sound. The more I thought, the more I was convinced that without realising it at the time I'd heard the same thing the previous afternoon. The haze that I'd seen hanging over the view when I first arrived at the Patricks' door – now I had the feeling that I'd not been seeing something but *hearing* it. It had been a sound so soft and subtle that it was more like a change of mood than anything audible. And then I began to think that that mood had been there all that previous afternoon. That electricity in the air at sunset that I'd put down to Clifford Patrick's presence had in fact been something different, something outside the three people on the terrace. It was as though the villa were wrapped in a web of sound.

Later Madeleine Patrick revived, and apologised for having snapped at me. She brought out drinks. It puzzled me that she didn't seem to have servants, like the other burghers. I asked her about this.

'Oh, but we do,' she said, handing me a glass of that delicious lemonade. 'They're just very discreet.'

She winked at me when she said this, switching on that Alice-in-Wonderland girlishness again. At the same time as the day before, Clifford Patrick came out on to the terrace in his evening dress. Again he looked impatiently down the hill and told his wife that it was time she got dressed. She put him off, teased him, pretended to be wrapped up in how my painting was going. Clifford Patrick heaved under the ruffles of his dress shirt. They were both far sunk in the groove of marriage, their performances clockwork. But there was nothing dead about this relationship. Sparks were flying. I thought at first that his impatience for the guests to arrive was a desire to be master in his house again. But as time went on I saw that there was no pleasure or anticipation in his mood. It was more the mood of a man who wants to get something over and out of the way. That was very much Clifford Patrick. He was an angry man. Life for him was an annoyance. It was one of those things to be gotten out of the way.

I say 'as time went on' because the Patricks entertained every night for the two weeks that I spent painting Madeleine Patrick's portrait. Clifford Patrick came out on to the terrace at exactly the same time every evening, and every night when I left I would pass the arriving guests. Wellfleet's *haute bourgeoisie* would be moving slowly, ghost-like, upwards through the dying light to the villa on the hill.

There was a spot out on the shingle beach from which you could see the Patricks' villa. Curiosity took me out there a few times after I'd got back to the apartment. At midnight there were still groups of young people sitting on the shingle. Some of them had built small fires out of driftwood. Through the darkness, over the rustling, metallic sound of the shingle being shuffled by the waves, you could hear their laughter. I'm old enough now almost to have forgotten the reality of those adolescent rites, those French kisses and all-night arguments. But back then I was closer to them. I was on a cusp. A year later Helen and I would be in America with a baby to look after, but those nights in Wellfleet when I stumbled across the shingle I still felt closer to the cross-legged figures whose arrogant gestures seemed to reach out to me through the fires. I felt closer, but not close enough to join them.

I walked on. The tide was out, and soon I was walking on damp gritty sand. It was from out here on the strand that you could see back over the seafront hotels, over the shoulder of West Hill and over the Old Town, to the lights at the top of East Hill. Those lights in the Patricks' villa burned long after the gas lamps along the front had been extinguished. One warm night I wandered up and down below the tidemark till three. When I finally went home they were still burning. On my way back I walked close to the huge iron pillars of the pier. They were green with slime and weed. At their base, where they disappeared into the sand and mud, pools of bilgey water shimmered in the moonlight.

I hadn't told Helen about the Patricks' social functions, or about those strange sounds. I didn't think she'd be interested. It was getting to be more of a jolt than ever to come down off the hill into the workaday crowds that filled the street below our window. Helen, happy but bored, tried to take me out more in the town. There were brass band concerts in Churchill Square, a fine old square in the New Town with three sides lined with down-at-heel hotels and the fourth open to the sea. Nowadays, reconstructing the scene in my mind, I can appreciate the democratic spirit of those events better than I could back then. Kids weaved across the grass. Families lounged artlessly around lunch hampers. And through it all blasted the brassy public sound of the band, as bold as the whiteness of the gulls that screeched against the blue sky. But back then my mind was fixed on that aristocratic place, that strange temple of villadom on the top of East Hill. When we walked through the steep streets of the town together, it wasn't the popular cafés and amusement halls that interested me, it was the antique shops and costumiers that kitted out Wellfleet's all-year residents. These were hidden discreetly up side streets, where carriages, negotiating the bends with difficulty, waited while their baroquely dressed passengers made their purchases. Helen got impatient with me when I lingered at the windows of these shops, gazing through the glass at arrangements of lace and elegant opaline vases. She couldn't understand my growing fascination.

Madeleine Patrick was always standing over me, especially when her husband was around. I began to associate the painting with the sound of her quick deep breathing next to my ear. She was friendly. She started to confide in me about her 'pig of a husband'. She seemed to trust me. So when I came up the hill for our final sitting, I had high hopes that she'd recommend me to one of the other burghers, maybe to one of those evening-dressed figures who trudged up to the villa every night. I finished the painting towards the end of the afternoon. All it had needed was some more warmth in the yellows and orange-browns of Charlie's plumage and Madeleine Patrick's skirt. Now it had that atmosphere of heat that I'd been searching for, I called her over to see.

Madeleine Patrick came round the easel to look at herself. She clutched my arm excitedly. The palm of her hand was sweaty. The head of the figure in the painting was tilted slightly towards the viewer, as though being pressed by the weight of the setting sun. Her black hair fell forward around her cheeks and neck. Balancing the forward and downward motion of the head were the eyes, looking straight up, and the lips, which wore an ironic twitch of a smile. I remember being surprised at its eroticism. The woman was curiously androgynous, with her mannish legs and arms slung out and her coquettish face bowed submissively. The whole painting was bathed in a kind of red languor that I'd hardly been aware of when I was executing it.

Madeleine Patrick took a step back. 'Oh,' she said, clasping her hands together in front of her neck. 'It's – ' She took another step back. 'It makes me feel – ' Another step. 'I must get Clifford to see this. It's overwhelming. It's – '

With the same motion that I'd seen that first afternoon, she walked backwards as she talked, then whisked around and sprang up the steps into the house. I was left alone with the painting. Madeleine Patrick, caught forever in false stillness, watched her double depart with that ironic smile.

She came back a few minutes later with her husband. It was the first time that I'd seen Clifford Patrick out of his evening dress. He looked rumpled. His old creased cream cotton jacket and trousers hung on him like a second skin. But there was still strength and anger in those horned bushy eyebrows and in the way his mouth was constantly wrestling with itself, the lips pursing and loosening again in spasms of tension and release. Out of his evening dress he had the look of a man who knew he was getting old before his time, and was determined to fight it.

She led him up to the easel.

'Doesn't it just make you want to shout with joy?' She clutched his arm, just like she'd clutched my arm a couple of minutes before. 'Doesn't it make you feel *alive*?'

Before he could answer, she released his arm and said to me, 'My husband finds it difficult to respond naturally to art. He spends too much time on his accounts. When I look at something like that, I respond with my whole being.' She said 'whole being' like a child who'd just learnt the words.

'For God's sake, Madeleine. What do you want me to say? It's a very good painting.'

She laughed. 'Very good? Is that what you have to say? Now what do you think, Mr Abrahams? Is my husband a thick-skinned animal?'

Clifford Patrick's mouth writhed. Whatever it was he wanted to say was being bitten back.

'I want to see it again.' She pushed him aside and stood square in front of the painting, jiggling her arms like a sprinter loosening up. 'Brrr. Those colours. It's making me all tingly.' She spun round, her arms still swinging slackly, and looked straight at her husband. 'Well, Clifford? What do you say?' A freighted look passed backwards and forwards between them.

Then Clifford Patrick did something surprising. He stepped past his wife and shook my hand.

'My wife's enjoying herself, Mr Abrahams. The fact of the matter is that I admire your painting enormously. Believe me.' He gave me a serious look, holding my hand firmly in his for a fraction longer than was necessary.

'Facts, facts,' said Madeleine Patrick petulantly. She wandered over to the edge of the terrace and, gripping the balustrade, looked down at the town. In a different deeper tone of voice she said, 'I don't want to let you go, Mr Abrahams. You have a great talent. I'd like you to do another picture.'

I glanced at her husband.

'Clifford,' she said. 'I want Mr Abrahams to meet Paul. I'm sure Mr Abrahams can be trusted.'

Clifford Patrick turned to me. 'Excuse us a moment, Mr Abrahams.' He took his wife by the arm and led her to the far end of the terrace. I looked at the view. Out of the corner of my eye I could see them arguing. The sunset had begun. There was that electricity in the air.

Madeleine Patrick burst out laughing. She'd broken away and was coming back towards me across the terrace. 'Don't be silly,' she said over her shoulder to her husband. 'Mr Abrahams isn't going to start telling tales to his wife. Are you, Mr Abrahams? No, of course you're not. Mr Abrahams knows about being discreet. You do want to paint another picture, don't you, Mr Abrahams?'

'I'm happy to have another commission,' I said, lamely.

She smiled at me with condescension. 'There. That's nice. Isn't that nice, Clifford?'

He said nothing.

Now that she had control of things, she became skittish. 'I have a wonderful idea. Mr Abrahams can stay for the party tonight and meet Paul. You'll need some clothes, Mr Abrahams. Clifford has a spare dress suit. I'm afraid it might be a bit big on you.'

So for the first time I got to see inside the Patricks' villa. I stepped through the doorway into a large entrance hall. Ahead of me was a staircase up to the next floor. The landing above formed a kind of gallery around the stairwell. To the right was a large reception room and to the left a mantel. Above the mantel was an enormous chinoiserie giltwood mirror, at least six foot wide and almost as high, divided up by leafy branches and scrolls. In the central section, projecting out from the surface of the mirror, was the frame of a two-tiered Chinese pavilion, with fret balconies and pillars decorated in red and black. There was even a pagoda roof on top, made to look like leaves. The hall itself was festooned with rugs and wall-hangings, and when you walked in there it didn't shade you from the heat so much as seem to concentrate it. Plum reds and russets predominated. I followed an old servant up the stairs, around the landing, and up another, more cramped, set of stairs.

We were about halfway up these stairs when it happened. I find it hard to describe. It was as though a burst of music shot across the stairs. Imagine you could turn an enormous piece of music – an opera or a symphony or something – into an object, and throw it through the air. That was what it was like. This large piece of music seemed to fly past us, coming out of the wall on one side of the staircase and disappearing into the wall on the other. It was the strangest thing I'd ever experienced.

I stopped. 'What the hell was that?' I said.

The old servant didn't say anything, didn't even pause in his stride. He just kept walking on up the stairs. When we got up to the next landing, I took his arm and said again, 'What was that noise back there?'

The old man looked at me with his lifeless creamy eyes and shook his head. He was deaf.

I was deposited in a spare room and given tails, velvet bow-tie, dress shirt, polished black shoes and black dress trousers with braid down the outside seams. I was still going over that incident on the stairs as I got into this stuff. The room I was in was at the side of the house. A window looked out on to a swathe of lesser villas cutting down through the woodland at the edge of the town. It was almost dark. I had no idea how long I should wait before going down for supper. My heart was beating fast.

I went back into the corridor. The dress suit hung on me like heavy black sacking. In front of me was the staircase down to the first floor. The corridor led away to left and right. I went to the left, towards the back of the house. The last door was ajar. I pushed it open and entered a room full of clothes – silk petticoats, mantles dripping with jet, sleek bodices, velvet dressing gowns in blues and purples. They were hanging from racks, wrapped around dummies. I walked in and out between the racks, absorbing the colours and textures. The dresses displayed on the dummies invited prolonged attention. The eye lingered on them, disentangling the layers, peeling them away one by one. It was a pleasurable transgression, alone in that stuffy room, to reach out and feel the material between my fingers.

I went back out into the corridor. I thought I'd heard a noise. No one there. I walked slowly back to the staircase, then past it towards the front of the house. The corridor turned a corner. Here there was just one door. From the layout I guessed it must give on to a room running the width of the front of the house. I went up to the door and listened. Nothing. Then suddenly there was a gentle strain of music. It was there then gone again, like the noise on the stairs. But this was quiet, like someone trying out an instrument. I put my ear to the door. A few seconds' silence, then a man coughed. It made me jump, not just because it was so close, but because it sounded so human after that music. The cough was followed by a kind of groan, and I heard feet shuffling across the floor. I retreated to the staircase.

Downstairs the guests had begun to arrive. From the balustrade of the first-floor landing I looked down and saw them stream in and begin to circle around the entrance hall. Madeleine Patrick was at the centre of them, dressed in a cream evening dress with a train. Her stiff black bodice was scooped out at the waist like a violin. On her bare arms were white elbow gloves. She looked up and saw me.

'Mr Abrahams! Come down and meet some people.'

I went down the stairs and was met by the deaf old servant, who was handing round glasses of lemonade on a tray. 'You'll have to forgive our little ways, Mr Abrahams,' she said, drawing in a group of guests, 'but we don't like artificial stimulants at our little soirées. Music and conversation's all we need.' Her guests murmured in agreement.

I wasn't stimulated by the conversation. The burghers seemed tired and sad. Roland Hinchcliff and his small evil-looking wife were there, and Freeman Du Cros. I couldn't see Barbara Du Cros. They were all old and dull, apart from Madeleine Patrick. She was playing the hostess bit to the hilt, circulating frenetically. When she joined a group, she injected new energy into them for a moment, and when she moved on the only thing that seemed to sustain those stuffed shirts was the momentum that she'd left behind. Clifford Patrick was always several steps behind her, offering cigars to the men.

The guests moved into the dining room for supper. I was getting bored. There was a limit to the excitement even of watching Madeleine Patrick at play. Last week I found some small sketches I did that night. I remember retreating to an elegant tan suede sofa and pulling out my pocket book and pencil. My hostess was delighted when she saw this. She kept taking men's arms and pointing me out to them. Her pet artist. I drew some of the guests squaring stiffly up to each other, clutching their glasses of lemonade. Then I drew the folds of the dark green velvet curtains; an arrangement of dried flowers under glass; a large tapestry of birds and fruit. The room was stuffed with glassy elegance, more so even than the other Wellfleet rooms I'd been through.

When supper was finished, Clifford Patrick clapped his h'ndr and everyone in the room went quiet. 'Ladies and gentlemen,' he said, 'I think it's time we took our seats.' Some panelled doors at the end of the drawing room were thrown open and the guests started moving through into a large ballroom. There were three rows of chairs round the edges of this room, and a small stage had been built at one end. There was an overwhelming impression of giltwood, and of deep red wallpaper. There weren't enough chairs to go around, so a few of the men stood against the wall. When everybody was settled, Madeleine Patrick walked confidently into the centre of the room and spoke. Her voice was hoarse with excitement, and her arms hung loosely at her side, the way I'd seen them do out on the terrace.

'Is everyone here? That's great. As you see, we have an addition to our little number tonight.' She swung around and looked at me with that mincing smile that was beginning to get on my nerves. I felt everybody else look at me too. I was awkwardly conscious of my sketchbook lying on my knee. 'Mr Abrahams has done a breathtaking portrait of me.' She looked at me, as though seeking confirmation. I made a kind

384

of affirmative grunt. Clifford Patrick's trousers were making my legs itch. I uncrossed them.

'Now,' she continued, 'Mrs Beatrice Barrett is going to give us a recitation.' She started clapping her gloved hands as she walked back to her place, then scooped her train around as she sat down. Meanwhile, Mrs Barrett was fussily climbing the three steps on to the stage. In her fifties, she was like a walking armchair, wrapped in a muddy brown satin dinner dress that was stuffed with flounces and a large bustle. When she reached the middle of the stage she turned, and with her chin self-consciously tipped up, said in a voice too loud for the room: ' "The Lady of Shalott" by Alfred Lord Tennyson.'

So this was it. These mysterious nocturnal gatherings were poetry recitals. I slumped in my chair, bored and disappointed. Mrs Barrett delivered the poem in a cavernous drone.

Madeleine Patrick waved the polite applause down after a moment, while Mrs Barrett made her way uncertainly back down the steps. 'And now,' she said, 'Mr Roland Hinchcliff has asked to recite "The Scholar Gypsy".' She patted her hands perfunctorily.

Hinchcliff's poem seemed to go on for hours. I soon lost its drift. Hinchcliff's lips slid together and apart, the creamy words slipping out from between those sharp, nipping teeth. I drew Madeleine Patrick, who was swinging her leg, looking as bored as me. Then I noticed Freeman Du Cros standing against one of the mantels. I took the opportunity of catching that face, and made the quick sketch that was the first I found when I started going through those old drawers again. I put down my pencil when I'd done that. I was beginning to feel sleepy. It had been a long day.

After Hinchcliff came an elderly woman. Tassels hung from her dark purple dress, and two sets of chunky amber beads from her fleshy wrinkled neck. She had something small and feathery on her head.

' "The Triumph of Time",' she said, 'by Algernon Charles

Swinburne.' Her voice was high and quavery. The poem slopped this way and that, like water in a bucket. I couldn't make much sense of it. But I looked it up in the 52nd Street library the other day and there was one verse that I remembered. It came towards the end, and I remember the old woman's voice rising to a whine of complaint:

> The pulse of war and passion of wonder,
>> The heavens that murmur, the sounds that shine,
> The stars that sing and the loves that thunder,
>> The music burning at heart like wine,
> An armed archangel whose hands raise up
> All senses mixed in the spirit's cup
> Till flesh and spirit are molten in sunder –
>> These things are over, and no more mine.

After the last line –

>> . . . and in heaven
> If I cry to you there, will you hear or know?

– she lifted both arms up in phoney supplication while the pattering of palm on palm petered out around the room. Madeleine Patrick was up again. She looked around the room and smiled conspiratorially while the old woman staggered back to her seat. 'Music!' she said.

Something happened in the audience. People coughed and shifted their weight on their seats. Madeleine Patrick walked over to a side door and held it open for a tall, heavily built man. He was wrapped in a gold and black Japanese kimono, worn over brown trousers. The kimono was tied tight at his plump waist, constricting his legs and emphasising his naturally shuffling walk. His thin fair hair, which was receding, exploded in an untidy mop. His scalp was red and irritated, his face pale and jaundiced, with heavy blue-grey shadows under the eyes. As he passed Madeleine Patrick he gave her a nervous smile, and she stroked him reassuringly on the arm. He shuffled forward on a walking stick, heaved himself up the steps on to the stage, and made slowly for a chair that Clifford Patrick had put up there. The audience watched him in silence.

When he reached the chair he dropped into it and sat motionless, staring at the floor and breathing heavily. I could hear him from where I was sitting at the far end of the room. He looked up sharply, suddenly aware of his surroundings. His mouth, squeezed between two puffy, bloated cheeks, twitched into a brief nervy approximation of a smile. He leaned to one side, heaving one buttock off the chair, and fished around in a side pocket of the kimono. From the folds of material he pulled out a pair of headphones. A long wire was attached to them. Something got stuck, and he had to lean over again and fumble around some more until he'd pulled out the small black box at the other end of the wire. All this drained his energy. He put the thing on his lap and rested again, ignoring the audience. A hand, large with overgrown fingernails, was raised to scratch the red, inflamed scalp. Then, laboriously, he untangled the wire in his lap, lifted the headphones, and fitted them over his temples. He fiddled with them for a couple of minutes more, getting them in just the position he wanted. When he was happy with that he went back to the wires, running them through his surprisingly slender fingers to straighten them out, shifting the box around until it was just where he wanted it on his capacious lap. Madeleine Patrick, meanwhile, had closed the side door and slipped back into her seat.

By now, of course, it was dawning on me what was going on. The thing was a neurorch. In the silence while the man on the platform made his final adjustments I glanced across at Madeleine Patrick. She was looking at me, studying my reaction. I looked across at her husband and met his grey hard eyes. I gave them both an appeasing smile.

387

The man on the platform was sitting back with his eyes closed. His mouth was slightly open and his whole face had sagged. I thought maybe he'd gone to sleep. I looked across at the rows of Wellfleet burghers facing me. Some of them had their heads turned towards the platform. Others stared ahead. None of them was looking at me. A glazed look seemed to have come over them.

I was wide awake now. I'd been here before. That first moment on the terrace, looking back at the view. That music from the second floor, before Madeleine Patrick had shut the windows. It was the same thing. Flakes of sound were falling through the room, accumulating gradually in the minds of the audience. That sense of the music falling from somewhere above was so strong that I even looked up at the ceiling. When I lifted my head, a gentle shiver ran through the whole of my body. I was conscious in a way I hadn't been a moment before of the weight of my feet planted on the carpeted floor. Then something happened. It was like something sudden and violent – an explosion, say – caught out of the corner of the eye. It took a second or two to realise that it was just the music changing direction. Not that the music itself became violent or loud. It was more that the change, though completely logical, was so startling. There was something more rhythmic – almost machine-like – about what I was hearing now. There was also a layering of texture, an architecture, as though those tiny flakes of sound had become a foundation on which this new thing was being built. But it wasn't a machine that simply repeated the same operation over and over. It moved. There were patterns, but each time the pattern arrived back at its starting-point, you realised that the starting-point had shifted.

But what did it actually *sound* like? I find myself remembering it in abstract terms because I had nothing to compare it to. I'd heard nothing like it before. It was beautiful, I suppose. But 'beautiful' implies certain gestures and conventions. This was just too strange and unpredictable for that. No, it wasn't beautiful.

And I was becoming more aware of the house itself. This musical architecture that moved and hummed around me had rooms of its own to walk in and out of, landings to dwell on, doors that swung open. Suddenly I felt the urge to get up and walk around. I sensed the same restlessness in those around me. There was a kind of relaxation in the air, as though nobody was really paying attention to anything any more. It felt almost companionable. I turned to say something to the woman sitting next to me, maybe just to smile at her, but when I turned my head I found she was adjusting her clothing. I looked away again. Across the other side of the room Madeleine Patrick was staring at me, smiling. I could see her breathing. She was slumped down in her chair, her arms hanging limp on either side of it. She was heaving gently. Then, I thought, she laughed and sat up straight, holding her hands in her lap. Only again it seemed to be happening too quickly and too slowly at the same time to be sure of it, and already my attention had drifted on to something else, to Freeman Du Cros standing stiff as a poker against the mantel opposite. His eyes were staring off without focus.

The music was becoming more aware of itself. That rhythmic spiral that had seemed so complete was the setting for something else. Now I knew what was happening. The thread of sound that was coming into the foreground, switching frenetically between registers, was a melody. But this was a melody without a purpose. It held the attention without making promises. My moment of reassurance was left swinging in the air, without support. The accompaniment died. Whatever this thing was that was left sounded as if it would go on for ever.

With a rush, the air seemed to be sucked out of the room. The walls and ceiling deflated. The giltwood chandelier dropped through the floor with astonishing violence, drawing the

389

rest of the room around and down with it. People were moving, making a noise. The music had stopped. My sense of time gradually returned to its usual shapes. As the applause continued, the fat man in the kimono eased the neurorch off his head, wincing slightly as he did so. He heaved himself up into a standing position and bowed perfunctorily to the audience, giving us the same twitching apologetic smile.

'Thank you, Paul. Very interesting.' Madeleine Patrick had stood up again. 'But it wasn't to my taste.'

Up on the stage, the man's face crumpled in disappointment. He nodded, and again his hand went up to scratch his reddened scalp.

'And stop scratching yourself like that. It's disgusting.'

The hand dropped.

'Now, ladies and gentlemen,' Madeleine Patrick continued in a showy voice, 'the moment you've all been waiting for. It's time to take your places for the first dance!' She walked backwards to her seat, presenting the man on stage with a stiff extended left arm.

No applause. But there was a general movement of preparation, of fans being tucked away and dresses straightened. The man on the platform again went through the laborious process of adjusting the neurorch and straightening out the wires.

This time the music started suddenly. There was a pounding that seemed physical, like something heavy being swung from one end of the room to the other. Four times it swung back and forth, then an expansive lush-harmonied melody swept in on top. At once the room seemed several times bigger, the lights of the chandelier brighter, the people more numerous and younger. The chairs were being pushed back. Everyone was on their feet. Already some couples were twirling around. Above the pounding waltz rhythm, the close chromatic harmonies oozed deliberate glamour. The colours on the women's dresses looked brighter, the black of the men's jackets and trousers darker and more dazzling. I retreated to the edge of the room and watched. Madeleine Patrick was dancing with her husband, who seemed to have lost all his plump irritability. He'd become supple and slender. Once, as they turned, I saw him almost lift her off her feet. Even Freeman Du Cros had found a partner. He was smiling as he glided around the floor. There was something debonair about him that I hadn't seen before.

I'd lost all sense of time again by now. Had it been an hour since the poetry recital had ended? Or two? There was something frightening about this music. The motion and rhythm of it, swinging backwards and forwards, made me think of a fairground ride that I'd been on when I was a kid. About thirty people sat in a large boat, which was swung backwards and forwards. At the top of each cycle, as it climbed higher and higher, your guts leapt into your mouth and your head kept repeating, 'This time they've gone too far. There's a mistake. Something terrible's going to happen.' It was like that now with the motion of this waltz. 'There's got to be a mistake,' I kept telling myself. 'This is going too far.' But the swing of it kept getting higher.

Madeleine Patrick was suddenly standing in front of me, flushed, heavy with momentum. She said something, but it was drowned in a fresh surge of the music. She took both my hands. She started walking backwards, pulling me into the crowd of dancers.

It didn't seem to matter that I'd never waltzed before. Forward, side, together. Forward, side, together. Impossible to do all that and keep up with the music. I stumbled twice to begin with, and Madeleine Patrick guided me with gentle pressure on the back of my shoulder. Then I lost that first painful consciousness of my feet, and was aware only in a distant way that they were doing what the music required of them. Each of their precise rapid operations slotted into place like the movements of a an elegant oiled machine. They left me free to follow broader movements, the turning, bending, pushing forward and pulling back that Madeleine Patrick and I engaged in together. The roundabout rhythmic motion of the music was like a screw, tightening like the fear on the fairground ride. Then it loosened. Everything seemed to go looser and easier. That fairground fear I'd felt when I was standing at the side had been caused by my resisting the music. As soon as you danced and gave yourself to the motion, the fear relaxed. There was nothing to fear when that motion was inside you.

I don't know how long we danced. My back was dripping with sweat, like that first afternoon when I climbed up to the villa with my easel. The crowd of dancers had thinned out, and the music, without losing any energy, had become softer, more sensuous and insidious. We moved to the side and slowed down.

'I'm thirsty,' she said.

The old servant appeared at our side. His lemonade had never tasted cooler or sharper.

'Now can you see why we don't need artificial stimulants at our soirées?' She was pressing her glass to her cheek and laughing. 'Paul gives us all the natural stimulation we need.' Although we'd stopped dancing, she still had one arm around me, her hand resting on my shoulder. We were close enough that when she laughed I caught the musty intimate smell of her breath.

She moved away. 'Let's walk.' We went through the wide-open doors into the next room. The supper had been cleared away. Some couples were sitting about on the floor. There was no sense when we walked out of the ballroom of the music becoming more distant. It didn't seem to have a single source.

'As the evening goes on,' she said, taking my arm, 'we like to spread ourselves out. Clifford and I keep open house.'

She led me back into the entrance hall, where a woman was staring into the giltwood Chinese mirror. Madeleine Patrick walked over and held her from behind, pressing a hand to each bare arm. The woman sank back slightly, almost falling into her arms. She turned her head away from the mirror and Madeleine Patrick kissed her on the mouth.

The rhythm of the dance had changed. Still in triple time, there was a galloping feel to it now. Madeleine Patrick giggled and took my arm again. 'A polonaise,' she said. We danced backwards and forwards across the entrance hall. There were other guests dancing there too, and an old couple were lying on the stairs, holding each other and rocking from side to side with the beat. Again I had the sense of the music being thrown, of it chasing the dancers from one end of the hall to the other, wrapping itself around them. It was unpredictable, but your attention didn't wander from it for a moment. It would seem to have found a groove, then it would suddenly veer off, explode like a firework, transform itself into a thousand different gestures shooting off into as many different dimensions.

We'd stopped dancing. Madeleine Patrick was leading me up the stairs. The music never left us. It always seemed to be coming from inside you, like something you were making up yourself. She started taking me through the rooms on the first floor, showing me her guests. In an office at the back there was an old man by himself. With his arms stretched out like a kid imitating an aeroplane, he was turning around and around as quickly as he could. In a bedroom, three couples had crowded on to a four-poster bed. They were bouncing up and down in time to the music, in a trance. On the landing, the woman who'd been sitting next to me during the recital was wandering up and down, still fiddling with her clothing. Two men were sniffing at each other, like dogs. A third watched them intently, his tongue hanging out.

The sound seemed to be bursting from every pore of my body. The pressure of Madeleine Patrick's hand on the inside of my arm was mirrored in the curves of the music. She turned around on the landing and faced me, laughing. Then she pushed her groin against mine and stuck her tongue out, holding it rigid and curling it at the end. She laughed. I reached out to grasp her, but my hands met nothing. The music shivered. I found myself walking back down the stairs, passing the old couple who were still clinging to each other, still rocking backwards and forwards, gabbling inanities.

I walked twice around the entrance hall, pausing to stare at myself for a few minutes in the giltwood mirror. The motion was slower now, but more relentless. I wandered back through to the ballroom. The chairs were still askew against the walls. The floor was empty, the dancers dispersed through the house. One man was lounged in a corner, rubbing his leg convulsively. Paul Clearwater was still sitting on the stage – motionless, eyes closed, breathing lightly. He could just as well have been asleep.

I sank to the floor, dazed and jaded. That fairground feeling had come round again. The ballroom seemed to be tilting from side to side, syncopated to the music. Paul Clearwater was as still as a fulcrum, moving only a finger now and then, playing with the wire of his neurorch, shuffling his feet slightly on the platform to make himself more comfortable. This felt as if it could go on for ever. I got myself to my feet and walked as quickly as I could out of the ballroom, then through the drawing room, picking my way over the people on the floor, and out of the entrance hall.

Things felt better out on the terrace, breathing the cool night air. I hadn't realised how hot I'd been inside. I started walking away from the house, but when I was about a quarter of the way down the hill, the music still ringing inside my head, I realised that I still had Clifford Patrick's dress suit on. I'd left my own clothes upstairs in the house. I suppose I could have just left them and gone home in the suit, but something made me go back. The suit was making me itch. Wearing it felt like carrying something of that house around next to my skin. I wanted to get out of it and into my own clothes.

Inside, the music was still going. The guests were dancing, clinging to each other. I went back up the stairs, around the landing and up the next set of stairs to the second floor. Every step I took the music seemed to sneak around from behind me, so that I was always walking into it. On the second floor there were pools of moonlight. The music mirrored everything around me. There were patches of darkness in the bass, and in the middle registers shimmering pools of paleness. I groped my way through the darkness, through the harmonies, to the room where I'd changed.

The music seemed to help me out of Clifford Patrick's clothes and back into my own. Out on the landing I was held in indecision. Downstairs I could hear laughter, a door open and close, someone running. I looked down the corridor and saw that the door to Madeleine Patrick's room of clothes was open. I walked in. The melody turned a corner with me. There was a loud open chord in the room. Moonlight on the racks of clothes. I went on, into the room. A sense of something stirring, a presence. I pushed aside some dresses.

Frdeman Du Cros was staring at me with that sad defeated look that I'd wanted to paint. The white light from the window picked him out clearly. His jacket and shirt tails were rumpled up around his waist, his trousers and pants crumpled down to his knees. The chord continued, with just a suggestion in it of that machine-like repetition that I'd heard before. Madeleine Patrick was kneeling in front of him. Du Cros didn't react to me at all, just kept staring straight ahead. The moment seemed to go on for ever. They were utterly still. Madeleine Patrick had her back to me. Her dark hair gleamed in the moonlight from the window. Inch by voyeuristic inch, I moved around one of the racks of clothes, until I had a different view of them. They were unaware of my presence, they were unaware of anything. The music was wrapped around them.

Now I was side on to them, and at last I could see what they were doing. Madeleine Patrick's lips were slightly parted. Du Cros was stiff and absurd. But they weren't touching. They were inches away from each other, but frozen as if they'd been like that for centuries. I crept from the room.

When I woke up next day I remembered everything immediately. My mind felt clear, as though the music had sluiced out my brain and left every cell of it gleaming. The neurorch. Paul Clearwater. Ten years before, I'd still been at home in a housing complex on the outskirts of a large city. One of my friends was given a neurorch by his parents, and I remember trying it. It had seemed like a neat idea, but the experience was disappointing. Then there had been all that fuss about it. The whole thing had got political. I lost interest. It seemed as if you couldn't switch on the telescreen or open a paper without seeing something about the 'Neurorch Affair'. I switched off.

I only really learnt about it when I was at art college and the whole thing was over. Students liked to talk about the 'Neurorch Affair' because it fitted in with the whole anti-science, anti-technology thing. The neurorch was the epitome of the anti-human, evilly intrusive machine. An instrument of mind control. Getting rid of it proved that you could roll back so-called 'progress'. But then there were other aspects of the 'Affair' that made it rather more complicated and uncomfortable for my student generation. We liked to set ourselves against the authorities, but in this case the authorities had done the right thing. It was the authorities that had got rid of evil. It was hard to carry on being an anarchist when you had such a clear example in front of you of power being used for good. Also, young people had originally been keen on the neurorch. It was a new funky gimmick. They said it helped you express yourself. That support for the neurorch had been seen above all in New Venice – that weird hip city. But even there the riots and demos burned out soon after the ban was imposed. And besides, New Venice was a long way from where I was. Where I was, my generation was moved by a puritanical reaction against things like the neurorch.

With these big, difficult issues swirling around it, maybe it's not so surprising that we often steered clear of the 'Neurorch Affair' and kept to tidier topics. So that even at college my knowledge of the 'Affair' was piecemeal and partial. But I'd heard enough to recognise certain names and places. Cottimi. Teatro Miracoli. *Mindmusic*. Fela Kanuteh. These words associated with the New Venetian epicentre of the 'Affair' had acquired a patina of fame. And Paul Clearwater. That name was a bit more obscure than the others, perhaps because he hadn't stayed in the public eye like Cottimi or Lahbib. (Even now, thirty-four years on, New York radio stations play Lahbib's classic recordings. Cottimi, of course, is still 'the old sage of the European stage' – a phrase he coined himself. His name as *the* theatrical radical had been made by the 'Affair'.) But in the clearness of that day after the Patricks' soirée it came back to me: Clearwater had been the original composer of *Mindmusic*.

Helen was asleep when I got in. When I woke up she'd already left for her office. My first instinct was to go and tell her all about it. Being more politically minded than me, she'd remember all the background. But of course with Helen there were problems. Staring at the marbled reflections of water on the ceiling of our seafront apartment, I remembered Clifford Patrick's nervousness about Helen. I remembered Madeleine Patrick's secrecy when I first started hearing things on the terrace of the villa. No wonder. The presence of a neurorch in that Wellfleet villa for ten years must have been a carefully guarded secret. Madeleine Patrick must have dearly wanted another painting from me.

I stretched out with pleasure, as the watery light played on the ceiling above me and the sounds of the sea and the lunchtime crowds washed over me through the open window. 'GET YOUR FUCKING CANDYFLOSS HERE, YOU BASTARDS!' A man's voice, jocular, and then laughter and a confusion of different voices that were submerged in the general noise. Those burghers on the hill had to be mad to let me into their secret. Down here I was in a different world. I could bring the whole weight of the authorities down on them. Unlike some of our friends, Helen had never been in two minds about the 'Neurorch Affair'. 'Human beings have only done two good things in the past century,' she used to say. 'They got rid of nuclear weapons and they got rid of the neurorch. It's just a start, but those two were the worst.' It was this basic attitude of hers that made her so pleased to have been offered a job enforcing the Movement of Technology laws. In many ways it was the perfect job for her. Although maybe she'd found it a disappointment, I knew how she'd react to the news that there was a neurorch in Wellfleet. She'd want to do something about it.

So I decided not to tell her. I'd spent too long getting an entrée into the Wellfleet world to blow it all now. I got dressed, spent an hour or so wandering through the crowds on the seafront, then walked back up to the villa.

Madeleine Patrick was sitting on the terrace, fanning herself and gazing out over the town towards the sea. She exuded heat and boredom. Charlie was on the table in front of her, tweeting depressingly.

The old man brought us lemonade.

'I hope you had a good time last night?' She screwed her face up in the sunlight to look at me. 'You weren't shocked by anything, Mr Abrahams?'

'Not at all. It was a fascinating evening.'

'Fascinating.' She looked out across the town, seeming to consider the word, then dismissed it. 'Well, at least you weren't shocked. Some people can be so prudish.'

'Was that Stanley Blair's problem?'

'Blair. Don't talk to me about Blair.' She giggled. 'I used to call him "bleeeah" ' – she looked at me seriously – 'because he made me sick.'

'He disapproved of your soirées?'

'The man was a hopeless prig. Good riddance to him and his disgusting children.' She smiled. 'But maybe I shouldn't be too hard on him. I'm afraid last night's affair was very tame. Things get much livelier than that when Paul's on form. Music can be so inspiring, so invigorating. I hope you'll stay tonight.'

'This happens every night?'

She sighed, and began tapping the arm of her chair with her fan, rapping out her boredom in a steady, even rhythm. 'Every night. All year round. It's the thing that ties us all together. It's what *makes* Wellfleet society.' She said 'makes' with relish, like a child using a grown-up word. 'Clifford and I wouldn't dream of abandoning our social responsibilities. People look up to us because of our soirées.' She laughed. 'Before Paul came back to Wellfleet, Clifford was no one. Well, not *no one*. But he wasn't the big, important man he is today, mayor and head of the Corporation. *I* know, of course, that he's just a little boy.'

'I've remembered about Paul Clearwater. He was mixed up in that neurorch business in New Venice.'

She closed her eyes and yawned. She didn't bother to cover her mouth, so that for a couple of seconds I found myself staring at her pinkish throat and tongue. She shut her mouth again. 'I'm sorry, Mr Abrahams. I'm afraid all that stuff bores me silly. I'm sure Paul would *love* to tell you all about it. He tries to tell me about it. But I'm afraid I can't get interested in anything outside Wellfleet.' She looked at me with a kind of sneer. 'You'll think I'm a very shallow woman. But you see the thing is, life in Wellfleet is just too perfect.'

She leant forward, smiling to herself, and wound up Charlie again. His beak opened and he started singing into the warm motionless air.

'So Paul Clearwater came here when he left New Venice?' I said.

'Like a little waif. And we took him in. Poor little Paul had nowhere else to go. And we'd had a spare room ever since

399

poor Monsieur Grenier died. Of course, we all knew him from his first visit. But he hadn't made many friends then.'

'Only now he had the neurorch.'

'He couldn't always make that thing sound like it does now, Mr Abrahams. He had to work at it for a long time. And meanwhile, we looked after him. We protected him when the busybodies from the authorities came looking to see if any neurorchs had been brought on to the Coast. It was a kind of investment.'

'Was it worth it?'

'What do you think, Mr Abrahams? No one else in Wellfleet can lay on soirées like ours. This house is the *only* place to go. If we decide to cut someone, they're finished. That's what your Mr Blair discovered. Paul's done all that for us, and in return we've looked after him and protected him. Not everyone was happy about him coming back here with his little box of tricks. When he first arrived, Freeman tried to stop him bringing it into the town. Freeman can be very unbending about the technology laws. His stubbornness cost him his mayoralty. Poor Freeman. Now he just clings on. He hasn't got anywhere else to go either.'

'What about Hinchcliff? He was mayor too, wasn't he?'

'Only for a short time, after Freeman had fallen. Hinchcliff never liked Paul either. We soon got rid of him. Now Roland licks our bottoms just like he used to lick Freeman's.' She smiled at me sweetly.

'And now your husband rules the roost.'

'No, Mr Abrahams. I rule the roost. Clifford and Paul are just my little boys. My bad-tempered little boys.'

As if in reply, a rush of sound came from somewhere above us.

'Paul's up at last,' she said. She stood. 'Come and meet him. Bring your paints.'

My easel and paints were still where I'd left them in the corner of the terrace. I collected them and followed Madeleine Patrick into the house. There was still an atmosphere of the previous night in the entrance hall, a feeling of something lingering and gone stale. I followed her upstairs.

She didn't knock at the door of the large room on the second floor. She walked straight in and looked around disapprovingly, standing very erect with her hands on her hips. I was behind her in the corridor, straining under the weight of my easel.

'I thought I told you to clear up in here before Mr Abrahams came,' she said.

There was a low grumble of complaint from somewhere out of sight.

'I don't care what you think. Mr Abrahams is here and he's going to paint your picture. Come in, Mr Abrahams.'

The room was how I'd imagined it, stretching the whole width of the house. The windows looked out on to the terrace. Light flooded back in. Blueness of sky and sea filled the panes of glass, bursting in on the room and filling it with a strange watery light. The effect was all the stranger because there was nothing clean and airy about the room itself. It was dusty and crowded with things. At one end there was a grand piano, its lid off and a broken string hanging out over the bottom end like a single curly hair. In the middle of the room and against the walls, placed hapzardly, were four or five old sofas in faded sagging upholstery. In a far corner, a chaise longue had been made up as a bed with a couple of blankets and some cushions. Some rugs had been flung about on the bare boards. Strewn across them were piles of books and sheafs of manuscript paper.

Paul Clearwater was sitting in a wing armchair at the opposite end of the room to the piano. His feet rested on a footstool. He was wearing the same food-stained kimono he'd been wearing during the night.

'Paul, you might at least have changed for Mr Abrahams,' said Madeleine Patrick. She was opening the windows and plumping up the cushions on the sofas. 'We used to try to get

401

Paul to put on evening dress for his performances. But I've given up trying. He just wears that disgusting thing.'

Paul Clearwater, sunk defiantly in his armchair, his kimono clutched around him, watched Madeleine Patrick with a malevolent gaze.

'Mr Abrahams was at your performance last night. He was most impressed. Weren't you, Mr Abrahams?'

Clearwater met my eye for the first time. On his side, distrust. On mine, distaste. There was something unpleasantly white about him. He was like some fungal growth that had been forced in darkness. He looked pampered and overfed.

'I want some breakfast,' he said.

Madeleine went over and started plucking at his kimono and plumping up the pillows around him. 'It'll be brought up soon,' she said. He received her attentions in silence, staring at me now with the same ill will. I started setting up my easel.

He was treated like an invalid. When she'd got him comfortable, wiping his mouth where a dribble had appeared in the corner, she began brushing his hair. All the time he watched me arranging my things. I got out a sketchpad and started making some notes. Madeleine stepped back to look at his hair. Suddenly Paul Clearwater's mood changed. He kicked away his footstool, sat up more erectly in his armchair, and said, with scornful pleasure, 'So you were "most impressed" with my performance last night, were you, Mr Abrahams?'

'Impressed and surprised.'

'You'd heard nothing like it before?'

I shook my head.

He looked imperiously at Madeleine Patrick. 'Can this man be trusted?' Madeleine Patrick stroked his thin hair. 'Don't worry,' she said. 'He's not going to spoil things.'

He smiled at her gratefully and put out a hand for her leg. She slipped out of his reach. 'Don't be naughty, Paul. You've got to sit still for Mr Abrahams.'

Paul Clearwater grinned and looked back at me, holding himself stiff and still. Madeleine Patrick slowly paced the room, stopping at long intervals to gaze out of the windows. Paul Clearwater's eyes, two marbles pushed into the fleshy dough of his face, watched her. Nothing was said. From time to time she sighed deeply and looked over at how my sketches were coming on. She was getting bored again. Eventually she slipped out the door.

When I read that obituary notice in the *Times*, it was this moment when we were left alone together that I thought about first. Madeleine Patrick's departure seemed to relieve him of something. He was able to be more himself. He drew himself further up in his chair and looked at me with absurd theatrical contempt.

'I should inform you straight away, Mr Abrahams,' he said, 'that I have no respect for the visual arts.' Then he coughed and looked down at his lap. There was more bravado than real strength in his voice. Even the hostility came over as just a pathetic, blundering attempt to make contact.

'That's fine by me,' I said, 'so long as you don't mind sitting.'

'Why should I mind?' he said petulantly. He picked up a book from the floor and began flicking through it, shaking his head with disapproval. Then he threw down the book again. 'I'm afraid,' he said, 'I must do my exercises.' He picked up the neurorch headpiece from his lap and fitted it over his temples. My pencil hesitated over the page. I was tense with memories of the night before.

His 'exercises' were methodical, painstaking and exhaustive. First there were studies in pure volume and space. White noise, so quiet it was barely audible, grew louder until it was painful, then was slowly pulled down again. The same noise, at a constant volume, was moved slowly around the room – first clockwise, then the other way. Then it was thrown violently from one end to the other. Pitch was explored with scales, arpeggios and sliding chord clusters, from a bass of pure vibration to an almost inaudible, whistling treble. He moved through the registers slowly at first, testing the quality of each one, then at lightning speed. Rhythm was added to pitch. Different patterns were sustained at different registers, a maze of syncopation, moving in and out of phase like a slowly turned kaleidoscope. There were exercises in timbre. A simple chord – breathy, full of softness and air – was moved painstakingly across a spectrum until it had become hard, brassy and concentrated, but with no change in volume. A different tone colour was taken and the same operation performed. Dozens of different tone colours were rehearsed separately and then in different combinations. Individual notes were extracted, warmed with vibrato and allowed to cool down again. All these exercises were performed clinically and without feeling. They followed on quickly from each other in a well-rehearsed sequence.

At the end of two hours, he eased the neurorch off his head and opened his eyes. He looked tired but alert.

'Well?' he said. He had a boyish need to show off.

'Very impressive,' I said.

'Impressive.' He considered the word primly. 'Impressive. I suppose you think that's the reason I do this, to be "impressive". You have no conception – '

'Does it matter what I think?' I interrupted.

Suddenly he was in a rage. 'Does it matter? Do you have any conception – ' He was speechless, grabbing and pulling at his kimono as he attempted to pull himself upright in his chair. He'd slumped further and further down while he was doing his exercises. He was in bad shape physically. His face and neck were dotted with spots and sores, and his white, indoor skin carried a sheen of sweat. His legs were weak and swollen. Even the brief effort of his anger had exhausted him. He sank back again, breathing heavily.

I said nothing to appease him, and not just because I didn't think it would do any good. I'd taken a dislike to the man. So

404

I just carried on sketching, trying to capture the impression of dead weight in his legs. They seemed to be connected only tangentially to the rest of his body. The kimono was rumpled around them in an interesting way.

It was ten minutes before I looked up and met his eye again. His anger was gone. He was watching me intently. I was surprised by a tenderness.

I said, 'I never expected to see a neurorch again.'

He smiled eagerly. 'It's wonderful, isn't it? I risked my life getting it out of New Venice. I was chased by the carabinieri. They were trying to hit me with their sticks. But I was young and fit, like you. I had everything that was true and noble and good on my side. That helped me to run like the wind.'

He fell back into his seat again, smiling to himself. I couldn't think of anything to say. The man seemed to be living in a world of his own.

'This neurorch,' he said, picking it up from his lap and holding it in front of him, 'is an *instrument* for everything that is true and noble and good. When Cottimi and I were rehearsing my opera, *Mindmusic*, Cottimi was trying to ruin a beautiful relationship between two young people in the cast, Fela Lahbib and Zerlina Kousoulas. He told me what he was doing. We even had a bet about it. It was Fela Lahbib who helped me see what could be done with the neurorch. He set me on the right path. And at the same time I began to realise that I couldn't just stand back and see a beautiful relationship ruined by a monster like Cottimi. I decided to do something. And this was the same time as I decided to take my neurorch out of New Venice. Telling Fela what Cottimi had been trying to do was my final act before leaving New Venice. So you see it was the neurorch and me together that did this beautiful thing. We've been doing beautiful things together *ever since*!'

His small, intense eyes had lit up, and he was still holding the neurorch out towards me like some kind of sacrament. I almost laughed. For a start, most of Europe knew the sexual history of Fela Lahbib and Zerlina Kousoulas. It was hard to think of either of them as noble and innocent. They'd divorced each other twice, and between times Kousoulas had been through a good half-dozen co-stars and directors. But even if they had been such innocents ten years before, Clearwater was glorifying his own role absurdly. It would have been more appropriate to be ashamed of taking that bet in the first place. But Clearwater kept coming back to this episode during our sittings, always justifying himself and explaining how the neurorch had helped him perform this great moral act. I couldn't see the connection myself. And I couldn't see why it was an event of such importance. There was something pathetic about Paul Clearwater, if this was the one good thing he could point to in his life. It made me think how cloistered he must have been for the previous ten years. Events from his past had become myth.

'Do you get out into the town much?' I asked.

He laughed derisively. 'I haven't been out for years. When I first came back I used to walk down to the fishing beach sometimes. It's one of my special places. But already things had changed there. The people who'd been my friends weren't my friends any more. The people whom I'd tried to help had rejected me. The memories were too painful. And besides, I had no time. I needed all my energy for my work.'

'You mean practising with your neurorch?'

He looked at me and shook his head. 'You have no idea, do you?' He indicated his flabby, distended body slouched in the chair. 'How do you think I've ruined my health? I haven't always been like this. Not long ago I was as young and fit as you.' He was at his most natural and relaxed at moments like this, when he was feeling sorry for himself. 'Let me give you some idea what has been involved, "practising" with my neurorch as you put it. The authorities who banned the neurorch and tried to take it away from me misunderstood the nature of this machine. They thought of it as something that interferes with the brain. In fact it is a musical instrument, but the most difficult musical instrument that has ever been

406

invented. Take a pianist. What must he do? Control the muscles in his fingers, arms and shoulders. A violinist uses his limbs in a similar way. A clarinettist uses his breathing, his mouth and his fingers. In all these cases, contact with the instrument occurs at an extremely limited number of points. Gross movements of the body are used to manipulate the instrument into making the desired sounds. Now think of the neurorch. Do you know how many cells there are in the brain? About ten billion. To play the neurorch, I have to control what each of those ten billion cells is doing at every moment. Can you conceive of the kind of concentration and singleness of purpose that is needed for that? When a pianist or violinist performs, they can play their instruments quite effectively while thinking from moment to moment of something unconnected. A hundred different thoughts flick through their minds – money troubles, the supper they'll be having after the concert, the legs of that girl in the front row. The musician can get away with these things because, in comparison to the neurorch, the movements required of him are so crude. I don't have that luxury. The movements required of me by the neurorch are tiny, the tiniest breaths of thought. Now perhaps you can understand why I haven't left this house for ten years. I haven't had time to wander about on beaches. All my energy has gone into the neurorch.'

'And now you play it every night for the Patricks and their friends.'

It was only a casual remark, but Clearwater took the implied criticism seriously.

'Years ago,' he said. 'I vowed that I would make music to make the Wellfleet burghers' tea taste like gin. Well, now I've done that. They're in my power. It's not always the patron that has all the power. These people are addicted to my music.'

I described to him the scene I'd witnessed the previous night in the room along the corridor.

'I know, I know,' he said. 'Nothing happens during one of my performances without my knowledge about it, without my having a hand in it. Unfulfilled desire is a terrible burden, Mr Abrahams.' He smiled. 'To be trapped by it is a terrible burden. To be frozen like that every night . . . Music can be such a bad influence, the way it stirs the passions.' He laughed. 'Don't look so disapproving, Mr Abrahams. You must have noticed by now: these people are worthless philistines. Of course I'd like to play for different audiences. I'd like to play my symphony at big concerts for the whole town. But news of my performances would be sure to spread. My neurorch would be taken away from me. An artist must have patrons and protectors, but that doesn't mean he can't also have little games, can't pay them back in his own way. My justification is my symphony.' As he said these final words, he pulled his kimono tight around himself, like a cloak of rectitude.

I swallowed my distaste. 'I still can't quite believe what you're saying about the neurorch,' I said. 'How can you control what every cell in your brain is doing? That's a contradiction, isn't it? It means that a part of the brain is outside that control, doing the controlling.'

He looked at me pityingly. 'You don't understand, do you? There's no contradiction, no division. When I perform on the neurorch, I *am* the music. What you hear is my body, singing.' He smiled at me triumphantly.

Later in afternoon Madeleine Patrick came back to tell us that it was time to get ready for the soirée. Clearwater started grumbling and muttering to himself. She helped him out of his chair, and I was ushered upstairs to change into Clifford Patrick's clothes.

For the next two weeks I hardly saw Helen. Every night I was at the Patricks' soirées, and by the time I woke in the morning she'd left for her office. It didn't seem to matter. For those two weeks it seemed as if we were drifting apart, and neither of us cared. She told me later that most of those days she didn't even go to work. She got up in the morning and went straight to that cove along the East Hill cliffs. There she stayed, naked on the shingle, till sunset. She said she'd wanted to 'lose herself'.

For my part, my mind was fixed on those nightly rituals at the Patricks' villa. They were always the same. The dancers were stuck in a groove from which they would never escape. The music spun an endless thread of desire around them. They were caught in unresolved motion. It was a kind of immortality, and a kind of death.

The afternoon sittings with Clearwater were always different. His moods were unassuageable. He'd enter them with complete conviction, and when they were over he'd forget them instantly. When he was in a good mood he'd show off. He had party turns that he did with his neurorch – an entire Mozart piano concerto performed out of his head, with full orchestra; a Hungarian dance by Brahms that he threw out of the window and brought looping back like a boomerang. He was particularly proud of this ability of his to move music through space. 'The baroque composers attempted it,' he said loftily, 'with their antiphonal choirs. Stockhausen tried to simulate it with electronics. But I am the first to achieve it. A good singer projects her voice, of course. But I am the first musician to master the true art of projection.' To prove the point, he took a chord and threw it through the wall. I could hear it shoot along the corridor, then drop down to the floor below. I could hear the chord weaving about down there, going in and out of rooms.

'I'll let you into a secret, Mr Abrahams,' he said. 'Something strange happens when I project like this. It's as though the sounds were extensions of my body. I can sense with them. As I told you before, nothing happens at my performances without me sensing it.'

This was creepy. It made me think of the way Clearwater's music sometimes seemed to chase the dancers around the house, wrap itself around them, involve itself in them. It was

409

as though the sounds were long feelers growing through the house, smothering it from within.

On the floor around his chair were piles of books and musical scores. Sometimes, if he was going to perform for me a movement of a string quartet by Béla Bartók, say, or one of Sophie Pastureau's nocturnes for tuned percussion, he'd pick one of these up and flick through it to remind himself of the notes. Other times he'd leave me completely and pore over a score for a long time, forgetting that he'd broken off in the middle of a conversation. At times like that I thought I might as well not have been there. But there were other times when some little thing I said would cause him suddenly to break down in tears.

Why did all this matter? Why did I care whether Clearwater noticed me or not? After all, I didn't even like him. You can dislike someone because you sense that they're putting up barriers, but the barriers that Paul Clearwater put up as he retreated behind his piles of books and scores were flimsy and obvious. And at other times he could show his need for me quite openly. It wasn't because I couldn't sympathise with him that I disliked him, but because I knew his isolation all too well. He was only aware of me to the extent that I interacted with his shifts of mood. His feelings were just that – projections, like his music, that groped and blindly made sense of the world around him. They were like fleshy feelers put out by a mollusc, something soft and vulnerable extending from the safety of a hard shell. In the end, I suppose, I disliked Paul Clearwater because I wanted to be his friend and I came to realise that this was impossible. For all the sensitivity of the part of him that touched me, I knew that it could, and would, always be withdrawn into an impregnable fastness.

Maybe that's pitching it too high. There was more than a grain of straight competitiveness in our encounters. I took myself so *seriously* then – but there, right in front of me, was a man who'd made sacrifices for his art that I hadn't even dreamt of making. I couldn't help comparing us, and reminding myself that for all that he looked like an old man, Paul Clearwater was only about twenty years older than myself. Would I be prepared to sacrifice ten years for my art in the way he had? It was a train of thought that led down to our seafront apartment, and to Helen.

Clearwater felt the age thing more strongly than I did. A younger, fitter, more *virile* man had walked in on his territory. What's more, that younger man was an active witness to his shameful encroaching decrepitude. I stood over him and put everything down with petty pointed jabs of my paintbrush. I began to notice the ways in which Clearwater dealt with me. First there was the way that he tried to show sexual proprietorship over Madeleine Patrick, the way that whenever she was in the room he'd be trying to touch her and draw her close to him. But while Clearwater and Madeleine Patrick may have had a history, it was clear who'd been in charge. Often she'd just knock his hand away.

Then there was his own past. The way he used it was pathetic and obvious. It made him seem even more of an old man. 'I was like you once,' he'd say. (Hence: 'And soon you'll be like me.') I was talking one afternoon about how Helen and I liked to swim off the nudist beach along the East Hill cliffs. (I wasn't above playing this game of male competition myself.)

'That place?' he interrupted dismissively. 'That was the scene of *mon grand amour*.'

And then he launched into an account of how, before he'd gone back to New Venice to take part in the aborted *Mindmusic* opera, he'd had an affair with a woman called Luisa in a yacht off the cove.

'We loved each other as no two people have ever loved each other before,' he said sniffily. 'But fate drove us apart.'

He didn't explain how he'd come to be there, or how he'd met the woman, or how 'fate had driven them apart'. The important thing was that this had been 'the passion to end all

411

passions'. They'd 'made love as though love were dying out'. They'd 'drunk each other dry, like two people dying of thirst'. He kept coming back to this grand passion that he'd had off the cove – it was the episode from his past that he talked about most, after the business between Kousoulas and Lahbib in New Venice. But when he talked about it there was something idealised and not quite believable in what he described. He was just trying to impress me.

You see? I was just as competitive as him. Maybe he did have this love affair. I'm probably doing him an injustice. And anyway, it wasn't because of this competitiveness that I disliked him. I disliked him because he wouldn't acknowledge me. (Not that I took it too personally. I doubted whether he was capable of acknowledging *anybody*. That was another reason I doubted his story about a grand passion.) In fact, this element of competition between us was the closest he did come to acknowledging me. At least it recognised that I existed.

Clearwater realised that I didn't believe what he said about his '*grand amour*'. That was why he kept coming back to it.

'You no doubt have a steady, stable "relationship",' he said one afternoon, apropos of nothing, 'with your "girlfriend" down in the town.' He flapped a hand weakly towards the door. 'Madeleine has told me all about her. She tells me everything. Perhaps you find it hard to understand a passion like mine – a brief explosion of love that burns itself into the soul, leaving scars and memories there for ever.'

I held my tongue, and concentrated on working a fold of fat on his neck.

'Perhaps – ' He fell silent, looking at me thoughtfully. 'Perhaps I should play you my symphony, my life's work. The third movement depicts my love for Luisa. I'd play you just that, but I've vowed never to mutilate my symphony again. I did that once. Never again. So, the *whole* symphony. Perhaps – ' He trailed off, considering me and shaking his head.

412

It was in that way, like a new theme in a piece of music, that Clearwater's precious symphony introduced itself into out conversations. Sometimes his moods would bring it back to the surface, at other times it would be lost beneath the heavy layers of his introspection.

'You know, Abrahams,' he'd say when he was in a good mood, 'I think I might just play it to you. After all, you are an artist, of sorts. You might appreciate it.'

He was toying with me. One time I got so sick of his arrogance that I told him I didn't give a damn whether he played me his symphony or not. That crushed him. He said nothing for the rest of the afternoon, just watched me with reproachful, pleading eyes, like a lap dog. I'd had enough of that by the evening, so I apologised. That bucked him up. He told me haughtily that he wouldn't accept my apology.

'Apologies,' he said, 'are the vinegar of life. That's fine, Mr Abrahams, if your tastes run to vinegar. Mine run to sweeter wine.'

I think I might have smashed the canvas over his head when he said that, if it hadn't been for the fact that I really did want to hear that symphony of his. I couldn't help myself. Clearwater had begun to cast his spell on me. Sometimes, when he was in a good mood and he'd got bored with showing off to me with Bach cantatas and chunks of Wagner, he started playing me some of his own compositions. (These, he was at great pains to tell me, were not on the same level as his symphony. 'I haven't yet reached a decision on that,' he added judiciously.) They were strange, these pieces. They had many parts, many moods weaving around each other. They were more intimate than the showy things that he played at the soirées. They were equivocal – endless painful negotiations of the heart that reached only strained, frustrated cadences. Strong forces were at work, but none of them succeeded in taking control. Something would solidify, then find itself undermined by something new, some new, more energetic force. Everything was always shifting. Everything overlapped.

413

Everything moved by juxtaposition, in overlapping irreconcilable waves of unfulfilled intention. He played to me more often as our tense, hostile relationship developed, and as he did so his music began to absorb me. I felt myself being drawn into it. Sometimes, in the middle of a brushstroke, I'd feel myself being drawn down my brush into the painting itself. The music seemed to be guiding me. At first I rationalised this. I congratulated myself on what was happening. I'd always hoped to reach below appearances in my portraits, to capture through them some inner atmosphere and essence. Clearwater's features were as uninspiring as Stanley Blair's and Barbara Du Cros's had been. But there was something stronger inside, something more tangible. If I could reach through that doughy face, through the ugly hoop of technology hooked over his head, if I could reach through all that with my brush I could touch – what? The music. That was what I was painting.

That was how I thought about it at first. That was how I accommodated the rising tide of Clearwater's music. I convinced myself that we were engaged on a kind of collaboration. We were artists together. Through him I'd learn to sacrifice myself for my work. I started thinking like Clearwater. And it was at that stage, when I was thinking like that, that I most wanted to hear him play his symphony. I wanted him to give me that.

But circumstances were difficult. The Patricks were often in the room, keeping an eye on me, on Clearwater, on each other. Clearwater forgot about me and his symphony when she was there. He was always following her with his eyes while she skipped up and down the long room, plumping his pillows. Her husband often followed her in and watched her flirting with the composer. (It was something she only ever did when he was there.) As the nights passed, I became more and more aware of the circles of power binding these three together. When Clearwater was playing his neurorch at the soirées, it seemed that he was in control of everything. But in the light of day I'd see how he was kept by the Patricks, and how he was clothed and guarded by them. He was their prisoner, just as much as they were captivated by his music. Clifford Patrick looked on him with a long-reconciled blend of contempt, suspicion and grudging respect. He liked to remind everyone that it was only through his own financial acumen and hard work that they had reached the position in the town that they had. When he said that, his wife would laugh contemptuously, sit on the arm of Clearwater's chair, and start stroking his thin mop of hair. Clearwater would grin with delight and her husband turn away in disgust. Their parts were as over-rehearsed and stale as the nightly rituals during which the three of them together held sway over the burghers of Wellfleet.

One afternoon Madeleine Patrick came in and said, 'I do like to see my artists working together.'

With that, the unease I'd been feeling over the previous few days found a focus. I could see what was going on. The delicate mechanism of power and control that operated in the house was adjusting subtly to make room for me. Madeleine Patrick had seen how I could fit in. Already she'd made plans for the future. Maybe she'd made them even before I arrived there that first afternoon. When I'd finished the portrait of Paul, she said, I'd do a group portrait with Paul and both the Patricks. One time she got Clearwater and Clifford to pose with her to see how I liked the composition. Yesterday I found the sketch I did on that occasion. The mood of it reminds me of my mood at that time, when I was giving myself to the pull of the Patricks' villa – fevered, obsessive, covered with patches of close-hatched darkness. Clearwater and Clifford Patrick are seated side by side, at odds and uncomfortable. Madeleine Patrick stands behind and between them, a hand resting on a shoulder of each. Clearwater holds his neurorch, Clifford one of his account books and an old-fashioned pen. Madeleine – who had had 'super fun' arranging the pose – wears an expression of child-like satisfaction. When I'd done that picture, Madeleine said, there were other group portraits that I could paint, scenes from her soirées. She wanted me to paint murals in the ballroom and erotic frescos in the bedrooms, so that her guests would be surrounded at all times by the artistic stimulation of music and painting to revive their jaded appetites. Of course, to paint these murals, to fill the inside of the villa with them, would take time and dedication – just as it had taken Clearwater time and dedication to fill it with the music of his neurorch. There were plenty of spare rooms, and it would be such an encouragement for us both if Clearwater and I could work with each other.

Madeleine Patrick had seen the future. But I'd already rebelled against it. Like something thrown up into the air, I reached a turning point. During the day I was spending more time in our seafront apartment, leaving it later and later to go up to the villa. This annoyed Madeleine Patrick. But the portrait of Clearwater was almost finished, and it wasn't necessary now to have long sittings. In the evenings I was leaving before the soirées began, while Clearwater's private polyphonic music was still ringing in my ears. I walked by the sea – thinking, feeling a sense of relief that I was stepping back from something.

Helen was spending more time in the apartment too. It was as though the same gravitational force was drawing her back from the sun-dazzled cove where she'd been spending her days.

But she couldn't quite tell me yet how unhappy she was. For a while we were like intimate strangers – shy, anxious for each other, but defensive. Both of us knew – but neither of us could say – why it was we were being drawn back up the separate paths we'd been thrown down.

She told me how she'd become disillusioned with her work. 'That office,' she said. 'It was getting to feel so phoney. It's like everything else in this town. A front. A fraud. I got sick of pushing around pieces of paper that didn't mean anything.

Technology's not going to stay out of Wellfleet. They'll *pretend* it's staying out, they'll cover it up in all the old-world trappings, but the truth is that they don't really *want* to keep it out.'

Later, she said, 'I was getting so depressed. It was so hot, and I couldn't come back here because I felt I couldn't talk to you about it. You were thinking about those people on the hill. Every day I'd go into the office, look around, then come straight out again and walk along the cliffs to the cove. I've been spending hours swimming. And thinking.' She paused. Looked at me. 'I've handed in my notice. I sent the letter this morning.'

'So what do you want to do now?' I said.

'I don't know,' she said. 'I only know what I don't want to do.'

On an impulse, I told her about the neurorch. I didn't feel like keeping it from her any longer. She'd changed. There was no self-righteous indignation about the neurorch, no politics. She laughed when I told her about the soirées, and about Clearwater and the Patricks.

'That Madeleine Patrick sounds wild,' she said. 'I'd like to meet her.'

'I shouldn't think she'd like to meet you.'

When I went back up to the villa that afternoon I found I could make better progress with the picture of Clearwater. It hadn't been going well. I'd got myself into a position where I hadn't been able to step back from it. It lacked form. There was something cramped about it, like something scrubbed in obsessively by someone too close to the canvas, gripping his brush hard near the head, staring maniacally with his eyes right up against the picture.

But now there was a sense of distance. Moving back to Helen, I was aware again of light and space. Finally I could see behind Clearwater. He became a thing. With a few harsh lines I now delineated him, gave him presence, cut him from his context.

He could sense my new detachment. 'You will be pleased to hear,' he said, flattening his kimono over his knees and smiling at me graciously, 'that I am prepared to perform my symphony for you. You will be the first to hear it in its entirety.' With dignity, he added, 'And perhaps the last.'

I thanked him, of course, but it felt to both of us that it was me doing him a favour. He could be quite sensitive, when it came to something affecting himself.

A few days passed. Helen and I decided to leave Wellfleet. The crowds on the pavements seemed different now. They were real to me again. I'd dropped back down from the Patricks' villa and the crowds were rushing in over me like water. I was out with my sketchbook again. I was early to bed and seeing the morning now. We walked along the front and discussed the future. Already the outside world was lapping at us like the sea, pulling us away. Helen had heard from the authorities that she could leave Wellfleet soon and serve out her notice in the city we'd come from. An official from further along the Coast had volunteered for transfer.

We made no definite plans beyond that. Getting away from Wellfleet was an end in itself. We were still protective of each other, and each could sense that for the other the Coast had become a dead end, and probably something worse. But though we spoke of nothing definite, the possibility of America entered our conversations early on. Perhaps it was just the place we both independently thought of as being most unlike Wellfleet. It was as though America were already there in our minds.

Paul Clearwater and the Patricks took the news of my leaving in different ways. The Patricks closed ranks, acting as a team. Madeleine Patrick was cold and scornful. Clifford was aggressive. He drew up two documents that he demanded I sign. The first said I'd stick to my agreement to finish the Clearwater portrait, and the second was a promise to tell no one about the neurorch. They were legally useless, intended merely to intimidate me. I signed the first one, because I wanted to be sure of getting my fee. The second I refused to sign, though I told him that their secret was safe. As indeed it was. Helen had no interest now in enforcing the laws. Clifford Patrick accepted this, sullenly, as the best he was going to get. Madeleine Patrick informed me that I was no longer *persona grata* at her soirées.

Clearwater took it worse. Maybe I hadn't realised how much he'd come to rely on our conversations. His sense of himself was large and easily injured. Talking to me had allowed him to realise himself. He was the kind of person who needed to find himself through expansive outward gestures. He had his music, of course. He had his neurorch, and every night he had his captive audience on whom he could lavish his most extravagant gestures. But over the years, those celebrations of Clearwater's hard-won artistic freedom had become rituals, each one a separate gilded cage in which his music flew about with only the illusion of freedom. My arrival had made a difference for him. It had put him back in touch with something outside his cage.

'Well, thank goodness for that,' he said when I told him that I'd be going. He turned away to look out of the window. 'Now I might be able to get some proper work done in the afternoons.' The sun flooded in on the profile of his face. The light caught the film of tears standing in his eyes. His lips were pursed with concentration.

For the rest of the afternoon he sulked. But when I came back the next day he'd changed. And it wasn't just one of his changes of mood.

'I'll miss you, Mr Abrahams,' he said. There was an unexpected note of sincerity in his voice. It was like the way a child will suddenly surprise you by speaking with a maturity beyond its years. I was touched by Paul Clearwater that day.

For the first time he seemed interested in me. He asked what plans I had for when I left Wellfleet. I told him how Helen was leaving the civil service, and how we'd talked vaguely about moving to America. At that point he lost interest in me. I could see him turn in again. The hand went up and scratched the reddened scalp. He shifted abstractedly in his chair, pulling the kimono around him. 'America,' he murmured to himself, as though remembering something.

A few minutes later, he got up and shuffled the length of the room to the piano. Under it there were piles of paper. He spent a while rooting through these, then came shuffling back to my end of the room with a single small piece of paper in his hand.

'Ten years ago,' he said, collapsing into his chair and pulling his kimono painfully back around him, 'my younger sister Jean emigrated to America too. It was really rather hurtful, because Jean was very . . . very *important* to our family.'

'Five years ago,' he went on, 'I received a letter from her. There's been nothing since. I've had no time or energy to reply. The letter was forwarded to Wellfleet from the New Venetian hotel where my parents lived until their death.'

I knew some of this already. Clearwater's father had died soon after his son left New Venice for the second time. His mother had lingered on a couple of years, then she'd died too. It was a symptom of Clearwater's self-absorption that he could never remember when he'd already told you something.

'Jean told me that she was living in the west. She'd helped to set up some kind of community there, some kind of religious commune. Her letter was full of the most bizarre nonsense. She wanted people to turn into trees. She wanted their brains to be like cities. I'm afraid the dear girl's finally lost her head. Jean's like my father – an idealist. Thank God he didn't hand that on to me. Musicians can't afford to be idealists. They have to get their hands dirty with the stuff of life. Anyway, Jean sent me this crazy letter. She actually wanted me to go and join her. She gave me the name of the place where she was.' He leaned forward painfully from his chair and gave me the piece of paper. 'Perhaps, if you're ever in that part of the world, you could visit her. You could tell her that I think of her.' He turned away again.

He always seemed to reveal himself most when he was

420

talking about his family. And it was typical of him to turn away when he was at his most vulnerable, hiding what was in his eyes.

'I knew Jean would resort to religion in the end,' he said, and coughed awkwardly.

He reached out to you, and in the same moment he'd be turning in on himself.

Things changed between us now that we only had a few days left. He seemed to want to give more of himself. And on our last day he did finally give me his symphony. But he never really came out of himself, and deep down I never stopped disliking him. His fits of generosity seemed like just another inflation of himself. It was just that his ego was big enough to touch other people. And yet his ego was also a battered thing, bruised from having been pushed at other people so much, from being worn on the outside, from his endless internal battle between pride and self-abasement. Sometimes he seemed to need that punishment.

When we first left Wellfleet I was filled with Paul Clearwater. He'd made a great impression on me. But so far it was only an intuition. There was nothing formed about how I saw him. The finished portrait hadn't been a success, despite the improvements I'd made towards the end. It was still too scattered and too much in close-up, like a thousand miniature fragments of observation flung across the canvas. (Nothing, of course, would have pleased the Patricks. But Paul, reaching out to me as far as he could that last afternoon, said he'd 'always hold it close to his heart'.) Only when I met his sister, four years later, did I get a better idea of Paul Clearwater, a rounder picture. She was so like him in many ways. It was like hearing a variation on a theme, and hearing in that variation the shape of the original melody clarified. When I met her, Jean seemed to me like her brother transposed into a different, brighter key – the relative major.

We were living in Manhattan four years later. We'd had our

first child and Helen was teaching environmental studies to sixth-graders. I hadn't painted a single portrait since we'd left Wellfleet. Now I painted only buildings and water, and I'd recently had my first major exhibition. To celebrate, we'd bought a second-hand RV and decided to take it on an extended summer trip across the continent. Like everyone else, we wanted to get out west. It was never mentioned when we discussed the trip, but Helen knew that at the back of my mind was Jean Clearwater. It wasn't the only reason for going, or even the main one. But it was there. The place named on the piece of paper Paul Clearwater had given me was a small town about a hundred and fifty miles south-east of Portland, Oregon. It merited letters about a millimetre high in the road atlas. Arinosa. Right close by it on the map three peaks were marked. Three Sisters. It seemed like a good place to head for.

We took two months to cross the continent, stopping over in Chicago with friends. By the time we got to Portland, rolling down the Colombia River gorge from Walla Walla, the three of us were grimy, hardened travellers. Sally had taken to life on the road. She perched in the back of the RV with her own imaginary steering wheel in her hands, singing along to the country music stations. In Portland we visited the rose gardens, and looked across the Colombia to the broken summit of Mt St Helens. And the other way you could make out the torn profile of Mt Hood, blown twenty years before and still smoking.

We drove south. The broad lazy Willamette River meandered down its valley. To the east there was a black fringe of distant mountains, and to the west the rolling hills of the coastal range. There was snow on those mountains to the east, but our bronzed travel-battled eyes saw nothing strange in snow through heavy August heat. The road shimmered blackly in front of us and the music from the radio rolled on, song after song. The pleasures of the road had taken over, and I'd almost given up caring where we were going.

From the broad civic avenues of the state capital, Salem, we turned east, into the mountains. Nature closed in around us. At night we parked near a dam, a big concrete slab that raped the valley we'd been driving up. Pylons the height of apartment blocks gripped the mountainsides. Nature was big and ugly here, and men had taken big ugly measures to tie it down. In the morning I got up early, shivering in the mountains' shade, and filled half a book with sketches.

On the Pacific side of the Cascades the mountains were clothed in rainforest – dense lush pine forests watered by the storms that blew in off the ocean. But as we drove on up into the mountains, we began to reach the plateau. The trees became smaller, sparser, scrubbier. For a while we passed through a landscape of ancient larva, a landscape of violent dark-grey rock formations, a post-apocalyptic landscape. The reception on the radio wasn't good. I switched it off. In the back of the RV Sally was silent. Helen was silent too, watching things unfold past the windscreen. There weren't many other vehicles.

We drove on for about an hour, then things began to change again. We came out on to a plain. Scattered across the grass as far as you could see there were grey-brown rock formations, islands lost in the ocean of brilliant green. The air was clear, the colours bright. Up ahead, far away, a snow-capped peak floated above the plain, buoyed up by the blue haze of the distance. Sally saw it and leaned forward on my shoulder to watch it slowly coming. All across the plain I had her bony elbow digging into my neck. We were coming towards the mountain diagonally, moving crab-wise across the plain, and as we progressed our perspective changed and the mountain began to break apart. Pulled out of alignment, we could see that there were three peaks. Three Sisters. It was just as I'd imagined it from the map, only more so.

One road carried straight on across the plain towards the town of Sisters. We turned down a smaller road that passed nearer the three mountains. They were close now, and big and real. The blue haze had gone. Fifteen miles by the map and we were there. Arinosa was just four houses under the mountains – four dirty clapboard houses with an array of old pick-ups and trailers out front. There was a man leaning against one of the pick-ups, watching us. I pulled up and we got out. The heat smothered us. Behind me the engine ticked.

'Warm enough for yer?' I'd heard this wizened line from good ole' boys on small-town porches all across the west. And he seemed to recognise its corniness, because there was ironic laughter in his eyes. His mouth was hidden behind a thick walrus moustache. He was about fifty, I guess, and pear-shaped inside his grease-stained overalls.

'Getting there,' I said.

The reply seemed to please him. 'Where you headin'?'

'Right here. We've been heading for Arinosa.'

'Well, that's novel.' He glanced at Helen and Sally – they'd wandered across the road to look at something – then went back to what he'd been doing. He had a bundle of twine in his hand and slowly, idly, he was arranging it into patterns on the tailgate of the pick-up. There was a tumbledown shack the other side of the pick-up, and beyond that crickets shrilling in the long grass. The heat was heavy.

'Actually we're looking for a religious community in these parts. Calls itself New Harmony.'

'Funny kind of a name.'

'Do you know it?'

His eyes were laughing again. 'Sure. This is a small town.'

I looked at the four clapboard houses gathered around the road. There was no sign of life. 'Is it far?'

'They don't get many visitors. Keep themselves to them-selves. You wanting to see anyone in particular?'

'Jean Clearwater. You know her?'

'Sure. You a relative?'

'No, but her brother told me we'd find her here. We – ' I hesitated. 'We're on vacation.'

The man looked past me, out across the grasslands. 'We get a lot of folks on vacation up here. See your folks have made friends.'

I turned around. Helen was holding Sally on the top rail of the roadside fence. Sally had a bunch of grass in her hand, and she was holding it out tentatively for a white furry animal, the size of a small pony, with a long neck. It was ambling slowly across the grass towards them.

'What the hell's that?' I said.

'Llama.'

Now I could see dozens of them, dotted about across the grass. 'What do you keep them for? Milk?'

The man laughed. 'You ever tasted llama milk? I breeds 'em for the wool, hires 'em out to folks like you. Folks on vacation.'

'You can ride them?'

'Wouldn't recommend it. You load your camping gear on them. Makes hiking a whole lot easier. My llamas'll go up any trail in these hills. Tell you what, since you're going up to see Jean, I'll give you a discount. Ten dollars a day.'

'I was hoping we'd be able to drive there.'

'No way. That RV'd never make it up to New Harmony. Seven miles up a rough dirt track. You'd be better off with your own two feet and a llama. I'd drive you up there meself in the truck,' he added, and nodded at the twine on the tailgate, 'but I got things to do.'

'There's Sally, my little girl,' I said. 'There's no way she'll walk seven miles.'

The man nodded.

'Tell you what: you want to leave your lady wife and the little girl down here, you can put the RV in the yard here. My wife and I like company. Our boy moved to Seattle a year back. 'Spect my wife'll cook 'em a steak. Plenty of good meat around here. Straight off the hoof.'

'Llama?'

The man grinned. 'You got it.'

We crossed over the road and I put the plan to Helen. The man showed Sally how to hold out the grass so the llama would take it. To me they were the most evil-looking creatures I'd ever seen, but Sally was enchanted. She was still talking about llamas a year later.

I felt like a kid again, setting off up that track. I felt completely alone. Only I wasn't alone. There was the llama. By the time I'd gone a mile I was regretting having brought it. For a start it wouldn't keep up, kept dragging behind and stopping to eat grass along the way. If you let it stop you had to yank it fit to break its neck before it'd move again. Then it'd give an ugly snort and bare its teeth at you. And there's another thing about llamas. They spit.

The dirt track wound up into the foothills of the three mountains. Sometimes it traced the gradients, then dived down into a canyon with steep switchbacks and up the other side. Behind me the llama snorted and spat like an old hillbilly. We were moving slowly around the northernmost of the mountains, crossing the canyons that cut into its side. Sometimes the track came out above the timber line, and the snowfields would be only a couple of hundred yards away up the scree slopes. A couple of times I felt the impulse to leave the llama and scramble up to the top of the mountain. It didn't look far.

About six miles out the track gained altitude more quickly. We were coming around the eastern side of the mountain now. The track climbed a ridge, then we were over it on to the other side.

In front of me was a wide alpine valley. There were trees lining the meadows, and a creek wound down into the trees from the mountain. Over the sound of the water I could hear birds singing. I think I must have got heat exhaustion from climbing the switchbacks, because all at once my legs started to give. I sat down. I felt like crying. The llama broke away from me and ambled over to the grass.

The track followed the creek down into the trees. Somewhere down there I could see roofs. I sat there on the grass beside the track for several minutes, breathing heavily on the thin mountain air.

A man was walking up the track between the trees towards me. The deep bronze of his skin was lit up and doused as he walked in and out of the pools of sunlight. He was naked. Except that I thought I saw – but maybe I'm just imagining that now. What's for sure is that to begin with he didn't see me. He was carrying what looked like a couple of fence posts and a mallet. He was swinging them carelessly in his hands, and I thought I could hear on the soft thin air the sound of him humming or singing to himself.

Then he saw me. He stopped and looked up the slope to where I was sitting, with the llama munching the grass beside me, about six hundred yards away from him. He studied me for a couple of seconds, then ran back the way he'd come. There was no panic or fright in his movements. He just put down the things he'd been carrying by the side of the track, turned around, and started jogging gently back down through the trees. I waited.

About five minutes later I saw two figures coming up the track. One was the one I'd seen before. He'd put on a pair of shorts and sneakers. The other one had an Asian look about him. They were unhurried in the way they walked. I stood up and started down the slope towards them, pulling the llama behind me. We met about halfway between the trees and the top of the ridge, standing ten yards apart in the sunlight.

'Hi. How're you making out with the llama?' The bronze-coloured guy was easy, relaxing on to one leg and nudging the dirt with his other foot, squinting slightly into the sun coming from low behind me. The other guy held back a bit.

'He spits.'

'Yeah. He never tells people about that. Nasty habit.'

'You can say that.'

There was a moment's pause, just a breath of the mountain air.

'You looking for the tourist trail? It's a couple of miles back. Follows the big canyon down – '

'I'm looking for New Harmony.'

There was another pause, but less relaxed this time. The second guy moved slightly. But the first one was still easy, still smiling.

'Well, that's where we're from. How can we help you?'

'I'm looking for Jean Clearwater.'

'Why do you want to see Jean? You a relative?'

'I've got a message from her brother.' Then I added, 'I've come a long way.'

'Yeah. You look beat.' He studied me for a moment, thinking. 'You wait over there under the trees. We'll be back soon. Tie up your llama.' The man smiled. 'And stay out of range.'

I did as I was told, and the two men went back down through the trees. From my new position I could just make out the shapes of four or five large wooden buildings. There was the slightest of dry, hot breezes blowing up the valley from the east. I thought I could hear children laughing.

I must have dozed off against the tree, because the next thing I knew I was opening my eyes and seeing a woman about twenty yards away, wearing shorts and a singlet, walking quickly towards me along the track. I recognised her immediately. She had the same heavy bones as her brother, the same high forehead, the same blue eyes. But she was shorter, and thin and muscular. The blue eyes shone from a tanned, freckled face. Her dark hair was cropped short, streaked with dye, and beaded and braided in an old hippy style.

'I'm Jean Clearwater,' she said.

'I know.' I made to stand up, but she came and sat down on the grass opposite me.

'You've come from Paul.'

'I was with him four years ago.'

'Where?'

'Wellfleet.'

428

She laughed. 'So he did go back. I guessed that was what had happened.' She spoke slowly, as though she were choosing each word very carefully. She had none of her brother's brittle front. Everything seemed to be out in the open.

She was gazing at me. 'So. Tell me about him.'

I told her. Pretty much as I've told it here. I told her how I'd found Clearwater and got to know him, and about the neurorch and the set-up in the Patricks' villa. It all came back vividly. The sunlit scene around me seemed provisional. Behind every shivering blade of grass there were vistas of winding streets climbing away from the sea to the proud, portentous villas on the hill. Behind the trickle of the creek was the grinding of waves on a shingle beach. Behind the sweet smell of pine, the sharp, sour smell of the sea.

I'd played that story over in my head so many times that I hardly needed to think to tell it. Sometimes Jean Clearwater prodded me on, asking a question, taking me back over something where she wanted more detail. But she never jumped ahead or got impatient. It took an hour. While I was telling her – spilling it out like I'd been waiting to spill it out, like I felt I needed to spill it out again when I heard he'd died – I watched her reactions. I saw how like her brother she was. There was a Clearwater strength in her, an independence that in her brother had gotten hard and crusty, limiting and cramped. In her it was still fresh. She listened well. I couldn't have imagined her brother listening. He was only used to hearing himself.

There were other things. From time to time, as she concentrated on what I was saying, something deep in her genes would pull her hand up to her head. But where her brother compulsively scratched his reddened scalp with those long indoor fingernails, Jean Clearwater just held her brown slender fingers for a moment up by her head, the tips barely touching her temple, before letting the hand drop again. It had been a strange gesture in Paul Clearwater, and stranger still to see it played again in this different mode.

I ended by telling her about the symphony. Everything I'd told her before seemed to gather itself up into that moment (Moment? I don't even know how long it lasted) when Clearwater came closest to giving himself away. The creek slid down through the trees, slapping and gurgling. My own words faltered, like an eye trying to follow one spot on the surface of moving water. It was gone. Clearwater's symphony was gone.

When I'd finished she said, 'Why is my brother so stupid? Couldn't he see what I was saying in that letter?'

'How do you mean?'

She sighed, leant back on the grass, her weight on her elbows, and looked at me. A shaft of sunlight fell across her face. 'I trust you, Mr Abrahams,' she said. 'Paul trusted you. You're going to know a lot about the Clearwaters.' She looked away, down through the trees towards the wooden buildings. 'When I talked in that letter about people being like trees, and their brains being like cities, it was a kind of code. I was trying to remind him of the way I'd talked to him before about the neurorch. I was trying to tell him he could bring his neurorch here, that it was safe here.'

I still didn't understand. 'He seemed put off by the religion,' I said. 'He didn't like the idea of a religious commune.'

She laughed exasperatedly. 'This *isn't* a religious commune. It's got nothing to do with religion. That's just something we tell the outside world, to protect ourselves. I didn't know who might read that letter. It was a risk. That was why I used that code.' She laughed again. 'But my stupid brother didn't even get it.'

'But what – ' My voice trailed off. The sound of the creek was still there: constant, constantly moving. I still didn't understand.

'Come on.' She stood up. 'You may as well see. She gave me a hand and pulled me up. 'And that llama needs water.'

The ground sloped gently down through the trees towards the buildings. My mind felt as if it was on a slope too, being gently propelled. So that by the time we arrived at the first barn-like building I think I already knew what the answer was and what it was I'd see.

'Shsh.' She put her finger to her lips. 'They're having a meeting.'

We'd stopped at an open window. Sunlight fell on the clapboard outside walls and, through the window, on to the wooden floor. The windows and shutters were open on the other side of the building too, so that you could see right through to the wood continuing down the slope and, half-hidden among the trees, another building beyond. The thin bright-green pine needles were motionless.

There were about twenty men and women in the room. The air was still and warm down here among the trees, and some of the people inside were naked – like the bronze-coloured guy, who'd taken off his shorts and sneakers again and was sitting against the wall at one end. Some of them were standing, others sitting or lying on the floor. There was an air of physical fatigue in the room, as if they'd just taken a break from working. Some wore dirty shorts, and one or two a vest or shirt as well. They formed a rough circle. They were all wearing neurorchs on their temples, the small black computer-speakers strapped around their waists with string or leather thongs. The room was filled with strange sounds. Hummings. Percussive clicks. A wisp of something almost like melody floated up, then disappeared. A beat pulsated momentarily. Sometimes a particular strand of sound had prominence, then slipped back, giving way to another. It was quiet and gentle, yet completely exclusive. I'd never heard anything so alien. My mind felt as if it had reached out in the dark and touched something cold and unexpected. I remember wishing I'd brought a sketchbook with me. I wanted to sketch that scene.

I don't know how long we stood there. I turned to ask Jean Clearwater a question, but she put her finger to her lips again. 'Let's take a walk,' she whispered.

431

I tied up the llama and gave it some water, then followed her. There were half-a-dozen other buildings dotted about in among the trees, and some tents. We passed some kids playing, chasing each other round one of the tents. Above them there wound ribbons of excited sound from their neurorchs, like birdsong. We came out from the trees into bright sunlight. The valley formed by the creek opened out here, and below us there was a large orchard.

She pointed to the orchard. 'That's what they were discussing,' she said. 'They were making plans for this year's harvest. Let's walk up here. There's something I want to show you.'

We walked to the edge of the meadow, then followed a narrow trail up the side of the valley. We were going back on to the mountain. Not far above us I could see another snowfield. We were coming around to the opposite side of the mountain from Arinosa. Ahead of us there was a wide view to the east, across the plateau towards Idaho. It was cold. The sun was hidden by the mountain behind us, which cast a long shadow out across the foothills and on to the plain. Way out beyond the shadow, light played on the greys and browns of the desert and flashed on the haze of the distant horizon.

We sat on some rocks.

'When I first came to America,' she said, 'I drifted for a couple of years, moving between cities, picking up casual jobs. I kept my neurorch with me and always moved on if the authorities were doing a sweep in the area. My neurorch was always the *most* important thing in my life.'

She paused and looked at me to see if I'd understood this. It reminded me of her brother, this momentary doubt as to whether one could grasp the strength of their feelings. It showed a strength, and a weakness too.

'From the first moment I heard about it the neurorch became the most important thing in my life. I could see what was happening in New Venice. I could see which way the political forces were piling up. That's why I left. I followed the whole "Neurorch Affair" in the news, but it was all lies. I

432

could see through it. That farce at the Teatro Miracoli was all arranged. Believe me. The truth was *never* told about that. The authorities had planned long before that to have the neurorch banned. They planned it because – well, I'll come to that. But the point was that I saw it coming. I knew Cottimi. I knew his ingenuity and how far he'd go to publicise himself. And so I knew that there was no future for the neurorch in New Venice.

'I kept my ears open during those years when I was drifting around America. I listened out for vibrations, for words dropped here and there that told me I wasn't alone in how I thought about the neurorch. I wasn't interested in the politics of the "Neurorch Affair". People discussed that endlessly. I wasn't interested in that short-term stuff. It was something much more radical that I was listening for.

'And then gradually I did begin to pick things up. The further west I went the stronger the signals were. There was something happening. It was there under the surface, hidden from view. You had to tread carefully and keep your ears open. I was always listening. And that way I began to make contact. There *were* other people out there thinking like me. Thousands of them. And we were beginning to come together.

'I helped build this place, ten years ago. Then there were just twenty of us. We called ourselves a religious community, because that way people wouldn't bother us. You can get away with just about anything if you call yourself a religion. The years went by and things began to happen. More people came to join us, and others left here and went back down into the cities, or went to set up new communes. There are other places like this. Dozens of them, all down the West Coast.'

'I don't get it,' I said. 'You mean it's a kind of political movement?'

She smiled. 'Like I said, it goes beyond politics. It's the end of politics. Ever since the Tower of Babel, people have dreamt of a natural universal language. And why did they have that dream? Because they knew that the actual languages – all those separate babbling tongues that people talk – are the root cause of human misery. It's those languages that divide people, twist them into lying to themselves and each other, draw them into hiding themselves from each other. They cause wars, they set people against each other, they stop people understanding each other.'

'So those sounds I heard back there in the barn were a new language, a kind of Esperanto?'

'No. For a start you can't describe it in words. It isn't "language". You don't learn it and there are no rules. There's no correct or incorrect way of using it. It just happens. It's what you are at any moment. The hard part, the part that takes a long time and a lot of effort, is learning to listen.

'Our cells in the city make contact with young people. They're good at picking out the right ones. If they're receptive enough, they'll be sent up to one of the communes to use the neurorch and to learn to listen. Then maybe they'll go back down to the cities as part of one of our cells. That's the way it goes on. It's a quiet revolution, a revolution from below.'

'So it *is* a kind of political organisation – '

'There's no organisation, no structure. We don't need any of that. There can't be any misunderstanding between us. The people in our city cells act from their own initiative. They're tuned into what's happening on the streets. They know the kind of people to look for. And we all want the same thing, the same kind of society.'

'It sounds like brain washing to me. You want everyone to be the same.'

'No, it's not like that. The neurorch doesn't destroy individuality; it helps you express it. It helps others understand it. And when everything's understood, everything's forgiven.'

It all sounded too simple to me. 'Haven't the authorities discovered what's going on?' I said.

'Of course they have. They can't infiltrate us, because we can spot an informer immediately. But they know about us all right. Only they're scared to do anything. We're too big now. It would make the whole thing too public. And because we've got no organisation, there are no leaders to round up. All they can do is watch. That's why I'm not bothered about telling you all this. Even if you did go to the authorities, you wouldn't be telling them anything they didn't know already. There's a quiet revolution rolling across this country. It's going to take this society down brick by brick and build a new one.' She paused. 'Do you see that?'

She was pointing out across the plain. I hadn't noticed it up to now, but there was a city down there. The blue-pink light I'd seen playing on the haze of the horizon was the light of the setting sun catching distant skyscrapers.

'That's Idaho City,' she said. 'In a couple of days I'll be going back down there. I can't wait. I'm really a city person.'

That was the most personal thing she said to me. She was cold like that. She talked some more about this new world they were creating with the neurorch, about the new anarchistic Utopia that was coming into being in the mountains and cities of America. Her dedication to the neurorch was total, as total as Paul's had been in its different way. But her fierce abstraction alarmed me more. She talked about how her brother was wasting himself in that villa, and how he'd be happier up here in the mountains where people could really understand him. (I didn't say so, but I thought the thing about Paul Clearwater was that he didn't really want to be understood.) But the more she talked about the differences between herself and her brother, the more they seemed the same to me. They both had their certainties. When we were sitting on those rocks, looking out across the plain at Idaho City, she asked me if I wanted to bring Helen and Sally up to New Harmony and live there. She wanted us to become part of the movement. I wasn't tempted, no more than I'd been tempted to stay in the Patricks' villa. I wasn't made for those kinds of adventures.

'There's one thing I can tell you about Paul,' she said.

435

'Something he doesn't know himself. Did he tell you about Luisa Delaware?'

I nodded.

'Well, a couple of years ago she wrote to me. Frank Cottimi had told her where I was. I went to see her. She was living out in the desert in New Mexico. She had a daughter by Paul. Paula, she's called. She plays the flute. She reminds me of her father. I want her to come up here to New Harmony. I'd like to keep the family together. That's important to me.'

Paul had said it was his sister who'd bound the family together in New Venice. Now she had this dream of binding the whole of humanity together in one family. But there was something Olympian about her that reminded me of things Paul had said about their father. I didn't like her.

I was given supper and shown more of New Harmony's idyllic communal life. But the picture that stayed with me when I led the llama back down to Arinosa the next morning was of Jean Clearwater looking down at that city from the mountain. Paul Clearwater had put all his faith and strength into the present moment, into the musical instant, and his sister projected that same strength into the future. That was where she was political. And that was where I switched off.

Of course, I couldn't help but take an interest in whether she was right. I never went back to Oregon, but over the twenty years since then, in my own small way, I've kept my ears open for that quiet revolution that she said would roll across this country. I've done my share of listening. I've scanned every new youth cult that's come on the scene for the mark of the neurorch. I've looked for it in the papers, on the telescreens, in songs, in adverts. Nothing. Every year I switch on the State of the Union address and half-expect to see the President with one of those things hooked over his head, expressing all of himself to us. Then I'd know the revolution had really arrived. But it's never happened. Not a sign. But then again, maybe that just means it's all going according to plan. Jean Clearwater said it would be a quiet revolution.

You have to shout pretty loud to be heard in this cacophony of a country. And she never put a time scale on the thing. Maybe that grandson of mine will wake up one fine morning and find the world transformed.

Of the two ways of using the neurorch – Jean's and Paul's – I preferred Paul's. I'll never forget his music. Jean talked about the future, but Paul gave you something in the present. But maybe that's just the artist in me talking. I forgot to take my sketchbook up to New Harmony, so I came away from there with nothing. But Paul gave me the best drawing I've ever done. I found it today. I've got it in my hand right now.

The painting that the Patricks commissioned hadn't proved a success. Perhaps it was just that I took too long over it. It reflected all my changing feelings about Clearwater. There was no single vision. You can only rework oils so much, and I went up to the villa on that final day before we left Wellfleet not in any hope of salvaging it, but just to paper over the worst cracks.

I've said before that I disliked Clearwater. But when we first left Wellfleet I was full of him. That dislike only really crystallised in retrospect, after meeting his sister. I disliked Jean, with her hard, bright vision of the future. And in disliking her I saw more clearly the hardness that she shared with Paul, that in Paul had been hidden by layers of bruised self-pity.

He looked so unhealthy. You looked at him and saw a dying man. And yet in another way it didn't come as a shock for me to read that obituary notice and realise that, somehow, he'd lasted another twenty-four years. He was a survivor. He had that hardness. It must have been a strange kind of survival, sitting out the years in that villa, playing overwhelming waltzes for the declining, dying band of Wellfleet burghers, playing his symphony for no one but himself. But for him, at least, it was a life. He lived in the present.

That hardness was there in his symphony. It was there in

437

its constant fluid accomplishment. I had no doubts that it was the most wonderful music that the world had ever heard. But it still left a part of me cold. Despite everything, it was only music. I remember how it began, with a burst of bustling, confident activity. I'd relaxed before he began, expecting something diaphanous, some soft and ambiguous statement, to emerge from – as Madeleine Patrick would have put it – his 'whole being'. But it wasn't like that. The movement was loud, performed, driven. Waves of activity washed across it, blurring the lines of melody that moved in the upper registers. Its gestures were large and showy, but collapsed at the last minute into nothing – like an orgasm turning into a cough and a snigger of ironic laughter. It was windy music, constantly inflating and deflating itself. And yet for all its contrivance, it was in a way the most personal movement of the symphony. Its hardness was like a screen – a moving screen, a film perhaps; whole worlds were built and destroyed by its restlessness – on to which he'd hurled everything of himself. All the absurd messiness of his interior life was splattered on to that screen.

But it was only the most personal movement in that one sense, in the sense of its being his own projection of himself. That was just one side of Paul Clearwater, just as it wasn't enough to say that he had power over everyone in the villa. Because those in his power had power over him. And all those warm, expressive gestures of the first movement, all those assertions of power, had been bearings at the bars of a cage. They had a context. All through the first movement I'd heard hints of their real impotence – the way that a melody failed to reach its climactic note, but cackled down through the registers to a plummy and comical bass; in the way that a grandiloquent piling-up of harmonies would lose its footing and slip sideways into some surreal enharmonic modulation. But it was only in the second movement that the music stood back and became something more than the projections of this strong ego. The screen took on a life of its own. Things became objective. There were different voices, none of which were the solipsistic, self-creating voice of the first. Yet coming after that first movement, that first voice was still there, in its absence. There was more counterpoint in that second movement, more clashings, harder rhythms. In retrospect it made the first movement's bombast seem plush.

And then the second movement was finished. I had no idea how much time had gone by. By now I was sitting bolt upright in my chair, braced against the sounds that had been coming at me from every side, flying off the walls, zooming out of Clearwater's motionless shut-eyed head. Now there was ringing silence. Things settled. And as the opening of the third movement walked quietly into my consciousness, I suddenly became aware of my body again. It went soft. I looked down at my lap, through slow dust-laden shafts of sunlight. I saw that I'd been drawing Clearwater during those first two movements. I'd drawn him from the inside out, from the outside in. And now my pencil dragged listlessly over the rough surface of the paper, feeling it, enjoying it. I was drawing Clearwater's legs, those puffy white legs that showed where the kimono had slipped away from him. The sketchpad rested, glittering and slowly spinning, on my suntanned knees. The music moved in a single weaving line, sadly. I drew the contours of Clearwater's physical body. And in it I felt I was drawing both what he'd been, and what he could and might have been. He was there simply as flesh, as a man.

Then there was another side of him. The third movement had drifted away and the fourth arrived with that same sense of forward motion as the first had done. And musically it seemed to combine elements of the first and second movements. Its timbre and tone-colour – its *setting* – was like that of the second, but it moved in a different direction, back into the showiness of the first, as though that showiness were now being shown up again. And now the shape of the symphony was moving into view – an arrow that had shot itself out into the still distanced reaches of that slow central movement and

439

was now swinging back to the place it had come from, to the last movement. And it was swinging back to me. In that last movement I heard his presence most closely. I felt the hardness of his accomplishment. I resisted it. It was drawing me in. At one moment I was so close to it that I began to think I was composing it myself ('It was all a dream.') and then in the next I was convinced that he was composing me and that every bit of me was a note in Clearwater's mind. He knew me completely. I gripped my pencil. It felt like a fight. I think it was then, when I was closest to him, that I disliked him most.

Maybe I didn't hear the end of Clearwater's symphony. It might have been going on till the day he died. I don't remember any ending. I don't remember saying goodbye. I found myself walking down the hill from the villa, panting, straining against a tightness in my chest. It was almost dark. Ahead of me I could see the first dinner-jacketed figures processing up the hill. I hurried past them. Down on the beach, I ran heavily across the shingle, down to the sea, where an early autumn tide was swelling against the steep bank of stones that once had protected the fishing boats. I picked out a stone, a jet-black stone that was cold and hard in the palm of my hand. In my other hand was the sketch I'd done. I walked out along the groyne at the end of the beach. To the east were the crumbling cliffs, and below me a clear, still pool of sea water, harboured by the groyne. I dropped the black stone into the pool and watched it fall. It wobbled in the water, falling slowly. And as it came to rest, I thought that the light of the stone was in the water. It was because of the water that I could see the stone. And it was because of the symphony that I could hear Clearwater. And in my other hand was the sketch I'd done.